At Boiling Point

TEMPEST WICK

At Boiling Point

First Edition
Paperback ISBN: 979-8-218-56412-4

To the one who inspired this story: you will always hold a special place in my heart. Your influence shaped more than words on a page—it brought this story to life.

To my husband who holds my heart and believed in me every step of the way: your unwavering support and encouragement made this journey possible. For that, and so much more, I will forever be grateful. I will love you always.

Chapter 1

CASSIE

The almost transparent swirl of the hot oil gliding around the bottom of the silver pan was mesmerizing as my mind went to my conversation with Jack earlier that morning about my career taking over our marriage.

As I tossed in the bright green heads of baby bok choy, fragrant garlic, shallots, and pressed fresh ginger, I could hear his steely words.

"I feel like you are having an affair with your goddamn restaurant, for fuck's sake, Cass."

Then, with a deep sigh, I had the thought.

Well, this goddamn restaurant is going to feed your fucking face tonight, my love.

It rolled through my mind as I added a splash of sesame oil and soy sauce to the now lightly charred greens.

"Hot behind."

My line cook called out and moved past me with a pan of hot water, pulling me out of my daze.

It was no longer dinner service, and just a few dishes left to go out to the last guests for the evening. The hustle of closing wasn't my gig anymore. I did my time with that.

Shit.

I wasn't usually on the line anymore, but I decided to step in and help since we were short-staffed this week.

The restaurant was my biggest endeavor. My blood, sweat, and holy shit, the tears.

Sagi-Shi.

The name means imposter in Japanese. I named it that because I was a white, southern girl who, at only thirty-six, managed to talk six gullible people with too much money, including my parents, to invest in a high-end Asian restaurant.

The restaurant was located in San Francisco.

Pretty much an Asian food mecca since there were approximately four hundred fantastic places to choose from. For some reason, those trusting humans believed in me, and there I was, standing in my very successful imposter restaurant I opened three years ago, crying. The tears in my bok choy were because my marriage to Jack was falling apart.

"Why are you still here? I thought you were leaving early tonight?" Kyle, my executive chef, said as he passed me with a stacked hotel pan of marinating beef tenderloins for tomorrow's dinner service.

"Yeah, I decided at the last minute to take Jack and his co-workers' late dinner. They are burning the midnight oil on a case tonight. I thought since we had overshot it on the sticky ribs and we have to use up this bok choy, I would put a little something together and drop it off at his office on my way home," I said as I shrugged my shoulders.

"Damn. Lucky guy. My dog isn't making me shit." He laughed. "Don't stay too long, or you will end up with a grill brick in your hand, missy."

"Yes, I know this, Kyle. I'm taking the rest of this rice, okay?" I yelled as he vanished out of sight.

A distant, "Please take it all." I heard from the walk-in before the door shut.

I carefully packaged the hot rice, topped with succulently sticky Asian ribs peppered with toasted sesame seeds, and the garlic-charred bok choy in another container. They went into the paper bag with a lot of napkins and chopsticks for everyone. This was sure to bring a little peace offering to soften the cruel words of this morning's conversation.

I texted Elizabeth, our nanny, to let her know that I would be running about twenty minutes later tonight than planned.

She texted back, *no problem*.

I popped my head into the office where Kyle was going over tomorrow's order for any changes.

"I'm out," I said, holding up a peace sign.

He spoke with a smile, looking up from the laptop. "Thanks again for your help tonight. It was nice being on the line with you again."

"Yeah, it was fun. See you tomorrow morning for that delivery."

"I'll be here," he said, looking back down at the computer.

I bid goodnight to some of my staff as I made my way out the back door, where we had a small parking lot for only a few of us. Most of the staff lived close by or took public transit to work because parking was expensive and an absolute bitch. I owned the joint and got prime real estate for my little Mini Cooper.

The cool air hit hard after baking in the kitchen like a rotisserie chicken all day, but it was welcoming. I rolled the front windows down a bit and put some classic rock on to rid my ears of the day's worth of kitchen noise. The short drive through the bay area from my restaurant to Baxley, Riley, and Buckley Law Firm was only about fifteen minutes. I rarely drove out to his office. It was mostly errands, Cora's school, which was only about two minutes away from home if I even had to drive there, and the restaurant in the opposite direction.

Fuck.

I need to make more effort.

We had a lot of work to do if we were going to salvage this relationship.

Shit.

When was the last time we even had sex? A month? Two?

Fuck.

I ran my hand stressfully over my forehead and through my shoulder-length auburn strands as I whipped my car into the somewhat desolate parking lot of his office building. Parking right next to his silver BMW, I got out, grabbed the paper bag of appeasement from the front seat, and headed toward the expansive entryway, where I used the key fob on the side wall to unlock the main door.

Since it was after hours, only the dim lights came on to light my way toward the hallway, toward the law offices. They shared the building with two other firms, one being upstairs using an elevator and the other in the opposite direction in another wing on the first floor.

I slowed my steps as I approached his main office, feeling like an intruder being here after hours. I again used my fob to enter their main office, which led into the small but professionally furnished waiting room that was well lit with a few table lamps. Beyond that were four additional offices, his two partners on the left, the conference room on the right, and Jack's office at the end of the hallway. Slightly confused as to why they weren't all meeting in the conference room, I continued down the hall. I walked hesitantly, not wanting to disturb their meeting, when I approached Jack's office door, which was only slightly cracked. Just as I was about to knock lightly, I heard moaning, a moan I knew all too well.

I slowly pushed the door open to be shocked to see the side profile of my husband leaning bare-assed against his desk while a blonde female figure was on her knees with his cock in her fucking mouth. His hands were buried in her hair, his head bent back with his mouth agape, groaning her name, Beth, as she slid him in and out of her filthy fucking whore mouth.

What the fuck am I seeing right now? Is this really what I am seeing?

It had to be real because my heart was beating so loud, I thought it would beat out of my body.

Oh my god.

Wait. Was that really Jack? Was that Beth, his paralegal?

I squinted.

"Oh. Oh, oh my God," I yelled.

I dropped the paper bag onto the floor and covered my mouth with shaking hands. I was standing in shock in his office doorway, staring at this clusterfuck, frozen.

"Holy fuck. Cass." Jack yelled. "Oh Fuck. Oh Fuck."

He clamored to climb into his pants and raced across the room to me at the same time.

"Jack. Fucking…stop moving. Right now. I'll see you at home. Go straight home, Jack," I yelled.

Actually, I screamed it.

He stopped long enough to pull his pants up and looked directly into my eyes. I turned and ran.

Holy shit.

I didn't think I had run that fast since I was in my twenties. I blasted through the front doors of the building into the cold California night air. It was the first breath I took since I wasted my last on that motherfucker.

Okay, what now, Cass?

I needed to go home.

Oh my God.

Did I just tell him to go home like he is my teenage son, who I busted smoking weed in the woods with his buddies? Why the fuck would I tell him to go to our home? Oh God, he would be racing out of this building after me any minute.

Jesus.

I gathered enough of myself together to compartmentalize the nightmare to be able to drive. I only had to go fifteen minutes and then three minutes to say bye to Elizabeth, and then I could lose my ever-loving shit.

I turned the key.

Prince's *When Doves Cry* blasted out.

How fucking appropriate.

Not today, Prince.

I skipped the track.

Pulling into the driveway after having one of those drives, I was teleported with zero recollection of moving the vehicle. I calmly climbed from the car, took the biggest breath, wiped from under my eyes, fluffed out my hair, and scaled the steps slowly of our home of fourteen years.

The memory of the sweet little porch from our first date when he brought me home started playing through my head. The furniture and the lamp on the porch. It was beautiful. I was now standing on my porch staring at what would become past tense.

Fucking Jack.

I turned my key to Elizabeth, already in the entryway, gathering her things to head out. She was a college student at the UCSF for Dentistry, and being there late was never a bother since it gave her a quiet place to study.

Cora was also thirteen, well, almost fourteen, and took care of herself, but I hated her being home alone when we worked super late nights. Elizabeth hung out with her. It was a habit we hadn't quite broken yet.

"Thanks for staying later tonight," I said, trying desperately not to make eye contact.

Slinging her bookbag over her shoulder, she said, "No problem at all. I never care unless I have an early morning exam, and even at that, you two are never *that* late."

"Well, we appreciate it. Was everything good with her?" I asked, looking through the stack of mail on the entryway table, trying not to draw attention to my swollen, red eyes.

"Yeah, oh, she has spirit week next week and needs a different outfit every day. I am loaning her my scrubs. She wants to be a dentist," she said as she approached the front door.

I replied less than enthusiastically, "Awesome. Spirit week."

I have no more spirit, Elizabeth, and I need you to go so I can open a bottle of wine or whiskey, whichever is closest to the cabinet.

"Thanks again, girl. See you next Wednesday," I said and waved as she hopped down the front porch steps to her car parked at the bottom of the walkway.

Once I closed the door, I placed my face in my hands and breathed in my new life, which currently sucked balls, and now I could never use that phrase without thinking of Beth with Jack's in her disgusting mouth.

First, I headed upstairs to check on Cora, who I found sleeping soundly beneath her headphones. I usually removed them, but tonight I would leave them on just in case shit got real when my stupid pot-smoking son got home.

Yeah, let's just pretend that's what fucking happened for a minute.

I climbed down the rear stairs that led me right into the kitchen. I opened the glass-faced cabinet that housed our pretty extensive collection of spirits, from whiskey to cordials. Dinner parties with his partners and the wives were a regular affair, and Jack thought having every liquor was a damned necessity.

Not feeling it, I thought wine. I just needed calm, not drunk and angry. I needed to be strategic. I reached into the wine cooler below me and took out a nice cab, a glass, and had a heavy ass pour.

I knew I should be thinking about what I would say, but I was numb. Or was this what shock was? Or maybe I was not surprised.

Sitting at the oversized white granite island, I looked out at the open living room. Quiet, so put together with the white linen furniture, oversized artwork adorning the walls, and dim lighting. It looked like a page out of Luxe Interior Design magazine, for heaven's sake. It was obviously just a perfect little façade. The house came with Jack, and the beautiful design was already there. I simply fitted into his pretty little life.

My right hand slid over the cool, smooth granite surface. My left hand shakily lifted the glass to my lips. My mind stupidly decided to replay when we met.

When I graduated from culinary school, I scored a great position as chef de cuisine at Le D'ebut. My sous chef was Kyle. We were such a great team after the same dream, as we would say jokingly, because that was cool shit to say back then. Unlike me, Kyle worked his way up the culinary ladder with all the hard knocks of the profession. In the culinary field, a person could still make it if they didn't spend a hundred and twenty grand on a degree. It was hard, but more respect was given. Kyle was a workhorse like me, and we enjoyed learning everything we could. French cuisine was the base of everything we would ever do.

Eventually, I became an executive chef, and I made Kyle the chef de cuisine under me. We had our own unspoken language in that kitchen.Being the executive chef gave me some leeway and creative time to experiment. I was growing tired of rich sauces laden with butter. Foie gras, escargot, and Coq au Vin were no longer a challenge. Kyle hadn't broken a sauce in two years. We were on autopilot in our careers, and with late-night closing chats, we talked about what cuisine we really wanted to work with. Asian. Since I was a teenager, I was obsessed with the culture, so it was my dream. The part that was comical was that neither of us had worked professionally with that type of cuisine, and neither of us was remotely close to being of Asian descent. We would be impostors.

It was a typical night of service, and Kyle had things running smoothly enough for me to head into the dining room and mingle with the guests. This was the awkward part of the job as executive chef and far from my favorite. I was an introvert and ran on the shy side most of the time.

I changed my apron into a crisp, clean one. I checked my hair, which was piled high in a messy bun on my head, and headed out into the dining room. I stopped by random tables.

"How was your meal tonight?"

"Glad to see you back."

"Thank you for coming in."

I approached a table with three men who looked like they were simply grabbing a business dinner. They were all wearing the stand-ard, *we are over being professional today look, but we are still being professional.*

Suit jackets were off, and ties were a little less tight than they most likely were from earlier. There was good energy at their cock-tail-laden table, as if they had a successful day and were doing some celebrating.

I approached their table, politely interrupting them, and said, "How was everything tonight, gentleman?"

They all replied.

"It was wonderful."

"The Duck Confit was outstanding."

There was one guy who was more reserved. Dark hair, great eyes, and a strong jawline, if that was even a thing. It felt like he was checking me out as I stood, leaning my hand on his counterpart's chair. I wished them all a great night, thanked them for coming in, and headed into the kitchen to start closing it down.

About fifteen minutes later, Stacy, the front of house manager, handed me a napkin with a note.

I want to know you better. Jack Buckley.

His number was written on it. I was shocked since this was the first time someone had tried to pick me up at work.

Why? Was I really sending the, I'm single vibe?

"Hey, Stacy. Which one was it?" I asked in surprise, with my hands in the air.

Shaking her head as she turned to walk away.

"The brunette with the dark eyes. You got it, chef, and you don't even know it."

I finished the night without another thought about it until I reached into my chef coat to retrieve the restaurant keys. The note. My heartbeat sped up for a minute as my mind wandered to somewhere other than work.

Should I call?

This is too weird.

I locked up and took a cab home.

I plopped onto the couch with excitement as I called the only person who told me what to do in this predicament.

Britt.

"Hey. I need help," I said immediately.

"Holy shit, what's wrong, Cass?" she answered with an urgent tone and a gravelly voice.

"Oh, nothing bad. Well, I guess it could be, eventually. I had a guy at the restaurant give me his number tonight. I never even talked to him. Just me visiting their table during service. Is that freaking creepy? Should I even think of responding?" I asked as I rambled all my thoughts hurriedly.

"You asshole. You always text me. Not call. And you scared the shit out of me. It's 3 am here. First, chill the fuck out. It's not like he's stalking you...well...yet," she said with a deviant yet tired laugh. "Second, yes, you should take the risk and at least throw out a text. What do you have to lose? Oh, wait. Was he hot?"

In a questioning tone, I said, "I think? I don't know. I was over my work night and not thinking much of it, but I was getting the vibe that he was checking me out. Ugh. I'm so awkward with this shit." I said, rolling around on my couch like a nervous twelve-year-old having an awkward penis talk with her bestie.

Britt paused a second while muffling the phone, then said, "Avery said to text him, *let's just fuck.*"

I laughed and said, "Hi Avery. Sorry I woke y'all up. I forget where I am sometimes."

I let out an audible sigh. "Fine, I'll text him."

Britt asked I tell her all about it tomorrow before she hung up. She seemed slightly more interested in her husband than me at the moment.

We said our goodnights, and I sat staring blankly at the napkin with Britt's voice in my head, saying, "What do you have to lose?"

First, a large pour of Pino Grigio went into my glass, and then I typed the number into my cell.

Hi, it's me…Cassandra from Le D'ebut.

I took a massive swallow of wine and hit send before I changed my mind.

Immediately, I got back a message.

Hi Cassandra, I'm Jack. I am glad you called.

Then.

I mean… texted. Sorry, this is awkward.

We texted back and forth for an hour while I obsessively paced my tiny apartment. I giggled at our immediate banter and polished off the entire bottle of wine. Jack asked if I would like to meet soon for dinner I didn't cook. I accepted.

And that brought me back to this cool, white granite countertop. I swallowed the last sip and poured more of the burgundy bliss into my glass. This house was where he brought me on our fourth date. This very countertop is where he made love to me for the first time.

I could see myself clear as day, right in front of me on this very counter. I picked out the lace bra and panties just for him. Expensive. Black. I went from commenting on how amazing his kitchen was down to the six-burner gas stove to him peeling off my jeans and black tank top within seconds. Him fisting my long, auburn hair back and ravishing my neck and down my chest, taking my breasts in his warm hands and lightly biting my nipples through the lace, causing me to gasp with need.

He lifted me up onto the counter and then stood between my legs. I could feel his hard cock pressing into my wet panties as he undid my bra with one move like a professional, then sucked my nipples one at a time. I lay right there on this cool counter, and he made his way down my stomach. I looked down and watched him take his jeans off, then slowly slid my panties down my legs. He told me I was so beautiful. Jack made me come over and over. He put me before himself, making love to me. He was so gentle and caring. We never left the counter that night.

The car door shut, the distant vibration of footsteps on the front porch, the jingling of the keys, and my heart pounding out of my chest yet again for the second time tonight were all I could hear.

I could feel the heat of him standing behind me, and in an almost whisper, "Cass?"

Chapter 2

CASSIE

I sat at the counter, feeling Jack approaching me from behind. My heart raced. My mind was a scrambled mess of unorganized thoughts, anger, and confusion. We were both incredibly non-confrontational, and this was beyond our comfort zone. This past year, we ignored every issue, so we didn't have to go to blows.

But there we were.

I didn't exactly know the blowing would be coming from someone not in this room, though.

I dragged my wine glass by the stem in small circles on the countertop, watching the liquid race around the glass. I gazed at my wine so I didn't have to look at him.

"Cass, can I please talk to you?" he pleaded softly as he stood next to me, obstructing the view of our picture-perfect living room.

"Jack, I don't think I want to hear what you have to say right now except for one thing. Do you want her? Like, love her? Be with…her? This is your moment to be fucking honest with me," I say in a calm but stern tone.

He sighed and said, "Yes, it's been…"

"Shh. That's all I want to know right now." I look up at him with tear-filled eyes.

"Oh my God, Cass, what have I done to you? Us? I'm so sorry."

He cried as he paced the kitchen.

"Jack," I said, trying to interrupt him.

Still pacing and running his hands through his tussled black hair, he said, "I mean, I just wasn't…"

"Jack." I snapped. "Sit down."

I point to the stool across from me.

He sat as I poured more wine into my glass.

Man, this bottle is going fast.

I continued to stare into my glass, praying the words absorb into me through osmosis from the alcohol.

Be tough, Cass. No time to be a pussy right now. This is business. Deep breath.

"So, this is how it's going down. You will go upstairs and pack a bag for at least a week. No coming for this and that bullshit. I need some time. Tell Cora you have a work trip," I said in a matter-of-fact tone.

"Okay," he replied slowly, waiting for the holy shit moment.

"You will not touch my restaurant, I will not touch your law firm, you will make sure I have a good place to live to finish raising Cora. Keep this house. She needs something familiar."

At that point, my hands ran wild through my long hair, and I looked down at the counter.

Don't make eye contact, Cassie.

"I'm not going to drag expensive fucking lawyers into this and get ugly. If you do, I'll fuck you up, Jack."

I said that with venom and that time with eye contact that seemed to have connected with his soul.

"We will not use Cora as a pawn. This won't be a war. To the outside world, we are divorcing because we just fell out of love. The only person who is going to know what happened is Britt because I must tell someone for my fucking sanity."

I took a deep, sharp breath and then chugged the remaining wine from my glass.

"I don't even know what to say, Cass. I…" He shuttered words.

"I suggest you go start packing, Jack," I said with little emotion.

He slowly passed me and went up the stairs to do just that.

"Another thing," I said.

"Okay. What is it?" He asked, turning towards me.

"I'm going to fly Britt here, first class, and I'm putting it on your American Express," I said with a slight smirk.

"Seriously? First class?" he asked with hands out.

"That's for today's horrific visual. You are lucky I'm not going Lorena Bobbitt on your ass right now," I said with squinted eyes and pointing my empty glass in the direction of his dick.

"First class it is," he said, holding his head low in shame, then proceeded upstairs.

I emptied the rest of the bottle into my glass and put it into the recycle bin under the sink.

Am I numb?

I seriously didn't understand the feelings I was having.

Am I...okay? Relieved?

This is fucked up. Maybe I had to go through all the stages of grief. Maybe I was going to do the steps in twenty-four hours. God, that would be great. Just be done with it all and move on. I didn't know how we were going to tell Cora. She was going to be devastated.

This was where my emotions lay. The tears were moving in now that I was thinking about breaking up our family.

Damnit Jack.

I retrieved my phone from my purse to text Britt.

Shit.

It was 10:45 pm, so almost 2 am in Charleston. I'd text her in the morning. If I text her now, it would be an all-nighter, and I didn't think I had it in me.

I opened the sliding door to the patio and stepped barefoot, touching the cool, dewy wooden decking that sent chills through my body. The rush of cool air hitting my tear-streaked face burned as I took a long, deep breath, trying to calm myself down. The sky is perfectly clear, and the stars were incredible.

Damn.

I wanted a cigarette. How odd was it that intense stress and anxiety mixed with the rush of fresh air made me want a damn cigarette?

Fuck it, I want one.

I went back inside and opened the upper cabinets and the drawers nobody ever used when Jack appeared in the kitchen with a suitcase and his suit bag draped over his arm. He was no longer in his sex suit, but a relaxed pair of blue jeans and a white t-shirt that fitted him perfectly. I felt nauseous that I was losing this man. I felt sick that I didn't try harder to make him stay, that he didn't try harder to keep me.

Then I heard his words.

"What are you looking for? Hopefully, not a knife to dismember my member," he said jokingly, covering his crotch.

"I'm only allowed to make jokes right now when I see fit. Emergency cigarettes. The ones Jeff's wife left at the last dinner party we hid from ourselves," I said as I opened more odd cabinets.

He reached above me into the cabinet over the refrigerator. The one I always forgot existed until the holidays. He took out the pack of hidden Marlboro lights. His strong bicep moved past me, peeking out from under the sleeve. The smell of his cologne, woodsy and clean.

I really fucking hate you, Jack.

"Ah, sweet Jesus." I said as I grabbed them from his hand.

I retrieved a grill lighter from the drawer and went outside, where my wine sat on the table.

I struggled with the cigarette, lighter, and wind combo when Jack took the lighter from me and, wrapped his free hand around it to block the wind and lit it for me. I took a nice long drag, then a nice procession of ridiculous coughs.

"You are very out of practice, Cass."

He smirked.

"Thank God, but I will practice until this pack is gone…or I puke. Probably puke," I said, turning it and looking at the bright red cherry on the end.

He took one out of the pack. "You mind if I join you?"

"Might as well. There is nothing normal about this evening, anyhow," I said as I took a sip of my wine, then another slightly less torturous drag.

Leaning up against the rail of the deck, I said, "I can't believe I am having a lucid fucking conversation with you right now, but other than Britt, you are my best friend."

The tears fell again down my face and my chin, and my lip quivered.

"Your life cannot continue only being your work, Cass," he said. "Don't Jack."

I held my hand up and my head down to stop his words.

"This isn't all going on me. You could have fucking told me you were done. You could have tried. We could have tried." I wailed.

"Cass, you are right. We became the best roommates, best friends, and we always came together to be amazing parents to Cora. That will never stop. You do know I will make her well-being number one, you know that, right?" he asked.

"Yes, Jack. I never doubt your ability to be a wonderful father," I said softly. "I just wish we could have been better partners for each other. We should have been first. Us, goddammit."

I stared at my feet, which were crossed at the ankle.

"Babe, I'm so sorry. I'm sorry I fucked up."

He came in for a hug.

"Yeah, not so fast." I put my hand up. "I'm not wanting your *handsy babe* comfort right now. The vision Jack, it's really fucking fresh."

He nodded his head in agreement, took a drag off his cigarette, and then put it out in the potted cactus by the door.

"I'm going to go. Are you okay for now?"

"Golden." I said sarcastically.

"Let me know when you aren't. I'll call Cora tomorrow morning before school and let her know I'll be out of town for work this week. Just…tell me what you need, Cass, and I will deliver," he said sadly.

"Goodnight, Jack."

I turned to lean on the railing overlooking the bay, taking in another drag and the last sip of my wine.

I turned in time to see the front door close inside the house, then moments later, the headlights from his car back out of the driveway and down the street.

Motherfucker.

I couldn't believe this had happened. Like...Fuck. One more cigarette, and I would take a shower and try to sleep.

I decided the pity party for one was getting lame, so I cleaned up any incriminating evidence that Cora may find in the morning. She would be very pissed to know I smoked and Daddy and I were divorcing, too.

I dragged myself upstairs to the master bedroom. Thankfully, the memories were enough for one evening. After scrubbing myself clean, I ran out of energy to feel much of anything. I curled into the fetal position, and sleep took me faster than expected.

My alarm went off at 6:00, and I swore I had only been asleep for fifteen minutes. My eyes felt so heavy, and my head was not well. The cigs were not a good idea at all.

Damn, I needed to get Cora's lunch ready and get ready for work. I had a damn delivery, and I need to be there at eight.

You can do this, Cass. Water, ibuprofen, banana, coffee.

I jumped in the shower again, just to wake up. I threw on a clean black chef uniform, which, in all fairness, never felt clean, no matter what I cleaned it with. My hair went into a messy bun, and I brushed my teeth. That was the extent of personal hygiene the universe was getting today. I walked down the hallway to Cora's room and knocked on her door.

"Cora? You up, baby?" I called in a fake, happy voice.

"Yeah," she replied.

The real teen years hadn't hit yet, where I got the big attitude. I dreaded it. She was so sweet and kind. It was going to break my heart when she told me she hated me someday and slammed her door every chance she got.

Shit.

That might start sooner than I thought once she realized her happy world was about to change.

I headed downstairs and started my day just like any other.

Just stay on task, Cass. Keep it going.

I scooped the coffee, poured in the water, and pressed it to start.

Bread, mayo, lettuce, turkey, cheese.

Yogurt, apple, water bottle.

Coffee was ready, Jack's travel mug, poured the coffee…Jack's mug. What was I doing? Poured it into my mug.

I was just standing there, staring, and the tears fell. I couldn't even feel them anymore, as if my face was numb to them.

Cora's feet bounced down the stairs, grabbing my attention. I quickly wiped my face clean and got my shit together the best I could.

"Hey, Mom. Did Elizabeth tell you about spirit week?" she said immediately.

With my back still to her, I replied, "Yeah, she did. We will get it all organized. How cool. Your lunch is there on the counter. I'm making your smoothie."

As I got out the blender from under the counter, I bought myself time.

"I'll grab the milk," she said.

"Thanks, honey."

When I turned back, she noticed my face.

"Mom. Why are you crying?"

"I'm fine, baby. I just had a horrible night at work last night, and I'm emotional. I'm okay. I'm also having my girl time, you know how I get," I said, making a crazy person look.

"Are you sure?"

She looked worried.

"I am sure. Let's get your breakfast and get you to school. Vanessa is going to be here in a few to pick you up. We don't want to keep her waiting," I said in a soothing voice to keep her from worrying.

"Wait, I need to say bye to Dad."

She started up the kitchen staircase.

"He's not here, Cora. He had to go to the office early today. He was going to call, but I guess he got busy this morning," I said.

"Oh, okay," she replied without a single doubt that I was being truthful.

I whipped up her smoothie, handed off her bookbag and lunch, and waved her out the door with a hug and a big kiss to ease her mind. I watched her skip down the steps to Vanessa's little blue Subaru with her long brown hair flowing through the wind. She looked exactly like I did at that age, with long tan limbs, dark eyes, and long hair.

As soon as the door closed, I rushed back to the kitchen.

Shit.

7:15. That meant it was 10:15 there. I pulled up my contacts to find Britt. The face I chose to go along with her number is her cross-eyed, which was a pretty accurate example of her answering the phone.

Me: Fuck my life.

Britt: Sup Whore?

Me: Talk?

Britt: In the middle of an order with Avery aka slave driver. Can it wait a few?

Me: I caught Jack with his dick in his paralegal's mouth last night.

My phone rings immediately.

"Holy shit. Please tell me you are joking right now?" Britt said.

"No, I am dead serious," I replied with almost no emotion.

"I'm going into my office. Sorry, we are in the middle of a meeting, and Avery is, you know, being Avery."

She whispered, but Britt couldn't really whisper, so it was kind of comical.

"I don't have a ton of time anyhow because I have to go to work too, but I needed to talk to you," I whispered as well, because well, she was.

"What happened?" she asked.

"I took dinner to his office, and there they were. I don't want to relive that again right now. It is what it is. Anyhow, when can you come? I am flying you here. Can you break free in a couple weeks? I can take some time off. I will fly you first class at cock-sucker's expense. Well, I guess he's technically not the actual cock-sucker is he?" I rambled.

"Girl, I…"

She started but was interrupted by Avery entering the office.

"Brittney, why did you leave the meeting?"

"Sorry. I'm on the phone with Cassie. It's important. She had something really important to tell me," she said, holding the phone away from her ear.

"She's finally professing her undying lesbian love to you?" he said jokingly.

"No, she caught some chick with Jack's dick in her mouth last night, and she needs me to come give her a hug and be her friend within the next couple of weeks."

"Um, fuck, Cass, I'm so sorry," he said, taking the phone from Britt and putting it on speaker. "I feel terrible."

"It's going to be okay, Avery. I'm a big girl. Can I borrow your girl, though? I sure could use my bestie. Pleeeeeeaaaaase?"

"Seriously, why couldn't Jack do this in say, I don't know, January or February when we were twiddling our thumbs? He had to wait until Food and Wine Festival?" he says sarcastically.

"Well, him not doing it at all would have been better, asshole. You can live without me. It's not your first rodeo," Britt says sharply.

"Sorry, I didn't mean it that way, Cassie. Babe, we are one of the main sponsors of the Food and Wine Festival, and we are a wine and cheese bar. I need you," he pleaded to Britt.

I quickly reply. "Hey, y'all, I didn't know. It's not that big of a deal. Maybe next month? It's okay. I will be okay."

"If something happened to you, Avery, Cassie would be on the first flight here without blinking," she snapped.

"Not during Food and Wine Festival. Fuck that, Britt." I said, laughing. "Seriously, I am not getting you two in a fight over this shit. Enough damage has been done by this dick-sucking nonsense. Can you at least keep up with my late-night sob sessions for the next month, though?"

"We got you," Avery said. "Again, I'm really sorry, Cass. You don't deserve this shit."

"I love you, whore. Shit, can I even call you whore anymore? It sounds mean now," she said sadly.

"Please don't change anything."

We hung up. I realized I was now running late for work.

I shot a quick text to Kyle, explaining I was running fifteen minutes behind.

No problem, Chef. The delivery truck is late as well.

My phone dinged with a text message.

Britt: It's not over. I'm working on him.

Me: Don't divorce over it.

Britt: But then we can be together forever.

Me: I don't eat pussy, and I don't have a dick.

Britt: Yeah, there's that.

Chapter 3

CASSIE

*P*ulling into my parking spot at Sagi-Shi felt different. I left this spot last night hopeful, and now I was back feeling so deflated and empty. How the hell could so much fall apart so fucking fast? The frigid morning air hit me hard the second I got out of the car. My eyes felt so swollen, and I wondered how many excuses I would come up with today for my looks and lackluster.

No sleep?

Allergies?

Stress?

How refreshing would it be to just walk in the door and say, "Good morning, Kyle. Sorry I look like shit. Jack and I are fighting. I kicked him out after I saw this chick swallowing his big dick last night. What a show. I'm freaking exhausted. I may need to cut today short and take care of my life since it's sort of in the toilet right now. Thanks pal. I owe you big time."

I pulled the heavy metal door open and walked down the short hallway to see Kyle leaning over the computer in the office. He barely looked up, "Good morning, Chef."

"Good morning. Sorry, I'm late," I said.

"All good. Do you want to go over this weekend's specials first while we wait on the trucks? The fish guys should be here first," he said.

"I need some more coffee while we do this, but yes, sounds good. Walk with me?"

We make our way to the coffee station where some angel sent from heaven, most likely him, made a fresh pot already.

He walked along with me as he flipped through the pages of a legal pad with the menu we had discussed previously for the week. It's pretty bold, and I'm realizing he's executing it this weekend when I'm not even helping on the line. Kyle has enthusiasm, and his excitement is contagious, even with my current situation. Sagi, as we all call it, is all Asian, meaning our menu is anything from Japanese, Chinese, Thai, Indian, and Korean. This opened up endless possibilities. This weekend, Kyle decided to do a twist on elevated Thai street food.

"For an app, I have Popia Sot, the fresh spring rolls with pork, crab, and Chinese sausage. These are the ones I made you last week. Um...eleven," he said.

"Yes, those were fantastic. Are you having them sit in that sauce? Just a smear. Last time, it was too much. And are there two rolls?"

I motioned with two fingers.

"Yes, two." He scribbled in his notepad.

"Then make it twelve due to that crab in there."

"Yes, Chef."

He scribbled some more.

"Next, Gung Foi Tort-the crunchy prawn cakes, sixteen."

"What sauce and garnish with those?"

He flipped back in his notes. "A Yuzu aioli and a simple seaweed salad with a charred octopus."

I nodded and said, "Nice job, but take out the octopus. Those prawn cakes were fantastic on their own."

I continued drinking my coffee and pulling chairs off tables in the dining room as I listened.

He continued, "Som Dtam Malakor; the Green Papaya Salad, fifteen."

"Hey, I know you love the heat of that salad, but easy on that one. I hate seeing chicks order it, and they are so disappointed that they can't eat it and have mascara streaming down their face. So, maybe go super light on the bird-eye and have the servers ask for a level of spice."

"Yes, Chef. Next, I have the prawns and chilli jam with Kanom jeen noodles, twenty-three, then Chicken and banana chilli curry with Assam, twenty-one."

"Raise the prawns to thirty-two. Did y'all already make that chilli jam?"

"Yes, Chef. Reggie made the chilli jam two days ago. Why?" he asked.

"Please tell me he made a double batch? That is the bomb. We can use it next week too."

"He did. We are all set then," he said with pride for thinking ahead on that one.

"Damn. You made quite the menu. Where are you in the mise en place checklist? What can I help with?"

"Well, the regular menu is almost prepped. Reggie is here in fifteen to finish that, then the rest of the morning prep line will be in. Carol should be in for pastry, not that I know what the hell she does." He takes a breath. "Where are our damn trucks? I need to break the fish down."

His hands and legal pad went into the air.

I could see the stress building in his entire body, and I realized I hadn't thought about one ounce of my stress since I walked in the door. This place absorbed it like a freaking sponge.

"Hey, I'm here to help Kyle," I said, patting him on the back like it was his restaurant and I was consoling him.

Noticing my face for the first time since I walked in, he said, "Jesus, Cassie, what happened to your face?"

"Why? Is something wrong?"

I touched my face with the hand that was not holding my coffee.

"You just look like you are having an allergy attack or something. Your eyes are really swollen over. I'm sorry I didn't notice until now," he said with a hand on my shoulder.

"Yeah, I don't feel great. As soon as we knock this out, I may head out if that's okay. Unless you think I need to come back and help you on the line tonight," I asked, praying he would turn me down.

"Oh no, we have this. Reggie, Soup Head, and I are solid," he said reassuringly.

I shook my head. "Seriously, how did Darius become Soup Head?"

"You will never know, Chef," he said with a laugh.

"Okay, boss lady stays out of it. If I don't get Goldfish Eyes by the end of the day, it will be a miracle," I said, laughing and walking into the office.

Kyle popped his head in.

"Hey, you know you can take time off, right? You pay me the big bucks and gave me the Exec title to do that six months ago."

While shrugging and looking down at my laptop, I said, "Yeah, where am I going to go, Kyle? All my friends are here."

Then I grin and look up at him.

He smiled and said, "Yeah, maybe somewhere with Jack and Cora? Just…just know you can trust that I have your back here, Cassie, okay?" Looking around the corner, he noticed the fishmonger arrived. "Help me get this order, will you?"

"I'm coming," I said.

We stood outside with the truck and all the crates of freshly caught fish. We inspected them for size, clarity of the eyes, and smell, and we signed off just as the produce truck pulled in. I did the same and went through the next order with Kyle. I scrutinized vegetables with the same careful eye, sending back slimy green onions and bruised and battered mushrooms, hoping for a better product to be delivered tomorrow.

The morning prep guys were busy unloading, prepping, and stocking the walk-in. They rotated, dated, and threw out anything past its prime. I was a stickler for this shit, and I liked my walk-in to look pristine. I was sure I had a better name than Goldfish Eyes behind my back due to this.

My phone dinged with a text in my pocket.

Britt: We have a plan. Call me when you can.

Me: Okay. I still won't eat pussy.

Britt: How can you manage to be this funny at a time like this?

Me: Survival

I helped Kyle, Reggie, and Soup Head get everything prepped for service. I met with Alicia, my front of house manager, and we talked about the night's specials. She printed off the cards for each table, talking about the significance and history of the Kanom Jeen noodles. I loved giving our diners a food lesson with every dining experience. It was our thing. I went over wine and drink pairings with our bar manager, Margaret, who would then go over it with our servers. There was a three-hour break, and Kyle and the morning guys headed out to do personal errands and grab a few stray items from our local vendors.

The rest of the afternoon crew came in and took over the remaining list of tasks. I made sure they had what they needed, and I headed home to meet Cora when she got home from school. This was my Friday ritual. That was what having Kyle allowed me to do. I got to be more of the owner-operator and less of the hands-on chef. I missed parts of it, but I also loved being a mom. Unfortunately, I seemed to have sacrificed the wife part in the process.

On my way home, I called Britt via the car phone. She picked up lightning fast.

"Hey. I think we have a kick-ass plan," she said enthusiastically.

"Okay, what's up?"

"So, oh my God, first I have to say, we are fucking geniuses, and we need a Nobel peace prize or some shit like that," she rambled.

"Dude, spit it out. Plan?" I asked with little patience.

"We want to fly *you* here for Food and Wine and pimp you out in our tent to be all, like, celebrity and shit. It's spring break for Cora, so bring her. She gets to see your parents and can hang out with Harper at the beach with my parents if she wants. It will be awesome. We have a black-tie gala at night, a total socialite fun-filled weekend. It will be great. Total win-win."

She said this with such joy I thought that she might cry.

"Wait, pimp me out? What is that about? Am I coming to work?" I asked with utter disappointment.

Britt pleaded. "No, well, we are going to work, but we would like you to be the face of our business this year at the festival. We would like to feature you as a celebrity chef from San Francisco. Avery even came up with the idea of a Buckley Board with all things from San Fran like sourdough, meats, and cheeses, and feature some California wines from there. You can sign... I don't know the menu of your restaurant. We can figure something out. Come on. What do you think?"

I breathed in deeply and waited for the extra drama effect.

"Fuck it. Okay, let me just double-check with my parents, the dates for Cora's spring break and make sure I can leave work because I have never left longer than four days, you know? I guess I should talk to Jack. Not one word from him today. He was supposed to call Cora this morning. Of course, nothing. What a dick," I mumbled.

"Sorry Cass. Fuck him. This will be good. All your people are here. It will be great. It's perfect timing for a trip home. Are you telling your parents what happened?" she asked.

"No. Not yet. I'm not going to tell them what he did. That's between us. I told him I'm not going to get ugly about this."

"You are way too nice. I would have his balls in a damn vise," she snapped.

"Nah, it's not me. It's not worth it. It's the same outcome, a divorce. Why make it shittier than it needs to be? I don't want to do that to Cora," I said. "I'm so sad for her, Britt. She really loves us together."

"Damn, Cassie. It's going to be okay. Get your ass here, and I will hug the shit out of you. Meanwhile, let me know anything else I need to do. Oh, we want to take care of your airfare since you are working for us."

"You don't need to do that. Jack needs to pay."

I laughed.

"We get to write it off. It's cool."

We discussed dates and logistics as I entered the house and then hung up.

I realized I hadn't eaten since yesterday. It was amazing how my body went into survival mode and needed very little to survive. I rummaged through the fridge, and nothing looked appetizing. I decided to grab the blender from this morning and start throwing random shit in. Coconut milk, almond butter, protein powder, a banana, a handful of spinach, and some blueberries that had definitely seen better days. I leaned against the counter, sipped my concoction, and stared at my quiet, perfect home.

I eyed my phone sitting on the counter.

Why haven't you even checked on me?

No call to Cora as promised this morning.

Coward.

I really wanted to call your ass out.

Don't do it, Cass.

Instead, I text Kyle.

Me: Since you brought it up, I think I am going to take you up on that vacation. Can you live without me March 29-April 5? It's also a work trip for Food and Wine Festival.

Kyle: Done. I have taken 2 weeks of vacation this year and it's March, you zero in 3 years.

Me: Your point is?

Kyle: Yes, Chef.

I checked the time, and I had thirty minutes before Cora got home. I should call my parents and tell them we were coming home. How did I do that and skate around the subject of Jack?

Shit.

I would have to tell them, but I would wait until I was there in person.

The phone rang twice, and she picked it up like she was expecting it.

"Hello, my darling Cassandra," she answered cheerfully.

She was the only person who used my full name.

I replied happily, "Hey, Mom. How are you doing?"

"I'm doing great. Your father is here too. Say, hi, Sam," she said, calling out to him. "Hey, baby girl," he called out from across the room.

"Hi, Daddy. I miss you," I shouted back into the phone as if he could hear me.

"How was your week, honey?" she asked.

I went right in with a long ramble. "It was good. We are very busy at the restaurant, Cora is doing great, so, spring break is around the corner, and I was wondering if you wanted to have us visit?"

With excitement, she said, "Oh, that is wonderful news, Cassie. Yes. Please. You know you never have to ask. It's been so long since you have been home."

"Sam. Cassie, Jack, and Cora are coming home for spring break," she yelled across the house.

I interrupted her. "Oh, Mom, it's just me and Cora. Jack can't make it. Sorry."

"Is everything okay?" she asked, worried.

"Oh, yeah, he just has a big case, that's all," I lied. "I will be helping Avery and Britt work the Food and Wine Festival, so it will be a mix of things. I'll send you all the dates and stuff as soon as I have it all lined up."

"Well, we can't wait, honey. It's been forever."

"I know, Mom, I will try to be better about that," I reply solemnly.

She interjects. "I didn't say that to make you feel guilty. We understand your career. We know the sacrifices you make. We are so proud of you, kiddo."

We chatted about random things happening and hung up for me to notice I could get in one more thing before Cora got home.

I found his contact. I should change this picture to a jackass.

Me: Change of plans. I want to go to Charleston for spring break with Cora to visit Mom and Dad. I'll see Britt then.

Jack: Sounds good. Cora home yet?

Me: Should be in 5

Jack: Have her call me

Me: Don't say anything. I haven't told her about spring break yet or us

Jack: I won't and wouldn't

Jack: I'm sorry. Very sorry.

My fingers hovered, and I decided I needed to learn to let things be.

Cora bounced into the house, excited it was Friday and her school week was over.

"Hey, Mom," she yelled as she closed the door behind her.

"Hey. How was your day?" I asked with more enthusiasm than the morning send-off.

She immediately went into an excited rant.

"It was good. Can I spend the night at Tiffany's tonight? We have cheer practice tomorrow morning anyhow and her mom can take us. Please?"

"Well, how can I say no to that?" I said with a smile.

She hugged me and bounded up the stairs to pack, saying, "Can I get a snack? I'm starving. Can you take me over there when you get a chance? Thanks, Mom."

I guessed this was the beginning of my lonely life.

Shit.

I had no friends or a husband. I had given my responsibilities away at the restaurant. I should go back to work on the line tonight.

I stopped her.

"Hey, before you go up, call your Dad."

"Oh, okay."

She came back to get my phone and scrolled to his contact. Good thing I didn't change it to *Jackass.*

"Hey, Dad," she said as she walked away with my phone up the stairs while I cut an apple and put some peanut butter in a small ramekin.

Minutes later, she scampered down the stairs carrying her book-bag busting at the seams along with her pillow.

"Dad is going to be gone all week he said."

I replied, "Yeah, that's the news on the street. So, what do we need to get for spirit week? I can do that this weekend with all my spare time," I said, skirting around the subject.

With a sad face, she said, "Oh, now I feel bad Daddy isn't here, and I'm spending the night out."

"Oh, my God, Cora. It's not your job to entertain your mom. I'm fine. I am going to enjoy some alone time. Or maybe catch up with a friend."

She looked at me with a screwed-up face. "Really? Who?"

Looking back and forth, searching for an answer, I said, "One of the wives of Daddy's partners. They are my friends. I don't know, I have friends."

I knew damn well they only came with my relationship with Jack.

Munching on her snack, completely clueless, she replied, "Okay, you should do that, Mom."

I made the ten-minute drive to Tiffany's house and listened to her bubbly chatter about how she would like a phone for her birth-day, who liked who at school, and cheerleading stuff. The child could pack ten minutes full of information without a single breath. That reminded me to call Britt, another person who liked to talk, as she climbed from the car bounding up the steps to the two-story Victo-rian-style house.

The phone rang twice, then she picked up.

"Yo Ho."

"Hey. You working?" I asked.

"No, Avery is tonight. I'm working tomorrow. What's up?"

I sighed with relief.

"Thank God. Cora is spending the night out, I'm not working, no Jack, and I have realized I have one remaining friend, you...on the opposite side of the country. I even lied to Cora and made up friends so she didn't feel bad for me. I'm pathetic, Britt."

"Well, you left all your friends here and basically went right into the chef world there. It's a hard living. Your crazy people have no life outside the kitchen," she said.

"You have a restaurant too."

She laughed.

"Girl, we have a bar that has an oven. We cut cheese, open jars of stuff, warm bread, and melt the occasional brie. A trained monkey can do it. Hence the reason Avery is there alone right now running the joint."

I said, hysterically laughing, "I still think you need shirts that say We Cut the Cheese."

"Right? I just need to order them. He keeps vetoing your idea," she said. "We need to keep it classy, Britt." She gave her best Avery impersonation. "It's bullshit."

"He's scared you will turn the place all low class. Remember when you ordered domestic beer?"

I laughed.

"Oh, I'm aware. His downtown high-class snooty ways mixed with my southern redneck ways, lord girl. You know how long it took for him to even get out of the friend zone with me with all the high-fa-lootin' South Battery shit? Damn."

I loved getting her all fired up. She got so funny and southern that she started to make up her own vocabulary.

"So, what are you going to do tonight since you are all… alone?"

She emphasized the alone part.

"I don't know. I've been on a destructive path for the last twenty-four hours. I only wanted wine, and I smoked old cigs I found in the cabinet. I think I want clam chowder and sourdough. Maybe just vegetate and watch Netflix?"

I started to question if that was destructive enough.

I got a long hesitation and then she snapped, "Seriously, that's destructive? I totally thought you were going to at least say you stopped by the dispensary and got a joint. You'll eat a heavy cream-based soup and watch a chick flick? You are so lame, Cassie."

"Thanks, dickhead. I have never gone through this before, and my support group consists of a fourteen-year-old, you, and the person who shit on my heart. What would you do? Go to a strip club? Go do lines on a homeless man's dick?" I barked back defensively.

"Woah," she said. "Calm down, sister sledge. First off, I am not against doing blow or hanging out with homeless people, but Hep-C runs ramped in that community, and I wouldn't do it off his dick."

I laughed, realizing I was a bit over the top.

"Second, I am always here for you," she said sweetly. "You are my girl, and if that is what you want to do, then fine. It's still lame, but you do you. Hey, the cigs are pretty reckless behavior on your part, though. Especially in Cali. People really frown upon that shit out there."

"I have more. I was going to smoke them with more wine tonight. I forgot how fun smoking was." I said with excitement. "Maybe I won't be crying and coughing this time, so I'll sit out on the terrace and enjoy it. Don't let me become a smoker, though. This is just temporary."

She laughed and agreed. "Totally, I will join you when you get here, then we will quit again. Hopefully, we won't need the patches, though."

"You need to get some toys and masturbate too. Don't forget to take care of those needs too, girl," she reminded me.

"I wonder if I'll ever have sex again. Sweet Jesus. I don't want to date and learn about another person. Oh my God. This is going to suck. Guys are older now. Shit. I am going to have to deal with a different set of balls, and what about a different dude's dick? Do they shrink with age? Do their balls get all old and saggy?"

I rambled and fretted.

"I don't think it's that bad. Maybe don't set your age range to eighty when you are setting up a profile online. Hey. We can get you some revenge strange when you get home. Test out the waters. Go get that kitty all waxed and ready, sister."

She giggled.

I gasped. "Britt. I am not ready for that. It's been twenty-four hours, and I'm pretty distraught."

"Better yet, text your boy. Get him to come to Charleston. That isn't strange. It's been like, two years since Lauren. He has got to be ready for something if he hasn't already. Guys move on faster than women. Y'all definitely know how to be discreet, good God."

"No. We have only been friends since I married Jack. It's been so long. It would be awkward now, and I'm just not ready and…I just can't. I'll order some toys. I'll be fine."

"Okay, suit yourself."

"If you text him that I'm coming to town, I will kill you. Britt, don't meddle," I warned her.

"Who? Me?" she said in a baby voice.

I had officially been sitting in my car in idle in front of the chowder house, having this conversation for twenty minutes. I put an end to it and picked up my to-go order of the most delicious New England clam chowder and sourdough in the bay area. I never ate clam chowder without sourdough.

I rolled the windows down in the Mini, took the longer way home along the waterfront, and enjoyed the cool air blowing through my hair. The last of the day's sunlight on my face.

Pulling up to the house felt so different. Jack's car not being there was disturbing. Since I gave control to Kyle, Friday night had been the three of us having dinner, watching movies, and sitting on the terrace watching the sunsets, and it had been nice. Now, I wasn't even expecting him. Where was he? I wanted to know, but I didn't because I knew.

There I was, walking up the steps with my lame-ass soup. Britt was right. I sucked at this, but I'd get better. I'd work my way up to one-night stands and cocaine, I promised myself, but I was too tired tonight.

Chapter 4

CASSIE

The warmth of his strong hands wrapped around my outer thighs. The feel of slight stubble on his face swept my inner thighs ever so lightly, and the coolness of his soft tongue rolled over my clit and through the folds of my pussy, intoxicating me. Reaching down, I ran my hands through his thick, dark hair, pressing his face harder into me. Needing more and more.

"Fuck this feels so good."

I moaned as I slowly ground my pelvis into him.

His one hand gradually disappeared from my thigh and made its way to slide through my slick opening, now dripping with a mixture of my juices and his saliva.

I gasped as one finger slipped inside me. Meanwhile, his tongue flattened and lapped up and down, over my now swollen clit. Two fingers reached deep inside, pleasuring my core as I bucked against his hand.

I moaned and with a lack of control of my hands, I ran wild through his hair and across his strong shoulders.

"I'm going to come. Fuck."

Taking his mouth off me for just a moment, he said, "Yeah, come for me, baby."

His low, raspy voice sent vibrations throughout my entire body, he proceeded to then suck my clit and thrust his fingers in and out of me with precision. He had years of experience with my body and knew exactly how to get me off.

I tightened and pulsed around his fingers with such an eruption that I could feel my juices flowing down to my ass. Once my body stopped writhing with pleasure and my breathing slowed, he gently slid his fingers from inside me and made his way up my body, kissing my stomach and my breasts along the way, taking my hardened, sensitive nipples into his mouth. He made his way to my face and looked into my eyes.

"I've fucking missed you."

I sat straight up in my bed.

"Holy crap," I said aloud as I looked next to me, completely expecting to see him there.

I swiped the bed sheets on either side, thinking it was all too real.

I lay back down with my heart pounding so hard. I was sweating.

Holy shit.

That was intense. I slid my hand slowly down my body. First, my tank top, where I found my nipples razor hard, breaching through the cotton fabric. I lightly rubbed over them, and I immediately felt my core tighten.

Next, I slid my hand down my stomach to my silky panties, where I found them completely drenched. I slid my hand underneath to find my clit, so hard, my pussy so wet, I must have actually come. That dream was so real.

I was left insanely turned on, and I could not stand it.

Well, let's continue that fantasy I guess, because there is no harm in that, a fantasy, right?

I closed my eyes, trying to relax, and went back to where my dream left off. His dark hair, the green eyes with flecks of gray. I started adding dialogue like it was a movie. Hearing his voice again made my heart swell.

"I miss this," I said.

"Shhh," he said, putting his finger over my lips. "Let's not talk, let's just fuck."

Yeah, the dialogue was overrated. Even my subconscious wanted me to shut up. I was there to get off, not recreate a love story that was clearly over. I took a deep breath, slid my panties down, then spread my legs. My fingers slid through my slick opening, revealing the velvety folds and my clit, which wasn't as hard as it was just moments ago.

I reached into my mind and found him waiting. Leaning over me, kissing me with those amazing lips I craved, especially the thicker bottom one. I ran my hand through his dark hair, his neck, and over his strong shoulders and arms. The body I never wanted to let go of. His tongue tangled with mine. I wanted to see all of it, so I motioned for him to go to his back, and he responded to my command without hesitation.

I ran my wet index and middle finger over my clit in circles as I imagined his hard body lying in my bed before me.

I straddled his naked body with mine as I licked and kissed my way down his chest, holding his arms above his head. I knew he hated to be restrained, but he let me, and this turned me on, knowing he was giving me what I wanted at his expense. I licked and sucked a line down and blew cool air as I went, sending chills over his skin. I could feel his cock hardening with small jumps beneath me with every inch I went. I stopped to take his hardened nipples in my mouth and brought them lightly between my teeth. He breathed in so deep, stifling a whimper of pain, or was it pleasure? I saw him arching his head back and Adam's apple bobbing as he swallowed hard. I continued my journey downward and loosened my grip on his arms. Giving him free rein to take hold of my long hair.

I was now sliding two fingers inside of me, then alternating my clit, then back to fingering myself again. Imagining his body in such detail and what I was doing to him had me so turned on. I was so close to orgasm. I didn't think I was going to make it to penetration in this fantasy.

I wrapped my warm hand around his now fully erect, thick cock, and stroked it from root to tip while I looked at him, now looking at me, with hooded eyes. I climbed between his legs and ran my tongue up and over his balls, which made him gasp with pleasure. I ran my tongue up and proceeded to wrap my lips over his swollen head. I slid over his thick shaft, then all the way down until I couldn't take in any more.

"Oh my God, Cassie, you do this so well. I've missed your mouth on my cock, baby."

He groaned as he fisted my hair and pulled it out of the way so he could see what I was doing.

I stroked his cock up and down with my hand and mouth with such a harmonious rhythm he couldn't hold back. I could feel his cock swell so hard inside my mouth, hitting the back of my throat. My saliva ran down his shaft all the way to his balls as I continued stroking.

"I can't hold on, Cassie, I'm going to come."

I continued stroking him as I felt his cock pulsating, then suddenly, hot streams of salty cum hit the back of my throat. I let him fill my mouth, and I swallowed all of him.

I was fiercely rubbing my clit and arching my back. Waves of warmth overcome my entire body. Tingles formed in the base of my spine as my pussy clenched down. I got wetter and wetter as my fingers moved faster.

I completely lost myself, yelling out loud, "Oh my God, I'm coming too, Stephen."

Chapter 5

CASSIE

We found our first-class seats, sort of complimentary of Jack Buckley. He got off easy, considering he only had to pay for Cora's ticket. I noticed a gentleman in the seat across the aisle had been eyeing me a few times. Once the passengers stopped walking through and Cora was enthralled with her new phone, he motioned to me.

"Excuse me, are you Cassandra Buckley?" he asked.

With hesitation, I answered. "I am. How do you know my name?"

With a slight grin, he said, reaching out a hand, "I'm Greg Langly, and I am the senior food writer for The San Francisco Eat. I am the one who did the last article on Sagi-Shi."

With wide eyes, I shook his hand.

"Oh wow, it's nice to meet you in person. Thank you for that glowing review. After that, we have been on a wait for almost two months."

"Really? That is good to know. Hopefully, I can drop my name for a last-minute reservation in the future for that," he said, winking.

I laughed.

"Shit, I'll give you my cell and a chef's table in the middle of the kitchen, Greg."

"Where are you headed?" he asked.

Surprised he would care, I said, "Charleston, SC. It's home to me, and I will be a guest chef for my best friend's wine and cheese bar's booth at the Wine and Food Festival. They are one of the main vendors this year and trying something new. They are pawning me off as a celebrity chef because nobody knows any difference on the East Coast. I keep trying to tell them a few awards don't make me a celebrity chef. I'm not on TV or have my own cooking line."

"Very cool. Well, I will be stalking you because that's where I'm going, too," he said with both hands out.

"No way."

"Yeah, they're sending me to do an article on East and West Coast Food and Wine Festivals, Upcoming chefs, and things like that. I'm actually meeting with a panel of food writers, chefs, and TV producers as well when we are there for a project back here in San Francisco," he said enthusiastically. "I may be stopping by your booth and chatting you up some more if that's okay?"

The flight attendant came over the intercom and rudely interrupted our very in-depth conversation to go over instructions for when we dived into the ocean or needed to put masks on our screaming children.

Oh shit, I have a kid.

I looked next to me really quickly to see Cora. Six days into being a phone owner, I lost her in the social media vortex, and the outside world no longer existed. I had every parental control known to man on there, so she couldn't look at porn like I had been doing obsessively every night with my new selection of battery-operated boyfriends. I found out they have an acronym of BOB. How fucking cute is that?

"I've got a date with Bob." Then, followed by a cigarette on the terrace. Who really needs a man?

"That's awesome, Greg. And yes, I would always be available to chat it up about the food and beverage industry, anytime."

It was a very early flight, so Cora was fast asleep twenty minutes later. My coffee had kicked in full force, yet it didn't stop me from accepting more when the flight attendant asked to refill my cup. I was in a great conversation with Greg across the aisle, and the sun was beaming through the few window shades that were slightly cracked open.

I felt like I could breathe. I was leaving so much bullshit behind. Cora still didn't know about Jack and me splitting. We had been lying through our teeth because he hadn't been living at the house. We told her we were working on some things, and she asked tons of questions. He picked her up from cheer practice and took her to dinner. He took her out of town last weekend to a concert for her birthday, and we acted like I had to work. After this trip, we needed to come clean.

We landed in Denver, and I reached for my phone.

Me: We are on time. 3:09 arrival.

Dad: You bet. Can't wait.

Me: I'll update if it changes. Love you

Dad: love you more, Bug

Cora was officially a fourteen-year-old with grumpy teen posture and required more than regular feeding. It seriously happened overnight.

We grabbed a salad and sandwich and made it to our next gate just in time. First class was nice. The seats were big and comfy. I thought I needed to travel that way more often. I needed celebrity status. I was nice and comfortable when Greg walked by, wishing us a nice rest of the flight. He was only lucky to have an upgrade on that first leg. Poor guy had to sit with the peasants back there.

We landed in Charleston, and the second we got to baggage, I spotted my dad.

The picture of the older Ted Danson. Full head of white, beautiful hair, standing about six foot three, round glasses, and a wingspan so wide it could hold both of us at one time.

"My babies," he shouted, squeezing us tight.

"Hey, Samsie," Cora said.

"Dad, you look great. I see you are wearing your uniform."

"Stop. You and your mother leave me alone."

He rubbed my head like I was five.

My dad wore an outfit one day about fifteen years ago, and I commented that he looked really good. He had worn the same outfit every day since, unless he had to go to a special event like a wedding or funeral. Khaki shorts, long dress shirt with the sleeves rolled up, and flip-flops. Charleson was mild, so in the winter, he might put on khaki pants...maybe.

We grabbed our luggage and made our way to the garage. As soon as the doors opened, the humidity hit me like a hot, wet washcloth. I instantly didn't think I was wearing enough deodorant or owned enough.

"Good God. I feel like I'm being waterboarded. I forget how humid it is," I said in shock.

Dad just laughed.

As I wheeled my bag next to him and Cora walked hand in hand, I said, "Dad, you could have just picked us up at the curb."

Shocked, he replied, "What kind of animal would I be if I did that? A real man walks inside to greet his family."

I guessed chivalry died when convenience was born.

We got to his car. Oh, bless it. His burgundy 2008 Honda Accord sat waiting for our arrival.

I did everything in my power not to laugh.

"Dad. When are you going to get a new car?"

"What is wrong with my car, Cassie?" he said, making a Vanna White movement with his arm.

He knew damn well it was ridiculous.

"She only has one hundred and seventy-three thousand miles on her."

"Samsie, it's really old. Maybe we could go buy a new one when we are here. I'll go shopping with you," she said.

"So far, I am greeted with you making fun of my clothes and my car. We aren't getting off on the right foot here, are we girls?"

He laughed.

I had to admit, the car drove really well. My dad took impeccable care of his things, and they lasted.

We made it home just fine.

Just as the car doors closed, my mom rushed out the house to greet us in the driveway. She was small with her little five-foot-three frame and full of energy. I got my dark complexion from her Spanish side of the family. Anne Patterson had the same dark hair, dark eyes, and skin. My dad looked like he was our Uber driver, standing with our luggage, and his translucent bird legs and white hair were standing next to us three. We had just got home from a cruise from the Bahamas.

My parents, Sam and Anne Patterson, were two of the most wonderful people I knew. My mom was so kind and patient. She came from money, but no one would ever know it. She helped to manage commercial properties in Boston that she and her brother inherited from my grandfather.

Dad was a contract attorney. He never had to go to court because he simply looked over contracts for corporations and individuals all day from the comfort of his home office. He worked up the contract sealing the deal on my restaurant. We were about to see how good my dad was with my pending divorce.

Fingers crossed.

My parents had money, but they spent it on the important things that were considered an investment. They lived in a very nice home on the peninsula downtown for thirty-eight years. It was worth two million, but my dad still drove his Honda, and Mom drove her older Volvo. I went to a private Catholic school and the best culinary institute their money could buy. Education was an investment. We traveled a lot, and international travel had always been our favorite.

I was fifteen years old when we went to Japan for the first time. I was absolutely amazed by that country, especially the food. That was the exact moment I realized I wanted to be a chef. I was obsessed with the flavors. Beautiful curries, delectable pho with lemongrass, fish sauces, creative sushi, the beloved Okonomiyaki, Udon, amazing Ramen, soft tamagoyaki, and pillowy dumplings.

Oh my God, the dumplings.

I came home from that trip Japanese. My room was transformed full of Japanese lanterns, fans, etc., and I wanted to learn all the recipes. My parents supported this whim, and this shaped me into a culinary-obsessed teen. I could eat curry and pull the spices out, one by one, off my palette like a sommelier tastes notes of cherry, chocolate, and oak.

I was going to be a chef, and they were my biggest cheerleaders. My parents sent me to culinary school camps in the summers, and I offered to stage at any restaurant that would let a kid in their kitchen. My dad had chef friends and invited them to support my dreams. I knew I needed to learn all types of cooking, not just Asian.

I applied to the Culinary Institute of America in California during my senior year and was accepted. I was terrified to leave home and go all the way across the country, but I was so excited to make this dream happen. I owed all this to my parents' support and encouragement. Those two humans were who I owed all my success.

"How was your flight?" my mom asked as she helped us into the house.

"It was great, Gram. We flew first class," Cora said.

Taken back, she said, "Wow, that's big-time, kid.".

She hugged me. "I'm so glad you are home, Cassie."

"Me too Mom," I said.

The house hadn't changed a bit. Classic Charleston style. They lived a block off the historical waterfront Battery. There was amazing ocean breezes, especially at night. Horse-drawn carriages passed by doing tours during the day, and tourists walked by, pointing at how beautiful the gardens were. For as many years we had been there, we didn't notice it until they blocked the driveway when we were trying to leave in a hurry. Wrap-around porches to die for on all sides of the house, complete with joggling boards. Five bedrooms, three bathrooms, and a kitchen. They remodeled this extremely outdated beauty along with all the appliances about four years ago. It was extraordinary with the white granite counters, green lower cabinets, and copper fixtures. Completely functional for any chef's heart.

I designed it, and they had top-of-the-line appliances. That may be why my dad was still driving a 2008 Honda, come to think of it.

"Cora, you have your room, the one with the bathroom. I put fresh towels in there for you," Mom called up as Cora dragged her suitcase up the stairs.

"Thank you, Gram," Cora replied.

I put my suitcase into my childhood room. It was completely void of all things Cassandra. I was glad. I always thought it was weird when parents left their children's rooms like a shrine when they left home. It seemed eerie, like they'd died. Also, if I had to come back to a single little girl bed, I would be pissed off. I liked this. A very classy almost blue-gray, white luxurious fabrics, cozy chair, the fireplace, and bookshelf stocked with classics and sweet childhood pictures. It was really inviting.

I made my way downstairs to the kitchen, where my mom was putting together a tomato pie. My absolute favorite thing she made. I sat at the counter-height island and watched her.

"I like what you did with the room. Super cozy," I said.

"Robin came over and helped me redecorate it. She has such a good eye," she said as she layered beautiful red tomatoes and slices of red onion in the bottom of the homemade crust.

"I'm taking Cora on a bike ride for ice cream. We will be back soon," Dad said, waving goodbye.

Mom shook her knife at him and said, "Sam, don't ruin dinner," just as the back door closed behind him.

"I opened a bottle of prosecco honey. It's in the fridge," Mom said, pointing her knife at the fridge.

"Since when did you start drinking that?" I asked.

"I had it at book club and found it so refreshing, and now I'm an addict."

I grabbed a stemless wine glass from the cabinet along with a water glass. I poured a tall water and half a glass of bubbly. I then topped my mom's off before putting it back in the fridge. No sooner was I sitting down on my stool I heard her say, "So? What is really going on with you and Jack?"

I almost choked on my water.

"Why do you think something is going on?"

Without even looking up from slicing and layering her pie, she said, "Well, you have been avoiding us and haven't said his name in one conversation when we have talked. Also, Cora told us he hasn't been home in two weeks."

My heart drummed hard like I got busted sneaking out of the house. Why was I scared to tell her? She loved me.

"Cassie, look at me, baby," she said looking directly at me, putting the knife down and leaning onto the counter.

My eyes filled with tears as I looked into hers.

"No matter what, your father and I will always love and respect your decision. We know you will do what is right for your family. Don't be scared to talk to us, baby. We are here for you. What happened?" she asked with a saddened brow and tilted head.

I got up from the counter and went around to hug her tiny frame. I just needed to do this. I needed to let the tears flow and hug my mom.

"We just fell apart, Mom. He decided I wasn't enough, and we are calling it quits," I said in between waves of tears.

She stroked my hair. "It's going to be okay."

"I know. I'm strong. You made me that way," I replied with a shaky voice.

"Damn right, I did. Good thing you didn't get your dad's softy genes."

She laughed with tears.

I sat back across from her and got control of myself. We had a long talk about my plans to move on. I was going to find a new place. Jack would keep the house. I needed to talk to Dad about the restaurant and make sure all was secure, even though Jack swore he wouldn't touch it. I did okay when I kept it business.

"Does Dad suspect something is going on?" I asked.

"Why do you think he is on an ice cream run, and you are alone with me?"

She smirked.

"Y'all are dirty." I sneered.

"Your dad comes across as clueless sometimes, but he knows everything. He knows all the bad things you were sneaking around doing in high school. He's like a little neighborhood detective."

She laughed deviantly.

"What are you talking about?" I asked.

She made lips with a zipper motion.

"Woman. What do you know?" I yelled.

She turned to put the pie in the oven.

"No can do, Cassie, my lips are sealed," she said, laughing.

I headed up to freshen up and change into less clothing since it was much hotter than San Francisco was at 5:30 this morning. I just needed to get rid of the travel clothes.

I got my phone and saw I had missed a slew of texts.

Britt: Are you here????

Britt: Bitch...I feel your presence.

Britt: Did we break up?

Britt: I'm coming to your parent's house. I know you are there.

Britt: As soon as I find my keys

Jack: Hey. Just making sure you made it there safe. I hope you have a good time. Hug Mom and Dad for me.

Fuck you.
You don't get to call them Mom and Dad anymore, Jack.
Ugh.
Why does that piss me off so much?

Greg Langly: I hope you enjoy your time back home. Loved talking to you today on the flight. I seriously want to get up with you this week about some possible business opportunities back in SF. If I stop by your booth, I promise, I'm not stalking you. Greg

Huh...that was interesting. I wondered what that meant?

I was pulling on a little blue t-shirt when I heard a loud commotion coming from the front door.

"Britt. Wow. I haven't seen you in so long," I heard my mom say.

I heard my girl's scratchy voice saying, "I know. I am so busy with the restaurant and the kid and all. You and Sam need to come in. We'll take care of you."

I ran down the stairs, and it was as if we had not seen each other in years. I thought it was only five months. She screamed. I screamed. We were ridiculous. Nobody should be in their forties acting like that, yet we did.

Just then, my Dad and Cora walked in the door as well.

"Well, look who it is," my dad said as he hugged Britt tightly.

"Hey, Mr. Sam. You look great. Stylish as always, I see."

She held his arms out to check him out.

"See? She knows style," he said.

Mom and I rolled our eyes.

Cora said, "Hi, Aunt Britt. Am I going to see Harper this week?"

"Yes, baby, she is so excited to see you. Do you have her number?"

"Can you give it to me? I have my own phone now. I can text her."

She shared her number, and Cora ran up the stairs to start a text thread immediately, which would inevitably take up the rest of the vacation.

We went into the kitchen, where my mom opened another bottle of prosecco, and we all caught up until the pie was done and Dad was pulling the BBQ chicken off the grill.

"Are you staying for dinner with us Brittany?" Mom asked.

"No, ma'am. I just wanted to lay eyes on Cassie. I need to get back to the island," she said.

"So, what is the plan for this weekend?" I asked.

"Can you come by the restaurant tomorrow around ten or eleven and go over everything? We have tons to do, not necessarily you. Did you bring something hot for the gala?" she asked.

"Sure. I brought two dresses because I wasn't sure, long or short. If it's this hot, I'm not wearing long. I'm sweating my ass off. I'm not used to this humidity anymore."

"Yeah, you are used to lizard-land."

She laughed.

We hugged and talked all the way to her car for the next fifteen minutes before she left. I went inside to enjoy a great evening with my family.

Dinner was amazing. The tomato pie was insanely good. There was nothing like a southern tomato pie with the creamy, herby layers of tomato goodness and flaky, buttery crust. I wished I could take one home.

It was a long day. I took a nice long, hot shower and got into my cozy pajamas.

One last check on Cora.

I knocked lightly on her door, then popped my head in.

"Hey, you need to get to bed. It's late."

"I'm just talking to Harper," she said with an eye roll.

"Okay, please shut it down Cora."

I glared.

Lord, that phone would be the death of me.

I crawled into my bed. Mom made it with heavy layers of blankets, just the way I liked it. I was going to sleep great. She also had a sound machine. It was as if she emulated my guest room when she visited me. I took out my phone, the blue light illuminating my face in the dark room. I checked to see if I had any new messages.

Britt: We are going to have a great time.

Me: Of course we will

Britt: It looks like a bunch of people are going to go to F&W this weekend.

Me: How do you know?

Britt: Facebook

Me: Anyone I need to know about?

Britt: I don't know.

Me: Britt.

Britt: Just a certain friend group

Me: huh?

Britt: The jock group from high school. He's not on FB, so I don't know if he's going. I swear I said

NOTHING.

Me: It is what it is. It's fine. I'm fine. I have to go to bed. Night

Britt: Did you bring your BOBs?

Me: No. They are too loud. Lol.

For as many times my heart beat this hard, I should be the new sound effect for the next Jumanji movie. Ever since she brought him up. Ever since I had that dream, I have had a new obsession.

So, I went to my Google toolbar and typed in Stephen Harlow. Among all the information that came up, there were only two profiles that were him.

The first, a black and white headshot for his company website, Southstar Security, Inc. He looked serious. His hair was dark and had a slightly tousled look. He had his beard in the picture. It was one of the many looks of Stephen that I didn't really get to enjoy. He looked right at me as if he was saying, "I want to fuck you". And it was really hot. I guessed if I was hiring him professionally to save my company's ass, I would see him as, *this dude is serious as fuck.*

When I found the picture, BOB and I had a date or two with it. Okay, maybe four... or eight.

The other thing I found in my search was an article from two years ago. The article about the kidnapping of Lauren, his fiancé. It was a grainy picture of him walking in handcuffs. Pretty disturbing, and it did not entice me to take BOB for a spin. They quickly accused him of her disappearance when they ran out of leads and dragged his name through the mud and the media. I remembered hearing about it all the way in California. He made his millions with his cyber security firm and maybe that made him a target. He was ultimately cleared as fast as he was charged, but that scar was still in the search engine somehow. That really sucked.

That made me sad. I needed to go back to the headshot. Yeah, that was better. God, he was so damned hot. What if he showed up this weekend? It was not a good time for me at all. I was a total head-case and I would feel like I was cheating on Jack, as crazy as that sounded. Britt would slap me across the face right now if she was in my head. There was no way Stephen could be okay either. Lauren was still...missing. How did someone deal with that kind of pain? It wasn't like he could just move on, knowing she could be out there somewhere or trying to get back to him.

I shut down my cyber-stalking and lulled myself to sleep with thoughts about the next steps of my life. What it would look like to be single again. I wished my life included Jack. I wished he was there moving forward with me, but he made his decision. The tears were becoming fewer and fewer.

Chapter 6

CASSIE

I made my way down into the sunny, bright kitchen and poured myself a cup of coffee.

"Good morning," came from my mom on the side porch who was watering the pots overflowing with flowers and green ferns hung strategically by hooks between columns.

I pushed the screen door open and stepped out with bare feet onto the wooden porch, with coffee in hand.

"It's not hard to keep up with this watering until it's ninety-eight degrees out every day in late July."

"I know, some day I'll get a system to do it, but this it so therapeutic for me to do it by hand."

"Y'all have such green thumbs. You always have the most beautiful gardens," I said as I ran my hand down a lush fern leaf.

"Thank you, Cassie. It's easier when you don't have a full-blown career and little kids to chase around. These are my babies now," she replied, moving the hose down to the lower patio.

Just then, Dad came out.

"Are you almost ready, Cassie? You need to be there at ten, right?"

"Between ten and eleven, Britt said. No rush. Is Cora ready?"

"She was finishing upstairs when I saw her last, I'll check. What time is our reservation tonight, Anne? I don't want to be too long today."

"It's at six, Sam," she said, winding up the hose and turning off the spicket.

"I'm so excited to see Mike again and eat at his new place. I can't believe we got in," I said.

My dad chuckled.

"It pays to be best friends with him. I don't think there was anything available for months. This place is a lot smaller than his other one. I don't know. We haven't been there yet."

"I'm sure it's great," I said, patting him on the shoulder as he walked past. "So? She really talked you into going car shopping?"

I laughed.

"That girl of yours can talk me into anything. I am just looking at what is out there. I don't plan on buying it today. Just looking," he said, shaking his long finger at me.

Cora came walking out saying, "We are getting you a new car, Samsie. Wait until you see all the new technology that has come out since the cavemen built yours."

I sucked both lips into my mouth, stifling a laugh and walking past them.

"Nice one, Cora," I said, slipping on my sandals and grabbing my purse and leather bag.

"I'll see you all back here later then?" My mom asked.

"Yes, ma'am. Britt will drop me off and pick Cora up at five," I said.

The fifteen-minute drive to Avery and Brittany's restaurant was pure entertainment. I missed those moments shared with my family. Life in San Francisco was just Cora and me. We had no family close by. Jack's parents lived two hours away, and we always had to trek to them, but it wasn't often.

Avery and Britt opened this little gem twelve years ago before wine and cheese bars were a thing. Charcuterie wasn't a fad yet. Between them, they knew everyone in Charleston, so people flocked to support their business. The location was primo as well. Not downtown with downtown real estate prices, but close enough to shops and walkable to a slew of neighborhoods.

They recently rebranded it to Wine on Board, which has a travel vibe. Charcuterie boards, wine, and beer flights curated for Italy, Spain, etc. Britt even had little postcards for the markers. The charcuterie boards were locally made and were in the shape of the countries. I could buy a South Carolina board, and she could put together full-sized local cheeses, honeys, jams, mustards, and such for me to give as gifts. This was the stuff we sat on the phone and geeked out on. Marketing and cool ideas for our restaurants. Well, vibrators and the possibility of me getting laid again some day had been the latest hot topic for her, but mostly restaurant stuff.

I pushed the door open, and the contrast was so dark compared to how bright it was outside.

Before my eyes could adjust, I heard, "Look who it is."

I was enveloped in a full bear hug by Avery. He stood about six feet, with dark brown shoulder-length hair, crystal blue eyes, burly, and as huggable as they got.

Avery Manning was your quintessential southern guy, born from a Southern lineage going back to the Civil War. His family had a plot in the Magnolia cemetery.

That was when a person knew they were born and raised there.

He had a family so deeply rooted in Charleston that they had been in politics and real estate, had names on bridges, and been in the news for picking up prostitutes and DUI convictions. Depending on what part of the family tree you looked at, you may not like the Mannings. His particular line was the good one, in my opinion. His parents were kind and generous, and they raised a great man. He had been the best father to Harper and husband to Britt. He was patient beyond measure. He chased Brittany for years before he broke her down. She wasn't interested in *his type,* and it wasn't until she broke down on the side of the road and he rescued her that she finally gave him a chance. Like a balloon, Avery held onto her string, connecting her to the ground but gave her freedom to float around the sky.

"Hey, you."

I hug his big strong body.

"I am so glad you are here and are doing this with us. It's going to be great. Wait until you see what just came in."

He walked me over to the side of the bar, and I put my bag down.

"It's a life-size write-up of your article. We will have this set up behind you. How cool, right?" Avery said with excitement.

"Holy shit. I'm huge," I replied with wide eyes.

They did an article in the San Francisco Times about up-and-coming female chef entrepreneurs and a picture of me standing in my chef's apron up against the wall, looking slightly badass. It was a great article, and I did have a take-no-shit vibe in the entire article and photoshoot. Avery picked a good one.

"I like it Av," I said, nodding in approval.

He wiped his brow. "Phew. I was worried you would hate it and I didn't pass it by you first."

"I also ran off menus for your restaurant to sign for people if they want and figured you can ask questions and such while we hand out food," he added.

"Sounds great."

Britt then made her way from behind the back into the bar area.

"Hey. I'm sorry. I was finishing up a wine order. Did you see your big ass cut-out?"

"Yeah, it looks good," I said, standing next to it and mimicking the bad-ass pose again.

"So, what else are y'all doing for your booth?" I asked.

Avery stepped in and said, "We are doing a 100% biodegradable, because you know how it is in California." He chuckled. "A personal charcuterie board with a wine stem holder cutout. We are calling it our Buckley Board, which we will be putting on our permanent menu here."

I covered my chest with my hand. "What? Guys. That is so sweet."

"We love you, Cass, and you are so cool, so we decided to make you the California thing," Britt said.

Avery continues. "We will have sourdough instead of the classic baguette. The cheeses are Foggy Morning, Humboldt Fog, Mezzo Seco Jack, Burrata, and Red Hawk. I have the standard cured meats, mustards, almonds, and jams as well. I picked six wines for people to choose one from for this weekend. We like small boutique vineyards to rotate here in the restaurant. People really like that."

"Sounds like it will be fantastic," I said enthusiastically.

"All right, is there anything else, Av? We have important business to discuss over lunch," Britt asked.

"You are free to go, my ladies."

He bows.

She slapped him on the ass as he turned to leave. "Thanks, babe."

"You two are so sweet."

"He's a pain most days. He's just kissing my ass because I didn't leave him and go running to you. I also gave him a blow job this morning, so he's extra nice."

She laughed.

"You are a horn-dog," I said, shaking my head.

"Ooh. Come look at the new stuff I did."

She took me by the wrist and pulled me into the dining area. There were tables that sat in nooks where map-adorned wallpaper lined the walls. Bookshelves held travel books spanning the world. Old vinyl suitcases sat high on shelves, brass lanterns with amber lighting created a warm, inviting glow.

"Look at all my new plants. I have been able to keep things alive now. Doesn't it look so good in here now?" she said twirling in her proud space.

"I love it Britt. You need to put this on your Instagram page. I haven't seen a tour of inside in a while," I said.

She took her phone out and snapped a selfie of us. "There, I'll tag you, so our followers are together too," she said. "I'll do it all weekend."

"Smart cookie," I said. "Just keep the drunk ones out."

She then broke out her notorious devious laugh.

Britt introduced me to some of her staff that was hustling to get things ready for the intense festival weekend and regular hours at the restaurant for Thursday night. Due to having such a small staff, they were closing down for Friday and Saturday nights and only working the festival.

We headed out and went to meet friends for lunch downtown. I hadn't seen some of these girlfriends in five years, so it was nice to catch up. Most had not ever even met Jack, so now that I was splitting up with him, they didn't know anything different. A great lunch, a couple cocktails, and reminiscing about the past. It was a nice distraction. It was also nice to see that I actually had friends.

Britt and I drove back to my parent's house to be greeted at the driveway by the one and only, burgundy Accord.

"Seriously? What is wrong with this man? Why won't he come off his money for a new car? Is he that sentimental or just that cheap?"

I laughed.

"I think it's hilarious that he drives that car and lives here."

We walk up the driveway, then into the house.

"We are back," I said.

"How did it go?" my dad asked.

I shook my head. "I should be asking you that. I see you didn't buy a car."

I pointed outside.

"They wouldn't come down on the price at all. I think it was because I wore these expensive leather flip flops and designer glasses."

He took off the glasses and pointed at the designer label on the side.

"Nah, it was probably your address on your license when you went to take the car for a test drive." I smirked. "You can't hide money, Dad."

He laughed and made his way up the stairs.

"I think your car is just fine Mr. Sam. You don't need a new fancy car anyhow," Britt called out.

"Finally, someone with sense. Thank you, Brittany," he said down the stairs.

Cora appeared in the kitchen with her bookbag full as can be. "Hey, Mom, hey Ms. Britt."

"You ready to party?" Britt asked.

I laughed. "Yeah, you better behave yourself over there. They do the heavy stuff at the Mannings."

"We do. Coke, not that diet crap. The white stuff, not wheat. We like red food coloring and MSG," she said smiling.

"I can't wait," Cora replied.

"Don't kill my kid," I warned.

She laughed. "Just with junk and love," she said as she hugged me. "Love you."

"Love you too," I said.

Cora hugged me. "I love you, Mom."

"I love you too, Cora. Have a great time with Harper and be respectful. Text me, okay?" I asked.

"Okay. Bye," she said bouncing out the door with Britt.

Before showering and getting ready for dinner, I checked in with Kyle.

Me: Checking in. Is the order ready for tomorrow?

Kyle: All set Chef.

Me: I will be at the festival when everything comes in.
If there is a problem, call me. My phone will be on.

Kyle: There is nothing I can't handle, but okay.

Kyle: Breathe.

Me: Trying.

Kyle: I got you.

Me: Thank you

Mike Tanner was one of Charleston's top chefs and restaurant owners. This was his third endeavor, Red Door. It began with a tiny ten top speakeasy bar underneath, which was strange considering nothing was ever underground in downtown Charleston since the city sat only five or six feet above sea level. After we waited on our table with a unique craft cocktail that my dad couldn't believe people pay eighteen dollars for, we made our way up to the main restaurant, which was a renovated old bank. The dark black and red rich colors against white, crisp linens and brass give it a cozy, inviting feel. The menu paid homage to the Lowcountry and was quite simply, a culinary experience and history lesson for your tastebuds.

Our incredible server, Landry, was impeccably attentive and had just cleared our dinner plates and emptied our bottle of wine into our glasses when Mike appeared at our table.

"Wow. I can't believe this is my little chef Cassie, all grown up," he said with outstretched arms.

I stood, and hugged him. "Aww, Mike, how are you? You look great."

"I'm doing well. I haven't let the industry kill me so far."

He laughed.

Holding my arm out, I said, "This place is wonderful, and our dinner has been nothing short of amazing."

"That means a lot coming from you, Cassandra Buckley."

"I learned from the best."

"I hear you are going to be a celebrity chef at the Food and Wine Festival this weekend?"

"Oh God. My friends are ridiculous. You should see the life-size cutout of me of an article I get to autograph in front of," I said with my hand on my forehead.

He laughed. "Enjoy it. We don't get the recognition we deserve being behind the scenes all the time. Our art is eaten, and it's gone."

"Thank you for getting us in on such short notice Mike. I wanted Cassie to enjoy it while she was here," my dad said as he took his napkin to his mouth.

"Anytime. You are my family. I need to get back to the kitchen, but I wanted to come and say hi. I'll come see you in the culinary village if I can sneak away this weekend," he said placing his hand on my shoulder.

"Please do Mike," I replied as I hugged him goodbye.

We finished up dinner and walked home. This restaurant was only about five blocks from our house and the night felt incredible. There were more people bustling around since it was spring break season and Food and Wine Festival. Unfortunately, tourists came and when the weather was this amazing, they bought and stayed, driving up our population and home prices. It had changed so much over the years. You couldn't keep a beautiful place like that a secret forever I supposed.

I thanked my parents for a great evening and checked in with

Cora, Britt, and then my front of house staff. Everything was running smoothly. I lay on my bed, went to my Google search bar, and let my heart flutter off to sleep.

Chapter 1

CASSIE

✗

I saved pristine monogrammed Sagi-Shi chef coats for days like this. Mike Tanner told me back in the day to save a few clean chef coats for photo opportunities when you made it big and had to go into the dining room to talk to your guests. He also drilled into me to always treat your staff like family and the days of yelling in the kitchen were long gone. I lived by it all. So, as I was getting dressed, I felt so fortunate that I had my chef family taking such good care of my restaurant back in San Francisco. I believed they loved it and its success as much as I did, and I was so proud of that.

I put my hair up into a twist and clip and pulled pieces down to frame my face. I would love to have had my hair down, but I would also hate to have my hair be part of their Buckley Boards. I put effort into some makeup and a few pieces of jewelry. Since Cora wasn't with me today, I slipped off my wedding set and wore a ring on my other hand. I was trying to ignore the naked feeling on my finger and the emptiness it just left in my heart as I slipped them into my jewelry bag.

I grabbed my tote and headed downstairs to be greeted once again by the happiest couple on the planet eating their daily toast and drinking coffee at the intimate corner table.

"Good morning Cassie," they said in unison.

I laughed. "I would like you to come home with me and greet me like this every day from now on. Good morning."

"I got you a travel mug out, so you can take your coffee with you, bug," Dad said.

I leaned down and kissed his forehead. "You are the sweetest."

I poured my coffee, added cream, and said, "I am ready when you are."

"Have a great time Cassie. Don't let them work you too hard, okay?" Mom said.

I leaned in with a side hug while balancing coffee in one hand and my large leather tote over my forearm. "Never. This is still vacation."

After the five-minute drive to Marion Square Park, I made my way to the tent through the dewy grass where Britt, Avery, and their staff were finishing up with the set up. It looked fantastic. Basically, a small version of their bar. Plants, suitcases, they set up my area like a little sitting area for people to come talk to me with chairs, a small round table, and big palms in the backdrop.

Umm, how cute?

"Britt. I love it," I yelled, placing my tote down.

"Really?"

She ran to hug me.

"Yes. You did great. It's so cozy. You even gave us fans. I love you," I said.

"Oh, that is Avery. His chunky butt needs air, girl." She laughed. "They have the panels up on these tents in case of rain, so there isn't much air movement back here."

"We ordered breakfast sandwiches and shit, so I hope you didn't eat," she said.

"Damn, I figured I was on my own today. I like this gig," I said.

She shook her head and headed back to help her staff as I found my VIP/VENDOR lanyard on the table and placed it around my neck. Just as I was organizing my materials and studying the map of the vendors, Greg Langly caught my eye, making his way over to the tent.

"Well, if it isn't my stalker, getting an early start," I said, laughing with my hand out for a handshake.

He reciprocated with a tight grip and said with a big smile, "I knew you would be busy this weekend and thought I may have a second to bend your ear."

"Bend away," I said as I sipped my coffee.

"We have been meeting the last few days, and I brought you up. We watched some of your footage from the cooking demonstrations you did on the Mid-Day Show on News 4, studied your social media presence, and we are intrigued," he said, bobbing his head.

I shook my head lightly as I said, "Okay, I am confused. Intrigued about what?"

"Well, of course, nothing is solid, but we would like to talk to you about coming aboard as an actual celebrity chef back in the Bay Area for our new upcoming program. We are looking at someone who would like to go all the way with their own show and branding, like cookbooks and cookware. We think that could be you, Cassandra," he said with a huge smile, pointing at me with his coffee cup.

I did a complete turn, looking around me, thinking I was being punked, before asking him, "Are you for real? Why me?"

"Well, you are a tough businesswoman. I mean, look at you." He pointed to my cut-out article behind me. "You have managed to work your way into a male-dominated profession and thrived. You have such a magnetic personality, you are funny, you have a Michelin-star restaurant, and you aren't pretentious at all about it. We think you would be relatable to the audience we want to reach. We want to make your cuisine more relatable to our type of audience," he said with a smile.

"Well, damn. I didn't realize my day was going to start off this well. That is a lot to think about, Greg. I don't know what to do with all that information. That is me staying in the Bay Area, though, right?" I asked.

"Yes. Absolutely," he said.

"Okay. I have a daughter and I'm a single mom and all," I said, trailing off, realizing what I just said for the first time.

He said with a hand on my shoulder to assure me, "No problem. We know you have your restaurant and family, and this would be a big commitment. We still have a lot to discuss with the team, and it's not written in stone. Dan Satterfield is the lead on this project, and he is here in town this weekend as well. He knows I am talking to you today and wants to stop by tomorrow to introduce himself as well, if that's okay? Unfortunately, he is tied up with all the food demonstrations today, or he would have been here with me this morning."

Britt caught me off guard and was now standing by my side, introducing herself with an outstretched hand. "Hi, I'm Brittany Manning."

"Hi, Greg Langly, I'm a writer with the San Francisco Eat. Cassandra has talked highly about your place, Wine on Board, Brittany. We talked about it on the plane," he said as he shook her hand.

"Oh wow. That's great. Please come back by once we are set up and eat. If you are in town long enough, please stop by. Unfortunately, we will be closed this weekend because we are here," she said with her bubbly personality. "Well, I'll let you two get back to it. It's nice meeting you, Greg."

Greg shook my hand and said, "We will be in touch then? You have my number if you have any questions and I'm around. Dan will be by and stalk you with a surprise visit tomorrow. You will like him. He's very personable. This will be fun, Cassandra, I promise. I wouldn't wrangle you into another hard career."

He smiled.

"Okay, thanks for all this. I'm really in shock right now. I honestly don't know what to say, sorry."

I just stood there.

He laughed. "Yeah, I knew that would be your response. Have a great day, Cassandra."

"Oh, Greg."

He turned back. "Yes?"

I tilted my head. "I go by Cassie. You can call me Cassie."

"You got it, Cassie."

He shot me a finger gun and walked off.

I walked over to Britt who was bent over in an ice chest.

"Oh my God," I yelled.

She stood abruptly and yelled, "Fuck. Don't do that. What?"

"I was just offered a celebrity chef position on a network back home with cookbooks, a show I think, and a cookware line. Oh my God."

"Holy fuck, Cass. This is freaking awesome. I thought he was hitting on you and was trying to give you a possible out."

She bent over laughing.

"Is this day even happening? I can't do this. I have a restaurant, a kid. I don't even have Jack and his help. What am I going to do? I can't do all this Britt."

Reality started to hit me.

"Hey. Stop this shit." She lightly slapped my face pulling me out of my place of darkness. "You don't even know the logistics of it all. You are already talking yourself out of an amazing opportunity. This isn't her." She pointed to my cut-out. "That's some weak-ass bitch talking. Cassandra Buckley can do any-fucking-thing. Look at this logo on your coat, Cass." She pointed hard into my chef coat embroidery, reading, "Cassandra Buckley- Executive Chef- Owner Sagi-Shi, you did that. You made that dream come true. You can do anything. If you decide you want this, you can have this too. Damn. I need a drink after that."

She bends over, laughing with exhaustion.

I bend over and look at her sideways and said, "I love you forever."

"I love you too."

She stood upright and hugged me tight.

"I'm so insanely proud of what you have done as well. Y'all are going to knock it out of the park this weekend," I said as I hugged her tiny body.

"Thanks. Oh, there is vodka soda in this cup at all times in case of emergency if you need it."

She pointed to a ridiculously large insulated metal Yeti cup with a straw embossed with, We Cut The Cheese. Wine on Board.

I laughed way louder than I should, and then she said, "Yes, I ordered more," with a big smile and a wink.

It was a beautiful, sunny, seventy-five-degree day with zero humidity. This was absolute heaven in Charleston. People were so receptive to coming up and talking to me and asking questions about my restaurant, menu, and about the San Francisco food scene. I signed some autographs for those who knew about my restaurant and followed us on social media. We did some interesting posts on there, thanks to my staff, and people from this far away actually knew about us due to it, which I found quite crazy.

The food line for Avery and Brittany was jamming, and I loved how they really took the time to talk to people. You would think they knew everyone they handed out to with how they made small talk and bantered back and forth. I had never known two people with so many friends. We would joke about how packed their funerals would be. We would have to rent out the coliseum for theirs. My living room would suffice for mine.

Just then, a tall, sandy blonde kid came walking up with an outstretched hand.

"Hi, I'm Benjamin. I'm such a fan. It's great to actually meet you."

"Well, hi, Benjamin. You are a fan of me?" I said, pointing to myself with my other hand.

"Yes, ma'am. I am in food and bev, and I want to be a chef. I follow your restaurant on Instagram. I know you are from here and I think it's really cool how your career developed and all. I also follow Kyle and his dog Rocco and how they skateboard together. He is awesome."

"Oh wow. That is awesome. So, you want to be a chef? Where are you working now?" I asked him.

"I started in a dish pit at fourteen, and I have moved up a couple of places. I have worked my way to grill and fry over at a fine dining place called Salt down here on the peninsula. Hopefully, I can make it to sauté someday soon," he said with a smile.

"That's great. You like that kitchen? They treat you well?" I asked.

"Yes, ma'am. The Chef has taken me under his wing, and he has shown a lot of interest in showing me a lot. He thinks I have what it takes," he said.

"It's really important to have a good mentor. I had Mike Tanner when I was your age and some awesome professors and chefs at the

Culinary Institute who believed in my talent. Make sure if it is the profession you want, stay out of the drugs and stuff. It will ruin your chances of going far. Look at it as an art. Surround yourself with good people, Ben, okay?" I said with so much sincerity. "Also, if you ever make it out to San Francisco, please let us know and come stage with us. We would love it."

"Yes, ma'am. That would be a dream come true. Could you sign an autograph for me, and can I please get a selfie with you?" he asked.

"Hell yeah," I said. "I'll take one as well to text to Kyle and tell him he has a fan club."

"That's awesome," he replied.

We took a few pictures, and even one with rocker hands and tongues sticking out. I signed his menu, saying, "Come cook with us," and sent him off with a hug.

Just as I was looking down, smiling at my phone, texting the picture to Kyle of me and Benjamin with the caption, "This kid is your biggest fan." and hit send, Brit stood directly in front of me and put the straw of the big cup in my mouth.

"Take a sip," she said.

I laughed. "Umm...why?" I asked as she was standing directly in front of me.

"Do it and look at your twelve o'clock past my shoulder."

I looked through her blonde strands and sipped the strong vodka concoction to a group of about fifteen people straight ahead of our booth. I was trying to make out faces, and some were coming in as familiar. Okay, I saw Sarah, Collette, and Brandon from high school. Oh, there was Kent. Oh, wait... that meant... I scanned... I could not breathe. I could not swallow.

Britt could obviously tell as she said, "Hey. Take a sip, babe."

I tried, but my tongue became thick and no longer wanted to work within my mouth. My legs felt like concrete, and my face felt...weird.

I panicked and quickly looked at her face and said to her, "I need to go."

She laughed. "No, you don't. They are walking over here. You need to act like a human being and say hi. It's fine. Take another big sip, put your big girl thong on, you got this." She turned and said under her breath to me, "Fuck. He's so damn hot."

I swallowed a large gulp and we turned and greeted everyone with all the normal conversation and hugs I did when I hadn't seen them in years. Once everyone had sort of moved on and Britt moved them along to the food side of the booth to see Avery, he made his way over. I felt like he was moving so slowly it was to torture me, like a lion hunting his prey.

He was wearing dark blue jeans and a light blue short-sleeved shirt with dark sunglasses. He looked like someone tailored this simple outfit specifically for his fit body. Like, who looked that perfect in two things? His body, Jesus, I wanted to lick him from head to toe.

"Hi, Cassie Buckley," he said in his low, rumbling tone that I felt right to my inner core.

"Well, hi to you, Stephen Harlow," I returned in a shaky reply.

With a hand outstretched, he said, "This is Allen Boyce, my business partner, and his wife Bianca. This is Cassie Buckley, one of my dearest childhood friends and most talented chefs around in San Francisco."

I shook their hands. "It's a pleasure to meet you both. Stephen and I go way back, and I can't wait to catch up." I shot him a small wink, which I had no idea where it came from.

They moved on with the others, leaving Stephen alone with me, and that was when the nerves really hit. Where was that big freaking cup now?

"It's really good to see you, Cass. It's been a long time," he said softly, with a nod.

All I was focusing on was his fucking lips. His brilliantly white teeth peeked out between the words. The lightly moisturized pouty bottom lip, slightly smaller top. The succulent lips that I wanted to kiss. I wanted to slide my tongue between them.

"It's good to see you too, Stephen."

I was still staring at his mouth.

He pulled me from my gaze with his hand gesture, pointing to my lanyard, which sat between my breasts. "Are you going to the Gala tomorrow?"

I took it in my hand, looking down at it. "Oh, yeah, I am going with Britt and Avery."

"Not Jack?" he asked.

Back to looking at his mouth. Why would Jack's name be coming out of Stephen's mouth?

"Oh, no. We aren't together. There's no Jack." I stumbled on my words.

He slowly removed his sunglasses to reveal those stormy gray eyes with specs of green that brought me to my knees. He then slid the arm of his sunglasses into his mouth, drawing my eyes back as his wet tongue wrapped around the plastic in a seductive motion. He totally knew where I was staring. The corner of his mouth curled upward at the mention of, *there's no Jack.* My pussy instantly clenched, and I could feel heat pool between my legs.

It was contagious and completely wrong because I did the same. I reciprocated with the same small smile back.

"Well, it is so good to see you, Stephen. Maybe I will see you tomorrow night at the gala?" I said with a business-like tone, trying to get my composure back as I went in with a hug.

He reached forward, and as he did, he whispered in my ear in nothing short of a seductive manner, "I'll text you."

He left behind an intoxicating scent of clean, masculine behind.

I couldn't swallow, and I could feel my panties becoming wet instantly, then smiled as he walked away to meet up with everyone else.

Britt, once again, was instantly at my side. "I think I may have come watching your exchange."

"Holy shit. Was it that obvious?" I said, rubbing my face.

"Just to me, I think."

She shoved the big drink into my face.

"I'm in trouble, Britt," I said.

"Fuck yeah, you are. It's going to be great. This is turning out to be the best day ever for you."

My phone vibrated with a text in my pocket, and I almost pissed myself as I fumbled to get it out. It was Kyle responding to the picture, and I gasped for a breath.

Kyle: I love that. Tonight is all set. No problems at all. Menu is on point. Prices changed per last night's conversation.

Me: Great. I have some more exciting news to share. Super crazy.

Kyle: What?

Me: Long story, I'll share later.

Kyle: Tease.

Me: HA.

Kyle: Oh. Found a new mushroom farmer. I'm over our current vendor.

Me: Nice job.

Kyle: Go back to vacation. We are good.

Me: I'm so thankful for you Kyle.

Kyle: Back at you Chef.

I talked to a few more people and just as I was back in my chef groove again, my phone buzzed in my pocket. A text message from Stephen appeared on my screen.

Stephen: That was disrespectful for me to smile due to your split with jack. I'm an asshole.

I had to walk to the back of the tent to text him back. My smile was ridiculous. I was immediately sweating. I found myself behind the palms like a schoolgirl.

Me: I'm an asshole too then. I smiled back, remember?

Stephen: I'm a mess.

Me: Me too.

As the three dots danced as he typed, my pussy got wetter, my mouth got dryer.

Stephen: Can I see you tonight?

Me: Okay. What are you thinking?

Stephen: Casual. I'll think of something. I'm over crowds.

Me: Okay. I have to do this again tomorrow and then the Gala, so nothing too crazy.

Stephen: Well, you are making me crazy

Me: Oh really?

Stephen: Yeah, I am having a hard time walking around right now.

Me: That's hot.

Stephen: I may need to run to the carriage house.

Me: Enjoy.

Stephen: Are you at your parent's or Britts?

Me: Parent's

Stephen: Pick you up at 7? Casual...easy access

Me: Yes sir.

Chapter 8

CASSIE

I lifted the glass of wine to my lips as I tried to cool my nerves while I got ready.

"This is fine, Cass," I told myself.

We knew each other so well. It was not like it was our first date. More like our eightieth. When I really thought about it, I guessed that we hadn't gone on many proper dates. We had hidden our relationship from the world for about twenty-five years, mostly keeping it at the sexual level, hooking up at every chance we could get, every moment we had been single. This had been the longest stretch by far, my sixteen-year relationship with Jack.

As requested, I chose a little short, flirty dark green sundress for the easy access aspect. I knew Stephen, and I loved how he asked for what he wanted, and I loved to give him what he requested. I already knew where his hand would be immediately, and I was turned on already thinking about it. I would wait until the last moment to slide my panties on.

I took another sip of wine and then a moment to close my eyes and unleash the memories in my mind like an old movie on rewind. I could see him like it was yesterday. His short sandy brown hair, broad shoulders, and infectious laugh right there in reaching distance. Right in front of me in Mrs. Vernon's junior year English class at Holy Trinity. He was a football player, but on the quiet side compared to all the other guys. Me, not into sports and didn't really relate to that crowd. I was quiet and kept to my close friends who weren't in that particular class.

I was brought back to the day I had to present my writing assignment with a slide presentation. There was no PowerPoint like today's world, but a little button on a tethered line to an actual slide projector to change as you went. We were to write about someone in Black History that was influential in your life. Everyone wrote about Martin Luther King, Nelson Mandela, Rosa Parks, or sports stars like Michael Jordan. I did Bob Marley. I thought he was a legend after-all, and I wrote a great fucking speech including music, slides, and all the facts that were possible. I got applause, dammit. Stephen gave me a high five as I headed back to my desk. He turned around and said,

"Damn. That was really awesome."

Something in that exchange was the beginning.

That day, I was riding my beach-cruiser bike to the record store when I heard, "Cassie."

It came from a house I had just passed. I slammed on my brakes to notice Stephen sitting on the steps of a house waving his hand. I climbed off my bike and walked it over to him down the cracked and uneven sidewalk.

"Hey. What are you doing here?" I asked.

He replied, "Umm, I live here."

"Oh shit. I didn't know you lived downtown," I said.

"Where are you going, Cass?" he asked me.

Pointing down the street, I said, "The record store they just opened. I know everyone is listening to tapes, but I still love vinyl."

"Can I go with you? I need some new music. I mean, if you want me to," he said shyly, looking at the ground.

"Come on," I said without hesitation.

He locked his house, and we rode bikes side by side, talking about anything we could come up with. Once at the store, we looked through albums, tapes, and posters. We talked about music, but now and then, we made a different connection. We talked about our family. We talked about his older brother, Ethan, who had just left for the Navy that year, his relationship with his mom, and how his dad had passed away when he was only eight years old.

I remembered the feeling he gave me. It was the same one he still gave me to this day. It was slightly mysterious. I could never quite tell what was on his mind.

A week later, we got the grades from our presentations back. Mrs. Vernon gave me a D-. A fucking D-. When I stormed to the front of the room to demand a reason for the horrible grade in the middle of the class, she told me the assignment was to be an honorable and influential person in black history, not a drug addict. I was crushed and defeated. I was so pissed that I stormed out of her class and straight out the doors of the school and right to my house without thinking of any repercussions.

Later that day, when school let out, I rode to his house, where he listened to me rage. He hugged me as I cried and kissed my salty tears as they flowed down my cheeks. Those kisses on my cheeks turned into kisses on my lips. His lips were the softest pillows that perfectly matched mine. We never even fumbled with the process, never. The kiss turned into passionate breathing and petting. Then, skin on skin. Two kids experimenting and completely vulnerable with each other, and neither of us knew what we were doing. We would inch along at our comfort level each day, revealing a little more of ourselves as we went.

I would ride my bike to his house every day over the next few weeks. We would talk, then it turned into passionate kissing, then finally, sex. The sex I experienced was what I honestly wished for every young person to experience for their first time. Someone gentle, caring, and loving walking you through it and all its awkwardness together. I was so lucky to have that. That feeling of sheer trust in someone.

With his mom not home for hours after school, we had the house all to ourselves. I could still remember the distinct smell of freshly baked cookies or bread, but there were never any cookies or bread that I could remember. The creaking of the floors. I would always think someone was home when we were having sex when they weren't, with all the odd noises. Just like mine, it was an old

Charleston home with all the uneven floors and history that came along with it. Heavy wooden doors that never really matched the frames.

Hours spent lying next to each other, talking, laughing, kissing, and touching. Exploring our new bodies and what they could do. The feeling of his hands lightly running over my skin.

I ran lotion down my smoothly shaven tan legs and fingered the dainty ankle bracelet I had bought myself for the trip. Something sort of sexy and a little different from my normal selection. I slid on a pair of wedge sandals, revealing my freshly painted pink toes. These shoes made my calves look good, especially with this little dress. I stood up, and in the mirror, I saw a sexy woman for the first time in a while. My arms and legs look pretty damn strong. My hair flowed down my back in waves of amber with honey highlights.

My phone vibrated with a text on the dresser, causing my heart to flutter rapidly.

It was Cora, and for a moment, I realized I had a child.

Cora: This beach house is so fun.

Me: Oh good. Avery's parents are the best.

Cora: We are going out to dinner.

Me: Awesome. Me too.

Cora: Are you having fun?

Me: Tons.

Cora: Yay. Call me tomorrow. Miss you.

Me: Hey. Did you talk to Daddy?

Cora: Yes. He's good.

Me: Good.

Cora: Love you

Me: I love you more

I smiled, knowing she was having a great time and not worrying about me and Jack. This might be one of the last great weeks we had for a while, and I hoped she would enjoy the hell out of it.

My phone buzzed in my hand as I was about to take a sip of my wine and head downstairs. My heart dropped at the sight of his name on the screen.

Stephen: Hey. Is it even cool I pick you up there?

Me: Yes. I told them we are going out as a group and you are picking me up.

Stephen: What happens when I don't bring you home?

Me: You have to, I have to work.

Stephen: We will see. Be there in fifteen.

I made my way downstairs and stepped out onto the expansive front porch, where I found my parents with their evening cocktails and snacks. My mom with her Prosecco, and my dad clinging to his Gin Gimlet. They had happy hour every day since the beginning of time. Since my dad worked mainly from home, it was how he made the transition from work to home, even though he never changed locations.

"Wow. You are a sight for sore eyes," my dad said with a big smile, looking up from his rocking chair.

I did a small twirl. "Thanks Dad, I'm heading out in a few."

"Y'all got a bunch of Holy Trinity or food and beverage friends going?" my mom asked.

I started making up the first elaborate lie of the evening. "A mix, I suppose. Stephen Harlow from high school is picking me up because he is right around the corner, and we are meeting some Trinity friends. I guess there will be some people from the Food and Wine Festival there."

"Where are you going?" my dad asked.

Fuck. I didn't think this through.

"I don't actually know. I think a party. I won't be too late because I have to do this again tomorrow, plus the gala," I said quickly.

Just then, a black Cadillac SUV pulled into the driveway.

"Well, that is my ride," I said, grabbing my purse and stepping off the steps just as Stephen exited the car and made his way up the driveway.

I wanted to interrupt this entire exchange and just get in his car, but I knew that wouldn't fly with this southern tradition.

He wore Khaki shorts, flip-flops, and a black golf shirt that once again fitted perfectly, revealing his strong biceps and showing the flow of his back and chest muscles as he moved towards us.

As he climbed the porch steps, he removed his sunglasses with his left hand and reached out to shake my dad's hand with his right hand.

"Great to see you again, Mr. Patterson. It's been years," he said with great confidence.

Then he reached over and did the same with my mom.

"Mrs. Patterson. Wow. You still look the same as when I was seventeen," he said with a gleaming smile.

"Nice to see you again, Stephen. I see your mom at Junior League whenever she isn't traveling the world. She keeps me posted on you and your brother," she said as she rocked in her chair, sipping on her bubbly prosecco.

"Yes, ma'am. She is always somewhere these days. Italy right now," he said.

"Well, you kids better get going and stop talking to us geezers." My dad laughed.

"Good night, y'all. Don't wait up," I said.

"We won't. We are old," my dad said.

Stephen waved and said, "Good seeing you again."

He gently took my hand, guiding me down the four steps down the stairs so I didn't break my neck.

He let go so as not to make it seem as if it were anything more of a safety precaution.

He opened my door and I slipped in, then he walked around and let himself in. His cologne took over my senses immediately. Not too strong, it was perfectly intoxicating with its woodsy cedar and clean scent. He backed out of the driveway, and as soon as we were out of sight of the house, his hand immediately slid to my thigh, and I directed my eyes to him. He was smiling so big with that mouth and those white teeth.

"You aren't wasting any time, Mr. Harlow, are you?" I said, putting my left hand on his thigh.

"Jesus, woman. So much time to make up for. I can't wait another second."

He grabbed my hand and showed me the excitement between his legs.

"This is what you do to me."

I could feel his hard cock through his shorts.

"Oh my God." I moaned.

He pulled over to a side street into a parking spot and threw it in park. He abruptly reached across the seats to grab my face, fisted my hair into his hands, and kissed me hard. Our mouths joined together like they had never been apart all these years. His tongue was hungry for mine, darting in and out of my mouth. He ran his warm hand over my breasts, down my body, and then between my legs. He urged me to open them, and I did.

I would do anything for this man.

He slid his hand over my lacy panties, and he unsealed his lips from mine to look into my eyes to say, "You are already so wet for me, Cass."

I whispered, "I have been like this since I saw you today"

Just then, he slid a finger underneath my thong and caressed over my smooth mound, then down into my slick opening to my clit that definitely had his attention.

He rumbled in his low tone into my ear as my head was lying back in the seat.

"You want that? You want me to make you come, Cass?"

"Fuck yeah, Stephen. Please?" I begged.

His fingers moved in tiny circles, then dipped through the layers of my pussy for more wetness, pooling it upward. Then, more circles.

"Come for me, baby," he whispered into my ear as he added more pressure.

He continued this pattern and breathed into my ear, driving me insane.

Warmth grew in my lower spine. Heat built in my belly. I bucked against his hand.

"Fuck, I want you to fuck me, Stephen."

I gasped as I reached over for his cock.

"Don't you touch me, I will fucking explode in my pants, Cass. This is just for you," he said.

Just then, I climaxed and cried out.

"Fuck yeah."

I completely forgot where I was, on a side street, in my parent's neighborhood.

He slowly pulled his hand from underneath my dress and slid his wet fingers into my mouth. I sucked them clean as he watched me do this with hooded eyes saying, "You are the sexiest woman alive, Cassie. Jesus Christ."

I reached over and lightly dragged my hand over his hard cock busting through the seams of his shorts.

"What are we going to do with that?" I said in a sultry voice as I leaned in to kiss him.

"I have jerked off three times today, and it hasn't helped at all, obviously. It can wait a bit. I have a plan. Come on," he said as he straightened himself into the seat and threw the car into drive.

"Where are we going?" I asked as we headed over the bridge to Mt. Pleasant.

"A little surprise." He smirked.

"Can you not smell the pizza in here?" he said with a smile.

"I could only smell your cologne at first, then I thought it was sex." I laughed. "Do you realize we haven't really done dates in all these years? Mostly just fucked in cars, alleyways, random apartments during the holidays, and stuff? The most romantic we ever were was in high school," I said, reaching over, running my hand over the nape of his neck and staring at his profile. Feeling in complete awe that he is sitting next to me right now.

"I know. I realized that too," he said, taking and kissing the back of my hand while keeping his eyes on the road.

"We really haven't been together as a couple as real adults, I guess. You deserve so much better, Cass. I'm sorry," he said in a sad tone.

"Don't be sorry. It's not your fault. This is just our thing. Don't forget, I was the one who went and got married."

I laughed.

"Oh yeah, there's that," he said. "And don't forget you got on your little bike and left me forever."

"Really? I'm never living that down, am I?" I pursed my lips and squinted my eyes.

"Nope."

He smirked as he pulled his hand away to park the car in the beach access parking lot.

"Aww. You brought me to our favorite stargazing spot," I said.

"Only the best, my love," he said as he reached over and kissed me sweetly. "And it gave him a minute to calm down," he said, pointing to the now smaller bulge in his shorts.

We got out of the car, and he opened the back of the SUV to a cooler, a blanket, and a pizza from no other than Ginos, our favorite neighborhood pizza place, waiting for us.

With hands on my hips and leaning back, I said, "Damn, Stephen, you really put some thought and planning into this."

He gathered up the cooler, a tote bag, and the blanket. I grabbed the pizza as he closed the hatch to the car.

We set up a nice romantic spot with a view of the waves rolling in and the dunes to our back. This was my favorite time of day on the beach, which I call golden hour when the sun was low, its golden glow was warm, and the beach had a more inviting feel to it. In the past, Stephen would take me there at night, and we would watch the stars and have sex on the beach. He would always have a blanket in his car for those warm summer nights.

This was our spot.

We sat on the blanket after kicking off our flip-flops and sandals, then he cracked open the cooler.

"I wasn't sure what you are into these days, so I got an assortment of everything. You have a few different choices. Assorted beers, a bottle of Italian Pino Grigio, I figured that was basic, and these girly seltzers. Oh, Diet Coke, in case you quit drinking and went back to your old habit," he said, holding up the can with a smile.

"Oh, man. I haven't had one of those in years. I was told it was going to give me Alzheimer's, and I quit immediately. I went through withdrawals like a crack -head. I'll take the wine, please. This is so sweet, Stephen." I said, smiling at him.

He placed a kiss on my lips and silently turned and rummaged in the tote to retrieve the wine tool and two tumblers. I held the tumblers as he opened the bottle, poured my glass, then opened a beer and poured it into the other tumbler for himself. Drinking alcohol on the beach was prohibited, so we had to try to keep it under wraps.

The pizza, even though it was cold, was like eating my childhood. Always consistent with its large floppy slices. Half cheese, half pepperoni. You never needed anything more than that. Ginos was the king of the perfect-tasting crust and sauce. You didn't need to cover it up with a bunch of toppings. We lived in this place since it was only blocks between our houses and right down the street from the school. $2 slices after school. I must have eaten hundreds over my high school career.

"We have so much to catch up on. I don't know where to begin," I said as I finished chewing and sipped my wine.

"I know. It's been a ride since we last saw each other," Stephen said, looking out at the ocean.

"You want to tackle the elephants in the room first or just ignore them all together?" I said before gulping down a huge sip.

He laughed. "You always know where my mind is, Cass."

"See, I actually think the opposite. You are always a mystery to me."

He took a big sip of beer. "Nah, you got me pegged. Always have."

"Jack and I are over. He left me for his paralegal. Our divorce will be final in about two months or so. We are keeping it amicable for the most part. Cora still doesn't know. We will tell her when we get back. She knows something is up. It's been over for a long time," I said, looking down into my wine.

He leaned over, and after a single soft kiss, he said, "I'm so sorry, Cass. I really am. As much as I'm happy to be sitting here with you right now, I really don't wish this shit on you."

"I know," I said, touching his face and kissing him back.

He took a very deep breath, a large sip of his beer, and then said, "Since we are chewing on the elephant first, I guess it's my turn to share." He paused, then said, while looking towards the ocean, "I miss her. I am still searching, well, as much as I can. I still have an investigator on staff, but there are no more leads. Her parents are always in touch, and constantly giving them nothing breaks my heart. I have guilt. I should have protected her better. I was supposed to be running with her that morning. Fuck, when do I stop? When do I start living again?"

Stephen drank down half of his beer, then looked down between his legs.

I rubbed his shoulders to comfort him, not knowing what to say. I was regretting starting with the hard conversations first.

He looked at me and said, "I am honestly pretty fucked up and broken, but I can be here, in this very moment. That's about all I can give you right now."

"Oh my God, Stephen. I can't give you anything more than this moment either. I'm a train wreck. I'm a month out of a broken marriage. I caught my husband cheating on me. I am still in our home. I can't move on right now. This is perfect," I said, smiling at him, climbing to my knees to take his face into my hands and kiss him passionately.

"I have missed you so much, woman. You always walk into my life when I need you the most, every time," he said between kisses and looking into my eyes.

I closed and pushed the pizza box to the side, then straddled his thighs.

"You are asking for trouble, Ms. Buckley," he said with a devilish look as I could feel his cock hardening underneath me.

The sun was now going down, and the air had gotten much cooler, sending chills over my skin.

His hands propped him up as he leaned back, and his legs stretched out in front of him. I ran my hands over his strong chest and down towards his waist.

"You are so sexy. When I saw you today, I almost came undone."

"Pretty much the same feeling here. It was all I could do not to run over to your booth and maul you," he said. "Then, when you said you were now single, I almost came in my fucking pants right there."

I lightly slapped his chest.

"Stop. You are awful."

"I know. I admit it. I figured once you got married years ago, I had lost my chance of ever being with you forever. It was over. Never again. I just got that chance back the second you said that. I felt like I had just won the lottery. Unfortunately, it was with the cost of your marriage," he said.

"It's okay. I feel the same way. I just like busting your balls."

I laughed.

"Speaking of busting my balls. You sitting on me like this isn't helping the cause," he said with a smirk.

I ground my hips against him as my dress flowed over him, blocking my movements from public view.

"What, like this? This is bothering you?"

"Oh fuck. Girl, I don't think it's dark enough for me to take you right here. There're children out here on the beach," he said, looking up at me.

"What are we going to do, Mr. Harlow?" I said innocently, taking my wine tumbler and finishing the contents before putting it down.

"We have two options. We can wait until dark, and I can fuck you out here under the stars like I planned, or we can pack up, and we can go to the carriage house where there is privacy and no chance of sand in our special places."

He smiled, then bit his bottom lip, and groaned as I continued grinding my warm pussy up and down his now hard shaft beneath his shorts.

"Your call," I said, breathing harder.

He lightly pushed me off him.

"Carriage house."

We quickly packed up and headed to the Cadillac.

Once in the car, it was kissing and hands all over. We lost all control of ourselves until he said, "Cass, let's get home. Like you said, this is all we ever do. I really want to make love to you properly, in a bed. If not, I'm going to throw you in the back seat and fuck the living shit out of you, and I don't want to do that."

I looked into his eyes and smiled mischievously.

"Okay. But can I still touch your dick all the way there?"

He shook his head. "Yes, I would like that."

Chapter 1

CASSIE

The carriage house used to be the maid's quarters with the original house before Stephen's family owned it. When we were in high school, it was the best hang-out area ever, like a mini house with all the discarded furniture his mom didn't care if we spilled drinks or what she didn't know, had sex on.

We pulled into the driveway, and I noticed that the property had a major facelift since I had seen it last.

"Wow. Your mom has been busy," I said.

"Yeah, she did a nice renovation on the carriage house and rents it out for short-term vacation rentals. It pays for all her travel expenses," he said.

We grabbed the items from the back and made our way down the moss-covered brick walkway through the small iron gate. The sound of that iron gate was imprinted in my mind from the late-night sneak-out sessions, trying to be quiet. The up-lit live oak trees draped with Spanish moss, lined the path to the sweet little porch. It was still the same with its Charleston charm, just shined up like a new penny.

The carriage house was a tiny replica of the main house. White house, white columns, with three steps leading up to the gray porch. A porch swing sat to the left of the front door, adorned with decorative pillows, lanterns with candles, ferns, plants, and sitting areas were strategically placed on the other side. Its quintessential Southern charm flowed along the space so beautifully.

Stephen placed the cooler on the porch along with the sandy blanket and tote. We kicked off our shoes as he punched a code into the keypad, unlocking the door, and we entered the cottage. Absolutely adorable. As much as I wanted to attack this man, I was in awe of the interior design of this space. It is small but perfectly executed.

I placed the pizza box onto the quartz counter in the galley-style kitchen when I was whisked in another direction and turned to face him. He looked at me with such adoration and desire at the same time. Without a single word, he gently took my face in his hands and kissed me deeply, taking all my air in with his. My arms wrapped around his hard body, and I reached upwards on my toes to meet him. He lifted me as if I weighed nothing at all and walked backwards towards what I thought might be a bedroom, never breaking the seal of our lips and embrace. There, he laid me down on to a tall bed of soft pillowy linens. He stood before me, and I could see him pulling off his shirt with just the dim glow of a small bedside lamp and the back light of the kitchen adorning his chiseled arms, abs, and the way his shorts sat on his hip bones.

Damn.

He unbuttoned his shorts, and they slid to the floor, revealing his raging hard cock beneath gray boxer briefs that outlined every strong muscle of his ass and legs. He came to stand between my spread legs, and I was almost panting with anticipation. He kneeled, then reached underneath my little green dress and slid his hand up my legs starting at my ankle, toying with my little anklet for a moment. Nothing got past him. He then slid his hands up my legs slowly, taking his time as if he was inspecting all he had missed over the years. I could feel the heat rising in my core, and instantly, I want more of him.

I moaned low with the feel of his touch. My hands wandered over my stomach and breasts, tugging at the fabric of my dress to mimic his movements. Heat built throughout my whole body.

His hands moved upwards, pushing the fabric until he reached my panties. He ran his thumb over my slit over the top, which made me throb underneath. He pressed and rubbed my clit while kissing my inner thighs with his hot lips. I ground my hips.

"You are getting so wet for me, baby."

Hearing his deep voice out of the silence simply turned me on. This man. Jesus. I wanted him inside of me so bad I was about to beg for him to skip all the amazing foreplay. Then, he slid my panties down my legs, and all I felt his fingers, then…his amazing tongue.

Oh my God.

My back arched as if I was being abducted by aliens. I officially had zero control of my body because his tongue and mouth were doing things to my clit I had never experienced before. He danced circles around and used perfect suction that drew me closer to an intense climax. I grabbed at the comforter, and my head arched back as a rush of heat pooled between my legs and my lower spine. He slid his fingers inside of me while he sucked my clit, and I came completely unraveled. In and out, his fingers dove through my walls of pleasure, and I exploded, releasing years of emotion, pain, passion, regret, anxiety, love, fear, and every other fucking feeling I had been holding in. I let it all go in one loud moan.

"Fuck."

My pussy clenched down with uncontrollable wave after wave of spasms around his hand. He licks me softly until I was calm, and my entire body became nothing but limp muscle.

He slowly slid his fingers from me and climbed up to meet my tear-streaked face as he had done times before. He kissed me, tucked some stray hair behind my ear, and because he knew me so well, he said with a smile, "I think you needed that more than therapy."

I laughed. "Fuck yeah, I did. Holy crap. Oh my God. I'm so sorry I cried. It was amazing, so amazing it warranted tears."

"That was so hot to watch you like that," he said as he took my hand and slid it to his extremely hard cock.

My heart dropped at the thought of what was on the other side of that fabric. This man had given me two orgasms already tonight, and I hadn't even had his dick outside of his pants yet.

"Time to set him free," I said with the enthusiasm of a teenager.

He laughed as he laid back on the bed, put his hands behind his head, and said, "I'm all yours."

On my knees, I lifted my dress over my head, revealing a strapless bra, then reach around and took it off. He reached up and grabbed my full, round breasts.

"Damn, I love your body. You are so beautiful, Cass."

I lightly pushed him back down to the bed.

"You have done enough, it's my turn."

He obliged and fell back to the pillow.

His six-foot-three frame took up the entire length of the bed, and I had a lot of amazing real estate to play with, and it was hard to pick where to start. So, just like he did, I slid my hands up his legs, kissing and licking my way upward. I then exhaled hot air through the thin fabric of his boxer briefs over his balls, then his hard shaft that jumped when my lips ran over his length.

He moaned, and when I looked up at him, he went from his eyes closed to looking down at me with a small smile. My favorite was biting his lip with a furrowed brow.

Next, I slid his boxers down and revealed what I hadn't seen in nearly sixteen years. Its familiar and glorious at the same time. I took his thick girth in my hand and stroked it from root to tip, sending his head back onto the pillow.

"God, Cass. Your hand. I never thought I would feel your hands on my cock again. This is amazing."

I slid between his legs and let him rest both of his over my bent legs and took his entire length in both my hands. Up and down I twisted and slid. Pre-cum seeped from the tip, then I reached down and wrapped my wet mouth around his swollen head.

He moaned.

"Jesus, Cass."

He fisted my hair to one side so he could see what I was doing.

I slowly slid my mouth down his hard cock, removing one hand at a time until I couldn't take any more of him, then back up. Up and down, I sucked and slid, adding my hand in unison, wrapping and twisting with my saliva from root to tip. I could feel his legs tighten, his balls tighten as I ran my tongue over them periodically, which made him almost whimper with delight.

He pulled my hair all the way to one side, and he said in his low voice, "I'm going to come, Cass. I know you don't swallow. Fuck, baby...I'm coming."

I decided to give him something I never had before. I ignored his tugging at my head and buried his cock deep into my throat just as he exploded hot streams of semen into my mouth. I continued stroking him with my hand and mouth, emptying him as he moaned loudly.

"Fuck yeah. Holy shit."

His legs were lengthening out before me. Once I swallowed all he had given me, I released him from my mouth and looked at him while I wiped the corners of my lips, smiling as if I had just eaten the most delightful thing of my day.

He looked up at me shaking his head.

"You dirty girl, Cassie. I leave you alone for sixteen years, and you get so, so dirty. I fucking love it."

He grabbed me, pulling me on top of his naked body.

"Stick with me kid, I have more tricks up my sleeve," I growled into his ear.

"Mmmm...I like the sound of that."

He smiled with his eyes closed, holding me in the crook of his arm and my naked leg resting over his waist, and now spent cock.

"I find it so crazy how comfortable I am with you. We can just pick back up where we left off," I whispered.

"I know. I was thinking when you were kneeling and taking off your dress, and I saw your amazing tits again for the first time. I have seen your body at all stages. Your teen body, your college body, and now this one. You have curves that are killing me and...I just can't get over you, ever," he said as he kissed the side of my head, holding it for a moment.

I leaned onto an elbow, looked at him, and caressed the side of his face.

"I'm a lucky girl to have all these moments with you. You have always been such a big part of my heart. I look for you in every relationship I have. I have always searched for someone who makes me feel like this. I come up empty every time."

Then, I kissed him deeply before he could respond.

He pulled away. "Hey. Remember how you said we only have sex and we don't actually have dates. Well, I was trying to have a proper date tonight, so let's try to finish it. Come on. Get dressed."

He rolled over and started pulling on his boxers, shorts, and shirt which were strewn on the floor.

I laughed as I watched him from the bed. "Are we going out?"

"No, come on."

He chuckled as he handed me my dress and walked into the kitchen.

I could hear beeping in the kitchen as I walked in and saw him turning on the oven.

"Are you cooking?" I asked.

"Ha. Fat chance, Chef. I'm reheating the pizza. We are finishing our date. I'm starving. You?" he asked, walking past me to grab the pizza box and planting a sweet kiss on my lips.

"Yes. I'll grab the wine. You want a beer?" I asked, walking out the door to the cooler on the porch.

"Yes, ma'am."

I still loved the sound of a Southern man.

I walked in, and he had already put the remaining slices on a cookie sheet into the oven and pulled out a wine glass for me. He was searching drawers for something when a lighter appeared.

"Ambiance, my lady."

Stephen went onto the porch and lit all the lanterns.

I poured my glass of wine, opened his beer, and took them outside to the little table.

"I hate to do this, but I need to check on my world for one second and make sure my business didn't burn down, or my kid isn't in a sugar-induced coma at Britt's," I said.

"Of course," he said.

I reached into my purse and swiped it open with one swipe and saw only one text, and that was an absolute record. Just Britt asking how my night was going. Of course, it was followed with a Gif of two frogs humping, which made me laugh out loud.

"I didn't mean to pry, but I noticed you don't have your phone password protected," he said.

"Yeah, that's a pain in the ass," I said, closing my phone and tossing it back into my purse.

"Oh my God. Take that back out, Cass. Give it to me," he said, holding his hand out and giving me the come-hither movement with his hand.

I obliged and handed him my phone. "Why?"

He gave me a stern look, then turned to peek into the oven on the progress of the pizza, then walked past me, holding the screen door open for me to come out onto the porch with him. I walked out to our sweet little candle-lit date, where we cozied up onto the pillow-covered porch swing. He motioned for me to sit closer so I could see what he was doing with my phone. I sipped my wine with full attention.

He explained, "So, if even as a mediocre novice hacker, I can load a simple shit app on my phone and sit next to you, at say, the airport or coffee shop and steal all your shit. Bank info, personal info, you name it."

I sat straight up and gasped. "You are shitting me."

"Not shitting you. Like, you have some pretty important apps in here. I'm sure you don't want anyone infiltrating, like, this one." He scrolled right to my POS app for my restaurant and clicked on it.

My eyes widened. "Umm, that's my everything. I can control virtually everything in my restaurant but cooking from that. Even my accounts."

"Okay, I'll stop freaking you out. So, let's just at least start by protecting your phone, okay? I'm going to guess you don't have your laptop protected either because it's a pain in the ass as well, so password protect that too, especially if you are traveling and working with it."

He went into my settings and said, "Here pick a five-digit code," then turned my phone facing me.

"Five? Ugh." I sighed.

"For fuck's sake, Cass." He laughed.

I punched in my new five-digit tether and said, "There, now texting and driving is going to be more difficult."

I laughed.

He lowered my phone and glared at me.

"I'm totally joking, Stephen." I laughed again and sipped my wine.

Stephen turned my phone and began to do more magic before turning it again, saying, "Here, right index fingerprint."

"Are you serious? I'm never getting in this thing again," I said, shaking my head.

He laughed at me. "This is once you are in your phone, and you want to open certain apps. I am putting it on your bank accounts, your credit cards here, and your POS account. Just double security. You can add it to anything else you want by going into settings and going here."

He scrolled faster than lightning, and I completely lost him.

"I have no idea what you have done, wizard. I just hope I can get in and do basic shit tomorrow."

He sipped his beer. "As long as you remember your five-digit code."

"Yep. 12345," I blurted.

"For the love of god, woman. No. Shit, the pizza."

He pushed out the swing leaving me grabbing onto the chains and ran inside pushing the screen door open.

"Phew. Just in time," he yelled.

He appeared with two plates and two pieces each on them. Then, magically pulled a shaker of oregano and napkins from his pocket.

"Here you go. Date resumed."

He topped off my glass of wine.

"Thanks, babe," flowed from my mouth as if it were water from the tap.

So easy, but I knew we both felt the small tension but carried on.

He took a bite of his pizza, a sip of his beer, then took my phone again and went back into settings.

"Oh no. We aren't done?" I whined.

"12345? Really?" He shook his head at me.

"Again."

He turned the phone towards me. I put in a better code this time.

"Okay. There you go, Sir." I smiled and took a bite of pizza. "Damn, this is good," I said, looking at my slice.

"Right?" he agreed, then looked back down at my phone.

He maneuvered through my phone with one hand as the blue light illuminated his beautiful face. Intently working, chewing pizza with his strong jaw, which wasn't covered in the beard like his picture on Google that I had been masturbating to. I just sipped my wine and found myself staring until he looked up.

"All done."

"Thank you. I really appreciate you taking care of me," I said softly.

He chuckled. "I'm glad I can. You are a mess."

I punched him lightly in the arm. "It's not my wheelhouse. I cook."

"I know."

"Why did you shave your beard off? I liked it," I said, rubbing the back of my hand across his jaw so as not to smear pizza grease on his face.

"Really? Wait, you have never known me with a beard," he replied with confusion.

"Oh, yeah. The only picture I have been able to stalk you with is the one from your company website," I said smiling veering my gaze, mischievously.

"Stalking, huh? What else have you been doing with my picture, dirty girl?"

He tossed his pizza crust to his plate and slid his hand up my thigh.

"Oh, you don't want to know. I've been very, very lonely and I sort of had a dream," I said softly, taking a very long, seductive sip of wine while not taking my eyes off of his.

His hand ran higher up my thigh and to my still-wet pussy because I didn't bother putting my panties back on. He leaned in to kiss me.

"We obviously aren't ever eating this weekend."

He took my wine glass from my hand and placed it on the table. I reached over and ran my hands to his chest over his muscles, ran them down as I kissed his mouth harder and harder. Our breath was getting heavier and my hands got lower until I felt his cock hard beneath my hand.

"You make me insane, Cassie, Jesus," he whispered in my ear, then stood.

He took my hand and guided me into the house, closing the door behind him. He turned off the light, and there were only a few small golden lamps lighting the room. We were standing in the kitchen now, bare feet on the cool hardwood floor, face to face. He slowly slid the spaghetti straps from my shoulders, and my little green dress slid down my body, and with a little push, became a puddle at my feet. I was completely bare before him. He twirled my hair down over my breasts and slid his fingers lightly over my tightened nipples. He took them between his fingers and pinched just enough to make me wince with pleasure, making me want so much more. He looked into my eyes, then ran his hands lightly down my arms, down the hourglass shape of my body, over my hips, and around to my ass.

I reached over at his waist and pulled his shirt up over his head as he lifted his arms. There was something so sexy about undressing someone piece by piece in silence. I unbuttoned and unzipped his shorts, then, with a small tug, they too, fell to his feet. I ran my hand over his tight ass and legs, then around to his swollen cock as he breathed in a large breath as I stroked this whole length. I seductively ran my fingers under the entire waistline before slowly sliding his boxers down but ending with my face directly in front of his fantastic erection.

I kneeled, then slid my hands around him, then ran my tongue around the now swollen head glistening with pre-cum. I loved the saltiness of him on my tongue. I craved more of him as I took him deeper into my mouth. He pulled my hair to the side and I looked up at him, and he looked at me, and he slowly shook his head and bit his lip. I twisted my hand up and down with my mouth, and he breathed heavier when he reached down and pulled up at my arms.

"Come on," he said and pulled me into the bedroom, where he turned me and laid me on to the bed, covering me with his body. I could feel his thick cock between my legs. God, I wanted it inside of me. He kissed me down my neck, stopping to softly bite my collarbone and shoulders, making his way to my breasts. He took one in his hand and then sucked lightly, then bit enough to make me squirm, followed by more sucking and licking. Then, the other side. This made me wetter and hotter. His hand moved down my stomach and to my throbbing pussy.

"Damn, baby. You are so fucking wet," he said as he fingered my clit, making me writhe with pleasure.

He slid off of me and went into the nightstand for a condom.

As he ripped the package open and put it on, he said, "I'm clean, but I'm assuming I should be wearing this."

"I have an IUD and can't get pregnant, but I haven't had time to get tested after Jack's little escapade. I'm sorry."

I winced.

"Shhh, don't be," he said.

He climbed back on top of me and spread my legs wide. Fuck, I hadn't had another man inside of me in over sixteen years. Get out of your head, Cass.

He sensed the slight nervousness after mentioning his name. He became tender and very sensual in his movements by stroking my hair, long kisses, and then he slid himself ever so slowly into me.

"Oh yes." I moaned as the first feel of his hard cock was intense and amazing. So big, stretching me out.

He took his time, and little by little, he pushed in and out, in and out, until he was balls deep inside of me, moaning and grabbing my ass beneath him.

"Fuck Cassie, you feel so fucking good. So, fucking tight."

He cried out, then climbed to his knees while holding one of my feet and looking down, watching his cock slide in and out of me.

"Damn, this is so hot."

He smiled and shook his head, then reached with the other hand to thumb my clit.

I grasped both breasts and arched my head back. Heat was building all over my body. My pussy ached to release.

I grabbed my breasts, nipples tight between my fingers. "Yes, yes, oh, fuck yes." I moaned.

He strummed my clit with a different motion and moved his hips differently. He was hitting something different, and I was on the verge of climaxing hard. I thought just then numbness had set in my lips, and heat rushed through my spine as my pussy pulsed around his cock uncontrollably. I became so wet it was now dripping down my ass. He slowed his pace burying his head into my neck saying, "Damn baby. I felt all of that. You are dripping."

Then kissed me deeply.

"I can't feel my lips." I laughed.

He laughed and said, "Here, flip over."

I did so, climbing slowly to my knees and spreading my legs apart. He ran his hands down my body, then over my ass.

"Damn, you are so sexy."

I felt his hard cock slide into me with a slow push and his hands on my hips, guiding himself in and out. I dropped to my chest. Damn, he was so deep. His palm was on my lower back.

His thrusts got deeper and deeper, and he grew increasingly thicker with every minute. Reaching forward, he pushed my hair to the side to see my face.

"Yeah, I'm almost there, baby."

He groaned.

Stephen thrust hard before his body went tight, then became limp over top of me. He kissed my back and neck, then laced his fingers within mine and squeezed, bringing back the memory of him doing the exact same thing since we were young. I smiled beneath the pile of sweaty auburn strands flowing down from my head over the bed.

We disconnected, and he discarded the condom. We held each other in a naked, tangled mess for a while, talking softly about everything and nothing.

I looked at the clock and noticed it was 1:30 am.

"I need to go," I said sadly.

"No, just stay," he pleaded.

"I can't. I have to be back at the park early and I can't roll up out of your car in the morning. Remember, I am technically still married in my parent's eyes."

"Okay. I get it. I'll see you tomorrow night, though? Maybe stay tomorrow?" he asked.

"I may be able to pull that off. I can act as if I'm staying with Britt and Avery after the gala."

Running a hand through his hair, he said, "Sweet Lord, I am going to die seeing you dressed up tomorrow night, aren't I?"

"I have a little something planned," I said with a smirk.

"Woman," he yelled as he climbed from the bed to get dressed.

The four-block drive home was quick and quiet.

"Thank you for everything. I'll see you tomorrow night. Don't kiss me. My dad may be looking out the window," I said as I was about to climb out the door.

"I'm going to walk you to the door, though," he said.

He did. No hand-holding. Just a wave goodnight as I let myself in. I watched through the side window as I saw his car back out of the driveway and down the street. I pressed my head into the front door and closed my eyes with a large sigh within the darkness of the house. My heart was beating so loud.

Fuck.

Chapter 10

CASSIE

✗

My phone vibrated me awake on the nightstand with a text message, and I slowly pushed the covers back and rolled over to reach it. I squinted and swiped, only to be denied access. Then I remember, shit. What is my code? I racked my brain by pressing my fingers into my temples and closed my eyes shut until it came to memory, and I punched it in. Yes. Her cross-eyed face came into focus in that little circle.

> Britt: You are killing me. I need to know about last night.

> Britt: My parents are taking the girls horseback riding at Seabrook Island today. Cora may never leave.

> Me: That's awesome. Getting in the shower now.

The three dots danced across the screen, and I already knew she wasn't going to be satisfied with that reply. My phone buzzed in my hand.

> Britt: Hello? Last night?

I knew it and smiled at how well I knew her, but I was too tired to text about every little dirty detail.

> Me: I'll tell you when I get to the park.

Me: Amazing...

Britt: I am dying inside.

I climbed from the coziness of the high-end thread count bedding, turned off the noise machine, and dragged myself to the sunny, white-tiled bathroom to shower and get ready for another day of talking shop and hanging out with my girl. I suddenly remembered I would be having a visit with Dan Satterfield at some point to discuss the gig back in San Francisco when a twinge of nervousness took over. I scrubbed my face trying to wipe away the tension and simply enjoy the moment. After all, I came here to relax, help Britt and Avery, and from the feeling of soreness between my legs as the hot soapy water flowed between them, I was having an extraordinary time catching up with Stephen. I smiled and let the elation from last night replace any other doubts and anxiety that I was having.

I took a quick look in the floor-length mirror, black-crisp chef coat and pants, hair twisted and up in a clip just like yesterday, and tote bag in hand.

"Not too bad, Cass," I said to myself.

I reached for my phone, and just as I was walking out of my bedroom, it buzzed with a text message. My heart stopped when I saw his name flash across the screen. Of course I had to go through Fort Knox to get to it.

Ugh.

I put my heavy tote down.

Stephen: I still smell like you.

I smiled and responded giddily.

Me: Unfortunately, I just washed you off.

Me: ...But I can feel you with every step

Stephen: Wait until after tonight...you may need a wheelchair.

Me: A girl can only wish.

Stephen: I'll reach out later.

Me: Sounds great. Going to the park now.

A winky face emoji appeared.

For just another moment, I forgot the crumbling marriage and the crazy career I have back home, and grinned like a freaking Cheshire cat as I slid my phone into my tote and headed downstairs to be greeted once again by the happy people.

"Good morning, Cassie," I heard coming from the side porch through the screen door as my mom held a cup of coffee in one hand and a hose in another as she gently watered her flower children.

I stirred cream into my coffee, then snapped on the lid, saying, "Good morning, Mom," while making my way onto the porch and leaned against a column.

Looking up at me, she said, "Did you have a good time last night?"

"I did. It was nice to be out with adults. It was also nice to have conversations about subjects other than work for once too," I said.

"Stephen looked great. I've talked with Margarite at length about the last two years with his fiancé. It's terrible. She says he's had a really hard time." A sullen look washed over her face. "I hope he got to relax a bit last night as well."

"Yeah, we talked a little about it. I think he had a good time."

I veered the conversation quickly in another direction before I started lying my ass off royally, saying, "Well, after tonight, we are all yours. Cora will be back from the beach house tomorrow early afternoon, I think. Hopefully, enough time for me to get over my impending hangover. Also, I might stay at Britt's after the gala."

"Sounds great. I'm glad you are having a good time, Cassie. I know you don't really get out much with friends back home," she said with a sense of sympathy.

"Why does everyone think I don't have friends?" I asked defensively, shaking my head.

Just as she was about to respond, my dad came outside. "I made you a ham and brie croissant for you to go, Bug. I don't want you to get hungry today." He held a tin foil wrapped creation in his hand and feeling the sliver of tension between me and my mom, he added, "Is something wrong?"

He looked back and forth between us.

"No, it's fine," I said, kissing him on the cheek. "Thanks, Dad."

Taking it from his hand I walked into the kitchen, placing it in my tote before picking it up. "I'm ready whenever you are."

"Have a good time, Cassie," Mom said with apprehension.

"I'll see you around five or so. Britt will drop me off so I can get ready," I said, stepping down the steps onto the lower patio where she was watering.

I leaned in and whispered in her ear as I walked past. "I'm just sensitive, I'm sorry. I love you."

"I love you too," she whispered back.

The short seven-minute drive consisted of me pulling up my POS and checking on last night's sales, which were fantastic. They knocked it out of the park.

"I'm so lucky to have the staff I have, Dad. They barely need me," I gloated.

"That's a great thing. It's an owner's dream. I'm proud of you."

He smiled as I climbed from the car.

"Thanks for the ride. I'll see you later," I said, pushing the door closed.

"I'll be there doodling around the house," he said cheerfully through the open window as he pulled away.

The day was cooler than yesterday, and it was welcome since I was wearing a thicker chef's uniform. I didn't want to sweat all day as I did in the restaurant, especially in my *going out* uniform.

As I approached the tent, I saw Britt and Avery busy with their staff, going over the day's operations and organizing inside a cooler when I walked up, with a startled, "Hey!" which was my new favorite way to greet her.

"Fucking…shit…why?"

She jumped, arms flailing, and turned abruptly.

I laughed, holding my chest. "It really doesn't get old. I know it's so wrong as a Chef to do that shit, but I can't help it."

"You are going to kill me one day, bitch. Now, stop fucking around and tell me what happened last night," she said between gritted teeth and a smile, pulling her shoulders up like a little mischievous girl, then rubbing her hands together, anticipating the juicy details.

I sipped my coffee and proceed to tell her. "Well, he picked me up, he gave me an orgasm within the first five minutes in his car on the way to the beach and..."

"Wait, he what?"

She put her hand on my shoulder, stopping my conversation with her mouth wide open.

I smiled behind my coffee cup, eyebrows raised. "Uh, huh."

She closed her eyes. "Sweet baby Jesus, this is hot." She made a *continue on* motion with her hand.

"We went to the beach, talked, and then went back to his place and did it some more. Girl. He is fucking amazing. I am so sore."

I laughed and motioned to my crotch, looking around, making sure nobody saw me.

"I love it." She smiled and hugged me with a slight bounce. "Are you expecting that dude Gary or Greg guy and Anderson Cooper?" she asked while in her tight embrace looking over my shoulder.

"What?" I asked.

I pulled away and looked behind me to notice Greg Langly and a man that did look remarkably like Anderson Cooper standing right outside the tent talking.

I made eye contact with Greg, and sure as shit, he was there for me.

"It's go time," Britt said. "You got this."

With a kiss on the cheek, she was gone.

Gary and Dan entered the tent with smiles, and with an outstretched hand, Dan said, "I have heard and learned so much about you this week, Cassie Buckley. Dan Satterfield. Is this a good time?"

"None of it is true, Dan, I promise," I blurted out a small chuckle. "Yes, this is just fine, I just got here."

I shook his hand.

I thought that was the winning moment, because it was downhill from there. Dan was easy on the eyes and easy to talk to, just as Gary promised. I never thought Anderson Cooper was hot-hot, but put him in front of me and he was a good-looking guy. I immediately wanted to go cook in the middle of a war-torn country with this man. Of course, I was having this ridiculous fantasy while he was talking to me, while I was sore from having sex with my current sexual fantasy, as I was devastated, in the middle of my divorce. I was completely rational and making perfectly logical decisions. I would say he was in his mid-forties but probably went white prematurely because he had a total baby face. The thick-rimmed glasses did it for me. I should probably stop looking at him that way if he was going to be my future boss.

Will he be?

For fuck-sake, focus Cass.

"So, Cassie, have you put any thought into going through the process of possibly signing with us? We don't need to do the complete interview and audition process since we have all that information already, with your cooking demos, and all. We could set up a meeting to see if it's all a good fit for you and us at this point. We would love to have you," Dan said with that damn fantastic smile.

I needed to be careful. I could say yes to pretty much anything to him right now.

Jesus.

What was happening to me? It's like my libido knob is turned on high. I was cooking on the power burner.

"This is all happening so fast, Dan. I basically came on vacation with my daughter and met Greg on the plane. This is just...so fast. Don't get me wrong, I'm interested. I am, but I just need to digest it and make a calculated decision. Sagi-Shi is my number one business priority, and I cannot jeopardize that."

"Cassie, we understand that completely. We have never asked anyone to give up their restaurants. We wouldn't have celebrity chefs, obviously, if we did that." He laughed. "We will work with your schedule. Also, Gary said you are a single mom?"

I closed my eyes and paused for a beat.

"It's new, but yes. I honestly don't know what schedule that will entail right now either, and my support system is, well...here," I said softly.

"I'm sorry. I've been there and it is a hard transition. How about we discuss everything when you get back to San Francisco? Just look at this as a possible new exciting endeavor for a moment until we talk, say, next week? Just let your mind be excited about a possible cooking show, a cookware line of your own, and cookbooks. Just let that run around in your head," Dan said, reaching out with his business card between his two fingers and again that damn smile.

"That sounds like a plan," I said, taking the card and a huge breath.

"I want you to enjoy the rest of your vacation. Chefs don't get them very often, and it doesn't look like you are completely taking one."

He motioned behind me.

"Oh, ha. Well, believe it or not, this is fun getting to be with my best girl and husband. I will be completely relaxing come tonight, I promise."

I immediately got a quick feeling of excitement run through me, sending a jolt through my heart, thinking about Stephen.

"That's great. Would you like my assistant to reach out to set up a time next week to come in and talk about what we can do for each other? Very relaxed. Just to see what it's going to be about. Greg has your number, I believe?" he said, looking at Greg.

Greg nodded in agreement and smiled at both of us.

"That would be fine. I will look forward to hearing from them."

He shook my hand again. "Her name is Stacy, and I will see you next week. If you have any questions before then, feel free to reach out to me, text, call, whatever."

"Thanks, Dan. It was very nice meeting you," I said, dropping his hand.

It was incredibly smooth, like I envisioned him with his hands in a paraffin bath nightly or some shit. That kind of removed him from a level of hotness. I liked a little more manly in my man.

Greg reached out. "Have a great rest of your trip."

They both walked away, leaving me standing there speechless.

"So?" Britt burst into my space, pulling me out of my moment of thought, scaring me.

"Jesus," I yelled, clutching my lanyard.

"Yeah, that shit sucks, doesn't it?" she said, laughing.

I shook my head. "Well, they are interested in me coming aboard as a celebrity chef. I don't need to do any kind of audition since they have seen me in action already with my cooking segments back home. I guess they already like my personality. I mean, who doesn't like all this?"

I moved in a swagger, running my hands down my body as I laughed.

Britt jumped up and down, saying, "I knew you coming here was going to be great, but holy crap."

"I'm not getting ahead of myself. He said just think about it and what it would be like over the next week. I just don't want to overextend myself, Britt. It will be a lot. I need to make sure I have Jack's support with Cora. I am completely alone in California. It's not like here. I also need to make sure the restaurant won't suffer. That is my baby," I said, holding her hands down, keeping her from jumping around.

"Man, enjoy the moment at least, okay? Be a celebrity for the next week and, roll around in it and see how it feels? Let me enjoy it if not you. I want a famous friend, Cass. Please?" she begged.

"Fine. For one week, you can be delusional, but if I don't go through with it, I'm not paying for therapy."

I shook my head, smiling at her.

"Deal."

She sashayed back to her side of the tent to finish getting her staff ready for the finale of a successful, busy weekend.

The day was smooth as people came in and out in a steady flow, intermingling with their charcuterie boards and wine, asking questions about the San Francisco restaurant scene.

Mike Tanner found time to swing by, which was a wonderful surprise, and he, of course, drew his own crowd when he was in the wild. I shared his thoughts on the celebrity chef gig offer. I got an immediate running of the hands through the hair, blowing out of the cheeks, rolling of the eyes.

"Come on, Mike. I know what you are thinking. It's a sellout.

We all think that, but you have to admit, it's a cool thing to roll around in the brain," I said, bobbing my head back and forth.

"Cass, you have one restaurant right now. If you have a great exec and staff that can run without you for you to take this vacation and you are thriving, you are doing great. If you have a contract to do this other thing and it doesn't pull you away too much, do it. Nobody gives up their restaurants for these gigs, in fact, their restaurants usually explode, so there is that, another problem. Your staff needs to be prepared for it," he said.

"I have a lot to think about. The other thing is, Jack and I are divorcing, and I am about to be a single mom," I said, not really knowing why I told him.

"Oh, shit, Cassie. I'm so sorry. Dammit, I wish this was all happening in Charleston. At least you would have all of us to help out and be support for you and Cora," he said as he grabbed me for a big hug.

"Thanks, Mike. I'm okay. I promise not to act like a sellout if I do it," I said, buried into his shoulder, laughing.

He pushed me out, holding my shoulders and looking into my eyes.

"I'm always proud of you like you are my own. You crush everything you do, and I wouldn't expect less of this if you decide to tackle it. I got to go, but if you need me, just call."

He gave me one more quick hug.

"Thanks, Mike."

He made his way out of the tent through the small crowd of rose day drinkers.

I felt the need to check in with Kyle. I was suddenly feeling very disconnected from my team.

I found his little circle of him and Rocco in my contacts.

Me: Y'all crushed it last night.

Kyle: Hell yeah we did.

Me: How is everything going for tonight?

I looked at my watch. It was 9 am there. So, the AM staff should be there, and he would have an idea if any wheels may fall off as far as enough ingredients for specials or menu items.

Kyle: Had to 86 a couple of things on the regular menu, but nothing major. We sold out of 2 specials, and I am replacing them with your tried and true. Roasted Oysters on the ½ with Ginger, chili, and soy dressing.

Me: Love.

Kyle: Stir-Fried Mung bean and soy bean sprouts with tiger prawns

Me: Fantastic. Are you okay?

Kyle: Had a moment LOL, but Reggie has my back.

Kyle: He needs a raise Cass. Maybe a bonus for this week?

Me: Bonus yes, take care of him. We will talk raise when I get back.

Kyle: Having fun?

Me: Yes. I will chat more Monday about something exciting. I'll call.

Kyle: Okay. I hate suspense.

Me: Lol. I have my phone on if you need me.

Kyle: We got it Chef. Party On.

I slid my phone in my pocket and thought to myself, maybe I could handle it. Maybe I could juggle both? Maybe I could do it all? Then, I remembered Jack's words on the deck that night.

"It can't all be about your work, Cass."

Is that me replacing my marriage with a new career?

A new distraction from actual life?

Jack, Cora, my mom, they are right, I had no friends. I had no life outside of the kitchen. What if I made friends in the studio world? Maybe that was where my new friends and life were waiting? I didn't want to live life with regrets.

Chapter 11

CASSIE

I pushed the tiny strap through the buckle on the side of my ankle.

"Lord, these are sexy heels, but I don't know if it's worth the pain," I muttered to myself as I stood and pushed the elegant fabric of my dress down my smooth thighs.

"Wow. That's quite the dress," my mom said, slightly startling me while leaning in the doorway.

"Oh, hey. Too much?"

I turned from side to side, examining myself in the floor-length mirror.

She muffled a small laugh. "Ah, no. You have that body, my dear, you wear that dress."

It was black, with a shimmer of silver running through it, which caught the light with each slight move I made. Tiny spaghetti straps adorned my strong, bronze shoulders, and the neckline dropped low with fabric draped perfectly at my cleavage. The dress was slightly form-fitting, but not insanely tight to where I couldn't move, hitting above the knee, with a slit up both sides to mid-thigh. The back was the money shot, as it dropped and fabric pooled just like the front, but right above my ass, revealing my entire muscular back. I envisioned standing with Stephen's broad, warm hand lying flat against my bare skin as we talked and laughed with friends, while sipping delectable cocktails. Yeah, it was my fantasy. Just one among many.

My hair flowed down my back with long auburn curls, which I was sure the Charleston humidity would destroy within the first fifteen minutes of walking out the front door.

"What earrings are you wearing?" Mom asked.

I didn't bring any. I didn't think about it. All I had was some little hoops. I figured the dress was enough of a statement, so bare lobes were it.

"Hold on. I think I may have something."

Holding up a finger, her little bare feet turned and took her to her bedroom down the hallway.

My mind slipped away for a moment to my last text with Stephen. Just a short, *pack a bag. See you soon.*

This man killed me. Right to the point. Meanwhile, I was dying with anticipation.

Just then, she reappeared, holding up thin, silver, long, shimmery strands and held them up to my ears.

"What do you think?"

"These are perfect." I slid them in and turned my head from side to side, looking in the mirror. "Thank you."

I reached down and hugged her. She was now feeling a microscopic four feet tall with my heels on.

Holding my face in her small hands, she said, "I'm sorry if I ever make you feel less than you ever are. This morning, I didn't mean to make you feel like you don't have friends or a life. I am sorry if that came out poorly or if I made you feel that way. I'm so proud of you, and I honestly don't know how you do it all. You amaze me, Cassandra," she said with tears filling her eyes.

"Mom. Don't make me cry. I have worked hard to look smoking hot. Do this tomorrow," I said, taking her little hands in mine and trying to turn it into a laughing moment. "It's okay. I know it's something I need to work on. I need a life outside of work. I'm trying, like this moment right now."

"You look amazing. Your dad may not let you out of the house, though," she said wide-eyed, looking me up and down.

The doorbell rang, and I could hear my dad, Britt, and Avery chatting with all their loudness downstairs.

"Well, shall we?" I said to her as I grabbed my bag for my supposed overnight stay at Brittany's.

I made my way down the staircase very carefully, completely regretting my choice of footwear.

"Holy smokes," Avery shouted as he stood with his hair pulled back in a well-made ponytail and classic all-black suit, looking absolutely gorgeous. "Here, I'll take that for you, Cass."

He reached to take my bag.

Britt, wearing a stunning emerald, green sheath silk dress with curves to kill, stood with her hand over her mouth, speechless for once. Her shoulder-length blonde curls laid beautifully around her face. Her crystal blue eyes, rimmed with smoky black liner and beautiful, long black lashes.

"You are smoking hot," she said, hugging me.

"Look at you, hot momma." I squealed.

I turned around, revealing the back, and she said, staring, "Oh my God, Cass."

Then, out of nowhere, my dad said, "I think you left the rest of your dress upstairs, honey." warranting him an elbow from my mom. "You look beautiful, all of you."

Once in the car, Brittany turned in the seat as Avery closed my door and was making his way around to the driver's side.

"He is going to eat you alive when he sees you."

"He told me I was going to need a wheelchair after tonight."

I shook my head with a smile.

"Damn. I want wheelchair-provoking sex."

She laughs as Avery got into the car.

"What are you sexy girls talking about?" he asked.

"Nothing. I wish we had a handicapped thingy for the mirror, like your Granny, so we could park closer tonight. That's all," she said, looking back at me, biting her tongue with a devious smile.

"Yeah, Avery, maybe you need to make Britt handicapped so she can qualify for one?"

I laughed.

Brittany covered her face laughing as Avery said, shaking his head, pulling out of the driveway, "This is obviously some sexual innuendo. It always is with you two. It's like being with two fifteen-year-olds when you are together."

Once again, the ride to the hotel was only minutes. Avery stayed back to deal with the valet as Brittany, and I went inside. The ballroom was a beautifully executed party. Platters of divine hors d'oeuvres by local restaurants were being passed around, and creative craft cocktails were being made with entertaining bartending skills. Everyone was dressed in their black-tie affair. I noticed some faces from the industry, but I had been out of the Charleston scene far too long to really make connections.

I sipped on the most amazing gin and tonic I ever had in a heavy crystal glass.

"Wow. This is fantastic," I said, lifting and looking at my glass as if it was going to tell me the ingredients.

"The bartender said the tonic came from a local soda maker that uses all-natural ingredients. I didn't know we had such a person here in town. I will be finding out who that is for our place," Avery said.

I spotted Dan Satterfield, who made his way over, looking fantastic once again, but this time, in a charcoal gray, form-fitting suit, and introduced himself to Britt and Avery, who, without surprise, ended up in a twenty-minute conversation talking about their restaurant. They really had a gift.

"Again, I'll talk to you next week, Cassie, enjoy your vacation."

He excused himself, letting me decompress and enjoy my time as promised.

I was enjoying my conversations with Britt and Avery and all the friends who joined us at the high cocktail tables that we stood around. They were mostly made up of their vendors and wine purveyors I had never met, with a few new friends. They were very interested in meeting me, and it was always easy to talk about the food and beverage industry with like-minded people.

Time seemed to be slipping by when I finally looked up from the small group we had gathered around us. He had to be there, when across the room, at another drink-laden, tall cocktail table stood Allen, Bianca, and a few other friends I had recognized from the other day. Everyone was engaged in conversation, but no Stephen. I scanned the room and was just about to open my clutch and check my phone to see if he had texted me when the sudden heat of a body pressed up against my back. A black suit-covered arm rested over my bare left, which laid on the table, his hand over mine, that grasped my drink, his right hand, warm and strong, now splayed wide across my low back, his fingers caressed my spine in slow circles.

My heart dropped straight to my pelvis and my lungs lost all air as his deep voice rumbled into my left ear through my hair.

"You are the most delicious thing in this entire room. I want to lick you from head to toe, Cassandra."

My hand tightened around my glass, mimicking what my pussy was doing beneath the lace of my panties. I did everything to stifle the largest grin ever as I faced the crowd outward or turned around and devour him with all I had, when suddenly, he slid his hand from mine and moved smoothly around, running his hand across my body in the process, then casually appeared in front of me at the table.

"Hi. How are you, Cassie. You look beautiful, darling," he said in the most casual, *we are the best of friends* tone, and wore the most devious smile.

With gritted teeth, I said, "Well played Mr. Harlow. I almost climaxed just now."

He smiled with that most amazing mouth at me, then down at my glass.

"It looks like you need another drink, love. Let's go."

He took my hand in his.

With his right hand, he reached through the small crowd and tapped Avery on the arm.

"Hey Avery. Thanks for everything, man."

"Ah, no problem, Stephen. Good seeing you."

He went back to his conversation.

"Brittany, you look gorgeous," he said when she turned. "Do you need another?" he asked, pointing to her glass.

"Not too bad yourself, Stephen. I'm okay, thanks. Be good to that arm candy," she said, pointing her glass in my direction.

Confused, I asked, "What did Avery do for you?" as we walked away.

"Oh, nothing. What are you drinking?" he asked, looking into my now empty glass as we approached the bar.

"Gin and tonic," I answered.

With a nod and raised eyebrows, the bartender asked over the noise of the room, "What can I get you two?"

"A gin and tonic, a prosecco, and two double Whiskey on the rocks, please?" he asked, then turned to me, leaning against the bar.

He was wearing a tailored, black three-piece suit. The vest had some sort of faint texture to it and the black tie as well. His crisp white shirt matched perfectly with his teeth, especially when he looked at me and bit his lip as he stared down at my mouth. I was staring up at his. I believed at that moment the room was actually silent, like a vacuum. Sort of like when it was fall, and the wind rustled through the trees, and all you heard were the leaves falling. All other noise seemed to stop, and your senses just focused on one segment of nature for that one tiny moment…this was what happened, for one second, but it was my heart beating inside my chest.

"Cass?"

His lips moved, and then all sound came back into the room.

He handed me my drink.

"Oh, thanks."

I took it from him with a smile.

"Can you carry Bianca's for me?" he asked.

"Of course," I said, sliding my clutch under my arm and taking her stemmed glass in my free hand. His fingers brushed over mine during the transfer, making my heart flutter. Those little things were going to get my heart in trouble. We were only able to give just this moment. I needed to keep reminding myself.

We made our way over to the other side of the room, and he introduced me to a few people I didn't know. I made fast friends with Allen and Bianca. I learned that Allen and Stephen were college roommates at MIT and quickly decided to go into business together after graduation. Allen and Bianca met and married shortly after that, and they had two children. Two daughters, a senior in high school and a freshman at the University of Houston studying Biomedical Engineering. Home-base was in Charlotte, North Carolina, due to the location factor for their company and the fact that they all hated an overly large city vibe. It was amazing what I learned about people in only thirty minutes.

"So, Cassie, we were discussing earlier today at lunch that we have a business trip to Silicon Valley next month. It's also my and Bianca's anniversary. I was thinking about making it extra special by sneaking away and doing a side trip to San Francisco," Allen said.

Bianca interjected in her beautifully flowing South African accent. "This also means he screwed up by planning this business trip and forgot it's our anniversary."

She winked at me, smiled, and took a sip of her prosecco.

Allen said sheepishly, "That too," followed by a larger sip of his whiskey.

Stephen shook his head from across the table.

"Oh, definitely. I would love to have you two come to my place for an evening out if you would like? We are booked months out, but I can make that work if you want?" I said, placing a hand on Bianca's shoulder.

"Well, we would like all four of us if we could?" Allen asked.

"Oh, well. I think I can make that happen." I made eye contact with Stephen and got an approving look. "I don't usually work on the weekends. So, of course."

I felt the blush in my cheek.

So, they were talking about me at lunch and Stephen was making plans for a month out that included me? I was having an internal meltdown while trying to maintain my composure in a lucid conversation. I threw back the remaining gin and tonic in my glass and smiled.

"I haven't been to the Bay Area in ages, Cassie, I will have to get all the latest places to go and things to see from you," Bianca said.

I shook my head and laughed. "Well, I don't get out much. I'll do my best."

I could see Stephen smiling at our conversation from across the table as he and Allen talked. Another round of drinks, more great conversation, and more laughs. I felt comfortable there and besides my feet, it felt really good.

Brittany and Avery made their way over, and I reintroduced them to Bianca and Allen from the previous day at the festival. Stephen, Allen, and Avery ended up in an in-depth conversation about whiskey. Serious man shit. People were beginning to disperse, and the night was officially winding down.

"I think we are heading out, Chica."

She leaned in for a hug.

"Okay. Ugh, I have my bag in your car," I whined, throwing my head back.

"No, Avery and Stephen took care of that earlier," she said, kissing me on the cheek. "Have fun, sexy girl. I would say break a leg, but I think that is actually too close to the truth," she added quietly, laughing into my ear.

I smirked. "Y'all be careful. I'll call you tomorrow morning from my hospital bed."

Everyone hugged and said their good nights.

The band ended with no better song than Marvin Gaye's classic, Let's Get it On. Stephen took my hand and with a smile, led me out to the small dance floor, and just as I had imagined, one hand splayed across my bare low back, another curled up into his chest. He pulled me into him, where I could breathe him in and become intoxicated by him for the first time tonight. The whiskey on his breath, the cedar, sandalwood, and the clean scent of his skin coming through his clothes.

The slow rhythmic movement of our bodies to this sexual song made me feel like we were completely alone. I wanted to slide his jacket from his shoulders, start untying his tie, and unbutton his shirt. I looked up, and he gently lifted my face with his hand. He kissed me so softly. It felt like the first time all over again, and the throbbing between my legs became hard to ignore.

"I think we need to get out of here before we start a show for these people," he said against my lips.

I breathed into him. "Okay, I don't know if I can make it all the way to your mom's."

He smiled. "Good thing we only have to make it upstairs."

Chapter 12

CASSIE

is hand slid down my arm to my hand as he guided me back to the cocktail-covered table, and I gathered my clutch. I must have a prodigious smile on my face when he looked at me when we turned towards the hotel entryway because he shook his head and stifled a laugh.

"What?" I asked with confusion.

"Your excitement is almost palpable. I love it," he said.

"You do this to me, and I love it," I admitted as he pulled me through the maze of tiny hallways of the oddly shaped hotel to find the elevator.

He pressed the button, and the large brass doors opened immediately. Excitement raced through my body as he pulled me inside as doors closed behind us in the empty elevator. He pulled me tightly into him, kissing me slowly and deeply, taking all my breath. He then pulled away with eyes racing back and forth into mine as if he wanted to say something. He refrained, leaving me in a state of bewilderment.

The short ride was over, the doors opened, and we skirted past a couple patiently waiting. I walked with my hand in the crook of his arm as we ambled the long hallway adorned with Charleston artwork and navy blue and pink lined carpet. Finally, we reached the suite, where he quickly swiped his room key, and once inside, he suddenly pressed me against the cool entryway wall before I could even take a look in the room, which was dimly lit by distant lamp lighting.

His strong physique, hard against mine, his hands pressed on either side of my face, tangled within my hair, his lips, tongue, and breath in a perfect dance, sending chills through my entire body. He pushed my hair from the side of my face and breathed in my ear.

"I have wanted you all night. God, Cassie, you are driving me wild."

He then made his way, kissing my neck and pulling my leg up under my knee, sliding his hand towards my now extremely wet pussy.

I whispered between gasps of pleasure, "Stephen, I need to get these shoes off. They are killing me."

He slowly lowered my leg, backed up slightly from me, tossed his suit jacket off onto the floor, kicked out of his shoes, and proceeded to then run his hands down my body very, very slowly as I leaned against the wall as if he was inspecting me. Inch by inch, thumbs stopping to trace over my hardened nipples through the fabric of my dress as he bit his lip, groaning.

"Mmm."

He then smoothed a hand down my stomach, over my hips, then my thighs. He squatted to trace rough fingers over my sore calves, unbuckle my heels, and slowly slid my aching feet out.

Instantly, I felt nearly a foot shorter and a hundred times more comfortable. I let out an audible sigh of relief as he made his way back up my body the same path he went down, but this time, he kissed his way back up.

Kissing my calves, stroking with his strong hands, then up my thighs. Switching back and forth between legs with his tender, succulent lips. My hands dove into his inky, thick hair as he was now between my legs, pushing the fabric of my dress up, breathing over the lace of my panties. Ripples of pleasure ran through me, and the throbbing in my pussy was now impossible to ignore. He was on his knees, his hands had pushed my panties to the side, and the first intrusion of his fingers had me gasp in pleasure as they found my clit, hard and incredibly wet. His other hand slid up my stomach and then reached all the way up to my breast. My head arched back, and I whimpered with delight when he pinched my nipple lightly.

"Oh my God. Oh yes, right there, fuck, yes." I moaned when he glided seductively with delicate fingertips over my clit. He massaged it with such precision, and it felt so fucking good.

Just when I was reaching my pinnacle of pleasure, he stopped everything he was doing for a moment.

"No, don't stop," I whined.

He took a minute to slowly run his fingers around my ass and slide my panties off until they dropped to the floor.

"See? Isn't that better?" he said, peering up at me as he held the small bit of fabric of my dress up again. I moaned with agreement as he pushed to spread my legs wider and went back to using the perfect pressure strumming my clit like an instrument with variations of circles and pressure. Periodically dipping into the juices of my pussy, making sure my clit stayed slick. It also teased me, making me want him deep inside me. His face was so close, and I wanted him to lick and suck me, but he didn't. Pressure built and heat exploded within me as he made me come within minutes with the rhythmic movements of his fingers.

My body tensed,

"Oh fuck, Stephen."

A rush of heat ran down my spine and through my core. Emotions washed over me yet again, but I contained it this time. My eyes were closed and my head tilted back against the wall as my legs became unsteady. I lightened my grip on his hair and ran my hands lightly through his strands as I thought about how I didn't want this moment to end. I truly didn't want to let him go, not again.

My body relaxed beneath his touch, and I fell against the wall when he suddenly slid his fingers into me with intensity, and his skilled tongue licked vigorously at my already incredibly sensitive clit. Oh my God, he was going to make me come again. I grabbed at his shoulder, the wall, anything I could as my body rippled with desire as he sucked my clit and rolled it within his hot mouth.

"Holy fuck," I yelled.

Grabbing his hair, I pressed his head harder into me as he moaned over my cleft. My lips went numb, I could no longer speak, and my legs shook, making it harder to hold myself up. Heat rushed through my pussy, and I climaxed again with such intensity I lost my breath.

Once I regained my composure and what I thought was consciousness, I took in long, ragged breaths and rested my palms on his shoulders to steady myself. He slowly withdrew his fingers from me, caressed my thighs, and kissed my stomach. He looked up at me with a mischievous smile and those amazing green eyes.

I looked down at his gorgeous face as I held my dress up and ran my hand through his soft hair, shaking my head.

"Oh my God. That was intense. Jesus, I want you so bad."

Then I reached down to pull up at his strong arm, guiding him up to me. He slowly stood and I looked around and laughed at the fact that we didn't even make it two feet into the room before one of us had an orgasm. Very Stephen and Cassie-like.

I kissed him wildly. His mouth was a delicious mixture of whiskey and my juices. I would say the night was exactly where I wanted it to be.

I pulled him slowly away from the entryway wall into the suite's living room area. Two lamps sat on either side of a couch that shed light on a nicely decorated sitting area with linen chairs and a dining area, giving the space a sense of warmth. An open area in front of a credenza held a large television. That was where I led him. I wanted space.

I stood before him in silence, and I needed silence because I would definitely say the wrong thing in that most perfect moment. I reached down, took hold of the hem of my dress, and seductively pulled it over my head, standing before him completely bare, except for my earrings. He slowly smiled with only the curves of his lips and ran his hands over my shoulders and down my arms, sending goose bumps over my whole body. I unbuttoned his vest and tossed it to the chair. I reached up and untied his tie, draping it around my neck and letting the cool silk lie between my breasts. Then I proceeded to remove his cufflinks, rolling the metal pieces onto the table, breaking the silence with a faint clinking sound. Then, I slowly unbuttoned his shirt, starting at the top as he intently watched my face and fingers until I slid it over his shoulders and down his arms. He silently watched my every seductive, naked move. I undid his pants, and they dropped easily to the floor. I slowly slid my fingers around the waistband of his underwear and down his strong body. His cock, hard and swollen. I wanted to stroke it so badly but refrained for a moment as I moved slowly down to remove his socks one by one. Just as he did, I kissed and ran my hands up his muscular legs until I was face to face with his virility. I wrapped my hand around his length and took his heavy, tight balls in my other hand. I stroked him slowly, up and down, then stood before him, looking into his eyes in silence, until his breath hitched and his eyes closed.

"Damn, your hands feel so good," he said softly as he reached with one hand around to my back and down over my ass. He made tender movements with his fingers as I watched his reactions to mine.

I stroked his hard cock up and down, then circled the ridge of the head with my thumb feeling pre-cum slickening the tip. I guided his body backward toward the bedroom, and he then came out of his slight dream-like state, opening his eyes, turning to take my hand, and guiding me to the bedroom.

The bed was a bit higher than expected, so I motioned for him to climb up first and left his legs hanging free. He had a questioning look but obliged. I pressed my naked body between his strong thighs, and I could stand. The bed was so tall. I slid the tie from my neck as I contemplated tying him to the bed for a moment, but I would save it for another time and tossed it to the nightstand. He lay back, and I took his thick shaft in my hand and ran my flattened tongue from the base slowly, all the way to the tip, making him moan.

"Oh God, Cassie, fuck baby."

I then wrapped my lips tightly around his head and ran my hot mouth slowly back down the entire length of him, burying him deep in my throat.

I made rhythmic motions, swirling with my lips, tongue, and saliva. Over and over, I continued doing this as I watched his desire build, and he fisted the comforter.

"Baby, damn, your mouth feels so fucking good."

I slid my mouth back down around his thick shaft and took all of him and slid my other hand around his balls to caress and run my fingers along the ridge between his ass, making him gasp with satisfaction.

He cried out, "Oh yeah, baby. Don't you stop that," as my hand and mouth were moving in perfect unison. He moved my hair to the side to watch me. "I want you up here baby, I want to be inside you."

He groaned.

I slowly slid him from my mouth, and he moved to the middle of the bed, rolling gracefully to the to the nightstand to retrieve a condom. I couldn't help but stare unabashedly at his body. His abs were adorned with that sexy vee of muscle at his pelvis and washboard abs. We weren't in our thirties, and he managed this body. It was impressive as hell.

I climbed up to the bed, and without blinking an eye, he was already on his back and ready for me.

"Damn, you are fast. I didn't even hear the package rip open."

I laughed.

He smiled. "I'm about to explode woman, come here. I want you right here where I can see all of you."

He motioned for me to climb on top of him.

I straddled him and took in his incredibly hard cock.

I winced as his girth stretched me wide.

"Are you okay?" he asked with a furrowed brow, tucking a stray hair behind my ear.

I leaned down to the side of his face, and my lips brushed against his ear.

"I'm perfect," I whispered as I pressed my pussy slowly down his entire length.

"Oh fuck."

He groaned as I glided my wet pussy up and down his rigid cock.

I rode him slowly on my knees, sitting upward as he palmed my heavy breasts and teased my tender nipples between his fingertips. Another surge of arousal overcame me as he reached down with one hand and ran his thumb over my already swollen clit.

"Damn, you are so sexy," he rumbled.

My hands splayed across his chest for leverage as I pressed, lifting one leg up, giving him a view of his slick cock sliding in and out of me. He peered between our bodies at this view, then, dropping his head back, moaning, "Oh, God Cass, I'm going to come. That's so fucking hot."

He then looked back between us again.

Just then, he pulled me down onto him tightly and buried his head between my shoulder and ear, breathing deeply and whispering, "Yes, baby. Fuck, your pussy feels so damn good."

I felt his dick swell so hard inside of me that it was borderline painful, and his whole entire body tensed. He held his breath for a moment. It was his tell, and it always had been. Knowing this, I ground myself deeper and deeper on to him. He guided me by my hips, slamming my ass down relentlessly, pulsating underneath me in long, deep movements as a guttural sound ripped from his throat. He grabbed a hold of my shoulders, pulling me down hard on to him as hot streams of semen poured from him, leaving him limp muscle beneath me.

I laid connected on top of him for a while as he ran circles over my sweat-slickened back and fingers through my knotted hair. Total silence. We were both in deep thought, still somewhat erratic breathing. Was he thinking about Lauren? Was he thinking about what his next move was with me? Work? Was he thinking about who the Philadelphia Eagles were going to draft at the center for next season?

Just then, he kissed my head, saying, "That was amazing."

"I don't even know what to say anymore."

I placed tiny kisses leading down his face to his ear, lacing my fingers tightly through his.

"Why?" he whispered into my hair.

I gently sucked on the lobe of his ear and released it, then kissed down his neck to his collar bone and up at his strong chin. My mind, racing with thoughts I could not dare release from my mouth.

I whispered back, "I just don't want this weekend to end. I'm enjoying this time with you."

He raised one of our interlocked hands and kissed the back of my hand with his eyes still closed, saying, "I wish I didn't have to go tomorrow afternoon. I would love to have at least one more day with you."

"Where are you headed?" I asked.

"Houston. We have a meeting with a client, and Bianca is going to go see their daughter. Our plane is scheduled to take off at 1:30, So I may move it later. Hold on one second."

He slid out from under me to discard the condom into a trashcan and laid back on the bed.

I sat up on top of him. He bent his knees, giving me something to lean against. I could feel his warmth underneath me, and his cock flinched as if it might come back to life.

I let out a giggle. "So, you are just going to interrupt everyone's plans to extend your time with me? Is there even another direct flight out of Charleston to Houston later?"

He laughed. "Babe, we have our own company jet, and Allen and Bianca obviously love you and will do anything for us."

"Oh, well, aren't you fancy?" I said, flailing my arms in the air.

He flipped me over faster than I could blink and pinned his hard, muscular frame over mine. His hands pinning my wrists to the bed. He sat on top of me and wrapped his strong legs around mine like a frog.

"Oh man, you play dirty," I yelled.

"I thought you like it dirty, Cass?" he asked with a smirk and biting his lip.

He looked up at the clock on the nightstand.

"What is it?" I asked.

He leaned down and kissed me quickly. "Oh, nothing."

He untangled himself from my legs and quickly climbed off me and the bed.

"Where are you going?" I asked, confused as he made his way into the closet and grabbed a pair of workout shorts out of his suitcase.

"Nowhere," he said as he walked into the living room to rifle through his pants.

I sat up just as there was a knock at the door.

"Damn. I love it when a plan is perfectly executed," he chanted from the other room as he disappeared around the corner. I heard the door open with, "Thank you man, have a good night," and the door closed.

Stephen magically appeared back around the corner, shirtless, sexy as fuck, smiling, and carrying a Gino's pizza.

"Oh my God. What kind of sorcery did you just perform?" I exclaimed, sitting naked on bent knees, holding my hands interlocked and arms over my breasts.

Grinning and placing the box on the dining table, he said, "I almost forgot I planned this earlier. I ordered Gino's last pizza delivery earlier tonight before we went out. I figured we would be drunk, hungry, and sexed up with no food options."

I climbed from the bed and walked into the room and kissed him on the top of his head.

"You are a God. Where did you put my bag?"

Scanning the room, he pointed over to the closet where he had retrieved his shorts. "Right in there." Then he proceeded to open the pizza box. "Hell yeah."

I pulled a short dusty blue robe from my bag and wrapped it around my body as I walked over to the table. I was in awe, thinking of the details this man had thought of ahead of time.

Who did that?

He made his way to the small fridge and I couldn't resist watching him bend over. The muscles of his back, his lean torso to his tight ass in those shorts. Damn. I could just stare at him all day.

"Bottled water? Perrie? Diet Coke? La Croix or beer?" he listed.

I replied, "Damn. Stop tempting me with that diet coke. Is this part of the twelve-step program? I'll take a Perrie. Thanks."

He returned with our drinks, and we spread out at the sofa and coffee table. I tucked my legs under me and he passed me a large slice of cheese, oozing from the edges. I folded it in half and piled the cheese in the center before tilting my head to the side and easing it into my mouth.

"Oh my God, that is so good when it's hot. Thank you for thinking of this."

Throwing his crust into the box, he said with a huge pizza-filled smile, "I have made nothing but good decisions this entire weekend. I am on a roll, baby."

I shook my head, smiling as I ate my slice in bliss.

He went in for another slice as I casually said, "I was offered a celebrity chef gig this weekend back in San Francisco."

I continued chewing my pizza.

He turned and looked at me in surprise. "What? This is awesome, Cass. Why didn't you tell me this?"

I tossed my crust into the box, wiped my hands on my napkin, and took a sip of my Perrie. Then I jabbered on.

"Well, I had a few small meetings, if that's even what you would call them. It was basically a chance run-in, if you ask me. I will know more when I get home next week. They are interested in me doing a cooking show, cookware, and cookbooks. We'll see."

He held his hands open in dismay. "Cass, that's freaking awesome." He reached over and hugged me, grabbed me by the shoulders, held me out and looked at me again, and said, "You are always a star. I'm so proud of you."

Then he kissed my greasy lips.

I laughed. "Don't get ahead of yourself, I don't know if it will work with my schedule with the restaurant, and I'm a solo flier now, remember? This is a lot on me. I don't have any support at home except for Jack. I need to talk to him and see what he will be doing to help. This is all new. I don't know what the fuck I'm doing."

While I rambled, and it all started to actually make me sad as I looked down into my lap and pulled at the hem of my robe.

I felt a tug at my chin as Stephen lifted it with his index finger, having me look him in the eye.

"Look at me. Don't doubt yourself, Cassie. You are the strongest person I know. If anyone can do it, you can, babe. If you need anything, I can help too."

I smiled and let out a chuckle. "Can you take Cora to cheer practice on Thursdays?"

He closed his eyes and dropped his head, then looked back at me. "Okay, maybe not anything, but if there is something I can do,

I'm your man. I'm a great listener. I can sext the shit out of you from across the country. I can even fly my plane to you and hug you in a time of need." He winked.

"Oh, hell. I may need a lot of hugs. I'm kind of needy," I said, biting my lip.

I just got butterflies thinking of what that scenario entailed. I could have a jet-delivered booty-call at my disposal? That is freaking hot.

He pushed me back onto the couch, spreading my legs open and pressing his hand between my legs. His lips brushed mine. "I feel something else that's needy too."

"Oh God, I am not going to be able to walk tomorrow," I whispered.

"I told you, you were going to need a wheelchair."

He smiled devilishly.

Chapter 13

CASSIE

✗

His tan forearms pressed on either side of my head, leaning against the cool tile wall. My nipples burned from the coolness of the frigid tile. Wet hair clung to my face as the hot water ran trails down my skin, dodging tiny goosebumps in its path. Our breathing was still labored while his cock was still hard, nestled inside me, and his body heaved against mine. He gently tucked my hair around my ear and sucked in my water-dripped lobe, whispering in his deep voice that echoed throughout the tile and glass enclosure.

"One month. I will see you in one month."

I sucked on my lip and curled it into a small smile.

He slowly slid himself from me, turning me around, and I wrapped my arms around his waist as we stood underneath the rain head that poured between us, making a pool within my cleavage and his chest. I slowly ran my fingertips over his eyebrows and down his jawline to his beautiful lips, just taking him in.

"I don't know what we are doing. When I go home, it's going to be complete havoc. When you…"

"Shh." He pressed a finger over my wet lips. "Just let this happen, Cass. Let's try something different for once and not control it. Let's just see what happens, okay? *We* are what has always gotten in the way of us."

I looked down and stared at the pooling water between us, and my mind wandered to the what-ifs.

He lifted my chin. "Remember what I said? I am a mess right now. That still hasn't changed. I have a lot to resolve and sort out. It also doesn't change the fact that I am crazy about you. I also don't want to promise you anything or hurt you, but I would like to give you some happiness while you work your shit out, too. I know you have a lot on your plate, and maybe we can just be a bit of good for each other when we can. No commitments, just when we can."

He backed up a bit, dropping the water between us in a violent splash, and ran his hands through his hair, shaking his head.

"I don't fucking know." He reached forward and held my face in his hands while looking at me with his intensely green eyes. "All I know, Cassie, is that I have lost you too many times. I may have lost another person I have loved as well. If this is what the universe is gifting me yet again, and I'm not paying attention, I may never get another chance. *We* may never get another chance."

His lips then sealed mine, taking all my breath. His tongue swept through my mouth, making me need him so intensely, not just physically, but emotionally. I felt so connected to him.

Pulling away slowly and placing my forehead against his, I closed my eyes.

"Okay, I will try. I am so scared I will hurt you again or that this will completely break me. I am already falling so…"

He covered my impending words with his lips.

Watching him put on a crisp suit was a damn aphrodisiac. He was lucky I didn't rip it off of him. We made mostly small talk as we gathered our belongings that were strewn around the room and packed up. I found myself standing in front of the expansive windows that looked out over downtown and the park where they were breaking down the tents where the Food and Wine festival took place over the weekend. I sighed as his arms wrapped around me, and he kissed the side of my neck, his face smoothly shaven as it brushed against mine.

"I can't get over this view," he whispered.

"It's pretty. I think I've grown to like San Francisco better, though," I replied, gazing out the window, holding onto his arms.

He chuckles. "I was talking about you."

I sucked my teeth and leaned back with a smile and kissed his lips that tasted like mint, his skin smelling clean and masculine.

"Let me get my things."

I stepped away to gather my clutch and phone.

I made a quick text to Britt.

Me: Stephen is going to drop me at your place. Aka Uber driver. Lol.

Britt: Got it.

Me: See you soon

"You ready?"

He stood leaning against the entryway wall, insanely handsome in his crisp navy-blue suit with his suitcase.

"Damn, I'm going to miss the many looks of you," I said, shaking my head as I reached down to grab my overnight bag.

He took it from my hand and slid it over the handle of his suitcase.

"I'm going to miss the many looks of you, too."

He lightly patted my ass as I walked in front of him, making the ruffles of my sundress lift, revealing my ass cheeks.

"Mmm…that gave me a rise."

He had to adjust himself in his pants.

The drive to Britt's over the drawbridges bordered by green marshlands and blue waterways was always serene and scenic. When you lived there, you tended to take it for granted. Visiting definitely made me appreciate the view once again.

We pulled up into their large circular driveway lined with live oak trees draped with an abundance of mossy-gray Spanish moss.

"Damn, I should have gotten my last kiss down the road. You are my Uber driver, according to Cora."

He quickly turned his head around, backed the car out of the driveway, and proceeded to the next block.

"What are you doing?"

I laughed.

He slammed on the brakes and threw the car in park.

"I'm getting my kiss."

He reached over and took my face in his strong hands and kissed me like it was his last. He ran his hands all over my body, up my dress, and over my panties. Fuck, I could almost come. This was close to a reenactment of when he picked me up the first night when we went to the beach.

With lips still pressed together, I moaned.

"If you keep going, we are going to be fucking right here in the car."

"Is that a bad thing?"

He smiled while kissing me.

"You are insatiable, Mr. Harlow," I whispered in his ear.

"You are fucking irresistible, Ms. Buckley."

"You need to go. It's 12:45," I said, peering at the clock on the dash.

He pulled away slowly, sighing.

"I don't want to."

Begrudgingly rearranging himself in his seat, he put the car in drive and turned it around. Right before the driveway, he reached over for one last sweet kiss.

"One month."

He nodded.

I walked into Britt's house to the mild chaos of TVs blaring that nobody was watching and slight disarray because that was how they rolled. I also didn't knock because I never had unless I knew she and Avery were alone, which they never were.

"Hello?" I called out.

"Mom," I heard from a familiar voice I hadn't heard in days as Cora came from around the corner and nearly tackled me.

"Well, hey, sweetie. Oh wow. You are so dark," I exclaimed, dropping my bag.

"I swear I wore sunscreen. I was just in the sun a lot," she said, worried that I would scold her.

"I know, we get dark. It just takes you longer than that at home in the summer, that's all." I giggled. "You have had quite the vacation so far, I hear?"

"The beach house was so fun, and we went horseback riding yesterday at Seabrook Island. That was awesome," she rambled.

"I can't wait to hear all about it when we get back to Samsie and Gram's. I'm ready to chill out." I said exhaustedly. "Where's Britt?"

"On the back patio."

She pointed to the back of the house.

I heard footsteps coming down the hall and a very much older Harper appeared from the shadows.

"Holy cow. Look at you," I said, mouth and arms wide open as she walked right into my embrace.

"Hi, Ms. Cassie," she said, leaning into me with a weak teenage hug.

"It hasn't been that long, and you turned into a dang woman. Wow," I said, shocked.

She blushed and I could tell she wanted to leave the conversation and go back to the comforts of her bedroom as soon as possible.

"Okay. Start to gather your things so you will be ready when we are," I asked.

"I'll be in Harper's room."

She bounced off, trailing behind Harper.

I weaved my way through the living room, the kitchen, and then finally to the large, expansive sliding doors that opened up to a gorgeous patio overlooking the harbor. Just like the front yard, large live oak trees shaded the well-appointed yard. Brittany and Avery were sitting on the screened-in patio with Bloody Marys, feet propped up with a Bluetooth speaker, playing music in the background.

"Hair of the Dog?" I asked, laughing.

Britt turned her head to see me approaching from behind her.

"Hey. Just a bit. We didn't overdo it until we came home and decided to have our own afterparty out here. Some of the guys came over, and it went a little later than it should have."

Avery held up his glass. "Want one?"

"Nah, I'm good. What else do you have?" I asked.

"There's a cooler right there. Help yourself," he said.

I rifled through the random bottles and cans in the icy water and pulled out a La Croix. I popped it open as I plopped into an oversized linen and wicker chair, propping my feet onto the coffee table, and crossed them at the ankle.

They both stared at me. After a beat, I took a big sip and looked at them. "What?" I said, holding my hand out.

"What is going on with emhem?"

She cleared her throat in case my child was within listening distance.

"We are just going to go with the flow. Nothing serious. We have fucked up shit in our lives right now, but we are going to…try?" I said, as I winced and shrugged. "Who am I lying to? I'm so fucked y'all. This is going to destroy me. I'm a mess and I can't have this right now. He's more than a booty call. I've held a flame for him for…forever."

I leaned forward and ran my hands through my hair and rested my face in my hands.

Avery laughed. "Sorry." He put his hand over his mouth. "I'm not laughing at you, I promise, but hasn't this shit been going on forever with you two? I honestly don't even know the real story. Why aren't you together? Like, did I just smoke too much weed or something? I don't remember you even dating, but I know y'all have been together since high school. Well, except for your marriage."

"Seriously? Britt tells you everything. She is the only person carrying all my secrets, and I always thought she told you. I just figured she told you the whole story," I said in surprise.

Britt finished the last of her Bloody Mary and placed the glass on the table.

With raised eyebrows, she said, "I honestly don't understand why you did what you did, Cassie. It was so long ago, and you two have managed to sabotage this relationship or whatever we want to call it… over the last, who the fuck knows, how many years now? Why don't you tell us what happened, and maybe we can finally figure this shit out?"

I ran my tongue through the inside of my mouth, not sure I wanted the Manning Doctors to dissect my past.

"Damn, I want a cig. I also may need a stronger drink."

I looked at my can.

"There's a pack someone left on the ledge over there," Avery said.

"There's stronger shit in the cooler. Grab me a beer," she said, smiling, getting more comfortable on the sofa.

I got up and grabbed two beers from the cooler.

"Avery?"

"Fuck it. Okay."

I grabbed three and glanced at the pack of Marlboros on the porch ledge. I couldn't. I'd smell like smoke and Cora was there.

Damn.

It's so tempting, though. Those two were such bad influences on me.

I passed them out, and we all got comfortable.

"Don't get excited. It's not a thriller," I began. "We know how it started. I secretly started banging him senior year. I don't really know why we didn't tell anyone except for the fact that we were really different. Not when we were together. We were awesome together, but we had completely different lives outside of us. His friends were completely opposite of mine and interests. He was a jock and not just that, but they were all the college bound, super intelligent kids. I hung out with, well...Colleen, Rachel, and Britt."

"Fuck you," Britt yelled at me.

I laughed.

"Not that we weren't intelligent. We just had different goals. We weren't the four-year college-bound kids. I was culinary, Britt wasn't sure what she wanted to do yet, Colleen was thinking about the military, and Rachel was thinking of art therapy or some shit. What did she end up doing?" I asked, looking at Britt with a furrowed brow and tilted head.

"She owns like... the busiest dog grooming place in Mt. Pleasant, I think?" Britt questioned.

"Oh shit. No way," I said, shocked. "Anyway, we were at the

beach, smoking weed, cigarettes, Britt was banging all the surfers."

I laughed.

Avery whipped his head to look at her. She shook her head, with hands in the air, acting as if I was crazy.

I continued my rant. "Totally not Stephen Harlow vibes. I wasn't hanging out with his football nerd friends and the cheerleaders. It just didn't feel natural, so we kept it a secret, and honestly, it was kind of hot. All the sneaking around. I went to his house almost every day on my little black bike. We had sex all over this town."

I swigged down half my beer as Avery moved to the edge of the couch. "Is this the part he rips your heart out?"

"Ha. Hardly." Britt blurted.

I fidgeted with my nails. "College acceptances started rolling in. We knew he was a freaking genius, right? Scholarships were thrown out like crazy back then, unlike today. He got into MIT, his first choice. Huge scholarship. I got my acceptance into the Culinary Institute, and he was genuinely happy for me. We knew this was it. No more Cassie and Stephen. This was so fun, but sadly, the game was over."

I took a deep breath and swigged from my beer.

"Two weeks later, he got an acceptance letter from Cal Poly, and he seriously considered taking it. Completely across the country, half the scholarship, and it wasn't his first choice. When I asked him why the hell would he even consider it? His answer was so he could be closer to me. I'm a chick. He didn't even have the balls to tell his friends he was seeing. Why would he do that?"

"That is so sweet, Cassie. Especially coming from a kid. He really loved you," Avery said.

A series of coughs came from Britt. "Sorry, I was choking on myself," she said, looking up at the ceiling.

"Nah. I'm a dick," I said, chugging the rest of my beer, putting it down on the table, and said, "So, the next day, I never showed up on my little black bike, I never went back, I never gave him an explanation, I didn't turn back, I just left."

The air left the porch. Avery just looked confused as Britt sucked her lips into her mouth and looked down into her empty beer.

"So…how did y'all hook up again?" he asked with a messed-up face.

"Christmas break, freshman year. Britt and I were at Cumberland's downtown, seeing this band play, and I felt this warm body up against me. I thought it was just some creep, but I turned around, and it was him. Smiling. Forgiving. We fucked in his car an hour later and every day over that break while I was home," I said, smiling in a daze, reminiscing.

Britt asked, "I don't really understand why y'all never really stayed together, though. You are so fucking compatible."

"Honestly? We are fucking stubborn. I won't give up my career and leave San Francisco. He won't leave Charlotte, so we just sat at a stalemate. I met Jack, then poof. Sixteen years happened. He met Lauren and, well, now here we are in this weird mess."

I stood and went to get another beer out of the cooler.

"I can't stay much longer. I need to go back to my parents' soon, and I can't be wasted."

"I'm so sad and kind of turned on by your story," Avery said with raised eyebrows at me. "I honestly didn't know. I thought you two just hooked up a few times in high school and college. I am invested in this shit now. I want this to work for you. I liked the dude, but Jack really fucked up. Stephen is a good guy, and he deserves happiness, Cassie. Fuck. He has been through some shit. You were ruthless," he said, laughing through his fist.

I tilted my beer back. "Thanks. I'm lucky he was so forgiving, though. Don't worry, he busted my balls about me leaving on my little black bike every chance he gets, and I take it like a champ. I am going to go home, get my life in order, and try to make it up to him if we can. He still has a mess, too. It's not all me."

"It's like the best soap opera ever. I love your life. As Cassie's Life Turns," Britt said, making a rainbow effect with her hands.

"More like Young and the Ruthless," Avery said through a laugh.

I chuckled, finishing my beer. "I'll take it. Now take me home, assholes."

Chapter 14

CASSIE

The house was buzzing with all my favorite sounds and smells. Cora and my dad were teasing each other relentlessly as he was heading in and out of the house, grilling his favorite Brazilian beef.

Oh my God.

When I walked into the kitchen that afternoon and saw him turning that glorious slab of beef in that marinade, I almost had an orgasm. Okay, a month ago, that might have happened due to my lack of sex, but I was thoroughly fucked in that moment, so I was able to hold my shit together this time, but it was…that worthy. My mom was singing and doodling around in the kitchen waiting for me to come help her to finish making the salad and our family recipe, Jack Hatch Chili Rice. I got the rice cooking, so I jetted upstairs to take care of a few things.

First, I needed to talk to Kyle as promised. I wanted to catch up on the weekend and how it all went at the restaurant. I could see the numbers, and everything looked phenomenal, but I wanted to hear his voice and how everyone there was doing. I also couldn't keep him in the dark any longer with the rest of the drama since he would be involved, even if it was indirectly.

I dialed his number, and he picked up on the third ring.

"Chef. How are you?"

I could hear music in the background, then becoming faint as if he was walking away from it.

"I'm great. How are you? If I'm interrupting you, call me back later," I said quickly.

"No, not at all. I'm just at a friend's having a few beers and getting ready to grill out. I'm trying to get out of cooking, so this is perfect timing." He chuckled. "Is everything okay?"

"It's great. I just wanted to catch up. Like I said, I was going to call," I said.

He laughed. "You are really into your vacation. You said you would call Monday. It's Sunday. I like that you don't even know what day it is. That's a good time off work. Well done, Chef."

I pressed my hand to my face with closed eyes in silence. "Fuck. I'm sorry. I am calling you on your day off. Ha. I didn't even question why you were drinking beers and grilling out on a Monday."

I laughed and threw my head back.

"No worries. We are here now. What's going on?" he said so casually, and I could hear him taking a sip of a drink. I could imagine him dressed in some tattered jeans and a softly worn t-shirt with his full-sleeved tattoo artfully gracing his arm. His hair gelled up in his mohawk, which he only sported on his days off. I rarely saw that guy, just the one who always kept his side-shaven scalp underneath Sagi-Shi hats and top hair pulled back in a ponytail. He had gorgeous gray eyes that complemented his sandy blonde hair. He was so good-looking. He was the skater dude. Every girl's best friend. Every guy's buddy. He was sweet and reliable.

"Can this conversation be between you and me as friends, Kyle? For god's sake, you and I have known each other for longer than…" I trailed off, realizing for the first time how many years? My internship, my marriage, opening Sagi, and my kid. "Shit, Kyle, forever," I said, questioning myself.

"Cassie? Are you sure you are okay?" he asked, this time more worried.

I almost giggled, sounding crazy, and just spat it out.

"Yeah, I'm okay… Jack and I are splitting up and…"

"Oh, shit," he said with a sigh.

I interrupted him before he got too worked up.

"It's okay. I'm okay, Kyle. If you noticed I was off my game lately... well, now you know why. Another thing. That little something exciting I wanted to tell you about?"

"Oh, yeah?"

"While I was here, I was offered a kind of celebrity chef gig back there in San Francisco," I said.

"Holy shit. Like, on TV?" he asked with enthusiasm.

"Yeah, and cookbooks and a cookware line. It's sort of bananas. It's not a done deal. I'm meeting with them next week, but I wanted to talk to you first," I said with sincerity.

Confused, he asked, "Why do you need to talk to me?"

"Well, this would take me out of Sagi a little more, not a lot, they say, but definitely more. I would need more of your help. Maybe move Reggie up? Darius up? Probably hire a couple more in their place. I don't want you to be overwhelmed, and we will make sure everyone is compensated appropriately. If this happens, and this is still a big *if*, Sagi could get even busier. I need to make sure you and our team are up for this." I realized I was rambling and had to look at my phone to make sure he was even still on the line. "Kyle?"

"Oh, I'm still here. Wow. This is freaking awesome news. I'm in. I know the guys will be too. Reggie ate up his bonus, by the way. I'm not sure anyone has ever done that out of the blue for him before. I kind of wish you were there to see the look on his face," he said.

"Aww. Well, I am talking to our accountant next week too about the raises and seeing where we are financially. I have to be strategic with all this. I can maybe lower my pay to cover everyone until the restaurant starts to pick up more with the excitement, but I will have the other income from the TV gig. I don't know what this divorce is going to do. Hopefully, not financially cripple me." I then immediately started to feel like I was going to throw up. "Sorry, I'm talking out loud about shit that doesn't concern you. I'm probably going more into the friend zone here than I should. I mean, it's been like, nineteen years?"

"Jesus. Nineteen? I need to get a life outside the kitchen. I'm in a ratty t-shirt, jeans with a freaking mohawk, and I only have the responsibility of a dog. I need to grow up and find a good woman."

He laughed.

Damn, I knew him so well that I knew what he was wearing on his day off? That was bizarre.

"Well, at the moment, I think a long-term relationship is highly overrated, Kyle, but I'm not really in the position to be your life coach right now." I cackled.

He laughed because he always found me funny when I was not in chef mode. He also managed to rein me right back into work mode. "Well, all went smooth as silk this weekend, and I will have this week's menu and order ready when you get back. Enjoy the rest of your time. See you Tuesday?" he asked.

"Yes. Unless I fuck that up and see you Wednesday," I said with sarcasm.

"All right, see you then," he said, then he paused. "Hey, Cassie?"

"Yeah?" I asked.

"As a friend, I think you were a star already, and I'm really sorry about you and Jack."

I sniffled and squeaked out, "Damn, thanks. Now, stop stalling and go cook your friend's dinner."

I then hung up.

I got downstairs just in time as the rice was done and fork fluffed in a bowl. All the ingredients were ready for us to start layering into a casserole dish. Creamy Monterey Jack cheese, sour cream, hatch chilies, and smoked paprika. This wasn't a match-up, just a Mexican side piece for the big Brazilian boy. A simple salad with a tangy vinegar-based dressing would cut the fat and heaviness of the other two. Everyone would be happy, happy.

I stood at the island, prepping with my mom, sipping prosecco, and talking about the random things that happened over the weekend. The gala, and pretty much lying my ass off left and right to match up stories. I wanted to steer our conversation in the direction of the new opportunity with Dan Satterfield, but I needed Dad in the mix as well. I also didn't want Cora to listen. So, once again, I was stuck with another thing I couldn't talk about.

Just as I thought it, she walked in with the other person I needed to speak to on FaceTime.

"Say hi to Daddy, everyone." She steered her phone between us, and we took turns with our fake smiles as she said, "Gram, say hi to Daddy," pointing the screen in her direction.

"Hey, Jack. Sorry we missed you on this trip, honey," she said with a head tilt and took a very large sip of her prosecco on screen, which I knew he knew was her southern charmed way of being pissed. At that moment, I also wondered if she suspected what had happened.

His face filled the screen of Cora's phone. Damn, I hadn't heard his voice in a week. I hadn't seen his face in what, two? He looked really good. His hair was a bit longer, and he ran his hand through the dark strands nervously as he was talking to my mom. I forgot how sexy he really was but in a very different way than Stephen. More of a younger, more playful version. More like a boy toy. That was it. He was a toy version of Stephen.

Holy fuck.

I never noticed that. Watching Jack talk and his mannerisms. He was Stephen, but on a smaller scale than him. Like...so close, but not quite there. Damn. Now, I understood my attraction to him so much better. I also felt my heart fall because I wondered if I ever made him feel like he didn't add up? Not intentionally, because I really loved and still loved Jack. Respected what he did? Fuck no. I guessed that was one of the thousand messed up things in Casandra's brain I would be working on in therapy soon.

My thoughts were pulled in another direction as Cora was now pointing the phone toward me as Stephen Jr. was staring into me. "Hey there, Cass," he said softly.

"Hey."

I barely squeaked it out as Cora turned the phone around to herself, "Mom had fun with friends this weekend, Dad. Can you believe that?"

My mom closed her eyes and took the world's largest breath on the other side of the island, reaching across and grabbing my hand. That simple, tight squeeze had all the words. *It's okay, she doesn't mean it, and hang in there, kid.* I added my own internal dialogue. *This sucked. Fuck that, get me out of here, and I don't want to do this anymore.*

But we all smiled and made Cora the happiest girl at that moment, including her father, who I knew was feeling the exact same way. Shit. Beth, the dick-sucking whore, was probably sitting next to him, holding his hand through it all like my mom was for me.

Just then, she whisked the phone to the porch where my dad was tending to our Brazilian meat dream. We watched through the door as he had a less awkward conversation, since they were obviously talking about grilling.

Mom, still holding my hand, said, "Well, I guess she has no clue?"

I shook my head. "I think she knows something is up, but I'm sure she doesn't want to speculate or believe it's true. I need to talk to Jack today or tomorrow before we come home. We need to do this soon. I have to find somewhere to live, Mom."

"Damn, baby. I wish I was closer to you," she said, squeezing my hand one final time before letting it go. Picking up the casserole dish, she turned to put it in the oven. After sliding it in, she stood there with her back to me, her little arms stretched on either side, gripping the range with her head down in silence.

I asked her in a worried tone, "Mom? Are you okay?"

She turned slowly with a look of dismay. "Did he cheat on you? If you are trying to keep him in our good graces, baby..."

"Mom, how did you know?" I whispered, shaking my head.

She looked to make sure nobody was listening before saying slowly and quietly, "He looked too good to be distraught. He looked, shall I say, taken care of." She sipped her bubbly with raised brows. "I won't say anything to your dad. This is your business. If you want to tell him, that's up to you. I just guessed that's all. I understand, honey. You are protecting Cora. It's what us mommas do."

I started mindlessly chopping the cucumber for the salad and said, looking down out of shame, "Thank you, Mom. This really sucks."

Tears welled up in my eyes, and my chin started to quiver. I placed the knife on the cutting board.

She walked by to get silverware from the drawer and pressed her head and hand against my back. She felt so small against me. "Your heart will be okay. You are so strong, baby."

My mom squeezed my shoulder and continued on.

I had to get my shit together quick because the house erupted into happiness with my dad coming in with his prize possession and Cora with her unbreakable happiness. We put everything aside and had an amazing meal with tons of laughter and so much to talk about, along with new experiences from the week. I really missed having my family. I didn't know how I was going to make it since I'd lost my only lifeline to any resemblance of it in San Francisco, and it would be just Cora and me. Like Mom said, I guessed I was strong and that it would be okay.

We cleaned up the dishes, and Cora went up to shower and get ready for bed.

"Hey, Bug. Come out here with me," he said from the porch as I finished in the kitchen with my mom.

"Go ahead, I'm all but finished here," she said, snapping my leg with a kitchen towel, laughing.

I grabbed my wine glass and joined him on the porch. "What's up, Dad?"

He was standing on the lower patio, and he motioned for me to come follow him, "Come on, Bug."

He took me around to the side garage door. "What are we doing?"

He turned the knob and hit the switch. The fluorescent bulbs cast light on the hundred or so unfinished projects. There sat boxes of lord only knows what, actually I knew, it was my shit that I kept promising to take, like high school yearbooks, photo albums, and memory boxes of bullshit such as old retainers and dingy stuffed animals that don't even resemble an actual animal anymore.

"Your mother gets on me about finishing projects all the time, right?" he asked.

"Yeah?" I asked hesitantly.

"Well, I found something I knew how to do, and I finished it," he said with great pride with his hands on his hips.

"Awesome dad. What?" I asked, bewildered.

"This." He dramatically lifted a painter's cloth from a bicycle.

"Wow. That's nice," I said.

"Cassie, that's your bike. I completely refurbished it," he said, incredibly proud of his work, holding his arms out like it was the Mona Lisa.

Once I realized it, my jaw dropped. It was like, completely restored. Original. Down to the flawless black paint, shiny chrome handlebars, and vintage stickers. I ran my long fingers over the detail.

"Dad, how did you…"

"I watched a lot of YouTube videos and went onto eBay and found the original Earth Cruiser stickers and even the tires that make the shells in the sand. Those cost me a pretty penny because most of them have dry rotted by now, and they don't even make them anymore." He pointed at the rims. "Look at your stem valve covers."

"Dad. They are little chef hats."

I put my hand over my mouth, then reached up and wrapped my arms around his neck and held on so tight. Tears flowed, and I sobbed uncontrollably. He squeezed me but then pulled me away to look at him.

"Bug. This wasn't supposed to make you sad," he said looking into my eyes with furrowed brows.

"No, Dad. I… I just don't know how I'm going to do this without you and Mom. I need you two so much. Y'all are so good to me. I always feel so loved."

I covered my nose and mouth to try to conceal my face contorting.

"Oh, baby girl. It's going to be okay," he said, completely enveloping me in his long, lean body and kissing the top of my head.

He let me cry it out for a few minutes, then pulled me out by my shoulders and said, "Hey. Let's take her for a spin," with such excitement.

With mascara and snot running down my face, I completely agreed.

Best bike ride ever.

Chapter 15

CASSIE

✗

Lying underneath my covers and lit by the blue glow of my phone, I anxiously pulled up my new favorite contact, Stephen. It was hard to believe that I was doing this giddy little secret charade in bed just days ago with the Google search bar and his profile picture. Butterflies still fluttered throughout my body just typing his name, feeling seventeen all over again. Now, I had the pleasure to actually talk and touch him once again. The entire weekend felt like a dizzying dream it happened so fast.

I found his circle with that faceless silhouette of a person. It somehow made it official when I added a photo in there. That person looked at me every time they called. I also didn't know if I wanted Cora to ask questions if his gorgeous face popped up on my car screen, larger than life. Especially since now that I realized he slightly resembled her father. It might raise even more questions, like, "Mom? Does Daddy have a brother?"

I felt excited sending him a message after a long day of not hearing from him. I wondered how his day was? What was he doing right now?

Me: My dad gave me the greatest gift tonight.

The dots rhythmically danced. Damn. Was he sitting with his phone in his hand waiting on me to text him?

Stephen: Damn. I've missed you all day. Well, it wasn't what I gave you all weekend.

I laughed and shook my head, then sent him the picture of my perfect black bike.

Stephen: That's sweet. He got you a new bike.

Me: No. He completely restored THE BIKE.

Stephen: I'm running it over with my car.

Me: OMG.

Stephen: Do you promise not to ride away again?

Me: Promise

Stephen: Your dad is really sweet. That looks terrific.

Me: The sweetest.

Stephen: The sweetest?

Me: Well, there's someone who is trying to move in on second, but come on, he's my Dad.

Stephen: I'm sitting in my hotel room trying to work, but all I can think about is you. You wrecked me woman.

Me: Do you want me to relieve some of that tension?

Stephen: Now we are cooking.

Me: You are in luck, that's my specialty.

After an hour of slightly graphic, somewhat comical, and intensely exhilarating sexting, he moved up to the top in the sexiest man category for sure. Damn, he had awakened the Kraken within my libido, and I didn't know how we were going to manage to be apart on the other side of the country.

Saying goodbye to my parents was tough the next day, but I was ready to get rolling with my new life back in Cali. I woke up early to have a private conversation over coffee with my parents about the enticing new opportunity awaiting at home. I really wanted them to be excited about something coming my way and not just this impending doom I seemed to have placed upon them. Their reaction was pure elation, just as I expected, with a hint of apprehension with me getting in over my head. I went through my ideas, just as I did with Kyle, and I seemed to have sold them on my plan.

Next was Jack. I waited until it was 7:00 am his time and shot him a text. He and I both agreed we needed to rip this Band-Aid off with Cora. Him not being in the house was shedding way too much suspicion, and we were just lying uncontrollably now, and that would only bite us in the ass in the life lesson department. We agreed he would come over for dinner, and we would break it to her then.

Sitting next to her on this plane, seeing her so happy, without a worry in her beautiful mind, made me want to crawl outside of myself and scream at how unfair this was. She was back in her zone with her noise-canceling headphones on, long, exceptionally tan limbs extending out from her shorts and t-shirt. Her beautiful long brown hair framed her dark face. She could feel my stare falling down on her, and she looked up at me with her big brown eyes, smiled, and pulled her headphones down from her ears.

"What is it, Mom?"

"Oh, I was just noticing how fast you are growing up, that's all."

I smiled and squeezed her thin, brown thigh, patting it before placing my hand back in my lap.

"Oh. Is Dad picking us up from the airport?" she asked.

She caught me off guard with that one. I was officially paranoid that she knew I was full of lies at that point.

"Um, no." I shook my head. "I think he has a late meeting. I'll just grab us an Uber."

Without another thought, she put her headphones on and went right back to Swifty-land.

They said kids were resilient. Well, I guessed we are about to put ours to the test.

Chapter 16

STEPHEN

The humming of the plane and Bianca talking to our flight attendant was white noise to me as I hazily stared at my laptop screen. I was not even paying attention to what was sitting in front of me. My mind was playing a reel of the entire weekend, and I was smiling internally, remembering her in the carriage house kitchen, naked, looking up at me with those mesmerizing hazel eyes. Swinging on the porch, setting up her security settings, and laughing at her ridiculous antics. It was so goddamn comfortable.

I was ripped out of my daydream by Allen's blurry hands waving behind my computer screen.

"Man, where did you go?"

He laughed.

Shaking my head, I looked at him and then my laptop as if I was completely focused.

"Nowhere. What's up?"

I took a sip of my water Silvia had just placed on my table, obviously dropping it off without me even noticing.

"I was asking you if you had the report from Rich with the breakdown of IT hours on this Houston job. You didn't answer me." He let out a laugh. "You just stared at your screen smiling, and you looked like you were going to laugh. Dude. I haven't seen you this happy in well, over a year for sure."

He raised his eyebrows, nodding with a knowing look.

"Sorry, I'm a bit distracted. I've got that email from Rich. I'll send it over to you now."

I tried going into work mode, searching my unending list of unattended work emails piling up all weekend.

"Hey."

He waved over my screen again to get my attention.

I looked up and sat back in my seat because he was obviously not going to give up easily.

"Yes, Allen?" I smiled and blinked excessively.

"You have something good going on for once. It's okay to enjoy it."

He smiled at me, placing his hands out.

I knew he wanted details. He was like a girl when it came to shit like that. We went so far back that it went beyond the business partner relationship. We were roommates in college. I was his wingman in the bars. I was his best man at his wedding. He even helped me navigate the complicated waters of my relationship with Lauren. When she went missing, Jesus, he gave never-ending love and support, both him and Bianca. So, if he wanted some juicy details from this weekend, why the hell not?

"So, what do you think about her?" I asked, leaning casually to one side of the soft leather seat and resting my face against my knuckles.

"Oh, this is all about Cassie?"

He played stupid.

I rolled my eyes and tilted my head back.

"Come on, we both know we are talking about Cassie, dickhead."

I looked past him towards Bianca. She was busy with her earbuds in, probably listening to a book or music while flipping through a design magazine. She had no interest in our chatter on a work trip. She mainly tagged along to come put eyes on their daughter as we checked in on our long-time client, who we probably billed the equivalent to Kendra's college tuition for the year just this month alone.

"B and I really like her. She is funny and talented, and she obviously knows how to run a business. Man," he turned around to see what Bianca was doing, then leaned in to say softly, "She's a smoke show."

I scratched my head and laughed. "Yeah, she is definitely all of that... and more."

I rocked my head back and forth in disbelief that that could be true.

"You two have tons of history, I know that. At lunch, you said she is divorced, right?" he asked.

"Well, not completely. California has a ninety-day, no fault. So, she is free to do whatever, but they are in the middle of the separation and working the details out. He has been living at his side-piece's house or somewhere else until she finds a new place. They also have a daughter. It's going to be hard for her, and she's really anxious about it. She has a lot on her plate. Not to mention her restaurant and she was just offered another really kick-ass opportunity. This isn't supposed to make her stressed out." I waved my hands between me and him. "I mean, me and her, not me and you," I said, laughing.

He laughed too, and then said, "Damn, her husband cheated on her? What an asshole." Then, the question I never liked to hear was brought up. "What's going on with the investigation with Lauren? We haven't talked about it in a while."

He slightly winced with the impending answer.

Immediately, all the joy and oxygen were sucked out of the plane cabin, but it had to be said at some point.

"My investigator hasn't had a lead in over six months. I think he is going to drop my case. He's made hints of not wanting to take my money anymore, but I refuse. I just don't feel like she is dead, Allen. Do you?" I questioned him with a deep look.

He shook his head. "Honestly? I don't have that connection with her, so I don't know. None of it made sense except that we really felt like it was connected to our government job. The timing and coincidence, yeah." He shook his head and pursed his lips. "That felt so off."

"I wrestle with not knowing when to move on." I blew out a

large breath and pressed my head into the seat and my palms into my eyes. "I don't want to miss out on having Cassie back in my life again, but fuck. The guilt of giving up and cheating on Lauren eats at me. I stood in an elevator on the way to our room this weekend and came close to telling her I couldn't do it." I shook my head and closed my eyes for a moment. "I couldn't continue that weekend with the guilt. I'm so glad the elevator doors opened, and that saved me because she was everything I needed. Sorry man, I sound like a fucking pussy."

"Shit. Don't be. You have had your ass handed to you these last two years. You deserve some happiness. Don't beat yourself up. Enjoy it. Cassie seems like the real deal, and this may be good timing since she is working on things too. Um, another thing? You two live nowhere near each other. How is that going to work?" he asked.

"I can't say we are planners, Allen." I laughed. "We need to pick up a shit ton of clients in California so I can expense the fuck out of my new travel itinerary with this beast."

I waved my hands around in the air of the cabin.

"That's on you, bro. I'm up to my eyeballs with the accounts I have," he complained, shaking his head.

"Whoever thought we would be this successful when we were two computer nerds at MIT, just trying to get laid?" I asked with a chuckle.

"You had no problem getting laid. You always looked like that." He splayed his hand out at me. "I can't believe I landed that sweet momma over there."

He smiled and pointed to Bianca, with her long brown hair flowing down her shoulders and delicate features of her side profile, bobbing her head to what must be music and looking out the window into the clouds.

Allen had always been your quintessential computer nerd type. I thought I flew under the radar because I was also athletic. He didn't have an athletic bone in his body. He had always had that tall, lanky build and never really knew what to do with his limbs. His hair was dark and curly and also unruly. He never knew what to do with that either. I loved his awkward ways. He was fun to watch him grow into the confident guy he was now, that was for sure. Definitely not muscular or graceful. I believe the hardest I ever laughed at playing a sport-like activity was the time we decided to give racquetball a go at the campus gym. He had zero ability to make a connection with the ball, and when it hit him, he sounded like a little bitch. I probably got the best ab workout of my life, though, due to laughing so hard. It definitely went down as one of the most re-told Allen stories in my repertoire.

I thought, gazing out my window, how much I really wanted what Allen had. I had it all, massive success, shit-tons of money, I was a pretty decent-looking dude, I built a huge house, except I didn't have anyone to live in it with me. I just wanted a woman to love and be loved like that like he had with Bianca. I was constantly so close, but they fell through my hands every single time. Nobody had stolen my focus, thoughts, and all my attention away except two women, Cassie Buckley and Lauren Malikov.

Once we landed, we had two meetings and an early dinner with our long-time clients. We wined and dined those guys, bringing along the wives, including Bianca. Of course, I was alone like usual, feeling the emptiness by my side. They were the bread and butter of our business because they were constantly expanding their hotel chains and needing our cyber security services more and more. Hotels not only had their own security risks internally with staff but also had to keep hotel guest's privacy secure. A hotel could be a cyber nightmare if not set up and monitored properly, from credit card processing, room key readers, hotel guest information, and staff information to on-site security. Once you build long-term trust like we have with this group, you are in. So, as Bianca drank the two-hundred and fifty-dollar bottle of expensed Chateau Marguax at dinner, and casually discussed recent vacation home purchases with the other wives, she knew Kendra's next semester at UH will be covered.

Back at the hotel, I tried to catch up on the pile of emails and bullshit I ignored all weekend while I played with my long-lost toy. I constantly checked my phone, looking at the time, and thought she should be done with family by now. Maybe she was waiting on me?

No, we didn't play those games. Just as I was about to give in and text her, I got, "My Dad gave me the greatest gift tonight."

She honestly could have texted me complete gibberish, and I would have been satisfied. I just needed to know she was there. I had grown to hate silence for long periods of time. I was not a needy guy. I just needed a daily something to know…you were alive. This was the first time I had had anyone romantically in my life since Lauren. I guessed this might be my new normal.

Great, something new for my future therapy sessions.

She showed me the bike her dad completely restored for her. What a great gift. If he only knew that bike was the devil for our relationship. Once I realized how happy it made her, I remembered it was the person who pedaled it, and not the actual bike itself. I forgave that beautiful, headstrong, relentless, wonderful soul, so the bike was safe from the wheels of my next rental when I came to Charleston.

I also never realized sexting could be so fucking hot. Maybe it was because we were so comfortable with each other, and we communicated so well already, but damn. I usually had to text two-handed but I was quickly learning the one-handed method so I could stroke my cock at the same time. She got dirty as fuck, and the pictures she sent… fuck me running. She started with her toes, which I found personally sexy as hell. I guessed it was because I still had the visual of them in my mouth and her staring up at me while I was inside her, and then she worked her way up. I almost blew my load by the time she got to the shot of her stomach with the view of her smoothly shaved pussy. All I could think of was my face down there as I licked and sucked, making her moan and grab my hair when I had her up against the wall in the hotel. I thought she was going to pass out that night.

I could get rock-hard instantly thinking about any of the moments of last weekend. When I saw her in the park for the first time in all those years, I thought she was fucking me with her eyes. The first time I picked her up and I made her come in seconds from sheer excitement of being together again, to the carriage house, and all the moments of the gala night. What a weekend that was not expected at all. Cassie managed to show up in my life when I didn't expect her, and I could not resist the woman.

I lay in my hotel bed, completely drained emotionally from the day, and now physically, because I had cum dripping down my stomach. My now spent cock lay lifeless to the side. I typed with my one semen-free hand.

Me: Talk tomorrow?

Cassie: Of course.

Me: Goodnight, sexy girl.

Cassie: Goodnight Stephen

Chapter 17

CASSIE

"So? What do you think?" I said, spinning in the expansive space with floor-to-ceiling windows and magnificent bay views of the bridge. "Come on, you can't deny that these floors don't feel great on our bare feet?"

She felt the cool, silky marble tile beneath them.

"It won't feel good when it's winter," Cora replied coldly, grumpily looking down, not letting herself feel any joy in the moment.

I closed the space between us, taking her two hands in mine and putting my eyes at her level.

"Hey, I know this isn't the perfect scenario or the fairy tale ending we hoped for. Look at me, Cora." Her eyes reluctantly looked up to mine. "This isn't the end baby. This can be a new chapter. It's just something new, that's all. I mean, look at this place." I let go of her hands and walked around, spinning with my arms wide in the air. She smiled just a little. "It's pretty awesome, right? I'm not putting you in a cardboard box behind a dumpster, kid."

I finally got a small laugh. Finally.

I signed the papers with the real estate agent and arranged the movers for the weekend. My personal things had been mostly packed. Some new living room furniture was ordered, along with new bedroom furniture for me and Cora. I was leaving as much as possible at Jack's so that she could keep some sort of familiarity in one space. I felt like I was taking one for the team, and he was getting away with murder. Lucky for him, I didn't have the will, energy, or time to fight. Fortunately, he was cutting a hefty check for me to start over. It was just…things, after all.

Everything was moving at warp speed. I met with Dan and the entire team at Bridge Culinary Enterprise Group. My eighteen-month contract would begin in two weeks, and I didn't know how the hell I was going to do it all. Kyle and my entire staff had been beyond extraordinary. I was almost non-existent in my own restaurant while I had been tackling all the changes. They had been incredibly understanding and Sagi was absolutely thriving through it all.

Stephen had been settling for the little bits of me at the end of the long, exhausting days. Listening to me stress, cry when needed, and yes, we managed to get our sext on here and there. Next weekend, we got to see each other, and I could not wait. I needed to feel him wrapped around me and in me.

Sitting at my computer in my office, I was suddenly interrupted by a knock on the open doorframe.

"Chef? Can I have a minute?"

Reggie stood with a wide smile on his round, happy face, waiting to come in. His tall frame took up the space, dreadlocks pulled in a thick ponytail. His uniform, black and untouched, yet his gray morning prep apron is covered in everything from the kitchen.

I looked up and slid off my reading glasses. "Hey Reggie, what's up?"

He entered the small office that originally started as my cozy nook, then slowly became a glorified storage closet after years of becoming a dumping ground for Kyle and me, with no extra time in our schedule to organize it all.

He entered with some slight apprehension.

"What can I do for you? Is everything okay?" I asked out of confusion because he was Kyle's right-hand man and usually went to him for everything, not me.

"No, everything is great." He smiled, but shyly looked towards my desk, grazing it with his fingers, slightly kid-like. Looking up at me, he said, "I just wanted to thank you, Chef."

Shocked, I sat back in my chair. "Thanking me for what, Reg?"

"Well, you took, you and Kyle, you guys took a big chance on me last year with that program right out of jail. I don't know where I would be right now if you didn't do that. I was really scared nobody would hire me being, you know," he said trailing off and looking down at the desk again, tapping his fingers lightly out of nervousness.

"Reggie, you came to us with skills from that program. You blew us away with your kitchen knowledge. You did the work. It wasn't a handout. You earn everything you do here," I said with confidence.

Looking up at me with bright eyes, he said, "I appreciate that, Chef. I work hard to not let you down. I love this job. Kyle is a great boss too and we have a good time on the line, even when it's hard," he said rubbing his hand down his face.

"Yeah, it's been ball-busting lately. Hang on. It's not going to slow down, either. Hopefully, I have some relief coming, though. I have a couple interviews for some help, but nobody seems to want to work these days, unfortunately."

I shook my head.

He puffed out a breath of air. "Well, ain't that the truth? Well, I just wanted to tell you that. I know you are busy, and I don't want to keep you."

"I appreciate you Reggie, we all do." I smiled as he turned and walked out.

I sat and had to think about that for a beat. I never thought about how my career and choices impacted someone else's life until shit like that happened. That just made it all worth it right there. I hope being pulled into this other direction wasn't going to change that. Was this a good move? It was only an eighteen-month commitment. Like Mike said, as long as I had the staff to support it, give it a try. I thought that just proved I did.

Kyle then knocked and slid into the room. He needed less of an invitation since this was his space as well.

"Chef?" he said without as much eye contact as he immediately went into looking for something on the desk. "Man, this place needs some attention. I can't find anything anymore."

He lifted stacks until he found his legal pad.

"I had a visit from Reggie just now." I caught him off guard as he was about out the door, then he turned.

With a worried look on his face, he asked, "Really? Was everything okay?"

I stared at my computer screen without actually looking at anything.

"Yeah, he just wanted to thank me, well, us, for giving him a chance. It was so sweet. I now want to cry," I said, looking up to meet Kyle's eyes with a fake cry face.

He took in a deep breath. "Yeah, he gets me in the feels all the time. He's a good dude. Wait 'til he bear hugs you after a night of feeling like you were struggling in the weeds." He laughed. "We do have a good team," he said, tapping the doorframe a few times and headed out.

My phone dinged with a text, and I immediately felt the tension of not having enough hours in a day to get everything done. Where the fuck was my phone? I lifted the stacks of vendor orders and the new job applications I promised to weed through for Kyle. There it was. I entered my code, and it was a text from Britt.

Damn.

Realizing I had been the shittiest friend.

Britt: Have you fallen from the face of the Earth?

Me: Yes. I'm in space. I need oxygen out here. Help.

Britt: That bad?

Me: Yes. Overwhelmed is an understatement.

Britt: I wish I could help.

Me: Got the apartment today. Cora is Eeyore. Went from biggest high to lowest low.

Britt: I'll have Harper cheer her up

Me: Thank you.

Britt: Stephen?

Me: Next week. Thank God. I miss him

She sent me a gif of a lady in a wheelchair in a full body cast, making me laugh loud enough to get an inquisitive look from Benny, my dishwasher, walking past my door.

Me: I needed that laugh. Thank you. You good?

Britt: We are all good. Love you.

Me: Love you more

I finished my day with three possible applicants lined up for interviews with Kyle for prep and line, went over the week's menu, and placed the order with two vendors. I sat down with my front of house manager, Alicia, and went over a few items she had been saving for me and a few questions from Margaret in the bar. I felt accomplished and somewhat part of my team today.

I climbed into my car to get home for Cora, well, soon to be Jack's home, when my phone dinged yet again. This time, it was Stephen.

Hell yeah.

I was in a good mood between feeling productive, tying up loose ends, and getting to talk to my people, it was going all right.

I start the car and got comfortable because I might be there for a few minutes.

Stephen: Hey sexy.

Me: Mmmm…I like being greeted like that.

Stephen: What are you doing?

Me: Currently sitting in my car

Stephen: Naked?

Me: That would be awkward in my work parking lot

Stephen: I'm in a fantasy, don't ruin it.

Me: Yes. I'm naked in my car baby. I have my fingers in my pussy

Stephen: Holy Fuck.

I laughed out loud and covered my mouth, knowing he was now probably rock-hard reading that. My eyes were watering from laughing so hard at the visual of where he might be right then.

Me: So, so wet. Wanna taste?

There was silence, then my phone dinged, but it was Jack. Well, that ruined my moment.

Jack: Why did you just text me that?

My heart raced out of my chest as I scrolled and sure as shit, I sent the last text to him.

I froze. I had no idea what to do. I got back to my text thread with Stephen and tried to figure out what went wrong.

Holy Fuck... I couldn't work my goddamn fingers. Yep, it just left with him saying, "Holy Fuck."

I must have hit Jack's contact instead. My eyes were blurry from laughing. I couldn't see shit anymore either without my stupid glasses.

Fuck. Fuck you age.

Sweat was now rolling down my brow. I didn't sweat. Great. Was that a hot flash? Was I going through menopause now too?

Another text came through and I was terrified, but it was Stephen.

Stephen: Thanks. My dick is hard and I'm sitting on my plane. Taking off for DC

I made sure I'm answering *him*.

Me: I just accidentally text Jack that my pussy was really wet and asked if he wanted to taste it. It was for YOU.

I got back a series of laughing emojis.

Me: It's not funny. What do I do? I'm freaking out.

Stephen: For one…yes…I would like that. A LOT.

Stephen: For two…Good on you. Karma is a bitch.

Me: What should I say? He asked why I sent that to him.

Stephen: Just say, sorry, wrong person and ask something else.

Me: Ok.

Stephen: It's over. Remember, he moved on. You can too.

Me: You are right.

Stephen: And…when this plane lands…we are discussing me tasting that wet pussy in detail.

Me: Yes sir.

Stephen: Talk soon sexy girl. Mmmmm.

I took multiple deep breaths and hovered my finger over Jack's icon. Stephen was right. Karma was a bitch.

Me: Sorry, wrong person.

I hit send and immediately, I wanted to throw up all the contents of my stomach. This was the first time I felt like I was an adulterer. I knew I wasn't, but we weren't divorced. I didn't want him to know I was seeing anyone, not like this anyway. I didn't make the time in my busy schedule for him during our marriage, but I was making it for someone else now? This crazy dialogue was happening as the dots were dancing for way too long on the screen. I could tell he was writing, then erasing, then writing, and erasing. Finally, he hit send.

Jack: Oh

That was it? I was having a fucking internal meltdown the size of Chernobyl over fucking, *Oh*? I literally looked around my car in disbelief.

"Oh?" I yelled out loud to myself in my running car, rattling my steering wheel. Then I remembered, Stephen said to ask something else, so I threw the shiny ball.

> Me: I signed the lease on the place at the Marina to-day. Cora is...okay at best.

> Jack: That was a really nice place, good choice.

Unfazed. What was I wanting? I didn't want him to question me. This was good. He didn't notice the text. I was good.

> Me: It's going to be a bitch for school though. I'm go-ing in the wrong direction.

> Jack: We will figure it out. We have the summer to come up with a plan.

> Me: The movers are coming this weekend.

> Jack: Want me to keep Cora at the house?

> Me: Let's let her decide. It will be strange you being there again. Can you keep her next weekend though?

> Jack: Sure. You probably need privacy with all that "tasting".

Chapter 18

STEPHEN

The second the plane landed at Palo Alto Airport, I felt closer to her. Two meetings and one more short flight, and we were there.

I shot her a text.

Me: Can you feel me?

Cassie: Is that why my pussy just got wet?

Damn. I was in fucking love with her.

We headed for our meetings which took all afternoon. Bianca got a ride into town for some lunch and shopping. It was their anniversary tomorrow, so the sky was the limit as far as the weekend went with her and Allen. He kind of screwed the pooch on this one, but I thought we would make up for it. Cassie promised to come through with a memorable evening at her restaurant and personally, I was extremely excited to see her in her element.

Finally, we sat on the runway waiting for our clearance to take off for the ridiculously short flight.

Me: On our way to you

I waited obsessively, staring at my screen as if she should be sitting with no life other than to text me.

Just then...I saw that she was typing, and my arousal followed along.

> Cassie: I'm rearranging furniture. You have my address?

> Me: Yes ma'am

> Cassie: Text me when you land and on the way.

Allen and Bianca opened a bottle of champagne to celebrate the fact we closed a five million dollar deal today. It was their nineteenth wedding anniversary, and I was getting laid for the second time in a month with more than my own hand. Huge deal.

Once the plane landed, a car took Allen and Bianca to their hotel, and they offered to drop me at Cassie's on the way.

> Me: Landed. OTW.

> Cassie: I kind of can't breathe.

> Me: Are you okay?

> Cassie: In a good way

> Me: Oh God. I thought it was because the furniture was too heavy. Lol.

> Cassie: SMH

I stood outside the car, thanking them for dropping me.

"Go, Stephen," Bianca said with a huge smile.

"Goodnight," I said, closing the car door and turned to see the huge apartment complex overlooking the marina.

I pulled out my phone.

> Me: I'm here. This is massive.

She answered quickwittedly with, "Just like your cock. Just give them your name."

I carried my bag, thinking to myself, yeah, I'm definitely in love. *Shit.*

I took the elevator up to the second floor and made my way to her apartment 2014. I knocked. She opened the door, and there she stood, in a little yellow sundress that sat no higher than the knee. So dainty. Her hair flowed over her shoulders and down her back. Tan and absolutely stunning in her bare feet, leaning against the open door.

"Hey," she said in almost a whisper. Like she was all innocent and not the same person who was saying the dirty things in texts.

"Hey," I mimicked back with an equally innocent smile.

She shut the door behind me, and I put my bag down.

I wanted to throw her against the wall and ravish her with all I had. I wanted to pull her hair, rip her clothes off, tug at her nipples, suck, and be rough, but I fought it. God, I fought it. I reached over and took her face gently in my hands, and I kissed her sweetly. I took her in slowly and ran my fingers over her bare skin as if I were reading braille, moving my fingers over every part of her so I never forgot.

"Go slow, Stephen," I said to myself.

She breathed heavily. "We never make it out of an entryway."

Her head tilted back as my lips were kissing down her neck and chest.

"Where do you want to go?" I asked in breathless laughter.

In a whisper, she said, "My new place. I have been decorating all day. I'm excited to show you."

She took my hand, guiding me down three steps to a large expansive living room surrounded by windows overlooking a park and the bay. A large white sectional couch was the star of the show. Green plants draped everywhere.

"Wow. This looks amazing," I said, shocked at what she had done in the short amount of time.

She turned to me and said, "I never really got to have my own sense of style since I moved in with Jack when he already had his place. So, I had a vision, and I went with it. It's completely different from what I had before, a new start."

"Cassie, it's really beautiful. It's so inviting, and well…you."

I kissed her in the middle of the room filled with white fabrics and green plants that overlooked the most beautiful panoramic view I had ever asked for in a city such as San Francisco.

"Oh, I'm glad you like it. I just got everything this week, and I'd been hustling to have it ready for you," she said in a stressed tone.

I took her face in my hands. "Babe, I could have taken you to a hotel and taken the stress off of you. I just want *you*. I appreciate all your effort and showing me who you are, I do. This means so much to me, but you have so much on your plate."

She smiled. "Come here."

She dragged me into the kitchen.

The room was bright and pretty, but pretty much just a large apartment-like kitchen with a fantastic view.

"I didn't cook for you," she said in a sultry voice.

"Oh, I didn't expect you to. We can do whatever you want. Order in, go out, starve to death, I don't care," I said, laughing.

Standing before me in front of the island and the wall of windows looking over the bay, she slid the thin straps of her sundress over her thumbs and off her shoulders as her dress puddled to the floor in one swift motion. She was standing absolutely naked before me in the empty kitchen.

I was completely caught off guard. I could do nothing but smile and shake my head in surprise. She got me. I lift her into my arms.

Fuck.

Her skin was so soft and supple. She smelled like cotton candy and summer. Just breathing her in made me feel younger. I lifted her naked body up onto the cold counter and spread her legs wide so I can fit between them. I kissed her passionately as I removed my pants, and she peeled off my dress shirt at the same time. Clothes could not come off any faster.

I pushed her back onto the large cream-colored quartz countertop, her hair flowing over the sides like an amber waterfall. Her arms were completely relaxed out to the sides, open to whatever I might do. She was so trusting. I spread her legs, revealing the sweetest pink pussy, so inviting. The second I touch her, she moaned like it was the first time she'd been touched. I slowly ran my fingers through the delicate folds of her flesh. So sweet. I leaned down to taste her, and she moaned louder.

"Oh God, yes."

I must be doing something right. I thumbed her clit, knowing how much she couldn't resist that. I alternated sucking and fingering her pussy. She writhed with my movements, and I could feel her getting wetter and wetter. She grabbed through my hair and at my shoulders.

"Fuck, Stephen. I'm going to come. I want you inside of me so bad," she moaned.

I pulled myself up from between her legs and stood between them. I wrapped her legs around me.

"Where is your room, baby?"

With her legs wrapped around me and arms draped over my shoulders like a rag doll, I carried her toward where she gestured. Splaying her beautiful body gently onto the King-sized bed, I lay on top of her. I spread her legs open for me, and as I looked into her eyes, I stroked my hard cock with my hand and ran my swollen head through her slick slit. Fuck. Going in bare was hot as hell. Up and down, I slid it through her opening until she started to beg.

"Is that what you want?"

"Please, baby."

She reached for it and ran her hands over my tight balls.

Dammit. She couldn't do too much of that, or I'd come too fast.

I slid my dick slowly into her.

Holy fuck.

It felts like heaven in there. So wet and tight. Her pussy was squeezing my dick immediately as she was moving her body in rhythmic movements.

Fuck yes.

I started pumping into her faster and faster, she kissed me harder and I was losing my goddamn mind. I knew I should have made her come before I stuck my dick inside of her. I realized this was too hot, I was not going to last long, and backed slowly out of her.

"No, what are you doing?" she whined.

I slid down her body, pushing her legs up and open, burying my face between them. I took her swollen clit into my mouth and rolled my tongue underneath it as I sucked gently. I slid my hands up underneath her ass and then underneath her back as it arched off the bed.

"Oh, fuck, fuck, fuck."

She fisted the bedsheets.

When she lowered herself down to the bed, I climbed back up on top of her and made my way to kiss her lips. Sharing her juices with her lips as I slid my dick back into her. This time, she was absolutely dripping, and it sent me so deep she yelled out.

"Are you okay? Too deep?" I asked.

She whispered, "No, God it feels so good. Just so fucking hard."

She ran her hands through my hair and over my shoulders.

It felt so hot, so intense, and wonderful. I reached down and grabbed her ass from underneath me and buried my cock deeper and deeper inside of her.

"Baby, I'm going to come, I'm…"

I pulled her into me as my whole body tensed and I came so hard, all stress and tension left my body, Jesus. It felt so fucking good.

"Oh, baby. You have had me worked up for a month," I said with my head buried in her chest.

I gave myself a minute to recover, then once I was out of her, I started to kiss her and suck her nipples, then a little harder. Then I massaged her clit with my fingers. I knew how to please my girl. I could make her come over and over if I wanted. And I did until she yelled mercy.

Chapter 19

CASSIE

This might be my new favorite pastime, watching him sleep. He looked so peaceful, spread across my massive bed, face down, arms wrapped around the pillow. The late morning light was trying to force its way through the long silk curtains, shedding light on the well-defined muscles of his back and arms. My eyes followed every beautiful striation from his neck, down his shoulder, over his triceps, and the triangulation of his back. His skin, a dark contrast against the soft white sheets. His hair, dark and tussled in so many different directions, with a sprinkling of gray strands that I now noticed were more prominent at the nape of his neck. I found that sexy as hell because with that, came more experience, knowledge, and wanted to be part of it all. This body I saw go from a boy to this well-defined man, from then to now in what felt like a blink of an eye. I felt like I missed so much, as if I had started a book and skipped right to the end, missing all the good parts and winning over my prince charming. Where was my storyline? I wanted to go back and read those chapters and know what had given him those touches of gray. What was in that beautiful, sleeping mind?

I placed his cup of coffee on the nightstand and traced tiny kisses along his neck down to his shoulder. He stirred.

He stretched with arms open wide and breathed in deep, moaning, then a yawn. With hooded eyes, he said, "Hey."

He saw me sitting next to him.

I smiled "Hey." I wrapped my arms around my naked knees.

He looked around. "What time is it?"

"Almost ten." I grinned. "You may have died for a while." I laughed.

"Are you serious?" he scanned the bright room, wide-eyed.

"Do you have somewhere to be?"

"Well, no, but damn," he said.

"There's jet lag and you probably need it, babe."

I ran my free hand through his dark hair. Damn, he was beautiful.

He slid up along the headboard, baring his sexy, strong chest and a thin ribbon of hair from his belly button that disappeared under the sheet.

"What's the plan for the day?"

"Well, I'm taking you somewhere at one, then we need to head to the restaurant for dinner at six-thirty. That's it. So, you are only required to take one shower, unless you decide you would like two, and two outfit changes. The rest is all on me." I smiled down at him, tracing my thumb over his eyebrow and down his jaw. "You make zero decisions today, Mr. Harlow. I don't even think you get to choose what you want to eat all day, come to think of it. Wait. I didn't know how you liked your coffee. I guessed black, but I wanted to put cream in it," I said.

He smiled and whispered, "Cream."

I nodded. "I knew it." I handed him his coffee from the nightstand with cream.

"So, we can lie around until close to one?" he asked, sipping on his coffee as I laid against his chest, tucking my body into his, and his arm heavy, wrapping across me.

"Yeah, it takes about twenty minutes to get there. Casual, shorts or jeans attire," I said.

He kissed the top of my head, and I closed my eyes, relishing the moment.

"We have time for me to have my way with you in that big, bad shower in there?" he asked as I felt him swallowing another sip of his coffee.

I looked back up at him, grinning. "Yes. I would like to break in every room in this house. Well, except Cora's. That's just wrong," I said, laughing.

The rest of the morning was spent bent over most of the hard surfaces available to us and spread eagled on anything wider than five feet. The excessive four heads in my shower were tested out and five stars were given. I now knew when I would need the lower one, the days when he wasn't there.

"This may be the smallest car I have ever been in." He laughed, trying to fit his wide shoulders within the confines of the seat.

Throwing my hands up, I laughed. "It's called a Mini for a reason, but it's fast."

I popped the clutch and took off.

We pulled up to the marina parking lot. "What are we doing?"

"Come on," I said, biting my lip with excitement.

"You and your surprises." He smiled as he climbed out of my tiny car.

Allen and Bianca were waiting at the head of the dock, waving. She was slightly bouncing where she stood with arms open wide with excitement to see us.

"Hey, friends," she yelled. Bianca was in classic white jeans and a blue and white sweater with large Jackie-O classic style sunglasses. Very California-esque sailing attire. Allen was in blue jeans and a black pullover, aviator sunglasses and his head full of dark curls shining in the bright sun.

Stephen asked in total surprise. "What are y'all doing here?"

Bianca took his face in her hands and said in her beautiful flowing accent, "Your sweet Cassie planned all this for us today. She is the greatest Stephen. She is a keeper."

She planted a kiss on his lips.

It was a fantastic cruise through the bay with a classic light lunch and endless wine served on a beautiful sailboat, visiting all the best water views of San Francisco, including the Golden Gate Bridge, Alcatraz, and skirting by Sausalito. It was a wonderful experience watching it through Stephen's eyes since it was his first time.

"I can see why you love it here so much. The weather is amazing for one, and there is something different to do around every corner for two. God. Look at this scenery," he said, looking out at the water, a spectacular vision of azure and green.

His dark hair was blowing in the wind, and his beautiful face was being kissed by the golden sun. I couldn't stop watching him.

I cradled my head against his shoulder, looking out at the water with him.

"I know. I rarely have time off to enjoy it. Watching you today reminds me of when I first got here. I was blown away, then I felt like I went inside the restaurant and life happened, and now I rarely come out to see it anymore," I said sadly.

He turned my face gently with one finger to kiss him.

"I think we have both sort of lost the meaning of what makes us happy. We drowned ourselves in our careers and did not do the things that fulfill us. We can change that."

He smiled and kissed me again. This time, whisking his tongue through my mouth, sending heat to my core, making me want him again. I forgot we were alone on this boat until I heard our friends' voices behind us. Once again, he sucked me into the vacuum.

We headed home and managed to not come completely unraveled, showering before dinner. We simply washed each other and talked while running soap over each other. The act was sweet. Just being this close to him for this long in my new space felt good, it felt right.

He chose a pair of tailored dress pants that hugged his ass and thighs so well I almost didn't want him to wear them out, along with them, a crisp white fitted shirt and coat. When my staff saw me walk in with this man dressed like this, I was toast. This already looked like a date, and there was no hiding my undeniable attraction to him. There was no way to tone down how attractive he was.

"You are so sexy," I told him, running my hands down his chest. "This dress."

He bit his bottom lip, running his eyes up and down my body.

"Oh no, really? I'm trying to look cute, not hot. I'm going to work." I winced.

"Ahhh, you are hot as fuck," he said.

I sighed, standing in my black one-shoulder, sleeveless sheath dress that hit above the knee. I thought it was simple. Not too much.

He stood behind me, looking at us in the mirror, wrapping his arms around my waist.

"For what it's worth, you could wear a garbage bag, and I would think you are sexy, so there is that. This is most likely perfectly appropriate for work attire."

He looked with a smile over my shoulder into the mirror.

I sighed. "Okay, I tried to not be hot, for the record."

"You tried. You failed, but tried." He laughed.

I organized our dinner as an evening with old friends in town to celebrate Allen and Bianca's anniversary, according to my staff. When Stephen and I walked in, it was written all over our faces that we most likely shared bodily fluids within the last twenty-four hours. It was impossible to hide, with the small touch on the arm when something funny was said, or his palm on the small of my back guiding me. We waited in the bar for our friends as I introduced him to some of the staff. Margaret instantly found him engaging, pouring him a rare twenty-three-year Shibui Japanese Whiskey, and they talked about rare finds in the bourbon world.

Bianca and Allen arrived. Once again, she was in her typical runway fashion, a gorgeous black Chanel sweater dress that hugged her curves perfectly with strappy heels that lengthened her already long, lean legs. Allen, a simple fitted black suit with no tie. Clearly, he was letting his wife be the star of the show.

"Your place is absolutely stunning, Cassie," Bianca said, holding her glass of Sauvignon Blanc, turning around to check out the dimly lit, Southeast Asia-inspired interior design.

"Thank you," I said. "My interior designer actually won an award for it the year we opened. That was a godsend for us because it put us in a well-known design magazine within the first three months of opening. How lucky were we?"

"That would make for a great start," Allen said.

We were shown to a more private area of the restaurant that had the best table in the house. It was a high, pub-style table level with a half wall of glass, showcasing the workings of our kitchen, which was a mix of white subway tile and stainless steel. Clean, unadulterated lines. Overhead was a blend of cherry blossom limbs and large rattan pendant lights that cast inviting golden light. The room was filled with blends of light and dark contrasting woods for an inviting feel. You felt like you were in a Japanese garden that backed up into a kitchen.

When we designed this, I wanted a concept so you couldn't hear the kitchen staff cursing when they burned themselves but could watch them do it. We called it the fishbowl table.

They say, *smile to the fishbowl table* all night long with gritted, fake smiles. They hated it, I loved it. It kept them from being slobs and doing stupid shit. Some establishments chose to have an open-concept kitchen, but I found it made for a loud restaurant. Some had a chef's table right by the galley you could pay a premium for. That was a solid no. We cursed too much, so that was the compromise.

We decided on a pre fixe menu tonight. That was basically the entire special menu the regular guests were being offered that Kyle and I created but with a few tweaks just for our table.

We started the night off with the peeled red ginger fritters, which were light and crisp. This was a pub fare item and was served with a Sapporo beer. We figured it would be a fun way to start things off.

I was surprised how much people were interested in the workings of the restaurant business. Allen was asking so many questions I thought he was either thinking of opening his own place or wanting to invest in mine.

Next, was the steamed snapper balls wrapped with chrysanthemum petals, laced with dashi. Super unique, and light.

"How do you come up with these ideas?" Stephen asked as he gracefully slid one into his mouth with his chopsticks. "I would never think of wrapping fish in a flower pedal."

"Well, it's a ton of collaboration, research, and trial and error. Kyle spends a lot of time researching where I like the trial-and-error method. That's why we have made such a good team all these years."

For a light vegetable, we chose asparagus with sesame vinegar dressing. This was always on our menu when we did our Japanese nights. It was super crisp and refreshing.

The black sesame-grilled spot prawns are another fan favorite. This was on rotation often.

"Oh my God, Cassie, these are insane. Do you only serve small plates? Because, I could have an entire entrée of these," Allen asked.

"We do mostly small plates, but it depends on the menu. Like when we do Chinese, Thai, and Indian, we tend to do more family style and sharable dishes. Most of the dishes like this are so rich and complex, it would just be too much on the palette to eat a whole lot of."

"Oh, that makes sense," Bianca said, as she savored her last shrimp.

Our final course was the star, the grilled duck breast with turnip. It was a beautifully curated dish, and I was so happy when it was brought out perfectly executed. Seared, medium rare with a gorgeous crust. The orange, persimmon, and grapefruit sauce were perfection, as the buttery white turnips were sure to melt in our mouths. I looked into the kitchen and spotted Kyle and Reggie looking to see our reactions as the plates were being handed out. Especially mine. I glanced in their direction and winked with approval. Kyle nodded, threw his towel onto his shoulder, turned, and sighed in relief. Thinking in my head, *well done boys.*

Stephen reached over to say something, and out of habit and sheer happiness, I kissed his cheek. Immediately, I paused, thinking, oh shit. Who just saw that?

Okay, just pretend you didn't do that, Cassie.

I straightened in my chair and jumped back into our conversation with ease.

Stephen smiled outward at my faux pas and reached under the table, placing his hand on my thigh for a second, knowing I was having an internal freak-out.

The remainder of our wine was served, and our conversation was getting loud and fun. Our last course, dessert, was to be served, and I put all faith into our pastry chef, who, this time, personally came out with her own creations. She never did this. She always stayed behind the scenes. She was a shy, slightly portly, red-headed woman in her late thirties. She had her own pastry room there and rarely mingled with the rest of our staff. I was very happy to see this moment. The guys in the kitchen looked just as shocked behind her in the glass cage.

I introduce her. "Hey, everyone. This is our very talented Pastry Chef, Carol."

Our server placed our desserts in front of us as she squeaked out, "Hi. Tonight, I made you all three different desserts. First being, the Okinawan-style sesame donuts. Second, is the Japanese matcha cheesecake with a black sesame crust, and third, a classic Dorayaki, which is a Japanese red bean pancake. I hope you enjoy."

She bowed to us before turning and leaving in a hurry.

I looked as she went back into the kitchen, and she high-fived the guys. Either she lost a bet and had to do it, or she wanted to, and they were encouraging her. I couldn't wait to find out the backstory on that one. Either way, our shy flower Carol was blooming.

When dinner was over, Kyle came out and met with everyone. He flashed his amazing smile as he stood with his arm draped across the back of my chair in an almost protective way. It was nice to see him taking on my role as Executive Chef and mingling with the guests while answering all of Allen's many culinary questions. He was a natural, and I was really proud of him. Everyone thanked him for his talent and time before he headed back to the kitchen to continue his night.

Stephen then leaned into me. "Someone thinks a lot of you."

"I know you do," I whispered.

"Uh, yes, but so does your chef. He has something for you," he muttered low.

"Are you jealous of my relationship with Kyle, or is this something you see? He's like, my protégé," I said, slightly unnerved.

He bobbed his head. "I see it. Sorry, babe."

"Shit. I'm oblivious. Who doesn't want to get in my panties lately?" I asked.

He looks around the room. "Uh, that dude." He pointed his head in the direction of the most metrosexual, best-looking server on my staff.

I laughed and whispered into his ear. "You are on the money. That's Kerry, and we all know he's gay, but isn't ready to come out of the closet. You're good."

Allen and Bianca thanked us profusely for the evening and of course, I took care of dinner and Stephen left a very generous $1,000 cash tip for everyone to share. I rarely got to do anything like that. Nobody came to visit. It was really nice to have people to treat. My staff seemed to enjoy it as well.

"Let's get out of here. I need to be able to put my hands all over you," Stephen said in a low whisper.

"Okay, let me thank everyone," I said. "Come with me."

We walked back into the kitchen.

"Hey, y'all. Thank you for an amazing time. You nailed it," I said.

"It was fun. I'm glad you all enjoyed it. Goodnight," Kyle said, looking down, back to what he was doing, almost emotionless.

"Thank you. It was nice to meet you." Stephen waved.

Kyle waved, barely looking up. "You too, man."

Once outside, walking to my car, I said, "You are right, he was not happy with me being with you. So jealous. How did I never see that?"

"You were married. I'm a different threat. I don't know. He may want to protect you from getting hurt again. He doesn't know who the fuck I am, and I kind of like knowing he's here watching over you. He looks scrappy." He laughed and opened my car door, and I slid in.

The night ended with drinking wine on the apartment terrace, watching the lights over the bay. The crisp, cool San Francisco air was something I could ever get enough of when I was used to the heaviness of the southern humidity. We lay in a chase lounge, me between his legs nestled up along his chest. His arms wrapped around me, tucked in warm sweatshirts to ward off the cool evening chill.

"I loved seeing you in your world tonight. You are nothing short of amazing." He kissed me on my head. "So, when did you know you wanted to be a chef?" he asked.

I sipped my wine and looked up in the sky. "Oh wow, I knew

when I was a teenager, but I was obsessed since I was really little. When my friends were watching cartoons, I was watching cooking shows."

He laughed. "What? What cooking shows did we have back then?"

I turned around in shock. "Oh my God. Julia Child for one. Then, the cajun dude, what was his name?" I tapped my temple trying to remember. "Justin Wilson. I guaraanteeee," I said in my best cajun voice.

He laughed at me. "You were a weird kid."

"Oh, Then the master himself, Chef Tell, a German Chef, I see you. That was his show ending catchphrase." I laughed at my childhood memories, thinking it probably wasn't normal.

"So? When did you realize you wanted to save the world with cyber security?" I asked.

He sipped his wine. "Well, computer science was my jam. I had a professor who pulled me aside telling me it was going to be a huge profession and to jump on it, so started taking those classes. I figured I should, especially since my dick isn't big enough for porn," he said, laughing.

I almost spat my wine out my nose. "Yes, it is. Whoever told you that lied. You could have made it to the top."

"Tonight, at your place, felt like high school all over again. Keeping us a secret," he said softly, kissing my head. My knees tucked up into me.

"Still kind of hot, isn't it?" I asked, knowing damn well, it wasn't.

"Yeah, but I am so ready to be completely out in the open. I'm proud to be with you. I don't care who the hell knows."

We sat looking up at the dark star-filled sky, the smell of the sea filling our senses.

"I know. It's just early, and I'm not divorced yet. You understand that, right? It's not that I don't want the world to know. It's not high school."

I reached up to kiss him.

"I want it to work this time, Cass. I don't know if I can lose you again," he said, looking down into my eyes.

My heart wanted to believe that, but my head spun with doubt. The distance, our careers, the lack of time. It was the same roller-coaster.

"I feel the same way, Stephen. I'm just scared to promise you something when there are so many unknowns in my life right now. Our lives," I said, reaching up to stroke his face.

He kissed my temple and breathed me in.

That night and the next morning, we made love repeatedly. Holding each other with long moments of silence, our minds reeling, trying to make sense of how this will work.

Breaking a moment in the silence, he asked, "I would like you to come to Charlotte next time. Come and stay with me. Can you do that?"

"I think so. I will look at my upcoming schedule and see what works."

"Okay, I would like that."

He smiled and wrapped his leg around me, flipping me on top of his naked body in one swift motion.

I laughed. "What are you doing?" I asked with my long hair flowing down around his face, his warm, hard body underneath mine.

"I just wanted to see that beautiful smile." He stretched his hand to tuck my hair behind my ears and reached up to kiss me. "I love this smile."

Hearing the word love made my heart pound, I so felt it, I didn't think I ever didn't feel it since I was seventeen. It was just new again. It was vulnerable.

His plane took off at nine that night. On the way home from the airport, I rolled my windows down, tears running down my face as the cool California air tried its best to dry them. As my hair whipped around my face, I put music on. Prince-When Doves Cry.

"For Fuck's sake," I yelled. "What are you trying to tell me, Prince? Every time I'm crying in my car."

As I was about to skip, I took pause, and turned it up...loud.

Chapter 20

CASSIE

✗

It's my fourth meeting of the day, and with deadlines quickly approaching, taping of cooking segments, and the buzz of people in and out of my office, it was finally wearing on me. Johnathan, my assistant, yeah, I was gifted an assistant, was chatting away and placing forms for me to sign onto my desk, just as I felt the vibration from my phone in my lap. With a half-ass attempt to stay on track, I didn't completely shut myself off from the outside world but just slightly muted it.

My eyes must have glazed over because Johnathan said, "I see I have lost you, Cassie, I'll get you some coffee."

He left the room, seemingly annoyed at my lack of response. My brain started to short-circuit when I realized I was being bombarded by an insurmountable number of texts. I opened my phone to reveal twelve missed messages from multiple people. Jesus. I was being pulled in a hundred directions and could barely keep my focus on one right now.

I have a few missed texts from Kyle. He was drowning in the restaurant without me, especially this week since we were in the middle of taping cooking segments, and I was here every day.

Kyle: Call me when you can. 910

We came up with a new code for non-911 emergencies, but important enough and can potentially be, therefore, being a 910.

He picked up on the second ring.

"Chef?"

"Hey, Kyle. I got your message. What's going on?" I asked.

He sighed. "Reggie's wife went into labor and he's out of commission tonight and tomorrow. I am short-staffed. I can swing tonight utilizing one of the new guys, but tomorrow, being Friday, can you help me? I hate asking Cassie."

"Hey. I actually can." I felt helpful for once. "I have taping until four, then I can be there. Will that be enough?" I asked.

"Yeah, that's great. What about Cora?" he asked.

"All good. It's summer, and she is spending the night at a friend's most of the weekend. 910 diverted." I laughed.

"Thank God. I was stressed out. We have a Fish Bowl Table, and you know that makes me anxious to be on display when I'm not at my best," he said.

"I can't believe Reggie is going to be a daddy. What hospital?" I asked.

"Mission Bay."

"Okay, I'm sending something. See you tomorrow," I said.

He breathed out an audible sigh of relief. "Thanks, Cass."

Just then, Johnathan came bouncing back in with a last-ditch effort to motivate me with coffee in hand. He had mastered it better than me. When he was hired, he immediately asked how I liked my coffee. When I told him, "I like it to be the shade of my skin."

He took that first task very seriously as soon as he knew my caffeine addiction was intense and necessary for proper brain function. People in my industry smoked cigarettes, took uppers and downers, drank heavily, and snorted coke like it was part of the job description. I refused to go down that path because I had bigger plans that needed a clear head. I was in an industry dominated by men. I had to keep my head in the game and out of a kilo to make that happen. I drank an obscene amount of coffee.

"Can you send some flowers for me to Mission Bay?" I asked.

"Sure. Just give me the information of who and what you want," he said. "You're meeting with Arie, your publicist, in fifteen. After that, your schedule is clear."

Shocked, I asked, "Like, I'm done for the day, clear?"

Looking around in confusion, he said, "Yes, Cassie. It's four. You can go home."

He then left me to my busy work.

My concentration on recipe editing for the upcoming shows was broken by a knocking on my door that was slightly ajar. A chipper British accent flowed into my office.

"Hello, you must be Cassie Buckley?"

She pushed through hesitantly.

I stood from behind my desk, leaving the amazing skyline behind me to reach for her delicate hand.

"I am. You must be Arie?"

"I am. I am your publicist. I am here to make you look good," she said with an impressively wide, beautiful smile, beautiful mocha skin, and long ringlet burgundy curls in an afro style that I was insanely envious about since my hair wouldn't hold curl for shit. She stood in front of me with such confidence, holding a small stack of files in front of her.

"Ahh, well, in that case, can you make me look like you?"

We both laughed.

"You are witty, Ms. Buckley. We are going to be fast friends we are."

Friends. Finally. I got to be friends with a late twenties British publicist who had curves to kill, an accent I could listen to all day, and a fashion sense I wanted to emulate. Sign me up.

She sat in the seat in front of my desk, and I followed suit by sitting back down as well.

"So, I will be in charge of arranging any of your public affairs and events when they arise. When we get your cookbooks and cookware lines on the markets, we will do ad campaigns and such, I will do that for you as well. When you look in your calendar, I will have things marked in purple," she said.

"Okay, purple," I said to myself as I jotted in my notes.

"Cassie, I will also handle things like the press and any good or bad things that may arise," she said.

I laughed. "Like, what? I'm a chef, not like a real celebrity."

"Ah, well, you will be surprised. People get crazy about their chef celebrities. Especially the pretty ones like you. They see you in their homes, they use your cookware, make your recipes, and follow your Instagram. It gets personal. You will be surprised by the fan base you will start to have. You may end up in a tabloid if we aren't careful, but that's where I come in, love," she said with a smile. "You work for this company, and I have to protect this brand, and I protect your reputation, okay?"

She stood.

"Wow. Okay," I said and stood as well.

She reached out to shake my hand. "If you need anything, text or email me. It was so nice meeting you, Ms. Buckley.".

"It was nice meeting you too, Arie, thank you."

Then out she turned with her sassy, beautiful self.

I didn't think she was planning on being my fast British friend. I thought she didn't want me to fuck up and embarrass this company.

Ugh.

I was hoping for some boutique shopping and a spot of tea, damn.

I gathered my things and headed out past Johnathan's desk.

"Hey, I'm heading home. I'll finish these recipe edits tonight for next week's tapings. Is there anything else?"

"No, I think that's it. See you tomorrow." He glanced into his laptop at the schedule. "Hair and make-up at 8:30." Then looked up with a smile.

I sighed. "Okay, see you then."

I made my way to the bank of elevators.

I pressed the down button, and the large brass doors opened. I stepped in and turned to press for the ground floor as a hand stretched in to stop the doors from closing.

"Whoa. Wait." The arm of Noah Foster, the Chef from Moxy and his latest endeavor, Yellow Jackets slid in, completely out of breath. "Thanks."

"No problem," I said as he took a double look at me.

"Hey. You are our new chef on the block. Cassie Buckley of Sagi-Shi, right?" he said with an outstretched hand.

I smiled and reciprocated with a tight squeeze.

"I am. You're Noah. I think we are sharing studio space this week. At least, that is what I've been told. I'm glad to see another chef," I said with relief.

The doors opened to the ground floor as we stepped out and squeezed through the few people waiting to go up without breaking in our conversation. Noah was in his early forties, with blonde wavy hair that he ran his hands through multiple times, drawing my eyes to it. Big blue eyes, and stood very tall, so much that I found myself craning my neck to talk to him. Sometimes, it was hard working with a tall chef if they weren't mindful. They would lay out their kitchen with things too high, not thinking of their staff.

"So? How is everything going? Big change from being behind the scenes, isn't it?" he asked as we continued walking toward the front doors to the large, bright entryway leading to the street.

I stopped. "Well, I'm getting the hang of it, but juggling my restaurant, home life, and this, is a bit overwhelming. I think once I get in the groove, I'll be okay."

"Well, once you get done with all the back-to-back taping, you are good for a while. Are you doing any other projects, like books and stuff?" he asked.

"Yeah, a cookbook and a line of cookware," I said.

He gasped. "Damn. They are keeping you busy. I'm sure they will be doing most of the work. You will mostly be just taking pictures and bam, you'll be done."

He laughed.

"I hope so. Well Noah, I guess I'll see you around the studio these next few weeks," I said.

He shook my hand again. "Welcome aboard, Cassie. See you around."

He dashed off, taking only a few strides before he was through the front doors.

My apartment was starting to grow on me, and I was becoming

one with my new space being Cora's and mine. Her room was starting to feel more lived in, with posters lining the walls and clothes strewn about. I now had pieces of art filling blank spaces. I knew the doorman's name. I chatted with a lady from the fifth floor in the gym downstairs for far too long on Tuesday. It was getting better. I was adjusting.

Before I drowned myself in editing, I pulled open my phone after sliding off my shoes, poured a glass of wine, and cozied up on my ridiculously comfortable couch.

He picked up almost immediately.

"Hey, sexy girl," he said.

"Oh baby, I am so glad to hear your voice. Am I interrupting anything?" I asked.

"No, not a thing. I was just sitting here watching people go by on their boats. Having a whiskey on the dock. The sunset is amazing," he said.

"Send me a picture."

Just then, a beautiful lake view picture with a sunset of pink, gold, and red reflecting on the blue water came through. His dock, with his legs outstretched and a low ball whiskey glass in his hand. I so wished I was there next to him. It felt like real time as I could hear the clinking of the ice in his glass and the boats going by.

"I miss you so much," I said softly.

He sighed. "I miss you too, Cassie."

"Send me a picture of what you are looking at," he asked.

I send a picture of my glass of red wine resting in my lap, legs draped over the white couch, with the beautiful blue sky and large windows above. My freshly painted French manicured toes being the focal point.

"Why do your toes turn me on so much?" He laughed. "I kind of want to scold you for having red wine on that brand-new white sofa, though."

"Maybe you should fly over and spank me," I said, taking a sip and laughing into my glass.

He let out a long breath. "If I didn't have meetings lined up here for the next week, I would be. I am about to die waiting on you to get here."

"Two weeks. It seems like an eternity, though," I said.

"I am just trying to stay busy."

"Are you okay? You seem a bit down."

Again, a deep breath and a pause. "I'm okay. Just stress and some things came up at work. I'm just out here decompressing. I'm so glad you called. You are making it better, I promise."

"Okay. Just know you can tell me anything, okay?" I asked.

"I know. I'm good," he said.

He says in a more chipper tone. "Tell me something about your day. Tell me something good, Ms. Buckley."

I said. "Okay, oh. I have a publicist. Her name is Arie, and she is British and fantastic. Oh my gosh, Stephen. She is so beautiful and curvy with tits up under her chin." I looked down at mine, which were not under my chin, like... nowhere close.

"She had an awesome sense of style that I want to copy. She walked in with her attitude of, *I am going to make you look good, Ms. Buckley, and keep all the blokes from talkin' about how they shagged ya in the papers Ms. Buckley.* I thought we were going to be friends. Then quickly realized she was just there to make sure I didn't fuck up the brand. I totally thought we were going to go to boutiques, have a spot of tea, and a biscuit, mate."

He was laughing hysterically now. "Please stop. You have the worst accents, and that was Australian. Also, do you want a friend or an actual girlfriend? I think you should stick to people that have things in common with you at the studio."

He was still laughing.

"No fun. She's cool. I want high-rise tits, a big bubble booty, and a cool accent. What do you think they would do if I started talking like that on camera tomorrow? Ello, everyone. Today we are going to mix in a wee bit of ..."

"Oh my god, stop. Ello? That's not British." He could barely breathe. "You make me so happy woman. You are ridiculous."

He continued laughing.

"You make me happy too."

We were interrupted by an incoming call on his end. "Hey, I need to take this. I've been waiting for this all day. I'll text you before I go to bed."

"Okay. Goodbye, mate."

I laughed.

"Bye," he said with humor.

I text Cora to make sure she was doing okay at her sleepover. She was happy as a clam in her teenage world with her friends. As shitty as this divorce was, we couldn't have planned it better with summer break right at the transition of the move. Summer and teen life. Who needed a mom? She would need me again come fall.

I pulled out my laptop and got back to editing for the upcoming shows and going through my placement and recipes for tomorrow. The newness of it all was exciting, but the nervousness started to take over. I hoped I wasn't becoming a sellout. I hoped I was doing the right thing.

I only had eighteen months. It sounded like a prison sentence when I said it like that. I took a big sip of my wine. I guessed it would be one of those white-collar prisons because I had a spectacular view, a publicist who will keep my prison-life business private, and my cellmate made a spectacular Ethiopian roast with double oat milk. I just needed to boost up these conjugal visits and I thought I could make it.

Chapter 21

STEPHEN

I was just getting out of a meeting with Rich, my head of IT, when I got a text message from Mark, my investigator hired for Lauren's case. He usually emailed me every couple of weeks with updates, so this was rare.

Mark: Call me when you can

Immediately, I knew he was dropping my case due to inactivity. I had felt it coming for a while.

I dialed his number as I walked into my office and shut the door.

"Hey, Stephen. How are you?"

"I'm doing well, Mark, and you?"

I climbed behind my desk and prepared for his words.

"I'm calling because I had something interesting come up this week," he said.

My heart picked up pace. I hadn't heard those words *something interesting* since the first couple of months of the investigation before it all went dry.

I took in a deep breath. "Okay, what is that?"

"I'm sending over an email with a file attached. Do you have access to it?"

"Yeah, I'm in my office," I said.

Pulling myself up to my computer and go into my email. "Okay."

"So, you know how I have surveillance on Lauren's parent's house, right?" he asked.

"Right?" I said.

"Are you looking at the pictures I sent over?" he asked. "The ones of the car?"

"Yeah, I got them. What am I looking at?"

"These two guys were sitting in front of their house three times in the past week. They have never been there before. I ran the plates. They were stolen. I'm not getting a good vibe from this. I was wondering if you guys can get any facial verification on these two in your database. They seem familiar. I have nothing in my files. It's off, Stephen. I just want to make sure Marek and Klara are safe as well."

"We should probably notify the cops, maybe get a patrol over there?" I said.

"I already did."

"I will have my guys run a facial recognition to see if anything pops up. I may also have someone on my end who I can reach out to. I appreciate it, Mark. Thanks for the heads up," I said.

"I'll keep in touch on what else happens. Something is going on," he said.

"Okay, please do."

I sat back in my chair, ran my hands through my hair as I stared at the grainy pictures of the men in the car. I wished they were clearer.

I went into my cell and found Zach Hatchell in my contacts.

Me: Can you come to my office?

Zach: Okay. Give me five minutes.

After pacing my office for what seemed like twenty, Zach knocked, and I asked him to come in.

"What can I do for you?"

"I was wondering if you could run some facial recognition for me?"

He said, in a questioning tone, "I can try. What is it?"

I turned my computer monitor and went through the photographs.

"They are pretty distorted and grainy, but I'll see what I can do. See what comes up. Send those files over to me."

"Great. Thank you, Zach," I said.

"No problem, Mr. Harlow. I'll work on it this afternoon," he said as he left my office.

My mind was reeling as I tried my best to get work done, but it was impossible. Why, all of a sudden, would someone be at Lauren's parent's house. I decided to check in with them. It was about that time, anyhow.

I chose their home number. They are still old school and had a landline. Klara picked up in her heavy Czechoslovakian accent.

"Hello?"

"Hi Klara, it's Stephen. How are you?" I said.

"Oh, Stephen. Yes, I am well. You?" she asked.

"I'm doing well. I was just checking in with y'all. I haven't called in a while, and I wanted to see how you and Marek were doing."

"We are doing okay Stephen. Okay. Marek is staying busy. He is at Jakob's. I can have him call you when he gets back, yes?" she said in her broken English.

"That's all right. Just give him my best. If you need anything, anything at all, just let me know, okay, Klara?" I told her.

"Of course, Stephen. We will."

"Take care. Bye," I said.

In a withering tone, she said, "Bye Stephen." and hung up.

Just making any contact with these two broke me. In one minute, they were making wedding plans with Lauren, and the next, they were in full-blown search mode, lost, and looking at me for answers. Knowing Klara, she had Lauren's wedding dress hanging in a spare room, and she went in to touch it daily. That was her one and only baby girl. They had Jakob, who moved to Charlotte from Miami shortly after she went missing to be closer to them, but there was definitely a bond they had with their firstborn. Their daughter was unbreakable. This had left them shattered.

I was sitting in a zoom meeting later that afternoon when a text from Zach came in.

Zach: I actually got something.

Zach: I'll come to your office when you have time.

Me: Give me 15 minutes

I had no idea what was said in the rest of the meeting. I hoped it wasn't important on my end. My mind was officially in detective mode once again.

Zach knocked and entered my office.

"So, I can't believe it, but I was actually able to pull something up. Can I?" he said, pointing to my desk to put his laptop down.

"Of course."

Pointing to the driver in the picture, blonde, early thirties. "He popped in our database." He went into another screen, pulling up another picture, this time clearer. "This is from three years ago." Then, another picture. "And this one a little over a year ago on our property, both with Lauren."

Shocked, I said, "Wait. What?"

He repeated. "Yeah, it looked like he was seen here both times, talking to her in our parking lot at Southstar. He didn't come in, so there was never ID run for our database, so I don't have that, but I got a facial recognition match. I don't have anything on the other guy, unfortunately."

Seeing Lauren again in a picture I hadn't seen before punched me in the gut, but seeing her talking to this guy who was now being seen sitting outside her parents' house the last few days, this was disturbing. She knew him.

What the fuck was going on?

"Can you email me all this, Zach?" I said as he whisked his laptop from me.

He smiled. "I already did, boss. Is there anything else?"

"No, not right now," I said in a complete daze. "Thank you for getting on that so fast. I really appreciate it."

"Sure thing. Let me know if there is anything else."

He turned and left the office, closing the door softly, like he knew I was in shock and needed to be left alone.

I called Mark, my investigator, as I pulled up the images in my email.

"Hey Stephen, any news?" he answered.

"Yeah, the blonde? He was seen talking to Lauren in my work parking lot on two separate occasions that we have on camera. One being not long before she went missing. Another about three years ago. Looks friendly to me by the way they are standing," I said, as my heart slightly broke, staring at the images on the screen.

"No ID?" he asked.

"No, he would have had to come into our building," I said.

"Okay, I'm staking out her parent's house this week and see if they come back. See where these guys go. Maybe get some traction on this case for once. I'll keep you posted," he said.

"Thank you, Mark."

I hung up.

I tapped my temple and contemplated making a call to someone who may have a way to know who these guys are if they are wanted, especially out of the country.

I dialed up my good friend Pete Maddox with the CIA. We had grown quite close, especially since Allen and I had been doing tons of government projects, and I was in DC more and more. We got up a good bit for dinner or drinks since he and his wife were there. He had been a great friend.

"Stephen. What's going on?" he answered.

"Oh, you know. Shutting down the pimple faces from infiltrating large corporate America computer systems." I laughed.

"It's scary that those little fuckers are more intelligent than we are most of the time. Fortunately for us, they stop and take too many jerk-off sessions to porn sites, and we catch 'em." He laughed.

I could hear his chair squeaking as he must be leaning back, maybe bouncing. His hands were behind his balding head, most likely, and his feet were up on his desk.

"I need something personal if I can?"

"Well, okay, I can see what I can do. What do you have?" he asked.

"I have two guys that have popped up on our radar. Sitting in front of Lauren's parent's house all of a sudden. Seems as if one has a past with Lauren. No ID. Can you see if you get any facial recognition in your database? Ours is, well, only as far as our personal company or client base."

"Well, yeah, I can do that on the down-low I suppose. Send me what you have."

"I appreciate it. I have my investigator on it, but he only has so many resources, local and you know, not CIA database. I'm sure these guys are not US citizens, being Lauren is Czech, and everyone she surrounded herself with was non-US," I said.

"Yeah, that makes it a little harder. I'll see what I come up with and get back to you as soon as I can."

"Thanks a lot. You doing all right, man?"

"We are doing great. Next time you are here, we should grab dinner or at least a drink."

"Absolutely. Again, thanks," I said before hanging up.

The rest of the day was a blur until the sunset called me to the dock. The colors were magnificent reds, oranges, and yellows. Bouncing off the blue, cool water. I propped my feet up onto the table. Swirled my whiskey in my glass and took a sip. It felt warm going down and tasted smokey on my tongue.

My phone rang, pulling me from my thoughts.

Her voice telling me she missed me. I needed that so much at that very moment.

She changed my entire mood, talking about her day, speaking in ridiculous accents that she could never get right, and just being, well...Cassie. She was nothing short of wonderful. As stressed as she was, she still made jokes and cheered others up. I didn't deserve her.

The situation with the case, I wanted to confide in her. She could read me and could tell something was on my mind, but this would only bring up the situation with Lauren. It would add unnecessary doubt into her mind, and I needed more information before I dragged her heart into it.

Just then, our fun banter was interrupted by a call from Pete.

"Hey, I need to take this. I've been waiting on this call all day," I told her. "I'll text you before I go to bed."

She got me with one good last laugh of, "Goodbye, mate," in her Australian/British accent.

She was fantastic.

"Hey, Pete. How are you?" I asked.

"I'm okay, Stephen. Listen, I started poking around, and it seems that I have kicked a hornet's nest. When are you in DC next?"

Now worried, I said, "Not until the week after next. Why, is there something urgent?"

He took a deep breath. "Um, I don't feel comfortable discussing this over the phone. I can't get to Charlotte..."

"No, this is not your problem, Pete. Let me move some things around. I'll see what I can do tomorrow and get there as soon as I can. Seriously? This is that urgent?" I asked.

There was a moment of silence, then, "It's important information for you, Stephen."

I shook my head and said, "All right, man, I appreciate your help. I'll call you tomorrow."

He replied quickly before getting off the line, "Okay, talk tomorrow."

Fuck.

What the fuck was going on? As I paced the dock and went to take a sip of my drink, I found it whiskey-less and only ice. I marched towards my massive house, which was dimly lit throughout. A house of glass, revealing my entire life, like a glass theater for everyone to watch my world shattering like a goddamn movie.

Once in my kitchen, I stood at my wet bar, poured more whiskey into my glass, and leaned against my counter. I looked out towards the lake, now almost completely dark. The water was more ominous than inviting as it just was moments ago. My house was large and cold. I felt anger rise. I just wanted this nightmare to fucking end.

Chapter 22

CASSIE

I wrote Margaret a note.

I took 4 Kirin-Cassie

Then I left it under the computer for the next day before making my way to the kitchen.

"Here, guys," I said, as I handed them out to Darius, our new guy Brandon, and Kyle.

"Nice. Closing beers," Brandon said, bouncing his head.

Kyle popped his open, pointed his at Brandon, and said, "Don't get used to this, man. It only happens when Chef works on the line, and that is rare."

He laughed, looking at me with a boyish smile.

"Come on, we are celebrating. Cheers to Reggie's new baby."

Everyone cheered and held up their beers.

"Also, here's to Brandon. You kicked ass on your first Friday on the line."

We all said *good job* and drank.

"Now, play some tunes, Kyle, and let's get this bitch closed down."

I laughed as I chugged some of my beer and went to scrubbing the flat top.

Kyle put Limp Bizkit-Break Stuff on the Bluetooth. This was our jam since our time at Le D'ebut. I looked at him as he turned his hat backward, and he grinned so hugely that his dimples appeared. I hadn't seen him this happy since before the night we had our dinner with Stephen, Allen, and Bianca. I smiled back and sang the words and got into my scrubbing like I meant it, throwing my hands in the air periodically to accentuate the angry words of the song.

After about fifteen minutes, I was heading into the office when Kyle approached me.

"Hey, we have it from here. You don't have to stay."

"I know. I'm good. I'm actually having a good time, and I don't have anywhere to be." I rolled my eyes. "For once."

"It's strange seeing you here, and look at you."

He snickered.

"What?" I asked with a small laugh.

"You have like, full makeup on, and your hair looks...good."

He looked away shyly.

I closed my eyes, shook my head, and said with amusement, "Are you crushing on the celebrity chef, Kyle? Do I need to make a call to my publicist and straighten this out?"

He leaned back hard against the hallway wall, and then I did too, looking at him sideways.

He took a sip of his beer in silence, looking forward, then down, holding the bottle at his waist with both hands, face serious.

He sighed, then said, "I've been crushing on you way before you were a celebrity chef, Cassie."

Then he looked sideways at me.

Oh shit.

What the fuck was I supposed to do with this information?

Fuck.

I gave him a smile. Then, I reached down, held his wrist, and squeezed.

He looked back down at his beer and his wrist with my hand.

"I know I don't stand a chance. I googled Stephen." He laughed, shaking his head. "I thought maybe for a second I had chance...since you and Jack..."

"I'm sorry, Kyle. I didn't know," I said.

He let out a small puff of air and looked at me. "Come on, Cass, would it have made a difference?"

I shook my head. "No, but I would have been aware and sensitive to it, maybe. I hope I never led you on or…"

Quickly looking at me, he said, "No, you never had, never. It's all been my grand fantasy." He took a swig of his beer and looked at the bottle. "You are so fucking awesome. I just… want to be around you all the time. I mean, you are the shit, you know? You can look like that," he splays his hand out toward me, "know every single word to Break Stuff, you run this kitchen like an absolute boss, you are the kindest soul, you are…" he puts his head against the wall looking at the ceiling.

"Chef, we are almost done back here. What do you need us to do in the walk-in for tomorrow?"

Darius interrupted as he came around the corner.

Kyle turned his head to look at him. "I'll be right there, man."

He took a big breath. "Well, don't let this be weird. I won't. Just, if for some reason you decide you don't like this millionaire or anyone else and you want to give this guy a try." He smiled really big and let out an uncomfortable laugh. "Just know I won't turn you down. I would actually really like it."

He walked away, leaving me completely speechless.

I headed into my office to sit in front of my computer, not knowing what else I should do. I couldn't even remember what I was supposed to do for the rest of my work night.

My heart was pounding. What if this changed our work relationship and he left? My hands went to my face, and I wanted to cry. I couldn't do this without Kyle.

I needed to get out of there.

I grabbed my bag and headed to the kitchen.

"Hey, I'm actually going to head out," I said, waving to the guys.

"We are right behind you," Kyle replied with a worried look.

I headed for the door and out into the cool air. It slapped me in the face as I took a deep breath, almost hyperventilating, as I headed to my car.

I unlocked it and climbed in. The silence was deafening once I shut the door, and I didn't know if I wanted to cry or scream. I just sat there and watched people walk down the sidewalk past me as I sat in absolute silence. Dressed up, laughing, celebrating, and thinking that it was the weekend, as they should, as friends should. Their joy started to anger me, then pulled sadness from deep within my chest as I could feel it getting tight. I was on the verge of an emotional outburst.

I reached for my phone. I wanted to text Britt.

Fuck, it was too late. I just needed my friend.

My day was so busy I didn't see the texts.

Stephen: Sorry I missed your call earlier.

Stephen: I hope you have a great time cooking tonight. Do your thing sexy girl.

Stephen: Goodnight, miss you.

I stared at it. And just so he woke up to it, I shakily texted a message.

Me: I miss you xo

I wanted to text Britt, but it was three in the morning at her time, but I knew her phone was on. I just want a fucking friend. Just then, a tap on my window makes me jump.

"Fucking shit."

I screamed.

Kyle laughed and threw his hands up.

I shook my head and opened my door. "Yeah?"

"Are you okay?" he asked.

I closed my eyes and slowly shook my head. My chin started to quiver, tears started to flow, and my hands covered my face.

He opened the door all the way and dropped to his knees.

"Oh fuck, Cassie." He reached into the car to hug me. "Are you okay? Why are you crying?"

The feeling of his arms around me made me explode. I didn't know why.

Why him?

I was shaking uncontrollably and sobbing.

He pulled my legs out of the car so he was kneeling between them, rocking me back and forth. Running his hands down my hair.

"Shh, it's going to be okay."

I buried my head into his chest and wrapped my arms around his lean body. He smelled exactly like me, the kitchen, the smell of Asian food mingling between us. Once I got a slight bit of composure, I pulled myself back and reached around into my console to grab a napkin.

"I must look like a mess," I said between crying jags.

"Slightly scary, you had a lot of make-up on from your cooking segment, I won't lie."

He chuckled.

I laughed and cried when I saw how much mascara was on the napkin.

He took his thumbs and wiped underneath my eyes while asking, "You want to tell me what set this off? Was it what I said earlier?"

He looked at me with furrowed brows and those stormy gray eyes.

I shook my head. "I don't know. I just really wanted to tell my friend Britt, and I realized it was three am there and..."

I started to cry again.

"Hey. It's okay. You feel alone?" he asked, blotting under my eyes with a napkin.

"Yeah. I'm really fucking alone. I thought about if you didn't like my answer of not being interested in you romantically, if you left me, if you left Sagi, Kyle, I...I can't fucking do this without you." I cried. "Everyone is fucking leaving me. My life is falling apart, and you think I'm the shit and I am *not*."

He reached up and pressed his lips against my forehead while saying, "I'm not going anywhere Cassie. I'm not leaving you." He pulled me from him and looked into my eyes and tearfully said again, "I'm not leaving you." Then he pulled me into a tight embrace.

"Why did you tell me you have been crushing on me tonight knowing that I probably didn't feel the same way?" I asked and sniffled while bent over his shoulder.

Pulling me out to look at him, he said, "Because I would rather live with rejection than regrets." He smiled, turning his head sideways trying to capture one from me. "I'm okay, and you will be too."

"You really are a good friend. See? We could have fucked it all up by having sex," I said with a small laugh as I wiped my nose.

His eyes raced back and forth. "Well, I mean, we can always see what happens."

I playfully hit his arm. "Thank you. I really lost my shit. I was having so much fun too, dammit."

"Are you okay to drive home?"

I nod. "Yeah, thank you for rescuing me. I owe you."

He stood, stretching out his legs. "Well, I mean we can give that sex offer a go if…"

I laughed again. "Stop. Seriously, you are the best. That was incredible friend shit right there. Thanks."

"Anytime Cassie."

He winked.

"Do you want a ride?" I asked.

"No thanks. I'm only three blocks, remember? I love the walk," he said. "Goodnight."

He turned and left the parking lot.

The next morning, I woke up and call Britt.

"Good morning, Sunshine," she said.

"Hey. I was dying and wanted to talk to you so bad last night, but of course it was another 3 am emergency."

"Oh shit. What happened?"

"I worked the line last night after taping all day, and Kyle kind of cornered me," I said.

"Do you do drugs? Like who has that much fucking energy? Do you hear yourself?" She laughed.

I sighed. "It's not that bad. Anyhow, he told me he has had a crush on me forever. Ugh."

She laughed. "Oh shit. Girl. You have more wieners being thrown at you than the Nathan hotdog eating contest."

"Oh my god." I laughed. "That was a great one. You need to

take it back because I seriously have like, two dicks, it's not worthy of that zinger."

She chuckled. "Yeah, I should wait until your segments come out on TV and men are really throwing the dicks at you left and right like a straight up, Bukkake."

I gasped. "Britt. What are you and Avery searching on porn? You are nasty."

She laughed so hard she couldn't breathe, and this was why I needed to hear from her at midnight.

"Isn't your divorce coming up soon?" she asked.

"Well, you know how to bring a conversation down, don't you? Yeah, in three weeks. I can finally close a chapter. I don't know, that's what people say. It doesn't feel real to me. I'm not sure when it will."

"I'm sorry you don't have any of us there. Do you want me to come?"

I sighed. "No, I'm okay. I mean, I say that right now. I'll probably lose my shit like I did tonight, and Kyle will have to let me cry it out on his shoulder again."

"Wait. What? He offered his dick and then you cried on his shoulder?"

I laughed. "Well, it wasn't really like that, but sort of?"

"You are a mess woman." She cackled.

"Yes, I know this."

We caught up on our week and the upcoming one seemed like a breeze with only taping Monday and Tuesday. I am due to work on Thursday to give Kyle the day off, and I fly to see Stephen Friday. Officially less than a week before my first conjugal visit. I couldn't wait to see what Charlotte, North Carolina had in store for me.

Chapter 23

STEPHEN

The flight was crowded but quick. I grabbed an Uber and headed to meet Pete at a coffee shop he had picked close to his office. I walked up, and he was sitting outside. It was a nice, sunny day.

He stood as I approached the teak table covered by an umbrella. Pete was in his late thirties, but this job has aged him. He was already balding, and he looked well into his forties. He dressed in simple suits and would just meld right into a crowd. He was probably one of the most relatable guys in the department, though, and this was why I was there. We have made a connection over the years outside work. We had gotten to know each other on a personal level, and he was front and center when Lauren was kidnapped. His department headed a massive search and stood up for my character, coming to my rescue when the local authorities arrested me.

He was a good dude.

"Hey, Stephen." Reaching out his hand with a firm shake. "How was your flight?"

"It was all right. I haven't flown commercial in a minute. Allen is in Chicago and has our ride," I said.

"Your way definitely takes out the sting of work travel," he said with a laugh. "Do you want anything?" He pointed inside.

"No, I'm okay actually, thanks."

He took a deep breath and pushed a file folder to me. I seriously wanted to vomit but chose to look at him and run my hand through my hair instead as I slid it in front of me.

Looking at him, I said, shaking my head, "I swear this shit is going to kill me, Pete. I want this to end, man. I want my life back."

I took a deep breath.

He looks at me. "I can't imagine."

He put a hand on the file and looked at me.

"I just need to tell you, this is going to change everything, and I am going to be in deep shit telling you what is in this. Like, I can lose my job, Stephen. It's important you know, though."

I looked at him and swallowed hard, then shook my head.

"Okay, I don't want to put your job on the line, looking around."

I looked down at the folder and he opened it. There sat a large picture of a man with Valton Kastrati written on it, and a red *wanted*, printed across his ominous mug shot.

"What am I looking at?" I asked.

Quietly, he said, "He's an Albanian drug lord we have been after for years. He went underground about ten years ago. We seem to have been dealing with his minions though, on and off, over the years, coming in and out of our radar. They have expanded their operations over the years from drugs to weapons and their latest, sex trafficking. He manages to keep things on the smaller scale, so it doesn't draw too much attention like some of the big guns, but over the last couple of years, he has gotten a bit ballsy, and we decided to really go after him."

"I have a feeling I know where this is going."

He flipped to the next picture. The blonde who was sitting outside Lauren's parent's house and even eerier, with Lauren. This time, a better picture. He tapped on his face.

"Alban Kastrati, Valton's brother."

I couldn't swallow and almost couldn't breathe.

"What the fuck are you telling me, Pete? Lauren was working with these guys?"

I put my head in my hands and closed my eyes. Was everything I knew to be true, a fucking lie?

I heard over the pounding of my loudly beating heart, "Stephen? Hey."

I looked up, and Pete was looking at me. "I know this is a lot, man."

"I think we should be doing this over fucking drinks. I'm about to have a goddamn stroke," I said, leaning back in the chair, running my hands through my hair.

"Yeah, that would have been better, I suppose."

He smirked then looked around. "There's a bar in that plaza right there. It's quiet. I know the owners. It's cool. Let's go there, and I'll call my office and let them know I'm not coming back." He places a hand on my shoulder. "You okay?"

"No, I'm not," I said, staring at the file of photos of the people my fiancé may have been involved with. "Definitely, not okay."

He stepped away to call his office, then headed back. "All right, let's go."

We drove over to the plaza and found a dark, secluded booth in the bar, away from the eyes and ears of others. I ordered a double whiskey on the rocks, and he ordered a beer. Once we got our drinks and I slammed half mine, we went back to business.

He proceeded, "Okay, so you remember the government job you were hired for?"

"Yes, of course," I said. "We had two main projects; we established a new Cybersecurity Fusion Center, and we were the lead on the investment of the quantum-resistant cryptographic methods."

"Yeah, all that Chinese. Way above my pay grade." He waved his hands in the air. "Completely not my department."

"Basically, we updated the government's cybersecurity measures so they can keep from getting hacked into and also hack into other systems that are attacking us. Just an upgrade from the archaic bullshit that was in place."

"Well, supposedly, shortly after you started your project, a shipment got through, and we weren't able to track it or some bullshit. That was my department," he said.

"Yeah, we really didn't have things set up and people trained in place yet to monitor correctly. These guys aren't just jumping in ships now and crossing borders. They are hacking into our security systems and fucking up our security measures. They aren't idiots," I said.

He sat back and took a sip from his beer, traced his hand over his mouth, and asked, "Stephen, how long ago did you meet Lauren?"

I swallowed...hard.

My mind wandered back to that hotel bar, funky, gray linen, black, and dark. Allen and I had just started our government job. It was the first time our company had landed a project this massive and important. We were over our heads, but we brought on the people to make it work. I was winding down from a long day behind computer screens and crunching codes and numbers. My head was complete mush. An arm appeared on the bar next to me, and a Cartier watch adorned it. Perfectly manicured nails and the scent of orange, jasmine, and cedarwood filled the space around us. She was an absolutely stunning blonde with hair trailing down her shoulders. The bartender came over and asked what she wanted. I was mesmerized by her every movement, and in the most beautiful accent of maybe Lithuanian or such, she said, "I would like a glass of Cabernet, please." Then she looked in my direction and smiled. Her eyes, so blue, teeth perfect, mouth fucking perfection. I almost felt like I was dreaming, she was so perfect. Then she said, "Hi, are you just going to stare at me?" And gave a slight laugh.

The rest of that night, we talked about everything. I found out she was a software developer, and we had the world of computers in common. She was from the Czech Republic, and I thought I fell in love immediately. She was fantastic. She was staying in the same hotel. I asked her out for dinner the next night, and then I took her to my room afterward. We barely made it inside before she was ripping my clothes off, and she had my dick in her mouth. Those succulent lips and her hot tongue, her blonde hair wrapped around my fingers. The morning came, and she was still there. Three years later, we were planning a wedding. Just two months before the wedding, we were planning to run a marathon together, but she went for a run without me and was gone.

I drank my whiskey until it was only the sound of ice circling the empty glass and placed it down,

"I met her five years ago. In DC, when I started the government project." I sighed.

"I don't know. I am not going to say for certain, but her being seen with Alban is definitely alarming. There is also this," he said.

"Jesus. What now? I don't think I can take any more," I said. "I'm scared to ask you anything else without another drink."

I closed the file and waved our server over.

"Another?" she leaned in as she walked by.

"Just a single this time, and another beer, please," I said as she walked away.

Once she was gone, he continued, "There was a ship that was actually stopped. The security measures your company put in place, directly, indirectly, however it works, supposedly was a large reason why we were able to stop it from entering our port. Stephen, it was full of girls. Fucking girls," he said with serious eyes looking at me and pointing hard at the table.

"Pete, that was the week Lauren was kidnapped," I said as my heart started beating hard.

"Yeah, I know," he said.

"Was this my fucking fault? Did they take her because of me?"

I felt panic take over because he was confirming what I had been speculating all along.

"I don't think so." He leaned in just as she brought our drinks and set them on the table.

"Thank you," I said to her, then took a large swig.

"When I opened your email and realized who was sitting in front of Lauren's house, it was like seeing a ghost. We had lost these guys. Months before Lauren went missing, they went missing too. We figured they may have either gone back to Albania and just stayed on their side or had been killed. They were too active here and too visible to have just vanished."

He opened the file and went back to the third picture. Pointing to what looked like the other guy we had in the car with Alban. "This is Fatmir Murati. He is what we think, Alban's right-hand man, security, not a hundred percent really, but he never goes anywhere without him."

At that point, I was just massaging my forehead relentlessly. I couldn't believe this was my fucking life. Drug lords, sex traffickers, gun smugglers, Albanian what? Hitmen? What the fuck were these guys? I was a cybersecurity fucking salesman who enjoyed working out, drinking expensive whiskey, and I just wanted to have the semblance of a normal relationship with my smoking hot, amazing chef. Was this too much to ask for? I felt like I would be killed for knowing all this information. I then threw back the rest of my drink.

"Can you just tell me what I need to do, man? Like, am I in danger? Lauren's family? Do you think she is alive? Dammit."

He took a deep breath, then a swig of his beer, and said, "Well, I am seriously only speculating, Stephen. This is seriously only my thoughts, well, a couple of the other guys think so too, but we haven't discussed this case in over five months now, sorry."

He winced.

"It's okay. We have all been trying to move on, I guess."

"I really didn't know how much Lauren could have been involved until I saw her in those pictures with Alban. I had no confirmation until that very second. We hit dead ends everywhere. All we had was coincidence after coincidence with your government job timing when you met, both in the same sort of field…"

I interjected, putting a hand up. "Not really, she just did freelance software development. It's kind of nowhere on the same level, not to boast, but…"

"Okay, we are going to say that is what her profession was for the time being."

Oh fucking come on.

More lies. My hand wrapped across my forehead, and my eyes closed. I kind of wanted them to close forever.

"Listen, this could be good. She could be out there, alive. She could be innocent in all this shit. We don't know. We now know these guys are not gone. Now that I have kicked the hornet's nest, I will open this back up, get some guys looking at Alban and Fatmir, and see where they lead us, maybe to her. Maybe we can catch Valton and shut this shit down once and for all as well. You not giving up and having an investigator still looking for her was great, man."

He placed a hand on my forearm as I stared at my glass of ice. "There's one thing, Stephen."

I look up at him, completely drained. "For fuck's sake, what? Like, do you have a piece on you? You can just shoot me in the goddamn head if you are going to give me any more shit news."

He laughed. "No man. I need you to keep all this between me and you. All this information." He moved his hand over the file between me and him. "You don't know any of this."

"What do I tell Mark, my investigator, I found then?" I asked.

"Just have him keep doing his job, following like he is. We will be there too, from a distance. We got it. Just tell him we came up dry as well." he said. "I'll stay in touch."

I took a large breath. "I am worn out. Do I need to worry about my safety, Pete?"

"Nah, I think they would have gotten ya back then if that was the case."

He laughs.

I raised my brow. "Gee. Thanks."

"No problem." He got serious. "Hey, we are going to try to end this nightmare for you this time around, Stephen, okay? You are a good dude. You deserve to move on. I consider you a friend, and I really mean that."

"Thanks, Pete. Thanks for being real with me and telling me the truth with all this shit."

I pointed to the file.

"Well, like I said, we didn't have confirmation until you handed it to us," he said. "Where are you staying? You need a ride?"

He started to slide from the booth and stood.

"Oh, no. I'm flying right back on the 5:10 to Charlotte," I said.

"Damn, you want a ride to the airport?" he asked.

I looked around at the dark, secluded bar with the four sad drinking patrons as it was only noon on a Monday.

"Yeah, can you drop me? I think I would rather drown myself with alcohol and free food in the sky lounge."

I sat at a small table overlooking the tarmac, examining my life. How the hell did I get there? I was just a computer geek. Anxiety welled up in my chest, and I took a sip of my amber liquid, trying to push it down, knowing that it was not the cure, but it was all I had right then. I stared at my phone in my hand. My finger floated over my contacts. I wanted to reach out to her. I wanted to tell her everything, but this would surely freak her the fuck out. She would run… shit, she would be peeling out on that black bike so fast sparks would be trailing behind her this time. I hovered over Allen's icon, he was my best friend. He knew everything about this case, but Pete said I needed to keep this between me and him.

Fuck.

I was going to have a mental breakdown.

I searched for her circle. I recently added her picture. It was one I captured over our weekend in San Francisco when we were on the sailboat. She was looking out over the water. The sun was shining, a golden glow was on her face, her hair was blowing back, and her sunglasses reflected the beautiful day.

Fuck, I could stare at that picture forever.

Me: Hey sexy girl.

I waited. Staring, hoping for dots, but nothing. I looked out and watched planes being loaded with luggage and all the inner workings of the aviation world, then looked down again. No response. She was busy taping, I was sure.

Allen knew I was going there. Sure enough, I could be vague. He was going to ask questions at some point.

Me: I'm heading back to Charlotte.

Allen: Me too in about 30. How did it go? What did Pete have for you?

Me: Not too much. Just opened up a ton of old wounds mostly.

Allen: I'm sorry man

Me: Yeah, I'll be alright. See ya at home.

Allen: Cassie comes soon, right?

Me: Friday. Thank god.

Allen: Let us know if you want to get together.

Me: Nope. I'm holding her ass hostage.

Allen: I hear ya.

I felt a little bit of sanity coming back into my body, just getting to hear from a friend, then an incoming text buzzed in my hand, drawing me away from sipping my drink and staring out the window. My heart instantly felt full again.

Cassie: Hey there. I love seeing that after stirring a pot of the same pho broth and smiling obsessively like a trained monkey for 45 minutes.

Me: I am heading back from DC in an hour. Killing time.

Cassie: I'm in my dressing room. Wanna talk dirty?

I laughed and kind of felt like I could get hard with the visual.

Me: I'm in the sky lounge, but after the day I had, screw it. Let 'em watch.

Cassie: Oh no. Do you want me to call? Want to talk about it?

I wished I could. God, I wished I could tell her everything.

Me: No, I want to talk about you, us. I can't wait for this weekend.

Cassie: Me either. 4 days.

Cassie: I have to go get Cora. Want me to call from the car for a few? Talk about your day?

Me: No, I'm okay.

She sent me a heart emoji, and that little freaking heart melted me. Little shit right now meant everything. I was a freaking mess.

I sent her one back.

I drove up to my dimly lit glass house. I built this house with the plans Lauren and I had custom-made. We had plans for kids to fill these rooms, at least one of them. Family to come and stay long weekends, go on boat rides, have cookouts, do family shit. I walked in, turned off the alarm, and looked out towards the black, dark water. I stood in my new glass house I built out of lies and deception, I was completely shattered.

Chapter 24

CASSIE

Me: On my way to you. Um…first class?

The dots dance.

Stephen: I would have picked you up in the jet, but that was a bit overkill.

Me: Yeah, too much.

Stephen: Enjoy your celebrity status.

I shook my head and smiled. That was comical, considering my segments officially started dropping this week, and so far, not one person had noticed me. No paparazzi lining my apartment complex parking lot as I got into my Uber that morning, clamoring for my autograph. Still just Cassandra Buckley, Chef, Owner-Operator of Sagi-Shi, who just showed people how to cook Asian dishes on TV. Pretty basic shit.

My flight was seamless, extremely comfortable, and champagne-filled. I was able to get work done, which was nice. I had never had work to do on my flights, so that was a change. I was officially in the cookbook business. Jesus, they didn't mess around. I thought they were going to give this to me slowly. I was told to take my time, and this would be spread out over eighteen months, but there I was with some time, so I figured I could work on one recipe. They want to do a back-to-*basics* approach, which I thought was kind of boring. I thought we should do something more like, turn up the heat, Motherfuckers. That would be a best-seller for sure. I wasn't in the marketing department, so there I was, coming up with my first basic pho broth and curry recipes. Any moron could look this shit up on Pinterest. I personally thought it was dumb.

Me: Landed

Stephen: I'm here

I rounded the corner to find he didn't just pull up to the curb; he came in, and I was enveloped by the biggest hug from his tall, muscular frame.

What was that?

Bergamot and coriander? Jesus, Mary, and Joseph. I was intoxicated by this man. He took my face into his hands and kissed me. I barely made eye contact with him before all this happened, and his tongue swept into my mouth. Thank god I jumped into the bathroom and brushed my teeth before we landed.

He pulled me away to look at him, still holding my face between his hands, his smile, so genuine and eyes, almost tear-filled.

"Hey, you," I said lowly.

He said in his deep voice, "Hey you."

He smiled and took my hand with one and the handle of my rolling carry on with the other.

We made our way through the maze of airport construction to the parking garage. He never let go of my hand, his, strong, as it wrapped around mine.

"This is a mess. You could have just picked me up at the curb," I said, trying to keep up with his long strides.

He looked at me, shocked, "My mom raised me better than that, Cassie."

My dad would be really proud of this chivalrous moment. He took his fob out of his pocket unlocking his car, lighting up, what appeared to be an extremely new all-matte, blacked-out Range Rover Defender.

"What? No Mini?" I asked, laughing into my hand.

He laughed as he opened the back to lift my suitcase in.

"As much as I was growing accustomed to claustrophobia on my trip in San Francisco, I like something a little roomier for my wing-span."

He walked around and opened the passenger side door for me, and I slid into what felt like a black leather-encased NASA control room. Looking up to an all-glass roof, buttons, and gadgets along the dash, the smell of new leather, this is so…him. I reached over and tried to open his door for him, but he beat me to it as he got in and started it up. It was barely a sound, considering the beast must have some major power. He reached over and kissed me with a hand behind my ear and along my jaw.

"Dammit, I've missed you, baby."

Looking into his eyes, I said, "I've missed you too."

The drive was just under an hour, and he listened to my banter about the studio world, how I constantly messed up, made people laugh, juggling home life, the restaurant, and he barely chimed in about his. He just rubbed my thigh obsessively. Never breaking contact. Looking over and smiling at me every chance he could take his eyes off the road.

"Oh my god, I haven't shut up. I'm so sorry," I said.

"Please don't apologize. I could listen to you all day. I needed this. I love hearing you talk about anything other than my mundane world. I love it, please don't stop."

"Are you okay? You seemed stressed this last week, and I wish you would talk to me," I said, worried.

He took a deep breath, which increased that feeling.

"No, just work shit, but you being here is exactly what I need, this is perfect timing. I'm so happy right now."

He smiled, big.

We pulled up to a large, dark, ornate wooden gate, and he punched in a code, opening up to what I would consider a field with a long driveway running through it. Sitting at the end, in the distance, was his house, if that was what we were calling it. It must span a football field.

"Stephen, is this your house?" I asked in shock.

"Yep, it's a bit much, I know. I've been told by everyone."

He let out a laugh.

It had a gorgeous, dark, almost black framework, tall glass windows everywhere, white gravel running between the landscaping of beautifully swaying willow trees and well-manicured shrubs. Meanwhile, it all sat on Lake Norman with its absolutely stunning backdrop.

I started to get out of the car, looking at him.

"I think it's kind of dinky, personally. I think you could do better," I said with a screwed-up face, and closed the door behind me.

After he disarmed his mini-Pentagon, we went in, and he gave me a general tour. I claimed my legs were getting tired and complained that I was now exceeding all my steps for the day, according to my Garmin watch, laughing.

"You are the biggest smart ass," he said as he hit a button on a remote that started opening up the entire accordion wall of windows of the back of the house that led to the expansive patio overlooking the breathtaking lake.

"Shut up," I said excitedly, looking at him. "Now, that's pretty freaking cool."

"Come on. Let's get our suits on and go enjoy this day, just me and you. I have been dreaming of this moment since I asked you to come here on your terrace that night and prayed that there would be perfect weather, and here we are."

He smiled. He hit another button on the wall, and music started playing throughout the house and on the patio. Chris Stapleton. Perfect.

He went to get my bag from the front of the house while I stood there wondering if this was real life. Like, who lives like this...alone?

He approached, rolling my bag, lightly slapping me on the ass. "Come on, sexy girl."

His bedroom.

It had large, stormy-gray walls and crisp white bedding. It was manly, organized, beautiful, and totally Stephen Harlow.

He rolled my suitcase into the massive closet, which was basically another room, and placed it on a low shelf.

"Here you go. Make yourself at home."

He turned to go into a drawer to pull out a pair of swim trunks.

When he turned, I was in my bag already with my bikini in hand and pulling off my shirt. I didn't stand a chance. I couldn't believe it took him that long, as I smiled, and he quickly made his way over to me, hands under my jaw, tongue deep in my mouth, breath hot. He pulled my head back and kissed and licked down my neck, down to my collarbone and bit my shoulder gently.

"I've missed your skin, every damn thing about you."

He picked me up, and I wrapped my legs around his waist. I laughed as I kissed him, walking me towards the bed and placing me down. My arms were wide, completely open to him. He stood before me, pulling his shirt over his head. Damn. Those abs and that chest. He unzipped his jeans and pushed them down, along with his boxer briefs.

I could feel him backing out of his shoes, never breaking eye contact with me, smiling and biting his bottom lip.

Sexy as hell.

He stood, revealing his cock, hard, thick, reaching up towards his stomach, fucking glorious. Then he reached down and under my chest, unsnapping my bra, letting out an audible breath as they tumbled from their lace housing.

"Damn, baby. You are so gorgeous."

Stephen kissed me and made his way down, kissing my nipples, teasing them with his teeth, making me moan with anticipation and excitement.

He unbuttoned my little white jeans and slid them from my body, peeling my panties down and spreading my legs. While running his fingers through my slick folds, whispering in his low, deep voice.

"If I put my dick in here, it's over."

So, he thumbed my clit, perfectly. He lay next to me, my eyes closed as he kissed my body, my neck, my lips, and watched my body move with his every touch, my every breath until I climaxed so quick underneath his fingers, so long, thick, so fucking amazing.

His dick, so hard, slick at my opening. It was absolutely

everything at that moment, and I wrapped my arms around his muscular body. I ran my hands to the nape of his neck and looked into his eyes as he slid slowly into me, causing me to arch my back.

"Fuck, yes," I cried out in pleasure.

"Are you okay?" He checked in.

"Yes, it feels fucking amazing," I said, breathless.

He started to pump his cock deeper into me, but still slow, putting his head next to mine, his breathing, small moans, and his voice gravelly.

"Damn, this feels amazing."

Our connection deepened every time. His dick was as if it was made for my body, fitting perfectly. It swelled and filled me. Then he tensed and grabbed my ass, getting more aggressive in his movements, losing control, sending himself deeper and harder inside of me, filling me with hot cum until he was nothing but limp muscle.

He kissed my ear. "I..."

He stopped himself.

I knew what he was going to say. I felt his heart race against my body.

I feel it too baby. I feel it too.

I ran my hands through his hair.

"Let's go have fun," I whispered and kissed his temple.

The day was nothing short of perfect. Swimming off the dock, laying in the warm sun, listening to music, laughing, talking about stories we lost in the years between, and then, together, we cooked a magnificent dinner in his unbelievable kitchen. He was a great prep cook, and it was so nice to have him by my side.

"Look at you finding all these ingredients I sent you on a scavenger hunt for," I said as I was dicing the green onions and bok choy with precision.

He grimaced, laughing. "Well, I cheated and sent my housekeeper, Gloria. She didn't know what that bok choy was though." He pointed with his unpeeled shrimp. "Or fish sauce."

We ate Pad Thai on the terrace with a perfectly chilled Sauvignon Blanc and watched the sunset change from light hues to bright florescent reds and oranges. I couldn't have asked for a better day.

"I think I could live here," I said casually, just completely in the moment, looking at the sheer beauty of the view.

He looked at me over the table while fingering the top of my hand. "You should."

My heart pounded, and I got flustered. "I mean, what a fantasy, right?"

I took a large sip of my wine out of nervousness.

Completely changing the subject, I asked quickly, "So, what is on the agenda for tomorrow?"

He shook his head. "You think you can throw shiny balls with me?"

Rubbing circles over my hand, and looking back out at the lake with a smile, he sipped his wine.

"I have a plan for tomorrow, but first, I want to shower with you and do all sorts of amazing things that last way longer than earlier."

I lean into him. "So far, I like your plan. I need a shower, I feel...dirty," I said seductively, biting my lip.

"Damn woman." He rolled his eyes and reached down, adjusting his crotch, saying, "You make me crazy."

He stood, taking his glass to make our way inside.

We did exactly that all night. We showered, and he pressed his hard body up against me, licking and kissing my wet skin, my pussy, until I came. I took his hard cock deep in my mouth until he made me stop in fear of coming. We washed each other. He washed my long hair. I thought I memorized every muscle on his brilliantly chiseled body as I ran my hands over them.

We eventually made it to the bedroom, where we continued. Our bodies connected for what seemed like hours. The moonlight shone bright through the room, shedding light on him, so beautiful to watch, pleasing me, over and over again. When he finally let himself go, it was a release of more than just a sexual one. It felt emotional, deep. I could feel it run through his entire body. I felt him let go of emotional pain at that moment.

He woke me up with coffee and kisses, "Good morning, baby."

I stretched, and once I realized where I was, I couldn't believe I got to see his sweet face smiling at me.

"We have a big day, and I can't let you sleep it away, unfortunately," he said.

I slowly sat up and leaned against the headboard, taking the coffee from him. With the first sip, realizing he got me. The coffee was the color of my skin, and I smiled.

"Where are we going?"

"I can't disclose that information, Ms. Buckley, but you have approximately," looking at his watch, then back at me with those gray and green eyes, "forty-five minutes until we leave. I have breakfast almost ready, so all you have to do is shower, and get dressed. Let's see," he looks up, "Shorts and t-shirt, sneakers attire," he says then kissed me on the lips, smiled, and left the room.

Damn. I loved this man.

I entered the kitchen and twirled around in my little white shorts that showed off my long tan legs. I knew legs were his weakness. He had disclosed this information on numerous occasions. I wore a light blue t-shirt and white sneakers. My hair was pulled back in a ponytail.

"Is this proper attire for our date, Mr. Harlow?"

He put the knife down from cutting up the fruit to make his way over and picked me up under my ass, holding his wrists, which put my face level to his.

"You are adorable, and perfectly proper."

He kissed me. His mouth tasted of melon and strawberries.

After he put me down, he said, "I made you a sourdough sandwich with ham, egg, and cheese. There's some fruit too."

He poured a small glass of orange juice and then sat at the bar counter with me.

We ate and tidied the kitchen.

"Where are we going?" I asked as he punched in the code and secured the house.

We made our way into the garage to get into the car.

"You seem to love the whole surprise thing, so I thought I would do the same," he said, opening the car door for me.

I shook my head, climbing in. During our drive, we had hilarious conversations about his college years, shit he and Allen used to do, and we reminisced about our college holiday breaks together. We also talked about things we missed out on.

"You really wanted kids, huh?"

He shook his head. "Yeah, I did. We were actually trying, even before the wedding. I am not getting younger, as you can see." He looked over at me, rolling his eyes. "I love my brother's kids, but I wanted more than just to be the cool ass uncle. I really wanted a family of my own, so we thought maybe we could at least get a head start. We weren't having any luck. She went and got checked out, then I did. Came to find out, I didn't have such strong swimmers." He shrugged his shoulders as he kept his eyes on the road. "She was gone before we could work on the problem and start the IVF process."

I squeezed his hand. "I'm so sorry."

I looked at his side profile.

Just fuck.

The guy could not just get a damn break.

"I wish I could make you a baby, but it would not be a good one. I am too old. My eggs are officially rotten."

I laughed, trying to lighten the mood.

He laughed, squeezing my hand. "Once she was gone, I realized it was a lost cause. I will be the cool uncle, or I am going to find someone who has kids, and I'll be a stepdad and a damn good one." He smiled. "Well, we are here."

I wasn't even paying attention to the fact that we had pulled onto the road leading to Carowinds, a huge amusement park.

"No way," I yelled.

"You said on the phone the other night you were so pissed and stressed that you wanted to scream. Well, I sure the hell need to as well, so ta-da…let's go scream our faces off," he said, pulling up to the parking lot attendant and flashing a QR code on his phone.

Once he put the car in park, I turned in my seat to look at him.

"What?" he said. "Is something wrong? Shit. You hate rides."

I shook my head. "No, not one damn thing. You are wonderful." I smiled and leaned over the console, and kissed him. "You are perfect."

I then turned to hop out with more excitement than I probably should have.

We rode everything we could. The lines were long, but we didn't care because it gave us time to talk and fill in more gaps. We screamed, we laughed, we completely let loose. We ate complete garbage, and it was fantastic. We *procrastinated* all day to wait in line for the Fury 325, the tallest and fastest in the park, and the line matched the hype.

"All right, last one," he said as we got comfortable with the rest of the other sweaty, thrill-seeking riders. We were chatting, licking away relatively fast at our soft-serve ice cream cones before they melted, when I heard, "Excuse me, are you a chef on The Foodie Channel on TV?"

I turned to see a woman looking at me, questioning, wide-eyed, at…well, me.

"Oh, well, yes, I am," I said, catching a melting drip with my tongue.

"I'm sorry to bother you. I'm actually from Charleston, and I knew the correlation. I saw you on TV yesterday, and then I noticed you. I thought this was so cool not to ask. I don't want to bother you."

"Aww, no worries. What episode did you watch? Did I do okay?"

I winced, waiting for her reply.

She laughed. "It was basic Pho recipes. It was really good. I didn't think it was that easy to make. We always go out for it. I'm totally going to try it at home. I DVR'd it so I can watch it again. I think you did great."

We all moved forward in line. "Thank you so much. It's new, and I haven't even seen how it turned out yet. I'm glad you liked it. I have some really good stuff coming up. Totally make those recipes at home, and Asian is so easy once you have the ingredients. Also, there's a great Asian market in North Charleston."

I smiled.

"Good to know. Well, it was nice meeting you. Good luck," she said, turning and moving up with her family, with a slight giggle.

I turned to Stephen and smiled, shrugging my shoulders. He

leaned down and whispered into my ear, "I'm fucking a celebrity, that's so hot."

I laughed, jamming the rest of the cone into my mouth like a chipmunk storing nuts for the winter.

The evening was wonderfully simple, just bringing takeout salads home, sitting on the dock watching the sunset, wrapped up together, and just enjoying our last night. He made love to me that night, it was very clear. There was nothing rushed, hard, or fast-paced, just soft and loving. He was trying to melt me with every last movement, and it was working.

Morning was spent naked intertwined mostly in silence, listening to his heartbeat. I didn't want it to end. He finally got up and made breakfast and coffee while I showered. When I came into the kitchen, he was standing, the wall of windows wide open, our breakfast set up on the patio, music playing. He was standing, just gazing out towards the lake in front of the table, coffee mug in hand. I walked up behind him and wrapped my arms around his chest and rested my face against his back. His free hand reached around to my back.

"I don't want you to go, Cass," he said.

I swallowed hard, and tears filled my eyes.

"I know, I don't either." I pushed to turn him and look up into his eyes. "Sooner than a month?"

He nodded his head and kissed the top of my head, keeping his lips there, breathing me in.

"Let's eat."

I stared out the window and watched the clouds go by feeling my heart so full and broken at the same time. I was heading back to San Francisco to end my marriage with Jack, to become this new celebrity chick, and it seemed I might have finally, after all these years, started something real with Stephen.

Chapter 25

CASSIE

X

"Are you sure you don't want me to come? Last chance, Cassie. The flights will be so astronomical, Avery will say no if I wait any longer," Britt said.

Pushing the heavy metal back door open to the restaurant, phone clumsily pressed between my face and shoulder, I said, "I'll be fine. I fit in these big girl panties now. Plus, I'm so busy, there's no time for me to spend with you anyhow."

I muffled the phone with my hand. "Hey, Kyle," I called out to him into the abyss of the restaurant as I walked into my office.

"Okay, fine. I tried. Don't get all shitty with me when you are having a breakdown on Thursday," she said.

"I would rather you come when I am done with all this taping, and we can actually have some fun. I'm so swamped right now. Maybe you, Avery, and Stephen can come out?" I said, rifling through the huge mound of mail on my desk.

"That would be fun. All right, I got to go. Love you," she said, rushing off the phone.

"Love you more," I said, hanging up.

I found my very unorganized to-do list had way too many things that were not crossed off. One by one, I needed to get through it. I had until four to tackle the mountain before getting Cora from Jack's and spending what needed to resemble some sort of quality time with her. I made my way into the kitchen to catch up with Kyle.

When I approached him, he was busy discussing the mise en place for all the sauces and vegetable prep for the day with our prep cooks and had just started breaking the fish down for service.

"Good morning, Chef," he said, looking up at me from under the brim of his hat.

"Good morning. How is everything going?" I asked.

"Everything is good. How are you?" he asked, leaning down and sliding his knife with precision down the entire length of the fish. I noticed the side of his head was no longer shaved clean to the scalp, fresh blonde hair filling in.

"Hanging in there," I said with a smile. "I'm going to tackle my list in the office. Let me know if there is anything I need to do for you on your end, okay?"

He giggled. "Oh, I have things you can do." He was still staring at the fish.

I laughed, shaking my head. "You are so funny, Kyle."

I made my way to the office. Ever since he came out to me with his crush, it's been non-stop sexual innuendos to keep it a joke.

I managed to do it all, the entire list, and organize my desk with plenty of time to spare.

Kyle walked into the office with a look of shock on his face when he saw the desk.

"Did you just toss it all and start over? That's what I have been contemplating for weeks."

"I'm the master when I set my mind to something," I said.

He leaned against the doorframe and looked at me with conflict.

"Oh god, What? Don't do it. Don't leave me. I'll fucking cry again, Kyle, I'll do it. I have my divorce this week, I can't..."

He put his hand up, laughing, "Cassie, no, I'm not leaving."

"What? What is it then?" I asked.

"I just wanted to tell you I have been on a couple of dates with someone," he said, shrugging.

"Oh, for fuck's sake." I leaned back in my chair and breathed a huge sigh of relief. "Really? Who?" I asked.

He smiled. "A girl I met out the night of our little thing. I went and had a beer to chill and... well, she's a chef over at Yellow Jackets."

"That's Noah Foster's place. I'm using studio space with him, nice dude," I said.

He nods. "Oh cool. Anyhow, I just wanted you to know, because, we are friends, and friends share this kind of shit."

He moved his hand back and forth between us.

I smiled and said softly, "Yeah, friends. Thanks, Kyle."

Just as he turned to leave, I asked, "Hey. What's her name?"

"Grace," he said with a sweet smile. "Her name is Grace."

I put my hand to my chest. "I hope she is nothing but that for you, Kyle, I really do."

He nodded, smiled, and headed back into the kitchen.

I pulled up to my once upon a life house. It still looked the same, except I was no longer in it. I made my way up the stairs, and this climb hadn't gotten easier since the night it all fell apart. I wished my kid would just come out to the damn car. I once walked in, now I rang the doorbell and waited.

Please, Cora, open the damn door.

Nope, it was Jack. Jeans, white T-shirt, perfectly fitting his now even better-looking frame. Was he in the gym every day now?

Jesus.

The divorce body was completely real. He ran his hand through his perfectly beautiful black hair.

"Hey, Cass, she's almost ready. Come in," he said, opening the door.

Damn you, Cora.

I smiled and casually stepped into my old life, realizing he hadn't changed a thing.

"So, how are things at the firm?" I asked, keys in hand, arms crossed.

He loved talking about work. Always a safe subject with Jack.

"It's great. We are bringing on a new partner. It's been a pretty big deal, but we have grown so much, we really need to."

Then a pause.

"So, you? Are you handling everything okay with all you have going on? I watched one of your shows the other night. It was so weird to see you on my TV."

He laughed.

"Yeah, it's going okay. I'm just struggling with feeling a little disconnected with her."

I pointed upstairs.

"Yeah, she's become so…teen and only wants to hang out with her friends lately. I think it's kind of normal, I don't know."

He shrugged.

"So? Thursday. It's *the* day."

He took a big breath, crossing his arms and looked down at his feet. "I guess so."

"What does that mean, Jack? I guess so?" I asked sternly, trying to get him to look up at me.

"I just still feel so much guilt, Cass. I'm so sorry," he said.

My heart was beating hard, thinking he had second thoughts. "Oh, yeah. Well, we already hashed this out."

I yelled upstairs.

"Cora. Come on baby."

I was feeling my blood pressure rising. The conversation pulled up the anger every time. I felt the need to get out of this house.

"I'm coming, Mom," she yelled back.

"Cass." He laid his hand on my shoulder. "You know I will always love you. You know this, right? I just don't think I will have a chance to tell you this before Thursday, and I never wanted to hurt you, never."

His eyes showed what he said was genuine, sincere, sad.

My heart was pounding.

"Jack, I know. We have had this conversation a hundred times. I will always love you too. It doesn't change the fact that you hurt me. You really fucking hurt me."

I said it low, in case Cora had decided to finally make her way down.

"It's going to take time for my heart to heal from this. Just give me that…time."

"Are you seeing that guy?" he pointedly asked.

"I'm not talking about my personal life with you right now. I am just trying to get through day by day. And I don't want to know about you and Beth. Don't bring her around Cora yet either, okay?" I said, sternly.

Shaking his head, he said, "Yeah, I know, we discussed this already, Cass."

I caught the eye roll.

Finally, Cora bounded down the stairs with her bookbag busting at the seams and hands full of all her many electronics.

"Sorry, Mom. I'm ready. Bye, Daddy."

She reached up and kissed him on the cheek.

"Bye, baby, enjoy your time at Mom's. I'll see you Saturday night for the concert," he said.

With excitement, she said, "I can't wait. See you then."

Once the car doors closed, she went into the old Cora mode, and it was so welcoming. Long rants of everything under the sun, who is dating who, cheer gossip, putting on her latest music obsessions through the car's Bluetooth, and, "Oh my gosh, Mom, I can't believe Daddy got fifth row seats to Pink. It is going to be so much fun."

"So, who did you decide to bring?" I asked.

"Tiffany. She is about to lose her mind." she squealed. "Oh my gosh, I need to text her what I decided to wear."

She went into her phone, two-handed fast texting, not to be heard from the rest of the car ride, except for random giggles as her bare feet went to the dash, painted pink toes, wiggling with excitement.

I didn't interrupt. I just basked in the glory that she was happy.

I pulled up to our complex and we unloaded our groceries, along with her bag to drag upstairs. As we walked up, we were greeted by my new friend and doorman, John, opening the door for us.

"Good afternoon, Buckley ladies," he said.

"Hey, John," We almost said in unison, smiling back and balancing our things.

"Do you need some help with all that?" he asked.

I let out a small laugh. "No, John, we got it. Women are born with extra arms. She is in training, but she will get the hang of it."

"Well, okay. Have a great day."

We had a great night, making homemade pizzas, swimming in the pool on the terrace, snuggling on the sofa, and watching movies. Girl time at its best. She fell asleep, head nestled in my lap, running my fingers through her long brown hair as I sipped my wine in the glow of the TV.

I took a quick picture of this fleeting moment and felt moved to send it to Stephen.

Me: What about this Step-kid?

My heart immediately dropped. That was probably a wine, and an emotionally induced mistake.

Shit.

I wanted to take it back, and I shut my eyes, then felt the vibration in my hand.

Stephen: Exactly the step-kid I was shopping for on a website earlier today, but they were sold out. How much?

Me: Just your heart

Again...what the fuck are you doing Cassie?
I closed my eyes and took a large sip of my wine.

Stephen: I stroked that check when you were here last. Sold.

I sent him two heart emojis, and he sent me *Ditto*

Me: Goodnight

Stephen: Goodnight sexy girl

Walking out of the courthouse, I felt crushed, alone, heavy, and on the verge of hyperventilating. I was instructed to call Britt the second I came out.

Thank God, she picked up immediately.

"Britt?"

My lip quivered.

"I'm here. I'm here, Cass. You dick. I told you I should have been there. Where are you?" she asked.

Tears started flowing down my cheeks.

"Walking out of the courthouse. Fuck. You were right. Why didn't I make you come?"

"Okay, well, it's California. Take in the fact that it's a beautiful day, okay? Take a deep breath, babe," she said in a calm voice.

"Yeah, okay."

I sniffled, then did just that.

"Where are you now?" she said.

"I don't know, walking to my car across the street. Fuck, that sucked," I said, trying not to completely lose my shit. "He looked so sad. I was so sad…"

"I know, baby. How far is your car?" she asked.

I looked up. "I don't know, half a block, maybe? I'll put you on Bluetooth in my car and talk to you all the way home. You aren't working, are you?"

"No, I took the day off to talk to you," she said.

I started to cry again over that sweet comment. "Dammit, you are the fucking best."

"It's going to be okay, Cassie. Stop looking down. You almost ran into that girl," she said.

"What?" I said, confused, as I turned to see a girl veer from running into me.

"Look at your car, whore," she screamed.

There she was. Jumping up and down, standing next to my car on the sidewalk with arms wide, blonde hair blowing around her face. I ran. I hugged her, and I bawled like a baby.

I pulled her out from me in disbelief.

"How the fuck? Like how did you do this?"

Laughing and crying, she said, "You told me what time your hearing was, I searched for your car, and waited." She shrugged her shoulders and hugged me again. "I got in late last night, and it was all I could do not to come see you and spoon you all night."

I covered my mouth. "I don't know what to say. You are the absolute best friend ever. I love you so much."

Tears, nonstop, poured from my eyes.

"Do you have something to clean yourself up with? I made a reservation across the street for lunch, and we're drinking bitch," she said with a big smile. "And you can't look like this."

I did just that, and we walked across the street arm in arm to a swanky place she had gotten a table for on the rooftop. The elevator opened, and we made our way to a great corner table. We were chatting and as we walked up, just then, realizing, we were not alone. Standing there, smiling, was my mother, Bianca, Allen, and of all people, Stephen. I just stood completely frozen with my hand over my mouth until Britt said in my ear.

"You are never alone. You have friends."

And then, I lost my shit.

I hugged them all, starting with my mom. "I love you, baby," she said.

"Where's dad?" I asked, completely tear-filled and so happy.

"He had work, but I kind of wanted to do this alone," she said, smiling.

I motioned to Stephen, and she said. "I know. I approve, and he is wonderful, Cassie."

She winked.

Bianca and Allen both hugged me, and Bianca said, "we just wanted to be here for you. You are so strong," she said holding both of my hands, smiling.

Allen said with a brow raised and a smirk. "I was told I was going to eat at your restaurant. It was a total sham."

I laughed and hugged him.

"You two are so sweet. Thank you so much," I said.

I closed my eyes and put my head down, then turned and made eye contact with him. I couldn't hold my tears back as he came over and wrapped himself around me. Running his hands down my head.

"Shh, baby." He kissed my head, then he pulled me out. "It's over. You get a fresh start," he said, looking into my eyes.

"You did this? You flew them all here, didn't you?" I asked with jagged breaths.

He nodded.

I just stood there shaking my head. Then, I took his face in my hands and kissed him so passionately, not caring who was watching, not even my mother.

We had a long, wonderful, loud lunch. I just sat in awe at those who came to be here from the opposite side of the country to support me when I needed them most. Stephen's hand never left my thigh.

"So, I have a feeling there is a plan I don't know about," I said as we were wrapping things up, emptying my glass.

Britt laughed. "What gave you that idea?"

Mom said, "Me and Britt are going back to your place and hanging out with Cora tonight and tomorrow."

Stephen looked at me. "I booked us a place." He smiled, coy.

Bianca said, "We are staying at the same charming place we stayed last time we were here."

She smiled at Allen.

"I cannot believe y'all went through all this for me." I shook my head. "You are crazy."

Stephen rubbed my thigh and kissed the side of my head.

We dispersed, getting in Ubers, my car, and a rental car. Stephen and I met Britt and my mom at my place so I could pack a quick bag before Cora got home. She was going to be incredibly surprised. I left them to their girl's sleepover.

"Thank you two so much. I love you," I said, bag in hand.

"Have a great time. Now get out of here before Cora sees you," Britt said.

Mom stood on her toes, taking my face in her hands, and kissed my cheek.

"It's all going to be okay. I love you. We all love you."

Stephen said, "Thank you," as we closed the door.

He took me to The Four Seasons right in the heart of the city. Our suite had insane city views from every window, and the décor was a sleek white marble bathroom with gray linen, rich reds, and blacks, with crisp white bedding in the bedroom.

"You have done too much," I said, wrapping my arms around his neck.

Looking down at me, arms around my waist, he said, "Nah, this was fun to plan. You wouldn't want to stifle my joy, would you? I was going to whisk you off to Paris or somewhere romantic, but Britt stopped me. She said you hate it over the top. Is that really the truth?"

"Yes, to a certain extent. It makes me uncomfortable when people do too much. You are walking a very fine line here." I breathed in, kissing him. "How did all that happen with my mom? I'm curious?" I questioned him.

"Britt said she thought you would probably love your mom here, and I told her I could play the *friend* no problem. Well, once we were on the plane and your mom had two glasses of prosecco, she interrogated me. She knew all about us in high school and college. Supposedly, her and my mom have been waiting for this moment."

He laughed.

"What?" I said wide-eyed.

"Yep," he replied with raised brows. "She knew when you came to town it was only a matter of time, and why would a friend be going to such great lengths to make me this happy if we weren't sleeping together?"

"She didn't say that?" I said, shocked, putting my hand to my forehead.

"That prosecco is truth serum for Anne Patterson," he said. "I was trapped on my plane with her for hours. I came clean. Sorry."

He shrugged.

I laughed. "It's okay. She obviously approves, she said so."

I shook my head.

"Now, about that sleeping together part. I kind of want to make sure we aren't just friends," he said, kissing me. "I want to make sure those lines are very," he kissed me, "very clear."

He pressed his mouth hard onto mine, making my pussy throb with need.

His mouth, warm, kissed down my neck, making me breathless.

"I'm definitely not feeling the friend zone."

I slid my hand down to feel his dick, hard beneath his jeans. Rubbing its long length, up and down through the fabric.

He breathed in my ear, "Look what you do to me."

I unbuttoned and unzipped his jeans, sliding my hand down,

his dick breaching his underwear, feeling the head, slick with pre-cum.

"We need to get these off."

Then we went into a frenzy of clothes removal.

There we stood, in front of a corner wall of windows overlooking the city, exposed, vulnerable, and it felt good. He took my breasts in his hands and began kissing and teasing them, my hands running down his back and ass. He pushed the round coffee table to the side with his foot and turned me to face the couch, guiding me to kneel. I held onto the back of the couch, pillows piled into my breasts, the view of the city displayed before me. He ran his fingers over the muscles of my back, then down my spine, sending chills over my whole body. I looked back at him as he was looking down at my ass, rubbing his hand over it, stroking his hand up and down his length with the other. He looked at me with hooded eyes, shaking his head slowly.

"Jesus, you are so beautiful. This entire view is outstanding."

He splayed his hand to encompass the window and my body as one.

I licked my lips and gave him a smile as he reached forward and kissed my back between my shoulder blades and leaned one knee on the couch, then ran the head of his hard cock through my wet pussy.

"Damn, you are so wet. Have you been thinking about this?"

I moaned. "Ever since you had your hand on my thigh at lunch, yeah."

He slid it inside of me, slowly, deep.

"Fuck, Stephen."

He felt bigger, thicker than the last time.

He whispered in my ear, "Are you okay?" as he backed off a little.

"Yeah, I just felt like a virgin for a second," I said with a small, breathy giggle.

"You are so tight."

He groaned.

He guided me closer onto the couch so he could get both knees on and spread my legs wider. Deeper and deeper he entered me. The sound of his skin slapping against mine was rhythmic, his strong hands gripped my hips, then on my ass, then the feeling of a finger, possibly a thumb sliding through my ass.

"Fuck baby, I…I don't know," I said.

"I got you, baby. I won't do anything you don't like. Just tell me, but just relax," he said.

His cock, so thick inside my body. His thumb rubbed my entrance, so erotic and dirty. I stretched my back and reached my arms towards the window. I relaxed and let myself go. I trusted him. He put a knee up on the couch, and he positions himself differently. His cock hit a spot inside my body that sends me flying. I climaxed almost immediately. He kept rubbing my ass.

"Fuck baby. Jesus, this is so fucking hot. I'm going to come."

He pounded me from behind, his dick hard, breath quaking, fingers grabbing at my ass cheeks, until he tensed his whole body, and released of all he had inside of him.

He collapsed over top of me. I could feel his legs shaking. I reached down and ran my hands over them.

"Woman." He sighed.

"That was hot," I said.

He laughed. "We are *not* in the friend zone."

"No, we are not. Especially when you stick your finger in my butt."

I laughed.

"I didn't put it in. Next time I will, though."

He laughed, kissing my back, and slowly pulled himself from me.

I shook my head and followed him to the bathroom to clean up.

We lay in bed naked and talked about everything and nothing until the sun got low.

"Dinner?" he asked, running his fingers through mine.

"I don't know if I want to go out," I said. "I'm emotionally toast."

"Room service? There's a rooftop restaurant and bar?" he said.

More excited, I said, "Ooh, that sounds good."

We rinsed off and changed, then make our way to the top floor.

It was a dimly lit rooftop space, and we made it just in time for the sunset. We cozied up to a railing where Stephen wrapped himself around me and pressed his lips to my temple, saying, "You make me so happy, Cassie."

I reached back and held his head in mine with my one hand. We stood there until the sun escaped the horizon and the lights of the city took over the skyline.

Dinner was exceptional for hotel dining. The wine went down smoothly, and our conversation was easy. His hand traced circles over mine as he sat back and looked out at the gorgeous night. The cool breeze was absolutely perfect.

"Now, I can get used to this," he said.

"You cannot beat California weather. No humidity," I said, putting my free hand in the air.

"Yeah, I could live here," he said.

I quickly turned my head to look at him.

"You should."

He kept looking forward, towards the view, smiling, and sipping his wine.

"I mean, this is where your step-child lives after all."

He looked at me, shaking his head and laughed.

The next day was more sensational sex and coffee in bed.

"Meet me in the shower," he said, slipping from the sheets.

He wiped the steam from the glass with his hand as I entered the bathroom. He stood tall and slender but very muscular in the large tile shower. He pushed the door open for me, and I stepped in. I wrapped my arms around his wet body, and he dipped my head back gently under the running water to wet my hair, careful not to get it in my eyes. When my face came back to meet his, he wiped the beads of water with his thumbs across my lids.

He kissed my forehead, looked in my eyes, and said in his low, deep voice, "I love you."

I pressed my head to his water-soaked chest. His heart beat fast. I took a beat to take in this precious moment. I slowly looked back up to his gorgeous face, which was looking down at me.

"Do you remember when you told me for the first time, before?"

"I do." He kissed my forehead. "You were laying on my bed. We were kids, what, seventeen?" He let out a small laugh. "We just had sex, and I went to get us water. You were naked, tan, laying on your side propped up by one arm, the sun was beaming in through the shutters. So perfect. I walked in and I was in awe of you." He kissed my head again. "I kneeled next to the bed and told you. It just flowed out so easily and I really felt it, like I do right now."

"I love you," I said. "I always have."

He reached down and kissed me, holding my face. Then wrapped my body in his.

They all flew back that afternoon, leaving my torn heart somewhat mended. What a gift. On my way home from the airport, I rolled down the windows, opened up the sunroof and let the bright California sun shine down over me, and let my long hair blow wild.

I was free.

Chapter 26

STEPHEN

"So, what time are we leaving tomorrow?" Allen asked as we briskly walked out of our meeting.

My stress level was so fucking high I could barely see straight. I was being bombarded with updates on the investigation by Mark every hour it seemed, with Pete chiming in periodically. I had enough work piling up to keep me buried until the New Year, but my favorite distraction seemed to keep me from going insane.

Cassie.

Damn.

Every text, every call. Every unsolicited foot or titty pic in the middle of my day, I could not get enough of her.

I could hear the stress in her voice when we talked about her upcoming divorce, and Britt obviously did too...and that brought me to my conversation with Allen.

We rounded the corner to where our offices branch off.

"I scheduled the plane for a 1:30 departure. We have that meeting in the morning with the Harris Group at 10:45. Britt and Cassie's mom are driving in first thing from Charleston and meeting us at the airport. Are you sure you and Bianca want to go?" I rambled.

He laughed. "Yeah, we really like Cassie, man, and this will be a nice quick getaway. It's really sweet what you're doing for her. I'm cutting out of here after I get out of this next call. I'll see you in the morning."

He tapped me on the shoulder before walking into his office.

"See you later," I said walking down, veering into mine, feeling my phone vibrating in my jacket pocket.

I swiped to see who was texting me.

It was Mark with no surprise.

"Call when you can."

I called him back as I entered my office and shut the door, making my way to my desk. He had been in touch so much lately that I no longer had paralyzing anxiety when he reached out.

"Hey, Stephen," he answered.

"What's going on, Mark?" I asked as I got comfortable in my leather chair at my desk, swiveling to my city view of the Charlotte skyline.

"I left Jakob's house about two hours ago."

He paused.

"What was up at Lauren's brother's house?"

Now, I felt slight alarm.

"They went inside Stephen, for like…an hour, then I followed them to the train station where I lost them. I have their car at the station and a tracker on it if they come back for it," he said.

"Why were they inside Jakob's house? Was he there?" I asked quickly, feeling my throat tighten.

"I don't know why, and yeah, he was there," he said.

I jumped straight out of my chair. "What the fuck? Is he okay? Have you seen him?" I asked.

"I couldn't make out anything going on inside, but when they came out, Jakob left in one vehicle, and they left in theirs. It looked casual, and he seemed fine. I chose to follow the guys to the train station," he said. "I will be putting a tracker on Jakob's car as soon as I can."

First Lauren was seen talking to Alban, and now these guys were in Jakob's house, casually coming and going? It was very clear they were working together. What next? Was Mark going to find Valton Kastrati, the Albanian drug lord, personally printing money, selling girls, and running cocaine out of Marek and Klara's basement next? Fuck it. Maybe they could all have a big family cookout in the back yard next weekend. I hoped I got an invitation.

"All right Mark, Jesus, this is insane," I said, pacing my office.

"Yeah, all this out of nowhere. I'm also pissed I lost them at the station. I'm sorry about that," he said. "Hopefully, they will at least be back for the car and can gather some more information."

"Thanks for the updates. Just please keep an eye on Klara and Marek, okay?" I asked.

"Yeah, I have a patrol on that too," he reassured me.

"Thanks. Also, I'm going to be out of town and a little out of pocket for the next two days if I'm slow to respond, just in case. I really want to focus on something I'm doing, okay?"

"I got it. I'll only reach out if it's something major," he said.

"Thanks Mark."

I hung up and sat down, wanting to bang my head into my desk, like really fucking hard.

I text Pete.

Me: Should I be worried? Jakob?

Pete: Not right now

Me: Ok

I breathed as my CIA backup seemed to be doing their job. I finished as much work as I could focus on, which was virtually nothing, and headed home to my glass fortress on the lake. I felt less secure with what was going on, even more alone and so much smaller in this big house without her.

I turned the lights on as I walked through, making my way to the kitchen, pouring myself a whiskey at the wet bar. I hit the lights that lit up the pathway through the yard to the dock leading to the lake. I leaned against the counter, eating what resembled half of a sandwich I had in the refrigerator. I wanted her there. I wanted that joy back.

Shit.

I didn't even care if it was there anymore. I just wanted

her…anywhere. I wanted that laugh, her talking, and the sound of her being busy all around me.

I took my drink to my bedroom and into my closet, pulling off my tie and discarding my suit from the day. I grabbed my overnight bag to pack, then headed for the shower. I hit the Bluetooth to rid my ears of the painful silence. I found myself not even being able to take a damn shower without thinking of her. The songs that come on reminded me of moments we shared. I was throwing her friends and family in my plane to surprise her on Thursday because I could not stand being apart for another minute.

When Britt called me saying we needed to do something, I jumped so fast at the opportunity that my pilot barely had time to change his underwear from his last flight.

I climbed into bed as my phone dinged with a text from my sexy girl. My dick almost got hard when I saw her face light up my screen in her little circle.

Her message was a sweet picture of her daughter sleeping in her lap. Not really the sexy pic I thought I was getting, but a sweet moment I was happy she was sharing.

Cassie: What about this step-kid?

Oh, wow. Definitely something I wasn't expecting. We are jumping ahead, but I liked it. I want all of her, and I knew Cora was the biggest part she had to share. I was not going to fuck it up.

Me: Exactly the step-kid I was shopping for on a website earlier today, but they were sold out. How much?

Cassie: Just your heart

Sitting there, shaking my head I wondered what I was going to do with her? My chest was all but exploding.

Be witty, Stephen.

Me: I stroked that check when you were here last. Sold.

The heart emojis were sweet. I dittoed her before saying goodnight.

Britt was beside herself at the airport when she spotted us.

"Oh my god, Stephen." She jumped up and down. "This is going to be awesome. She is going to be so surprised. Thank you for making this happen."

She wrapped her arms around my neck. Anne, well, she was more reserved, but extremely sweet in her approach, giving me a big hug.

"Thank you for doing this for Cassie, Stephen. She must mean a lot to you to go to such great lengths."

Oh Anne, if you only knew.

I smiled.

"I know this would make her happy and she's having a rough time. Come on, we need to board."

I steered the conversation away.

It worked, because Britt was very excited about her first private jet experience. I thought she ran her hands over all surfaces as she found her seat across from Bianca. Anne chose the one across from me.

Fuck.

I had a feeling I was about to get the Mom interrogation. I could deal. After all, I'd got going on with drug dealers, kidnappers, and sex trafficking, I could handle a five-foot Spanish Mom.

Two glasses of Prosecco in for her and two whiskeys for me, and I was toast. She had it all out of me. I would have told her I fucked her daughter on the kitchen counter back in high school if she hadn't changed the subject to my mom and her latest travel plans. I hoped I never got waterboarded by the Albanians.

Shit.

They just needed to give me alcohol, Anne Patterson, and a dark room.

The five-and-a-half-hour flight landed, and we all went to dinner. All I wanted to do was go get her. It felt terrible to be this close and not have her with me, with us. She must have text messaged me, her mom, and Britt while we were all together during that time. It felt like a conspiracy.

The next day, we all met at the rooftop restaurant, and Britt nervously went down to wait by Cassie's car. She text us.

"How long does this shit take?"

"I need to pee."

"I hope she doesn't faint because I can't remember CPR."

Then silence until a quick thumbs-up emoji.

Moments later, arm in arm, they appeared from the elevator, Cassie shocked to see us.

It was all worth it.

I would say every weekend we had spent together so far had been magical, but this was the most emotional, vulnerable, incredibly sexual, and just absolutely incredible. I flew home from San Francisco so sure of what I wanted from this relationship. I would do anything for her and would not lose her ever again.

I landed in Charlotte, late, tired. I texted her goodnight and sleep took me hard and fast.

I could feel the covers lifting and the weight of her body softly climb in next to me. The warmth, wrapping around me like a cocoon. Her skin, mostly bare except for the feel of some silk against my back. I could smell her scent, clean with vanilla and sandalwood. Her arm wrapped over my side, and I took it, pulling it up into my chest, kissing her hand. She kissed the back of my neck, then my shoulder. My dick woke with her touch. Her hand slid from my chest over my body, slowly down, over my ass, around to feel my arousal, making me breathe in deep at her stroking it. Her kisses moved to my back and she was moving her body rhythmically around mine, stroking my cock as it got harder and harder within her hand. I turned over to take her, I wanted her. I took her face in my hands in the darkness, her long hair tangled in my fingers.

My mouth hovered over her lips, "I love you so much," I whispered.

The most precious response.

"I love you too, Stephen. I'm still with you," came from her lips.

I was instantly confused in my sleepy haze.

It was the way she pronounced my name.

My heart stopped. I rushed for the lamp on the nightstand to find my large king-size bed empty.

I sat, drenched in sweat, naked, on the side of my bed, palms pressed in my eyes.

"Fuck," I yelled out loud.

I looked at my clock, and it was 2:34 and I was officially wide awake.

Why? Why was she haunting me?

She lied to me.

She fucking lied to me, and I was not going to chase her ghost anymore.

I was moving on from this goddamn nightmare.

Chapter 21

CASSIE

✗

The view of the city from my office never got old, especially when I felt like procrastinating. I turned my chair around, staring aimlessly at the endless city skyline. The lights of the camera and grueling taping schedule were over for the year, and we were simply working on the cookbook and the release of the cookware line. Who knew how picky I would be about putting my name on a wok set? I also never imagined how much garbage cookware was being mass-produced, either, until I was forced to test it out one by one.

The holidays were right around the corner, and everyone was up my ass about my plans. Jack had Cora for the holiday break this year and was taking her to Vail skiing with his family. I had her for Thanksgiving, and my parents were coming to help me give it the family vibe. However, Christmas was up for grabs, I either stayed here and worked, helping out my crew at Sagi, and Stephen came out, sacrificing his own family, or I could go to Charleston. Either way, this was my first holiday without my girl, and I was completely heartbroken over it. I was choosing to be a major bah-humbug and not make a decision about anything, pissing everyone off in the meantime. Gearing up for the holidays in California sucked. I couldn't get in the mood when it was in the 60s. I just wanted a fireplace, some sweater weather, or those adorable window displays like they had in New York City.

I felt like a child hiding in her room, pouting. It never lasted long though, they always seemed to find me.

This time, it was Arie at the door.

"Hello, Cassie," she said, knocking as she entered the half-open door.

I swiveled my chair. "You found me. What can I do for you, Arie?" I asked with a sigh.

"We need to go over your schedule for that photo shoot, but another thing..." She pulled something up on her phone and turned it towards me, smiling big.

I squinted because I didn't have my glasses on and couldn't see shit.

"What am I looking at?"

She laughed. "You are so blind. Your Instagram, the post from the other day, got quite the response we were hoping for."

She raised her eyebrows up and down.

"Yeah, you totally whored me out for likes and followers with that."

I groaned.

She snickered, looking at her phone. "Eighteen K new followers, Cassie. Like, fuck, all off one post," she said wide-eyed.

"What? Over a picture of me in the dressing room with curlers in my hair, in my silky little robe, getting ready for taping, laughing?" I asked.

She explains. "People like to see the behind-the-scenes, the real you. And the tiny robe didn't hurt our male followers by the way."

She laughed into her hand.

"I'm not posing for Playboy next, no matter how hard you beg," I told her, shaking my head.

She laughed. "Shit. A centerfold was the next endeavor I was going to ring you for, fuck. Oh well, then."

She started to stand and smooth out her pencil skirt, turning to leave my office.

"Hey, Arie?"

"Yeah, Cassie?" she said, turning half out the door.

"I'm okay being a hot mom, just not a whore. I have a teen kid, you know?" I said, pointing a finger at her with squinted eyes.

She giggled and turned to leave, shaking her head and wiggling her finger. "I like you, Cassie, I really like you."

I grabbed my phone from my desk and swiped it to Stephen's sweet face. I looked at the time and calculated. It was an automatic thing now. Add three hours…constantly when I looked at the time. It was noon there.

Me: I need to see my man.

Please don't be in a meeting or a business lunch.

Stephen: Hey sexy girl.

Seriously, that never got old. Hopefully he still said it when I was eighty-eight and I was wearing an adult diaper.

Me: I don't have work or Cora this weekend. Want me to come? Or do you have plans? I'm dying here.

Stephen: YES…… Only plan is to be inside you. Arrive Friday?

Me: Yes. I'll get a flight right now.

Stephen: I can have Catherine set it up.

Me: I have people too and income you know?

Stephen: Are we arguing about money? Because it's turning me on.

Me: What doesn't, fiend?

The week was smooth at Sagi. My new notoriety had definitely increased our business. We brought on a few more people in the kitchen, and the front of house was fully staffed. Everyone seemed really happy. Kyle had truly embraced his executive chef role and relinquished a lot of cooking duties to Reggie and Darius. I seemed to be slowly disappearing from Sagi and spending more time at my high-rise office. I didn't know if that was where my happiness lay.

The further I got away from cooking, the less content I felt in my career. That's all I knew.

Cora was doing really well in eighth grade. She had made some new friends and junior varsity cheer squad for the basketball season. Boys were now her biggest obsession and mine and Jack's biggest obstacle.

My first-class flight was comfortable as always, and yes, Catherine beat me to it. I may go for comfort plus, but he didn't bat an eye at going all the way. About thirty minutes before landing, I got an email from Stephen.

"Babe, please don't be upset with me, but I had a very important meeting come up that I can't get out of. I'm sending a car for you. My driver is Gregory, and he will pick you up when you get off the plane and take you home. I'm so sorry I won't be there to kiss you. Text me when you get in the car. I love you."

Well, that sucked, but I got it. He sent me a car, not, *Grab an Uber and I'll see you at the house.* I couldn't complain.

The plane landed, and as I came around the corner towards baggage, there was my driver, Gregory, tall, dressed in black, very unassuming, with a sign reading, *Sexy Girl Buckley* making me laugh.

When I walked up, he said smiling, "By the look on your face, you must be my girl." He took my carry on. "Is this all you have, Ms. Buckley?"

Still slightly laughing, I said, "Yes, Gregory, it is."

The cold North Carolina air hit my face when we exited the busy terminal.

"Whoa. Winter is here," I said, wrapping my arms around my body and pulling my head down into my sweater.

Gregory laughed as he hustled me across the crosswalk to the black Cadillac Escalade.

"Ms. Buckley, it's only forty-eight degrees. It's far from winter."

He opened the car door, smiling with a nod of his head.

"But I'll get those heated seats on for you in just a moment."

As soon as we were on our way, I pulled out my phone and found his sweet face.

Me: Gregory doesn't kiss as good as you. I also realize I don't like the feel of mustaches on my lips.

I felt giddy just being this close to seeing him again and being in the presence of something he set up for me. I stared at my phone. No reply for the forty-five-minute drive to his house. I now felt slightly sad. The gray sky and gloominess of the weather weren't much help as it was trying to push in, trying to match my mood. Between learning about everything Gregory and constantly checking for a missed text or call, we arrived faster than it felt.

As we pulled up, I said, "Gregory, did Mr. Harlow leave a code? I don't know it."

He looked at me in the rear-view mirror and said, "Oh, Ms. Buckley, I have it all, no worries. I do this all the time."

I sat back realizing Stephen's life was still a mystery to me.

Gregory pulled up and punched the code in, and the gates opened. Once we pulled up to the house, he came around, opened my door, retrieved my bag, and as we walked up to the front, a sweet older woman greeted us.

"Hello, you must be Ms. Buckley."

She held her hand out. As I took it, she introduced herself as Gloria, the housekeeper.

"Come on in from the cold, dear."

Gregory placed my bag inside.

"It was nice meeting you, Ms. Buckley. Have a great day."

I waved with a smile. "Thank you, Gregory, it was nice meeting you as well."

He shut the door, taking the brisk air with him.

"Come in, Ms. Buckley, make yourself at home. Mr. Harlow will be home shortly. He said to make sure you had everything you needed before I left."

I followed her, wheeling my bag. I felt strange being there without him.

On the way to his bedroom, we stopped by the kitchen, and she went to open the now fully stocked fridge with a sense of pride.

I laughed. "Gloria. Oh my." I placed my hand over my mouth. "You went nuts."

"Well, he gave me quite the list this week. You have odd requests, my dear. I'm learning about so many things, but I have no clue what to do with them."

"I am so sorry. I thought he was doing the shopping, not you. He is such a cheater having you do his dirty work," I said.

"Ms. Buckley…"

I interrupted. "Please, call me Cassie, Gloria."

"Cassie, Mr. Harlow is a very, very busy man. Ever since…well, I just do whatever I can to take things off his plate." She put her hands up in the air. "Then he builds this McMansion and doubles my workload." She laughed. "At least nobody ever uses the other ninety percent of it," she said breathing a sigh of relief.

"Right? Well, if that ever happens, I'm sure he will bring on more help for you Gloria." I placed a hand on her shoulder. "I will also be more thoughtful about my grocery list next time I come to town and decide to have a weekend of cooking in together like I planned."

She smiled. "No worries, dear. It's been nice seeing him smile lately. He's actually been somewhat pleasant at times when he isn't overwhelmed with work." She winked. "I'll get out of your hair. Is there anything you need to know about the house? Do you know how to work everything? It can be tricky."

"No, I think I can remember. Plus, I think he will be home soon," I said, hoping that was the truth because I really missed him, especially now, being there in his space.

"Okay, if you need me, my number is on the inside of the pantry door on the corkboard," she said with a smile. "Have a lovely time, Ms. Bu…Cassie."

She pulled on her coat, walking down the hallway, and shutting the front door behind her. Leaving me in silence in this large house, alone.

I wheeled my suitcase to the bedroom, into the closet to its usual spot on the shelf. I grabbed my makeup bag and went to the bathroom to freshen up. As I brushed my teeth, I saw his things, neat and tidy. The simple fact that he roamed this space excited me. I went to the kitchen, decided I wanted some noise, and fiddled with the pad on the wall, controlling the music. Magic happened, flooding the house. It was loud.

Jesus, Stephen. Party much?

I turned it down and rummaged through the kitchen, opened a bottle of cabernet and poured a glass, then I checked my phone.

Still, no text.

My heart fell with worry and disappointment.

I decided to wander. Room by room, I sipped my wine, running my fingers over surfaces and looked at things collected from travels, childhood memories, family heirlooms, and pictures of the past.

My phone buzzed in my hand with a text message. My heart flipped.

> Stephen: I have left you unattended so long, I wouldn't blame you for having sex with him by now. I am so, so sorry, baby.

I almost forgot what I had originally texted him, it had been so long.

Ahh. Kissing Gregory.

> Me: I was able to control myself. It's okay, I was worried though.

> Stephen: I know. I'll be there in 30. I have one thing I need to do in my office as soon as I get there for like 1 second and I'm done...I promise.

He sent me a gif of a cat driving a race car with goggles. He knew I was a sucker for animals doing stupid shit.

I laughed.

I decided now would be a great time to try on the little outfit I got for him since I had a minute to get dressed, and I had some liquid courage in me.

> Me: I'll wait for you here then and make that second count

> Stephen: I love you woman.

Black thigh-highs with lace tops, fucking sexy as hell. Strappy four-inch heels that are not made for walking, a lace thong, a matching lace push-up demi bra that my tits were spilling out of, and I found one of Stephen's crisp white dress shirts I left unbuttoned. I was ready for work.

I found my way to his desk in his office. Masculine steel gray walls and large silver foil world maps framed in black adorned the walls. His desk faced the wall of windows overlooking the meticulously manicured backyard, dock, and beautiful Lake Norman. I pushed the few files and papers over and sat on his desk. There, facing me was a bookshelf lined with historical novels and random books on travel with a few pictures. One I could not resist taking off the shelf. It was them, him and Lauren. I traced over it with my fingertips. They looked happy. A smile I saw when he looked at me, so genuine. She was stunning, just absolutely gorgeous with hair, long and blonde. Eyes, crystal blue. She was undeniably radiant. I put the picture back on the shelf and tried to get myself back to my sexy place, but I now felt like the other woman, like… Beth. My inner dialogue was off the charts and out of hand. I reached back over and put the picture face down. I climbed back onto the desk, took a swig of my wine, and assumed position again. Just as I moved the files to the side, a picture slid out. I saw that it was a grainy picture of Lauren and a guy in a parking lot. Like, surveillance pictures. I rifled a little more. Some guys in a car? I felt like I was snooping. I shoved them back in. This wasn't my business. I decided to put the papers and files back onto the desk and just simply leaned against it. I felt so unnatural, awkward.

I heard the front door shut and his voice, "Cassie?"

"I think you have work to do, Stephen," I yelled to him.

Chapter 28

STEPHEN

I looked at my watch. In a little over two hours, Cassie would be landing. I listened in on our team meeting through the intercom on my desk.

My phone buzzed in my pocket with a text message.

It was Pete.

"Call me when you can."

Fuck. Not today.

I shook my head.

Rich chimed in, pulling me from my thoughts. "Do you have those numbers in front of you? I sent them over this morning, Stephen."

"Yes, Rich. Everything looks good on my end," I responded.

Shit. I had no idea where I was in this meeting. I needed to pull the ripcord.

"Does everyone have it from here? I have another meeting I need to step into."

Everyone responded that they were fine, so I jumped off to only make a call to what felt like impending doom.

"Hey Pete, what's up?" I asked as he answered.

"Stephen, I have some pretty big developments that I think you may want to be brought up to speed on. Do you have some time?"

I looked at my watch. Time was moving fast, and I needed to leave to make the drive to meet her plane.

"A little, what is up?" I asked.

"I'm here in Charlotte. Can I meet you?" he asked.

Oh fuck. This doesn't sound good at all. In person, not a call.

"Hey Pete, is this urgent? I have something important I will need to rearrange if so," I said apprehensively.

Please say no, please say no.

"Yeah, it is, man. Sorry."

Fuck.

He gave me the address of a coffee shop and I asked jokingly if it should be a bar kind of meeting like last time.

He laughed. "I can't drink today because I'm still working, or I would."

I called Gregory, my driver, and set up for him to pick Cassie up from the airport.

"I'll text you her flight information. Can you do me a huge favor, though? This will make her laugh," I asked.

"Sure, what is it?"

"I need you to put something on her name card when you pick her up. I'll text it all to you," I said, laughing.

He snickered into the phone, "Well, okay. Whatever you would like, Mr. Harlow."

"You will like her, Gregory. She will probably entertain you all the way to the house," I said with a smile, wishing so bad it was me in his place.

"I will get her home safe and sound."

Then, the dreaded email to her. *Ugh.* I hoped she wasn't too pissed. I pressed send, grabbed my things, and headed to the coffee shop to meet Pete.

The day was gloomy and cold, a perfectly ominous setting for the stage for shit news.

I walked up to the coffee shop in the small shopping center. I spotted him at a corner table in front of a window as he held up a hand to get my attention. I stopped by the counter and grabbed a coffee before making my way over to him. He stood to shake my hand.

"Pete, how are you, man?"

"I'm all right, Stephen. How are you holding up these days?" he asked with a slight smile, sitting back down.

"Well, I'm missing something really important right now, and my life keeps getting derailed by this shit, but other than that, I'm hanging in there."

I sipped my coffee and placed it on the table.

He took a deep breath and said, "I'll get right to it. We brought Jakob in after he had that little meeting with Alban and Fatmir a couple months back."

"Okay," I said hesitantly.

"So, Jakob and Lauren were not working with the Albanians, Stephen. They are European DEA working with the US to dismantle transnational criminal organizations like Kastrati's. They have been working undercover to bring these guys down all these years."

He swallowed, leaning onto the table, lacing his fingers together.

I sat in silence, just staring at him.

He let out a small laugh. "Believe it or not, one thing is true, Jakob is her brother. They actually share the same profession, believe it or not."

I was still in shock and found very little amusing at this moment. I had no idea what was true in my life.

He cleared his throat. "So, she actually wasn't planted in your life. It seems it was an absolute coincidence, and Jakob warned her not to get involved once they realized they were working the same government job as you. She didn't listen, obviously. She couldn't tell you because it would have blown her cover, Stephen."

I just sat there, staring at my coffee cup, turning it with small, jagged turns, my mind wandering to little moments from my times with her.

The constant buzzing of the phone with work, needy clients, rushed breakfasts because she needed to go immediately, late nights with clients, no contributions of friends to our relationship. I felt like I could keep going on and on now that the veil had been lifted.

"Was my entire relationship a lie? Did she even love me?"

I looked up and asked him in a bit of a stupor, thoughts just bubbling out of my mouth.

He looked at me with a tilted head.

"It's not a question we asked him or that he gave us the answer to, buddy, sorry."

He took a sip of his coffee.

"Why were they here to see him? Is she alive?" I asked.

"He gave us some intel on why they were here, but unfortunately, I can't share that with you. As far as her being alive, they told him no."

He shook his head and placed his hand on mine that sat on the coffee cup.

"They claimed they killed her when they took her," he said with sadness in his eyes.

I dropped my head and closed my eyes, tears threatening to form underneath my lids. Anger rose from my chest.

I heard Pete say, "Stephen, Jakob doesn't seem to believe them. He has gotten encrypted messages, and he thinks they are from her."

I looked up at him, and he had a smile. I felt hope, false or not, but maybe some hope. Especially if it was coming from Jakob.

I ran my hands through my hair.

"Jesus, man. This is the worst rollercoaster ever. Zero stars given. I want off."

He chuckled. "I hear you. There is some pretty big shit going down in the next month, we believe. Buckle up. It may give us some more definitive answers. I just wanted to keep you in the loop on some of the things we discovered that involve you and Lauren."

"Oh, another thing, are Merek and Klara involved? Do they know their kids are agents?" I asked.

"They are definitely not involved. Completely in the dark. They still think Lauren was a software developer simply kidnapped for reasons unknown," he said.

"Does Jakob know that I know?"

"He does now. He knew that was your investigator outside his and his parents' house."

"Can I talk to him?" I asked with a sense of excitement.

He nodded his head. "I think it would be okay. I'm not sure what he will tell you, though. Keep it to your relationship with him and Lauren, okay? I mean, that's what you want answers to, right? Leave the big shit to us, okay?"

I nodded. "Yeah, I will."

"All right, just tread lightly."

I looked at my watch. There was fifteen minutes before Cassie landed. I might have time to run by Jakob's office since it was right around the corner.

"Thanks for filling me in, Pete," I said as I stood and shook his hand.

"No problem, Stephen. Someday, I hope to be giving you really good news, man, and we can have a celebratory drink."

I immediately dialed Jakob's number as I walked out of the coffee shop. I was eager to get some answers. He answered quickly.

"I figured I would be hearing from you soon, my brother," he answered in his thick accent.

"Hey, Jakob. I'm around the corner from your office. Do you have a minute to talk?"

"I do, I do. Come over."

I pulled into the real estate office that I now knew was a front. Jesus, now it made sense why he gave all the work to another agent in his office for my property closing. He claimed to be too busy. What did he do? Just rent this office? I shook my head as I walked up the steps, pulled the door open, and found his fake facade.

I was greeted by his receptionist, as she sat so small in her oversized moon-shaped reception desk.

"Can I help you?" she asked.

"Yes, I am here to meet with Jakob Malikov. I'm Stephen Harlow. He's expecting me," I said.

She picked up her phone, pressed a button, and said, "Stephen Harlow is here for you."

She put it down, pointing down the hallway. "His office is down that hall, third door on the right, Mr. Harlow."

"Thank you," I said and made my way nervously, not knowing

what information he had for me. I honestly didn't know how much more I could take.

I lightly knocked.

"Come in, Stephen."

There was no denying that Jakob was Lauren's brother. They had the same face, same crystal blue eyes as Klara, same tall, lean body. The only difference was he had Marek's brown hair.

He greeted me halfway across the room. He had always liked me. We had always gotten along since the beginning, which now baffled me since I now knew he didn't agree with Lauren's decision to be with me. Once again, was everything just bullshit?

He shook my hand, strong.

"Stephen, I am glad to see you."

I gave him a half smile.

"I wish it were for better reasons, Jakob, honestly."

His entire tone changed as he dropped his hand. He walked behind me to shut the door. His head bobbed in agreement as he backed up and leaned against his desk, splaying his hand out for me to sit in one of the chairs. He took a deep breath, running his hand through his hair and over the nape of his neck.

"You need some answers."

"I do, Jakob. I hear you have some for me," I said, looking directly into his eyes.

He took in a deep breath. "What do you know?"

I only told him I knew about him and Lauren being DEA agents and that they were trying to bring down the same people my government job was trying to as well. I didn't go into detail, not wanting to incriminate Pete too much.

I asked point blank. "I need to know if what Lauren and I had was a complete fucking lie? Was I just a pawn in this fucking game?"

He shook his head. "No. She loved you so much, man. That was the problem. All of that was real. She wanted to tell you every day and couldn't. Her plan was to come clean when we took Kastrati down, when it was safe. Obviously, that didn't happen."

He looked down at his feet.

"Pete said you think she's alive?" I asked.

He looked up. "I do. When I ask them questions about how she was killed, they are always vague. I think it's pure bullshit. I think they still have her. She is so valuable. She knows how to do things on a genius level, and they know it. That's why they took her. She has the brains and computer skill of you and Allen."

He laughed.

"What?"

I let out a laugh.

"Yeah, man. She is a hacker, a freaking mastermind. She can handle a weapon like no other. I don't think she is dead, Stephen, I really don't. I just don't feel it. I don't feel like she has left this earth. I have also gotten encrypted messages over the last year. I'm not on your or her level, so my people have been tracking them."

He rambled all of this, making my head spin.

Who the fuck had I been in a relationship with? I had been thinking she was a simple nerdy software developer. Had I been sleeping with a female Jason Bourne? Ms. Mission Impossible?

Jesus.

"So, there are some developments I don't think Pete or I are able to discuss, but hopefully we can get closer to some answers. Maybe we will be closer to finding her. I don't know." He ran his hand through his hair, blowing out a breath. "I'm so sorry you are going through all this. I want her back too. I miss my sister."

"Jakob, I want to move on. Just when I started to feel like I could, this all came up again." I put my head into my hands. I closed my eyes, now thinking of Cassie, without me in the car, waiting for me.

"I don't think she would expect you to put your life on hold all these years, Stephen," he said.

"I love her Jakob. I couldn't just turn that off. When I thought my whole relationship was a fucking lie, it was easier. Now this? Fuck. I…"

I stood and started to pace, running my hands in my hair and holding the back of my neck with both hands interlocked, eyes closed.

"I was supposed to protect her. I failed her."

Tears flowed from my eyes uncontrollably.

He walked over and looked at me.

"Man, my sister is a fighter. If she is alive, she will make it back. She will also never fault you for moving on. I know this. She is my blood."

He put his hands on my shoulders and looked into my eyes.

I shook my head and let out a laugh.

"Thanks. I guess I should go before the person I am trying to move forward with doesn't leave me too."

I wiped my eyes.

He slapped my shoulder. "Hopefully I get to meet her some day soon. Go get her. You deserve to be happy," he said, nodding his head.

I walked out of his office to my car feeling hopeful, relief, but still confused. Like, what the fuck? I'd throw some of that information in a corner of my mind to process later and focus on the task at hand, Cassie. My girl was the most important thing to me right now. She was my beacon of light, and I needed her more than ever right now. I climbed into my car and pulled out my phone to see her missed text from over an hour ago.

Damn.

Threatening to kiss Gregory, my driver. At least she had her sense of humor intact.

> **Me: I have left you unattended so long I wouldn't blame you for having sex with him by now. I am so, so sorry, baby.**

> **Cassie: I was able to control myself. It's okay, I was worried though.**

Wow. Someone worried about me. That was a change of pace.

I let her know I would be there in thirty minutes, and it seemed like she had a surprise waiting for me. My dick was instantly hard. My Defender seemed to be speeding without my knowledge.

I walked in the door to music playing through the house. Man I loved that. Someone waiting on me at home feels good.

I yelled, "Cassie."

I heard a distant voice. "I think you have work to do, Stephen."

It was coming from my office.

I rounded the corner to see her leaning against my desk. My dick instantly connected with the arousal of what my brain saw. My incredibly sexy woman dressed in my white dress shirt wide open displaying her beautiful tan body, a lace bra, Jesus…her tits. Lace panties, thigh highs wrapped around her long, beautiful legs, and strappy sexy fucking heels. Her legs were spread apart, inviting me in. Her long hair flowed over her shoulders, and she was looking seductive, yet trying to be innocent, biting her bottom lip.

"You said you have a second of work to do."

"Jesus fuck, woman," I said, leaning in the doorway, taking her in.

She then turned around, spread her legs, bent over the desk, pulling the shirt up, revealing her beautiful ass while looking back at me, saying, "I can help you get your work done if you want?" in a low, seductive voice.

I walked, removing my suit jacket, shoes, tie, and was unbuttoning my shirt by the time I reached the desk. She turned to help me. My hands at her jaw, pulling her head back, my mouth taking hers, I kissed her hard. I reached down with one hand and grabbed her ass, pulling her up higher. She moaned with need. Our breath became heightened. Our movements become desperate. She pulled my shirt down my arms and it dropped to the floor. She unbuckled my belt, unzipped my pants, and they puddled at my feet. She took hold of my cock through my underwear. I shook my head.

"Oh god, I'm so fucking hard. I'm not going to last long." I breathed the words against her lips.

I slid my shirt from her shoulders, her skin so brown and beautiful. I kissed her neck, her shoulders, then took her amazing tits in my hands and licked and kissed them.

"This bra, damn, I don't know what to do with all this," I said as I squeezed them together.

She laughed. "It's a lot." She looked down at them.

I stepped out of my pants and pushed the files and papers to the side of my desk, then lifted her up onto the edge. I ran my thumb over the lace fabric of her panties, finding her clit. Her head went back and exposed her neck. I kissed her supple, soft skin, then slid my finger under the lace, feeling her slick pussy.

"Oh, oh god," she moaned.

"You are so wet for me," I said, hovering over her lips.

"I want you so bad. I've been thinking about this all week. I want it hard. I want it rough. Can you do that, baby?" she said in desperation.

I nodded, and slid her back in a quick motion, pulling her thong off. I got on my knees and spread her legs, diving my tongue into her needy pussy.

"Holy fuck," she yelled.

I thought this might be what she wanted. She wanted to be taken.

I licked and sucked until her legs shook uncontrollably. I sucked her clit through her, pulling my hair and her saying, "Stop, stop, stop."

When I didn't, I made her come over and over again. Then, I climbed to my feet and pulled her legs down. I kissed her and let her taste herself in my mouth.

She reached down and ran her hand over the length of my rigid cock beneath my boxer briefs.

"Fuck baby, I'm going to explode." I groaned.

She pulled my underwear down to my ankles and I stepped out. She shook her head when she looked down.

"Mmm, that is one beautiful dick," she said as she stroked it.

I hadn't forgotten what she said, rough and hard. I motioned for her to turn around and face the desk and lie face down, her face against the mahogany. She obeyed. The view with her long legs with the lace on her thighs and those heels, damn. I thought the view might do me in, but I needed to make her fantasy come to fruition. I ran my fingers down her spine to her ass, then ran my hand around and around the bare globe, then lightly spanked her, finding her threshold of pain. She flinched, but moaned. I stroked my cock. This was a new turn-on for us. Again, harder, and she gasped, then moaned.

"You like that baby?" I asked.

"Uh huh." She whimpered.

I slid the slick tip of my hard cock into her tight pussy.

Oh God.

It was so fucking hot, so luxurious, so wet. How could something feel as good as the first time? I slapped her ass again as I pumped my dick in and out of her slowly. She reached back and grabbed my thigh, motioning me to go faster.

Oh god, don't come, don't come, don't come.

I sped up.

"You are so hard, baby, so deep." She moaned.

I grabbed hold of her shoulders, then I reached down and kissed the side of her neck, and then gave it to her like she wanted, rough, hard. I grasped the back of her long hair lightly in my hand and buried my cock deep into her, deeper and deeper, harder, and harder. She was loud. She loved it. I came…so fucking hard.

I collapsed over top of her with exhaustion. My damp skin is against hers. Our breathing matched each other's. She reached back and held my head with her hand. A simple gesture, but it meant so much. I covered her hand with mine.

"What work did you need to do that was so important?" she whispered.

"Shit." I looked at my watch. "I need to answer a quote before five. It's four-fifty. Good save, babe."

I slowly pull out of her.

"Sorry."

She slid out of her heels and laughed. "I cannot walk in these, only stand and fuck."

I laughed as I climbed into my underwear. She slunk off to the bathroom.

I make my way into my chair and logged onto my computer, pulling up my email. Cassie came back dressed in a pair of panties and a comfortable sweatshirt. I turned my chair and motioned, patting my lap.

"Sit here, babe."

I wrapped my arms around her, then turned back to my wall of three computer screens on my desk, and tapped at the keys.

"What are you doing?" she asked.

"Just confirming the quote on this job. All I have to do is click this..right..here…and..done."

I closed the screen out, kissing her on the temple.

"I could get used to this, Mr. Harlow," she said.

"Oh baby, you have no idea. Coming home to you has made my year," I said.

Her eyes fixed on something behind me. I felt her mood instantly change.

"What?" I asked.

She shook her head. "Nothing," she said quickly.

"No. Something is bothering you, Cass. What is it?" I asked.

She took a deep breath. "It's petty and childish."

"Tell me. It's okay," I said.

"I was in here waiting on you earlier, and I noticed you have pictures of you and Lauren. I don't know. Seeing you two, I got jealous. It's so stupid. I'm jealous of someone who isn't here," she said, looking down, pulling at her sweatshirt nervously.

"I'm sorry. I should have put those away. They have been there so long I don't notice them." I took her chin to look at me. "Hey. There is no competition. You are here, and I am not going anywhere. I love you."

"Another thing, and I promise I wasn't snooping. That isn't my thing. I am all about people's privacy. The files on your desk." She pointed to the ones right next to me. "I was climbing onto your desk at first, trying to be sexy, and some pictures fell out. The ones of Lauren and some guys in a car. Are they recent surveillance photos? Is there something I need to know?"

My heart dropped. I wanted to tell her everything. If she knew she can be alive, if she knew what was going on and the possible danger that was out there, she would run. I knew Cass. I couldn't risk it.

"Those are old. It's all from years ago when she first went missing. Just an old file, babe," I reassured her and kissed her head.

She nodded and kissed me. "I'm sorry. I'm just insecure some-times. Jack has my head fucked up a little, I think. I trust you. I do. I don't want to lose you again, Stephen. I just can't, not again."

She stared into my eyes.

"I don't want to lose you either, baby," I said, putting my head against hers.

"Now, I did some pretty extensive grocery shopping for this weekend of cooking in together, fires in the fireplace, and oversized sweaters. I think that was the orders, right?" I said.

She slapped me on the shoulder. "Cheater. Gloria did all the shopping."

I laughed with a smile. "Well, I will make sure you have constant fires and give you loads of wood all weekend, babe."

Chapter 21

STEPHEN

She sat on my counter with legs spread and me between, wine-glass in her hand, the most beautiful smile on her face. The sunlight was shining through her auburn hair from the window behind her. She looked like an absolute angel. I took a moment to soak her in, waiting for fresh bread to come out of the oven, nothing to be prepped, stirred, or carefully watched over at the moment.

Over the weekend, we made everything from homemade pasta, bread, sauce, Italian meatballs, pesto and strawberry preserves. Watching her in the kitchen, in her element, was like watching a pianist front row in concert. It brought me joy, and she let me be part of it. She was an amazing, patient teacher at that.

I kissed her and said, "I keep thinking every time we are together, that it's the best time I've had with you, then the next is the best."

I smiled, reaching for my wine.

"I feel the same way. We can sit in and do absolutely nothing. It's not even what we do. It's how I feel," she said, running her thumb over my eyebrow, her eyes tracing the outline of my face before landing on my eyes. "I want us to always be honest and open with each other. It's hard being so far away, this long-distance thing. If you decide it's too hard, too much, whatever, I need you…"

I stop her. "Hey. This isn't too much. I want this. Where is this coming from, baby?"

She breathed in deeply with a long exhale. "I don't know. I guess knowing I'm leaving tomorrow, the holiday stress, our conversation when I got here, I'm an insecure baby sometimes, because of Jack cheating…" She shrugged her shoulders. "I'm sorry. I probably seem crazy. Sometimes, I just shouldn't open my mouth."

She laughed, putting her hand over her eyes.

I reached over, pulled her hand down and kissed her lips. "Over time, you will trust again. I'm patient. I want to throat-punch Jack every time I hear your doubts, but I still want you to tell me."

She laughed. "That makes two of us."

"We have the money, and we are making the time for the distance part. Yeah, I want to be with you every single day, God I wish that." I shook my head. "But right now, I think we are making it work." I took her face in my hands. "I will be honest and open with you. I promise."

Just then, I wanted to vomit. I knew I just bold-faced lied to her because I was keeping all the secrets about fucking drug lords, sex trafficking, and the large possibility that Lauren could be alive. She should probably know I was currently working with, the CIA and the European DEA right now looking for her. I actually sealed that sentence with, "I promise."

I was an asshole. This was for her safety, right? Pete told me I couldn't tell anyone. I had to protect her. My lying ass needed to protect her. What happened if Lauren walked back into the picture? Jesus, this internal thread had me in knots.

I backed out from between her legs. I needed air.

"Are you okay?" she asked.

"Yeah, isn't the bread ready?" I asked, walking over to the oven and turning on the oven light.

"No, the timer still has twelve more minutes," she said.

I grabbed the bottle of wine and walked over to refill our glasses.

"Here. I'm going to go add another log onto the fire. Join me in there?"

I made my way into the living room, leaving her behind.

"Okay," she said, confused.

The living room was large and open with a tall A-frame wall of windows, exposed beams, and a large roaring fireplace casting a golden glow on the dark suede couches. The sun was now going down on the lake, golden against the water and trees, making it feel less cold than it was.

I sat on the couch, and once she sat next to me, she curled her feet up into her body, and I handed her, her glass. I looked down at her ankle and traced over her fresh, tiny tattoo on the inside of her ankle with my index finger.

"I still can't believe you did that," I said, with a curled-up smile.

She chuckled. "Why? It's so small. Plus, I thought my little black bike was a perfect first tattoo. Kyle thought it was a good idea."

I sipped my wine. "Well, Kyle thinks anything you do is a good idea," I said with a raised brow, "What does it symbolize to you? Isn't that the point of getting a tattoo?" I asked.

Looking down, she traced it slowly and said in a soft voice, "I want to stop running from my fears."

"Cassie," I said.

She looked up at me.

"Seriously?" I looked at her with a confused look. "You constantly accomplish the hardest shit ever. Look at you. What fears do you have?"

"This." She placed her hand on her heart. "I ran when this got hard. I ran from relationships, friendships, being vulnerable. Look at me. I have one solid friend, Stephen, and she doesn't even live in my state."

She got teary, looking back down at her little bike.

"Oh, babe. I'm sorry. Please don't cry."

I kissed her forehead.

I definitely knew that. It was the reason why I was completely avoiding telling her anything that would upset her. Knowing that she would run, leaving me...on her little fucking black bike. I couldn't believe she went as far as tattooing it on her body. I had to be able to tell her things without her running. Her being aware, maybe this would be a great segue, like therapy.

The buzzer on the oven pulled me from my really bad idea.

"I'll get it."

I practically raced to go to pull the loaves from the oven.

"Wow. These look amazing," I called out, placing them on the racks we set up. I then turned the oven off. My house smelled and felt like an actual home for the first time.

Turning to see her in the late afternoon glow of the sunset and the fireplace, only lit her beauty ablaze that much more. I couldn't take my eyes off her. I took her glass from her hand as she looked up at me. I slid my body over top of hers, pressing my mouth against her lips, sinking her into the softness of the sofa. My elbows were on either side of her head. I was enamored by her beauty.

"I love you, Cassie. I want you to trust that I will never knowingly set out to hurt you. I will never hurt your heart like that. You know that, right?"

She nodded and reached up to kiss me. "Is that your dick pressing into me?"

"Well, it's not someone else's." I smiled.

"You are insatiable."

She shook her head and reached between us, running her hand over my dick, that now throbbed beneath my jeans. She seductively bit her bottom lip, her hazel eyes watched my expression.

"Fuck, woman."

I groaned, closing my eyes, taking in a deep breath, enjoying the magical caress of her hand.

With one hand, she unbuttoned my jeans and slowly slid the zipper down. Her thumb, caressing the head of my dick that had breached the band of my boxer briefs, slick with pre-cum as it slid easily over the tip.

"Oh yeah, I need to get out of these jeans," I said as I pushed myself to my knees on the couch.

She looked at my body, and what she had done.

"Damn, your dick is just begging to get out of there."

She chuckled.

I was pulling off my flannel and t-shirt, then stood next to the sofa as she reached up to pull my jeans down, then my briefs, letting my cock spring free from its enclosure. I reached down, pushing my jeans and underwear to the floor, stepping out of them. I reached for her hand.

"Come up here," I said.

She stood and I pulled her sweater over her head. She never bothered putting on a bra for the day, which had me busy reaching underneath, playing with her nipples every chance I could get when my hands weren't busy stirring or in flour. I took them, squeezing them together, sucking them, biting the tight buds. The sound of her moans sending a surge of arousal straight to my cock. I ran my hands down her tight body and peeled off her leggings, her lifting her legs to help me. I reached around and slid her thong down as well, and it fell to the floor. We stood naked, with the only light being the glow of the fireplace, the sunset almost completely gone over the lake. Her hair flowed over her shoulders. The crackling of the fire. What a beautiful R-rated Hallmark moment.

I looked over and grabbed a fluffy sheepskin blanket from a nearby basket, and place it in front of the fireplace. I lay on the floor, motioning for her to climb on top of me. My cock, hard and waiting for her. I wanted to watch her. Watch her ride me, see her face as I was inside her.

She straddled me with her long legs. Her hair flowing over my chest as she leaned forward, guiding my dick inside of her now-drenched pussy.

"Fuck."

I moaned as she slid slowly down my shaft. It felt so damn good, hot, tight. I held her hips as she ground herself on me, looking into my eyes, hair flowing around her face, shadows casting on her gorgeous body by the flicker of the flames.

"You are so beautiful," I whispered.

She smiled and placed her index finger over my lips, pushing the tip into my mouth as her face tensed. I sucked her finger, her eyes closed, her head went back, and her momentum picked up. I reached between her legs and found her clit, hard, wet.

"Oh fuck, oh fuck," she muttered.

Her palms were pressed into my chest, fingertips slightly digging, matching the pressure I felt wrapping around my dick.

"Come for me, baby. You like that cock inside of you, don't you?" I whispered.

She whimpered ever so low. "Yes, I love it, baby. I'm coming."

My pressure increased on her clit as she arched back. She ground harder on my cock. Just then, my mind and dick connected. The sight of her turned me on so much when she reached and grabbed her breasts, tugging at her nipples. Her hair flowed back, her neck, her open mouth, her groan of pure ecstasy, and her pussy grabbing my dick...I was done. I came so hard I thought my soul exited my body for a moment, but thankfully, my angel was the one who brought me back as she collapsed on top of my chest.

I wrapped my arms around her. I only wished I could pull her inside my body and keep her there forever. I didn't know what I would do if I lost her. I was so glad I kept my mouth shut.

The next morning, we fell into our normal routine of departure day. Cassie packed and got ready. I made breakfast as we pretended it was not a sad day. I had the news on in the background on the TV, simply checking on the weather and the Charlotte traffic so I knew what to expect for my drive to the airport in a little while. Cassie joined me in the kitchen and handed me my phone.

"This was on your nightstand. It was lighting up like crazy, so I figured you may need to check it."

She kissed me as I handed her a coffee.

"Thank you," I said, checking to see what was so urgent.

"Man, I sure love me some Al Roker," she said.

I looked up at her with a questioning look.

"Most people say that about Chris Hemsworth or George Clooney, but you say Al Roker. I fucking love you, weirdo."

"I have a thing for weathermen. I have a crush on one in San Fransisco. He's in my building, so I get to see him all the time," she said, looking back at the TV, sliding on her boots.

"What? Who is he? I'll kill him," I said, joking.

She laughed, sliding her other sock and boot on.

I noticed I had a slew of missed texts and calls.

"Shit."

Mark: Call me.

Pete: Hey man, call me when you get this.

Two missed calls from Pete.

Missed call from Allen.

Oh, fuck me.

I looked at Cassie. I looked at the time. We needed to leave for the airport in a little over an hour.

"Hey, babe, I have some business blowing up. I need to take some calls in my office. I'm sorry," I said as I rounded the counter and kissed her. "Your breakfast is right there. I'll try to be quick."

"It's okay. I'm a big girl," she said without a care.

I headed to the office and closed my door, dialing Mark.

"Hey, Stephen, sorry, but this was urgent," he said.

"Of course. What's up?" I said, pacing in front of the expansive wall of windows displaying the view of the lake as if it was going to calm my nerves.

"I have been cut off by the CIA. The car at the train station has been seized by them, and I was told that they will be handling this case from here on out," he said.

"What case are they referring to?" I asked, confused.

"When I asked, he said anything related to the disappearance of Lauren Malikov, they had it from here," he said.

"Who did you speak to, Mark," I asked.

He answered. "His name was Pete Maddox."

"Okay, well, I guess something big is going on. I guess we will wait. Thanks for everything, Mark. I'll let you know if I hear anything, and you do the same I guess?"

"I guess so. I was on a roll, and the big guns came rushing in. I'm glad something may be happening, though. Maybe there's an end to this mess for you, Stephen."

"Yeah, I hope so. Thanks, Mark," I said sadly. "Take care."

I immediately called Pete. I got his voice mail.

"Hey Pete, it's Stephen. I talked to Mark and…"

My phone beeped, it was him. Thank god, I don't want to play phone tag all goddamn day.

I answered.

"Hey Pete."

"Hey man, well, things progressed a little faster than a month, I guess."

He laughed.

"What is going on?"

"Is it not on the news yet?"

"Oh fuck. What?"

I thought Cassie was in there watching the fucking news.

"We took Kastrati down last night. I'm surprised you haven't seen it on the news yet," he said in an excited voice.

"I actually wasn't really paying attention and just got my phone, I've been busy. Holy fuck. What does all this mean? Like did y'all get everyone, Alban, and the other guy?" I asked, rubbing my face.

I couldn't think straight.

"Fatmir? Yeah. We got them. The system Southstar Securities put in place for the US government helped stop a major deal. We were able to end this. Jakob is on the way to Albania as we speak."

My heart pounded out of my chest. I swallowed hard.

"Is he…"

I couldn't finish my own sentence. The line went silent.

"Yeah, he's going to go into their compound with the other agents now that they can and see if they can find her or at least get some answers. She is one of their agents too, part of the mission as well. So, fingers crossed."

"Yeah, okay. Thanks for calling me. I'm just… I don't know," I muttered.

"It's all right. If you need anything. Call or text me," he said.

"Thanks," I said. "Oh, Pete?"

"Yeah?"

"Am I allowed to say anything yet?"

"Well, anything that is public knowledge at this point is fair game, I assume. Oh, I took your PI off the case. I felt bad. He was all in, poor dude."

I let out a small laugh. "I know, he was working so hard. He never gave up these last two years. He probably didn't mind the steady paycheck either."

"Good man, there. All right. Let's get together for that drink soon, Stephen."

"Okay, bye, Pete."

I hung up and breathed deep.

I walked out into the kitchen, TV still going, Cassie sitting at the counter, half-eaten breakfast, looking down at her phone.

"Hey." I walked up to warm up my coffee.

She looked up. "Everything okay with work?" she asked, looking adorable with her glasses on.

"Yeah, I just have one more call to make to Allen. I was just checking on you. Did you get enough to eat?" I said, glancing at the TV in the living room to see if there was anything on about the breaking story about Kastrati.

"I did. I'll clean up in a second. I just had some work emails I got sidetracked with," she said.

"You can leave it for Gloria, babe. She will be here today."

She shot me a glance.

"Or not. I'll help you in a minute. Let me go call Allen real quick."

I smirked and went back into my office.

I found his contact information and hit send.

"Finally. Dude," he said.

"Sorry. I am chasing fires over here too," I said.

"What about that shit? When are you getting in the office dick-face? We have celebrating to do. Our systems in place brought down a notorious drug lord. Holy shit. Southstar Securities is about to fucking explode. I'm counting the days to retirement. What about you?" he rambled excitedly.

"You would never give it up. This is as close to living your John Wick wet dreams as you can without leaving the comfort of that fancy thousand-dollar leather chair behind your desk."

I laughed.

"You seriously hate that chair?"

"No. I just think it's stiff as hell, and why do you need air conditioning in it? You are skinny as fuck. That's for fat dudes."

I laughed, shaking my head. Damn, I loved busting his balls.

If he only knew this entire deal was connected to Lauren. While we are joking around and he was celebrating, I was having a freaking internal meltdown. I got to wait on Jakob, who was going to come home with my fiancé alive, dead, or once again, with no more answers than I have had over the last two damn years.

"I'll be in after I take Cassie to the airport." I looked at my watch. "In about an hour and a half." My heart fell. "I need to go."

"All right. Tell her I said hi," he said before hanging up.

I came out to a clean kitchen, the TV was off, and her suitcase was sitting by the door.

"Cassie?" I called out, nervous.

She came out of the bathroom. "Hey, you done?" She was completely clueless of the shitshow called my life, wrapping her arms around my body.

"Yeah, I don't want you to go. Can we cancel your flight? Stay here forever?" I asked, kissing her head.

"Jack isn't competent to raise Cora on his own, and I would be in breach of my contract with the studio," she said.

"Well, I guess we need to talk about Christmas on the way to the airport," I said.

"I don't want to." She pouted.

"We will make it fun. I promise."

Chapter 30

CASSIE

I walked into work at the studio Tuesday to a meeting, instantly bombarded with an insane holiday schedule. Arie sprung a last-minute trip to New York on me for a holiday cooking segment on the Today Show along with a shameless plug for the upcoming cookbook and cookware line.

"They had a cancellation with another chef, Cassie. We need to jump on this opportunity. You seriously can't say no to this," she demanded.

I sighed. "How long will I be there?" I asked.

"Three days, tops. I'll put you up in a nice hotel, I promise." She winked.

"Fine. What am I cooking in the segment?" I asked.

"Fuck if I know? That's not my job, Cassie."

She turned to leave.

I swore. I honestly didn't know what her job was sometimes.

I swiveled my chair around and pouted, looking at the city. I took out my phone. I needed to catch up on so much shit I didn't know where to start.

Sagi first. I called Kyle.

"Good morning, Chef," he said in a jovial tone. He was obviously getting laid these days, and it made my life more pleasant.

"Good morning to you. What is on the schedule for the week?

I am in my cell up here at Alcatraz-lite today, but I'm all yours the rest of this week," I said, joking with our banter about my second career at the studio.

"Really? Like, all week?" he asked.

"Well, I am working Wednesday through Friday for you, I thought?" I questioned.

"Oh, shit. Yes. Sorry, I'm on another planet today," he said. "Oh, Cassie. I have that kid, Benjamin, from Charleston staging this week. So, Reggie and Darius will finish up with him. He's freaking awesome. You will like him."

I thought, thinking back, Benjamin, Benjamin.

"Oh. The kid I met at Food and Wine. Right. I forgot he was here this week. I thought it was closer to Christmas. I can't wait to meet him."

"Also, can you mark me off the schedule for the week after Thanksgiving? I have to go to New York for a cooking segment on the Today Show now," I said with dread.

"Yeah, the Today Show. That's what normal people do around here." He laughed. "You going to make all your Al Roker dreams come true?"

Shit. Did I make my weatherman obsessions known to everyone?

"Leave my weathermen alone. Well, I may need you to mark me off for hurricane season, though, I heard Jim Cantore needs a personal chef when he hits the road."

I laughed.

"You are so weird," he said.

I chuckled. "Stephen said the same thing yesterday. I think I'm perfectly sane. I'll be in tomorrow. I bet I have a major list waiting for me," I said.

"Nah, not too bad. Reggie, Darius, and the crew are ready to go. You just have to babysit. I've potty-trained them well."

He laughed.

"Well, I hope you have a great trip with Grace," I said.

"Thanks, I will."

I got a knock at my door, which had me turning around from my city escape.

"Hey, Cassie," Johnathan said, as he entered my office.

"Good morning, Johnathan. How are you today?"

"I'm great. So, a couple of things, we scheduled a photoshoot for the cookbook, and I put it in your calendar. Here are a few ideas the kitchen has for the segment in New York." He handed me a handout. "And this is the final selections on the cookware they want you to sign off on when you have a chance."

"Got it," I said.

"Coffee?" he asked.

I looked up at him and smiled big. Blinking my eyes obnoxiously.

He just shook his head and rolled his eyes. He knew me very well.

My phone buzzed on my desk with a text message.

It was Britt. I thought I should ask her to go to New York with me for that segment. That would make it more fun. I opened my phone.

> Britt: Hey. What the fuck? You haven't called me about what is going on.
>
> Me: I just got home. I haven't had a chance, chill.
>
> Britt: WTF?
>
> Me: Why are you being aggressive? It's just a weekend of fireside sex. Lol.
>
> Britt: Dude. This is nuts. Aren't you freaking out?
>
> Me: Over what???

My phone rang.

"Hey," I answered.

"Cassie. Are you seriously unaware of the shit show that is happening?" she asked.

I asked, now officially freaking out, "What the hell is happening, Britt? You are scaring me."

"Shit. I'm sorry. I thought you were just avoiding me," she said. She took a deep breath. "So, there is some Albanian drug lord who was captured yesterday morning. Like the whole operation went down. Supposedly, they were involved in drugs and sex trafficking and all kinds of shit."

Confused, I laughed. "What the hell does this have to do with us?"

She snapped at me, "I'm getting to it. They mentioned new cyber security systems and government blah, blah, blah, and some crap that was involved, and Southstar. That's Stephen's company, right?" she asked.

"Yeah, Southstar Securities," I said slowly, now...listening.

"They brought up the correlation between the disappearance of Lauren and this Albanian dude. They showed her picture, Stephen's picture. It was on the national news, Cass."

My heart just lept from my body. What was she telling me?

"Did they find her or something? I'm so confused Britt."

"No, they are just trying to put stuff together and her disappearance, I guess. Like these guys have something to do with it. I don't know. Obviously, Stephen knows about this. His company is involved, right?" she asked. "What is he saying about it, Cass?"

Was this why he had been stressed? Was this why his phone was blowing up yesterday morning? The rush to his office? Why wouldn't he tell me?

"Maybe, I don't know. I guess I should call him and find out," I said.

"Wait. He hasn't talked to you about this? It happened yesterday morning," she said. "Call him and call me back. Man, I have celebrity and spy friends? Y'all are like, so much cooler than us."

She laughed.

"I wouldn't go that far. This doesn't seem like it's that much fun," I said and in a slight daze, I managed to ramble off, "Oh, speaking of the celebrity thing, I was going to see if you wanted to go to New York with me the week after Thanksgiving. I have to go for a segment for the Today Show and thought it would be more fun with you," I practically mumbled.

"Hell yeah, send me the dates. We are usually dead at the

restaurant then," she said. "Oh shit. Does this mean you get to live out your Al Roker fantasy?"

"Jesus. Do I tell this to everyone?" I asked.

"He's freaking adorable. I want to cuddle in a bed full of Oompa-Loompas, so there is that."

She cackled.

"Well, you are flat-out disturbed. That's been proven. Let me call Stephen. I'll call you later," I said.

"Love you."

"Love you more."

I contemplated. Did I call or text him? I even talked to him at great lengths last night when I got home. He had been out with Allen and his co-workers. He was in a good mood.

I found his face, I text him…

Cassie: I got a call from Britt about Albanians, your company, and Lauren?

My heart felt hollow. It borderline felt like it did when I sat at my kitchen counter waiting for Jack to come home the night I caught him with Beth. I felt like I had been lied to, and I didn't like it. My leg bounced as I just stared at the screen.

Come on dots…fucking dance.

Moments later, Johnathan brought my coffee that I no longer wanted. I tried looking at the task at hand and went over the ideas for the Today Show. My choices being holiday left-over egg rolls, Hoisin Asian meatballs, or crunchy shrimp wanton balls. Fuck. I don't care. I just reverted to staring at my black phone screen.

It rang. I was startled. It was my mom.

"Hey, Mom," I said, with a sigh.

"Don't sound so excited."

She laughed.

"Sorry, I was waiting for a different call. What's up?" I asked.

"What's wrong, baby?" she asked, worried.

"I don't want to get into it. Probably more than it needs to be. You know, me and how I overreact."

I rolled my eyes to myself, leaning back in my chair and biting my nails nervously.

"Well, you can talk to me if you want, okay?"

"I know."

"The reason I was calling is about Thanksgiving. We are very excited, and I just wanted to know if there is anything you need me to bring you from here. Two weeks. Is Cora excited?" she asked.

I thought of my conversation with Cora just this morning and how she was excited about taking my parents to some of her favorite places in town and doing homemade pizza and movie night at the apartment like we have made a tradition of doing. We even talked about going to get a Christmas tree early since we would have my dad's help.

"She is really excited, Mom. I am too. I hope we can manage to have some sort of resemblance to a holiday. I need to get into the spirit. Y'all are just what the doctor ordered."

"It's going to be wonderful, Cassandra. If you think of anything you want from here or you want to talk about what is on your mind, just call, okay?"

"Okay, Mom, thank you."

We said our gushy I love yous before hanging up, and once again, I was disappointed to see that more time passed and no returned text or call. I couldn't sit there and wait.

I dialed his number. I got his voicemail. The sound of his voice melted me, and then the dreaded beep. What I wanted to say confidently came out sad and low.

"Hey, I need to talk to you. Call me."

I didn't want that. I didn't want a long-distance relationship if I couldn't trust someone. I couldn't even trust my own feelings. I was too emotional for that shit. I was not ready. I just needed to drown myself in work and my kid. It was safe there. I couldn't handle this. I needed to get out of this fucking office.

I grabbed my things and headed out to Johnathan's desk.

"Hey. There really isn't anything here I can't do at home. If you need me, I'll be there or at Sagi, okay?"

He just shook his head. "Okay. Is everything all right?" he asked, slightly worried.

"I think so, probably not. I just need to get out of here. I have too much nervous energy to sit at a desk today. I'm sorry," I said, slightly neurotic.

Once I reached the cool air, I felt like I could breathe again. They wouldn't fire me, would they? I laughed out loud about that thought, and I made my way to my car. Just as I pulled into my complex, my phone rang.

It was Stephen.

My heart almost stopped. I was relieved, sad, confused, and mad all at the same time.

Control, Cass.

"Hello?" I answered through my car. I pulled it into a space and put it in park.

"Hey, baby," he replied.

"I am guessing you got my text. What is going on, Stephen?" I asked him.

He took a deep breath, and I could hear him let it out, like he had been holding it for months.

"Is this what has been bothering you all this time? That you didn't want to talk to me about every time I asked?" I pleaded.

"Yeah. It's been a lot on my mind," he said.

Tears started to fall. "Please talk to me." I sniffled.

"I am so sorry, Cass. I'm so fucking sorry," he said in a crackling voice.

My heart ripped open. What the hell did he do? Oh my god. Not again.

"Stephen. I need you to talk to me. Just tell me what happened, please," I begged.

"I have been hiding all this from you because I didn't want you to get scared and leave me again. Also, I wasn't allowed to share most of the information, according to the CIA. There was stuff that was put out today that was classified, the stuff about my company and Lauren, that was somehow leaked, I don't fucking know." He was now crying. "I have been dying inside, wanting to be truthful, I swear."

"So, what is happening now? What have they discovered?" I asked.

He sighed and sniffled. "So, well fuck it, I might as well tell you. Her and her brother Jakob are undercover European DEA. He went to their compound with the other agents after they caught the Albanians yesterday. All this time, they told him she was dead. Yesterday, they found evidence that she may very well be alive and possibly escaped."

"Okay. That's good. That's good, Stephen. We want that for you," I said nervously.

Meanwhile, I didn't know what my heart wanted. I didn't want her dead, for heaven's sake. I just didn't want her in our relationship.

"I feel like this is a betrayal to you, Cass. Me, even wanting her alive," he said.

Anger rushed in. "Wait. Why are you making me out to be a monster all of a sudden?"

"I just feel like I have to walk on eggshells to deal with the grief of losing her, or the possibility of her being alive, and hiding it from you," he said.

"Stephen, this is a narrative you have in your head. It's not true. I want her alive." I wailed. "I just don't want to compete with her constantly, for years, if she is dead, alive, missing. I want the Stephen who has moved on. I don't want you to hide shit from me in the first place or to feel like you have to walk on eggshells. Who the hell has CIA and DEA agents looking for their fiancés while they are in a relationship?" I stopped to take a breath to hear silence. "Are you there?"

"Yeah," he said.

"What are we going to do?" I asked.

"I told you, I'm not going to lose you again, Cass. I'm not," he said.

I started to cry. "Maybe we need to just take a..."

"No," he cried. "Please, Cass."

"Stephen, let's just slow down, okay?" My breaths become jagged. "Let's just focus on all the things we have going on and just..."

"Fuck, baby. Can I just come there? Talk this out in person, please?" his voice shook.

"I don't have much time. I'm working this week at Sagi. I have Cora, then my parents come for Thanksgiving, then I have to go to New York...I, I don't know."

"I'll fly there for thirty minutes if I have to, Cassie, you know this. Don't run. For fuck's sake, don't run from me," he said.

I took a deep breath. "I'm not running. I need a minute," I cried. "I can't compete with her, Stephen. I just can't. I need to be the only one in your life. Call me selfish. I don't want to be the other woman anymore. I played that part, and it didn't work out real well." I came unglued. "I love you so fucking much. I have given you my heart for nearly thirty years of my life. I'm not ready to quit you, but I can't share you, I'm sorry. I'm so, so sorry."

I bawled.

"Cassie, please, baby, please," he cried.

"I need to go," I said.

"No. Please, baby. Don't," he yelled.

"I'm in my car, Stephen. I need to go."

"I'll text you later?"

"Bye, Stephen," I whimpered.

Cora made me grilled cheese and cut up some fruit for dinner that night, setting it on my nightstand.

"Mom, are you okay?" she asked, running her fingers through my hair as I lay in the fetal position on my bed, tears flowing endlessly from my eyes. I hadn't even done this with Jack. I had no control over my feelings this time.

"Yeah, I'll be okay," I whispered, wiping my nose with a tissue.

"Do you want me to call Britt?" she asked.

"No," I said, shaking my head. "I just need a minute. Sometimes the heart just needs a minute, baby girl."

Chapter 31

CASSIE

I woke up the next morning to thirty-two text messages.

Holy shit.

I scrolled through them to check for the level of urgency before going into full freak-out mode. They were mostly from Britt, wondering what happened and why I had ghosted her with the news, and checking to see if I was okay. She had a fucked-up habit of breaking a text up into twenty tiny ones, which made me bonkers.

The others.

Stephen pleading with me to call him. I could hear the tears behind his words, making my heart wrench with pain again.

My mom with a simple message of worry and one from Jack.

Cora had called him, worried about me last night. Now he wanted to comfort me? I shook my head, wanting to just crawl back under the covers, but I needed to move forward with the day. I had business mode to go into, what I did best. I needed to wrap myself in it, like a cocoon, until I felt safe again.

"Cora," I called out, walking down the hall to the kitchen. "Time to get up, baby."

I flipped the dim lights on in the kitchen and made my way to the coffee maker, getting it started before heading to the shower. I took in a deep breath, stopping to look out over the living room, leaning against the counter. I gazed out at the morning view of the bridge. The city just starting to wake up for the day. I could hear and smell the coffee going behind me, waking my senses. It took me back to the weekend I first moved in there. Taking Stephen that first cup of coffee that morning, feeling giddy, just wondering how he liked it. My heart swelled, and I laughed at that little feeling. I remembered his face that morning, disheveled hair, and gorgeous body in my bed. My eyes brimmed as I looked at the kitchen island before me. Just minutes after he got there, I dropped my little dress, and he put me up there. His face was between my legs. My god.

"Mom. Where is my cheer jacket?" Cora yelled from her room and pulled me from my thoughts.

Startled, I wiped my eyes.

"Um, I think it's hanging in the laundry room, Cora, check there," I called to her, voice shaky.

I turned back around and poured a cup of coffee, some oat milk, and the tears flowed.

Fuck. How was I going to get through this goddamn day... this week?

I took a deep breath and got to my room, starting my ritual of making my bed, showering, and getting ready for work. I gave up on eyeliner and mascara for the third time.

The daydream drive to Cora's school consisted of listening to her chatter about boys and friends, trying to focus on her, anything but...him and this clusterfuck we were in.

Once I walked into Sagi, my mind was instantly wiped clean like a dry-erase board. This was the most therapeutic place to be, with lists to tackle, people busy with non-stop questions, decisions to make, and time just escaped me with how much there was to do.

Of course, I had forgotten we had Benjamin, the sweet nineteen-year-old aspiring chef from Charleston staging for the week. He was expecting me to be my charismatic, amazing self he met during the Food and Wine Festival, and I just wasn't in the right mindset. I rounded the corner, and he was getting a world-class lesson on dumpling making. Brandon and Darius worked on making more farce while Reggie and Benjamin rolled fast and precise, laying them out on floured-lined cookie sheets before going into the freezer.

"How are we doing?" I said, poking my head in on their work.

"I think I have it down," Benjamin said, holding up a dumpling for me to see.

"I think you do. It looks great," I said, walking over to the pot of water.

I stood over the pot, staring blankly, watching the water slowly coming to a rolling boil. I could hear the conversation to the left of me. Reggie told Benjamin, "The trick is to never overstuff your dumpling and make sure it's sealed real tight. Then, when it goes into the water, make sure it's right at boiling point. If it's rolling, and it's not sealed, all that farce will spill out and your dumping is a goner."

I thought to myself, staring into the water, just like my heart, Benjamin. I let it get too full. I didn't make sure it was sealed up. My world was at boiling point, and my heart was a goner. It was a fucking goner.

I didn't have much time to dwell on my exploding heart at the bottom of a pot of hot water because Reggie was too busy showing me pictures and videos of baby Violet with every spare minute he had. When I finally got a moment of quiet in my office to tackle orders, I was hit with my pending texts, and there one sat, heavy.

Stephen: Look at your ankle.

Chapter 32

STEPHEN

I sat casually slumped in a chair across from Allen in his sleek, modernly designed office, dressed in jeans and a sweater, completely out of work mode. I had officially spent the last hour spilling my guts about the entire Albanian-Lauren saga I had been holding in. That felt like therapy, sitting across from him, except his jaw was on the floor. Very unprofessional if he were a therapist.

"What are you going to do about Cassie, man? Has she responded to you yet?" he asked.

I shook my head, reached down, and put my head into my hands.

"I don't know." Then I leaned back, saying, "I came up with a couple of possible scenarios last night to win her back while I was texting her nonstop like a lunatic."

He nodded.

I started with, "I could stand outside her complex with a boom box in the pouring rain professing my undying love for her, but she's on the twelfth floor and, well, it's California, and it never fucking rains there." I throw my hands up. "Then I thought I could go super elaborate, I don't know…fly in on the jet and whisk her away like, in a limo with flowers bullshit…"

"Hold up," he said with a hand outstretched, stopping me,

laughing, "Have you been eating a fucking tub of ice cream, watching 80s rom-coms, man?"

I laughed. "No. Well, I may have tapped into that bottle of Pappy Van Winkle 23 you brought me last week while channel surfing and stumbled on Pretty Woman. That scene where she's wearing that prostitute mini-skirt get-up and drives the Lambo for him? Come on. That was fucking hot. You can't deny stopping for that scene."

"I don't know. I'm more of the piano scene guy," he said. "Wait. What the fuck are we talking about? Thank God nobody just heard that conversation."

We both laughed.

"What the fuck are you going to do?" he asked.

"I just dropped a thought-provoking text, and I'm going to give her space. I'm going to go to good ole Marguerite's, see some friends, and pray she comes to her senses. It's all I can do. As far as Lauren, I am going to pray they find her alive and figure my life out then. My life is a mess, Allen." I stand. "I am going to work remotely from Charleston for a bit. I just need to get the fuck away from here. Away from that goddamn house."

"Go. We got it," he said.

I turned to leave. "I'm not losing her. I'm not."

I dodged my new normal reporters in the parking lot of the office building.

Jesus.

The PTSD of two years ago came rushing back. I remembered that all too well.

What to say: No comment.

I climbed into the blacked-out world of my Defender and sped away.

I pulled into the driveway of my mom's house, the place that felt like a sanctuary from the chaos of Charlotte. She stepped out onto the spacious porch. Damn. It felt like it had been a year since I'd seen her. Marguerite Harlow was an exquisite woman, tall, slender, dark hair and eyes, flowing gracefully with every movement. She was as southern as you can get with her mannerisms, grace, and charm.

She walked down the steps to greet me halfway down the brick walkway, arms wide open.

"My sweet Stephen. Come here, baby."

She kissed me on the cheek, and her hug was so comforting, like a warm blanket on a chilly night.

"Hey, Mom," I said. "You look so good. Vacation does you well."

In her long southern drawl, she said, "Oh honey, I am blessed. So, so blessed. Come in. It's cold out here."

It was literally fifty-five degrees, and Charlestonians thought it was parka weather.

We caught up, and I spilled all the beans about my insane life. Unfortunately, she learned from the news about the Albanian kidnapping crisis, seeing our pictures across the TV screen, completely freaking her out, and I had to talk her off the ledge for over an hour on the phone that day already.

"I am so happy you and Cassie Patterson found each other. I just adore Anne and Sam," she gushed.

"She's Buckley now, Mom, and I hope I still have her. I hope this mess doesn't have her running."

I ran my hands through my hair and took a sip of my sweet tea.

"Do you want something stronger than that, honey? A beer? A drink?" she asked.

"I'm okay. I think I need to slow my roll with the alcohol. I hit the whiskey a little hard last night and binge-watched too many rom-coms and over texted her last night."

I laughed.

"Oh boy." She giggled.

"I'm going to unpack and see what some of the guys are up to this weekend if that's okay. Do you want to go to dinner or something tonight?" I asked.

"I was actually going to make your favorite tonight, if that was okay?"

"No way. Squash casserole and fried chicken?" I asked excitedly.

She smiled. "Yes."

"I love you, Mom," I said, placing a kiss on her cheek before getting up to leave and make my way over to the carriage house.

I walked in, and the memories flooded my mind of the last time I was here with her. Dammit. She was everywhere now. There was no escaping the memories. Just as I started to unpack, my phone notified me of a message.

I reached into my pocket, and there it was, a text from Cass. My heart fell. Just knowing she wasn't shutting me out was a first step in the right direction.

She sent me a gif of a girl on a bike with sparks flying behind it I laughed.

Cassie: I do love you Stephen

My eyes were now brimming with tears, and the words on my screen were becoming blurry, but I felt them.

I decided not to go overboard with a slew of texts but just one simple one.

Me: I love you too sexy girl. Whenever you are ready, I'll be here.

Then there was silence again.

Dinner was delicious and with my mom, it felt like home. We talked about the upcoming Thanksgiving holiday. My brother Ethan, his wife Meredith, and their boys would be here. I loved having family around me. It was what I always wanted and rarely seem to have. Hopefully it would drown the feeling of emptiness without Cassie there.

"I heard from Cassie," I told her.

"Oh, Stephen. Good, I hope?" she asked.

"Yes, ma'am," I said.

She pressed her palm to the side of my face, looking into my eyes.

"Just have patience, honey. What you have going on is a lot. She has been through a lot too."

She patted my face and got up from the table, clearing the plates.

I helped her in the kitchen, and we had a glass of wine on the porch, chatting some more before I went back to the carriage house.

I decided to text Anne, Cassie's mom. She had given me her number when I flew her to San Francisco for Cassie's divorce.

Me: Hi Mrs. Patterson, it's Stephen. I am in town, and I was wondering if I could stop by tomorrow? I have something I would like for you to take to Cassie when you go next week if it isn't too much trouble?

Anne: I will be home all day. Please come by any time.

Me: Thank you.

I texted Kent and some other friends. I decided to make the most of my time here in Charleston. I felt better, like I had hope that it was going to be okay with Cassie and me. I just need to give her a minute.

Chapter 33

CASSIE

I sat on my big, comfy couch, wine in hand, as the storm rolled in over the bay. The sky was gray and ominous against the dark blue angry, white-capped waters.

Cora came in.

"Can I watch with you?"

Thunderstorms were so rare there, so when they happened, we tended to stop what we were doing, and took it in, like a movie on the big screen. Fortunately for us, we chose this view. I knew deep down inside, she was thanking me for this location.

"Of course," I said, as she leaned her back into me, feet tucked up into her body. I ran my fingers through her long hair in rhythmic, flowing movements. We sat in silence, waiting for the rumble of the thunder to begin.

"You can tell me about him, Mom. Who has you this upset?" she said, breaking the silence, still looking forward. I realized her voice was no longer that of a little girl.

My heart beat fast, her question took my breath.

I said, almost stumbling on my words, "Oh, well, I have actually known him since high school."

She turned her head and looked at me in surprise. "What? Really?" she smiled.

I smiled back, looking away shyly. "Yeah, we have dated on and off forever. Well, except when me and your dad were together, of course," I said.

The thunder rumbled and streaks of lightning raced across the sky, sending her closer to me.

"Whoa. Watch the wine."

My mind wandered back to the conversation of Stephen wanting to scold me for having red wine on my stark white couch and the pending spanking I was still aching for.

"Do you have a picture of him?" she said, pulling my mind out of the gutter.

"You really want to see him, Cora?" I asked.

"Yeah, I do. He has you so happy, then upset. He must mean a lot to you. I should know about him too," she said.

I took out my phone and scrolled through my pictures. Trying to find the best one to show her and I realized they are all wonderful. This man was so photogenic. Damn. We had so many great moments, taken some sweet pictures. I chose the one on the sailboat. The one I used as his profile picture. I handed her my phone. It felt so special to be sharing the moment with her right now.

She took it.

"Mom. He is so cute. Wow. He looks just like Daddy," she said in surprise.

I laughed. "No, he doesn't."

"Um, yes, he does, but different. He looks happy. Tell me about him," she said.

And I did. I poured more wine, and we sat face to face and chatted like two friends talking about boys for over an hour. When I was done telling her all about him, it made me miss him that much more. I wished he had his world in order. I wished I knew where I fitted in it.

Cora looked down, picking at a loose stitch on her sweater, scared to make eye contact with me.

"Dad has a girlfriend, too. He said you know."

"I know. Beth."

"He said she's nice. He said I can meet her soon when I am ready," she said.

"Are you ready?" I asked her. "It's okay with me if you are."

"I guess so." She shrugged. "I just want you two to be happy. I felt better with him having a girlfriend when I found out you found someone."

I chuckled. "It's okay Cora. It's not a competition. I'm okay. We aren't always going to be happy at the same time. It's not how it works, honey," I said, tucking a stray hair behind her ear, trying to get her to look at me. "Mine and Stephen's relationship is, I don't know, very complicated. I don't know what will become of us. I support your dad's happiness, and you can too." I smiled.

"Okay." She leaned in and hugged me. "Hopefully, it works out with you two, and I can meet him."

"I would like that too, baby," I said softly.

I thought I might have just done some forgiveness shit. I was letting it go. I was setting my anger towards Jack and Beth free for Cora's well-being.

I looked out at the sky. It was over. We made it through this storm.

The next day at Sagi was the same as usual, except my mood was more optimistic than yesterday.

"Good morning, Reg," I called out, as I peeked in the kitchen before heading into my office.

"Good morning, Chef," he answered.

After a few minutes of rifling through the pending orders for the day and looking at the menu we had created for the weekend, I heard a knock at my door.

It was Reggie.

"Chef, you have a minute?" he asked.

"Yeah, Reg. What's up?" I asked, looking up, taking off my glasses.

"I'm having a great time with you this week. I am a bit nervous about being on the line with you tonight and tomorrow. We have Fish Bowl tables, and I've never worked those with you. I really don't want to mess up," he said nervously, pulling at the tie on his apron.

I wanted to laugh at how innocent and childish he looked for such a big, strong guy he was, but I didn't dare.

I said, "Hey. Reg. We are going to have fun. I am rusty as hell. I haven't cooked in so long. I should be your sous."

He looked up and smiled. "All right."

Changing the subject, I asked, "What trucks do we have?"

"Only produce from Mitchell Farms. They are the new mushroom grower Kyle found. Great find," he said.

"Love it. When I'm done here, let's go over the specials and the mese en plas with the line and make tonight a successful one, okay?" I asked.

"Yes, Chef." He smiled.

The night went perfectly. So perfectly, I was able to put on my clean chef coat and visit with my guests in the dining room. That felt so foreign and so much more comfortable now that I was used to being in the spotlight these days. People's heads were turning a lot more now as I walked through the dining room, hands to their mouths to whisper to the person next to them as I walked past. I noticed, smiled, and kept moving.

My first stop, our Fish Bowl Table guests of course, who paid a premium. They were blown away by their meal, service, and something that had never happened, now wanting pictures with me. I thanked them for coming and continued moving throughout the dining room until I made it to the bar.

"You made it," Margaret said, smiling as she was wiping a wine glass dry with a white cloth as I walked up.

"That seemed like a different experience tonight," I said.

She laughed. "From here, it looked like one too. The dining room seemed to come alive when you walked out."

I shook my head. "You cook on TV and things get weird."

She put the wine glass she was drying in front of a gentleman sitting at the bar, saying, "Here you go, Adam."

She poured him a glass of wine.

He turned and looked at me, reaching out a hand.

"I don't think we have actually met yet. I'm Adam Norris, your new wine purveyor."

"Oh, Chef. I totally forgot you haven't been here in so long. I'm so sorry, I thought you had met."

She clumsily tried to fix her mistake.

"No worries, Margaret."

I put my hand up, laughing, and shook his hand.

He stood, tall, blonde, slight curl in his hair and crystal blue eyes. Gorgeous man.

I smiled and motioned for him to sit back down.

"So, how long have you been my dealer?" I laughed at my own joke.

He laughed back, getting it, and said, "About two months, now?" looking at Margaret for confirmation as she nodded while dunking glasses in a sanitizing solution in front of us.

We chatted about wine for what I thought was only fifteen minutes but noticed he had finished his glass, and the restaurant was now almost empty. Margaret was giving me the eye of, *You need to go into the kitchen now* and time just seemed to slip by too easily with this man.

"Well, I need to get back to work before they call in a missing person for me back there. It was nice to meet you, Adam. Welcome aboard," I said, reaching out my hand.

He took it, looking into my eyes. Oh shit. That was a look that got the senses going. Fuck. I instantly got flustered.

"Alrighty. Bye now."

I turned and briskly walked back down the hall to the kitchen.

Closing the restaurant consisted of two beers and really taking cleaning to a new level while listening to music through my earbuds. What I didn't realize, my playlist must have gone rogue and a bit sexual, catching myself singing out loud.

"I like the way you touch me there, I like the way you pull my hair."

I looked up and saw my entire kitchen staff staring at me.

Once I was home, the Google search bar, the BOB, and I had a date.

Chapter 34

STEPHEN

I made my way up the steps of the Patterson's porch to be greeted by Sam as he was making his way out the door.

"Oh. Hey there, Stephen. I heard you were stopping by today at some point."

He reached out his hand.

"Hi, Mr. Patterson. How are you doing, Sir?" I asked, giving him a firm shake in response.

"I was just about to go to the store. Anne is inside. Anne. Stephen is here," he called, peeking his head inside of the house.

I turned to see her making her way toward me down the hallway through the glass door.

"You two kids have fun. I'll be right back if you are still here," he said, so friendly.

"Okay, sounds great," I said, smiling back at him.

Anne held the door open. "Come on in, hon."

She put a hand on my arm as I passed by.

"I won't stay long, I just had a card I wanted to have you hand deliver if you wouldn't mind?" I asked, handing it to her.

She tilted her head, gently taking it from me. "Is this really all?"

I took in a deep breath. "You are hard to get things past, aren't you?"

She laughed. "Yes, Stephen. I'm the master at this. What the hell is going on with you two? She is barely talking to me."

I shook my head. "Well, that's both of us."

"Oh my gosh. My manners. Come in here."

She waved me into the living room to have a seat on the couch. I sat.

"Mrs. Patterson, I don't want to put you in the middle of our drama. That isn't the purpose of this at all."

She went right in.

"She's stubborn as hell, Stephen. She is an only child, and we didn't spoil her rotten, but she definitely got showered with all the attention because, well, she was the only one." She sighed. "I just want to apologize out of the gate for that," she said with a screwed-up face. "Not to bring up a sore subject, but we have had to apologize for this with Jack a few times."

I laughed. "I don't blame you. She is the most amazing, strong-willed creature I have ever met. It's what I love about her. I just want to reach her. I pretty much said all I could, and I am giving her space."

"Perfect. She is a thinker. She will come around. Drop a crumb now and then, but she will come around. She loves you, Stephen," she said, placing a comforting hand on my shoulder.

"Thanks, Anne. I wish I could be with her this Thanksgiving, but I'm hoping by giving her what she needs now, by Christmas, it will be different. Maybe you will have a better gauge of that when you visit. Put in a good word for me?" I asked, shrugging my shoulders.

"You bet." She smiled.

I stood to leave when she caught me off guard.

"One more thing I would like to ask," she said. "Sam and I were watching the news, and we happened to see you have some dealings with some Albanians? Is there something we should be worried about? Our daughter's safety?"

She arched an eyebrow.

I shook my head and closed my eyes. "No, ma'am. Everything is just fine."

I chuckled.

She smiled. "The two of you choose to be celebrities in the strangest ways," she said, walking me to the door.

"I didn't choose this one, I promise. Thanks again for this and our talk. I feel so much better."

We stood on the front porch, and she reached out to hug me. I felt like I held a small piece of Cassie. I mean small because it was like hugging the tiny version of her.

The next week and a half consisted of remote work meetings, catching up with old friends, and having an amazing Thanksgiving holiday with my family. I drank and ate to excess and managed to laugh harder than I had in years. I continued giving Cassie space but dropped the proverbial breadcrumbs here and there when I could. I missed our usual banter, the sexual tension, and the closeness we had created. I wanted it back so badly. I craved it.

Thanksgiving night, I was helping my mom in the kitchen with dishes when I received a text message. My heart swelled when I saw it was her.

> Cassie: I got your card, seeing your handwriting made me cry.

That was what I was going for, but now I wondered, was that the good or bad crying?

Shit.

> Me: Happy tears, I hope?

> Cassie: Yes

> Me: I miss you

> Cassie: I miss you too. It hurts being apart.

> Me: We don't have to be, baby.

> Cassie: I don't know where I fit Stephen. Nothing has changed.

Oh fuck. I just went too far. Nothing was resolved. I had to get in front of her to have this conversation. I had to prove to her where she belonged in my life.

Me: When can I see you?

Cassie: I don't know. I'm so busy right now. I leave for NY in 2 days

Give her space Stephen. Give her space.

Me: You name it, I'm there.

Cassie: Okay. Let me think.

She was a thinker, Anne said. Jesus. I liked a complicated, free-thinking woman, but Cassie Buckley was going to give me a heart attack. I got an *Okay.*

The next day, I was wrestling and giving my nephew horseback rides in my mom's living room when I felt my phone vibrating in my back pocket.

"Uncle Tefen. Your butt is tickling me."

He laughed.

"Brandon, it's my phone. Grab it out of my pocket, buddy," I said as he was riding on my back.

"Oooh. She's pwetty," he said, looking at the screen as he passed it to me.

My heart raced.

"She is," I said, taking it out of his tiny, three-year-old chubby hand.

I quickly opened the phone.

"Hey," I answered, slightly out of breath, leaning on my elbows on all fours.

"Hey. Is this an okay time?" she asked.

I laughed as Brandon jumped back onto my back. "Hey, pwetty girl," he said, giggling, trying to talk into my phone over my shoulder.

She laughed. "Who is that?"

"My three-year-old wingman Brandon. We are out here trying to score chicks. Is it working yet?" I asked, laughing.

"Maybe. He may need to work on his game a little, but he has some time." She laughed.

That laugh. I missed it. I missed this so much.

"So, I was calling to take you up on that, *I'm there offer* from yesterday," she said.

My attention was instantly all hers, and my wingman was silenced by my quick shush and a finger in the air.

"Okay. What are you thinking?" I asked.

"Well, it's last minute, but I'll be in New York tomorrow for three days with Britt. I was thinking if you want to come meet me…"

"Yes," I answered immediately before she could finish her sentence.

She laughed. "Stephen, I didn't even finish."

"You didn't have to, Cass," I said. "I'll be there."

"Okay. I think it will be good. I would love to see you," she said.

I inhaled for the first time since our conversation on that horrible day.

"I would love to also, if you can't tell," I said, smiling, my heart feeling joy again.

She said, "Hey Stephen?"

"Yeah?"

"Tell your wingman that your moves are working. The pwetty girl likes you," she said.

Chapter 35

CASSIE

✗

I stood on stage, waiting nervously for our segment to start. It was going to be so quick. For these veterans up there, it was nothing, but for me, it was everything. Giada nudged me.

"Don't be nervous. Craig will screw up and make you feel completely competent," she said, laughing.

She was so tiny in person I realized, and absolutely stunning.

Sitting down at the tasting table across from us was Hoda, Savannah, and Al, who all waved. The cameramen got in place, and everyone was ready to roll, my nerves popped. Craig and Sheinelle made their way over to us, and we began the segment. It started without a hitch. Ina breezed through her Lazy Chai Cinnamon Rolls, which she mastered the clock with ease at no lie, two minutes, and with her smooth voice, it sounded like she did an entire show.

Next up was Giada, who made elegant but easy cheese-stuffed dates with prosciutto. Beautiful job. She flowed through her presentation like a fucking boss.

Craig moved over, introducing me and my restaurant Sagi-Shi, since I was new to the scene.

"So, what will we be making today, Cassie?" he asked with that great smile.

I instantly want to puke. I was fucking live. No thirty takes like I did in my studio at home, and I had under three minutes.

Let's get to work.

I took a deep breath and put my game face on.

"Craig, today we are making my family's favorite left-over egg rolls with turkey, mac and cheese, and collard greens."

I showed them how to stuff and roll them step by step.

"You can spray these down and pop them into an air fryer or deep fry them at 350 for two minutes. The dip was our gravy that I simply changed the flavor with some rubbed sage. If I used the stuffing instead of the mac and cheese, I would have used leftover cranberry sauce, adding half a juiced orange, the zest, and reduced that down as the dip."

I showed a pot on a completely fake-ass stove set up in front of me.

Hoda, Al, and Savannah, were eating and commenting on how much they loved it at the table across from me, and I knew damn well it's cold as hell because I made it over an hour ago. You gotta love the magic of TV.

Craig moved on from me and went to introduce the next segment. We were off the air, and I could breathe again. I made it. We all high-fived each other, and I was officially part of the Today Show chef crew. It was a sheer miracle that I didn't pass out or vomit on the stage.

Once that was over, I was whisked back to the green room where Britt was talking, or should I say holding court. When I walked in, it was as if she had her own comedy routine going on. She was standing at the front of the room and there were six people sitting in awe, listening to her stories.

She turned and saw me. "Oh, there she is now," she said.

Oh shit.

Was she telling stories about me?

One of the innocent bystanders stood and said before walking out, "Your friend Britt is a treasure. She adores you, that is for sure."

I turned to look at her. "What have you been doing in here?" I laughed nervously.

"Just making friends. Girl. You crushed it." She squealed.

"I wanted to throw up. I don't think I have ever been so nervous in my life," I said, putting my hand to my forehead.

"What's next?" she asked.

"Um, third hour with Hoda and Jenna," I said. "I will talk about the upcoming release of the cookbook and cookware line."

"Look at you." She held me by the shoulders. "Look at this." She held her hands out at the studio space we were standing in.

"I know. It's so surreal, right?" I said, covering my smile with my hand.

"It's so cool." She smiled.

Just then, Al Roker popped his head in. I thought Britt was going to stroke out for me, but we both managed to hold it together.

"I heard you were a huge weather nerd, Cassie?" he said.

"What? Who told you that?" I said, putting a hand to my chest, then turning to look at Britt with pursed lips.

What he didn't know was it isn't a weather nerd thing; it's a weather MAN thing. Big kinky difference.

"I am Al," I lied.

"Would you like a tour of the weather room while you wait on the third hour?" he asked.

"Um, hell yeah," I said like my ass was on fire. "Can my girl Britt come too?"

He laughed. "Yes, of course."

The personalized tour was wonderful. He was so funny and everything I knew he would be. The three of us joked around like we had known each other for years.

He looked at his watch. "I need to get you back. I can't play any more girls," he said, smiling.

We weaved our way through the studio to the green room where he deposited us.

"It was great meeting you, and I will see you at your restaurants when I make it to Charleston and San Francisco, okay?" he said before rushing down the hallway.

Britt and I just looked at each other. "Did that just happen?" I asked her.

"This is great." She squealed and bounced.

I reached into my purse to check my phone. I had multiple missed texts.

Arie: Great job on your cooking segment. You didn't puke Cassie.

Arie: Talk up that cookbook and Wok Set girl.

Stephen: You did great babe.

My heart swelled seeing his face, seeing his name, thinking that I would get to see him tomorrow.

Mom: That was so cool watching you.

A well put together blonde, carrying a clipboard popped her head in saying, "Cassie? Are you ready?"

Again, I wanted to vomit. Not as much as before because I wasn't cooking under pressure.

Hoda and Jenna were welcoming, and we breezed through talking about my restaurant, the San Francisco food scene, the cookbook and cookware pending release. They had a way of making me feel so relaxed I almost forgot I was on camera.

Once back in the greenroom I was greeted by a big Britt hug.

"Let's go drink," she said.

Britt and I roamed New York and did all the magical things. We ate our way through Little Italy and Chinatown, decadent hot chocolate in Sant Ambroeus, and ice skating in Midtown's Bryant Park that did not go well. Southern girls didn't ice skate, especially after a few cocktails.

We did a well-deserved and indulgent spa treatment the next day before Britt headed out to the airport.

I stood in the entryway of the hotel, refreshed, happy, as her Uber pulled up.

"I love you," I said, wrapping my arms around her.

"I love you too. That was so much fun. I hope you have a great time with Stephen." She looked in my eyes. "Give him some slack, Cass. Remember, it's just a missing fiancé and a drug cartel."

She laughed.

I shook my head, laughing, opening the door to her Uber. "Yes, I will."

"The dating pool sucks at our age. You could do worse, trust me. You could have found out he was the cartel."

She chuckled.

She climbed in and waved through the window as she rolled away.

I went back up to my room and got ready for the shift change. Stephen was due to arrive in two hours, and my sadness that Britt being gone had now been replaced with the excitement for his arrival. I was also nervous about how we were going to approach the status of our relationship.

I climbed from the elaborate marble and glass shower, hair piled up on my head. My phone buzzed on the bathroom counter. My feet hit the cool tile floor as I make my way across the well-appointed, steamy bathroom.

I tapped my screen, and I put in my code. I saw his gorgeous face, and my heart beat harder.

Stephen: I just landed. On my way sexy girl.

My entire body responded.

Chapter 36

STEPHEN

My excitement and anxiety was almost palpable as I climbed from the Uber at her hotel. The elevator ride up was basically torture, then standing in front of her suite door, pure exhilaration. I knocked, then there she was. It felt like it had been an eternity since I had seen her.

Her amber hair, cascading down her shoulders. Her big hazel eyes looking into mine.

I almost had to choke back tears, I missed her so much.

"Hey you," was all that squeaked out of my mouth.

She smiled. "Hey you," she said softly as she leaned against the door, looking fucking adorable and incredibly sexy at the same time.

She opened the door wider, inviting me in. I walked in, passing her, never taking my eyes off her. Taking in every inch of what I had missed over these last weeks. Absolute fucking torture. She closed the door, and it was over.

My voice cracked. "Cass, I…"

She put her fingers gently over my lips. Just looked into my eyes. Back and forth, then covered my lips with hers. Without a single word, she melted my entire being with her lips, her mouth, her tongue.

I ran my hands up her neck, to her jaw and held her head in mine, her hair flowing down my arms. The smell of her perfume, intoxicating me like a damn drug. The feel of her skin against my fingers like silk. I missed this so much. I never knew how much I needed her. I could not be without her.

My lips parted hers just long enough to break the silence for me to say, "I love you, Cassie, I love you so much, I am so, so sorry."

"I love you too. I'm sorry too," she whispered between kisses.

I slowly walked her backward into the large, sunny suite, that grew brighter as I moved, never breaking the seal on her beautiful mouth. She smiled underneath my kiss as we made it to the bed.

"Why did I even put clothes on?"

She laughed.

"I deserve to be tortured by this get up. What is this contraption?"

I stood back, hands out, and holding my head to the side.

She laughed. "Get up? Are you seventy?" She looked down at herself. "It's a leather jacket, turtleneck, skinny jeans, and thigh-high boots. High New York fashion, babe," she said with the most adorable smile.

"You should have just worn those sexy fucking boots," I said.

"Fiend." She laughed.

"Yes, I am. For you, baby," I said as I started peeling the layers of the bondage-like clothing off her body, one by one, looking into her eyes, kissing her as I went.

The coat, I tossed to the chair in the corner. I lifted her top over her head, revealing her magnificent breasts, full, inviting beneath a black lace bra. I ran my thumbs over her nipples under that fabric. Fuck. I wanted to get to them. I wanted to suck them, bite them, but I was taking my time. I didn't jerk off eight times the last two days for nothing, for this very moment. I was going to take this slow.

Damn, how did I get these jeans off? So tiny, so tight, fuck, I could almost eat them off of her. I kissed her and laid her on the bed, pressing my body over top of hers. Damn. Her amber hair splayed all around her beautiful face against the white linens. She was a sight, such beauty. I stood and unzipped her boots down her long, lean legs, pulling them off, dropping them to the floor, peeling her socks off, stopping to notice and laughed.

"Snoop Dog smoking a joint?"

She covered her mouth and laughed. "I forgot thin socks for my boots, and Britt had bought them on the trip."

I peeled off her Snoop socks, reached up and unbuttoned and unzipped her jeans. With some assistance from her, I peeled them off her legs, leaving on a black lace thong, and a very, very sexy Cassie on the bed. My dick was hard as fuck beneath my jeans as I stood undressing myself with her watching.

Her voice, soft, said, "I have missed that body. God, you are so sexy, baby."

I peeled down my boxer briefs, setting my dick free.

She gasped. "Oh damn. I don't know why I almost forgot how glorious that is. Come here, baby."

She motioned me on top of her.

I slid my naked body on top of her, between her legs, kissing her stomach, reaching underneath, unhooking her bra, and pulling the straps from her shoulders. My tongue and teeth grazed over her beaded nipples, her breasts heavy in my hands as I squeezed them. Her head arched back reflexively. The surge of arousal ran through my body, through my cock that pressed between her legs up against her now wet panties. I kissed down her stomach and ran my fingers down her body in my mouth's wake. I could hear her breathing quicken, feel her body tense as I kissed and sucked my way down. I breathed hot breath over her panties, sliding my fingers underneath.

"Oh, yes, fuck."

She moaned as my fingers made the first slide inside her slick pussy.

I slid her panties down her legs and dropped them to the floor, spreading her legs wide. She was so beautiful laying here before me, tan, smooth as silk, and here, all for me. I ran a skilled thumb over her clit, which is hard and responsive to my touch, every circle, every movement. Her moans grew louder, and then I buried my head between her legs. I sucked her clit and licked her luxurious pussy, leaving her grabbing at the bed sheets, grabbing my hair, and yelling, "Jesus fuck, fuck, fuck."

Then she was calm and completely limp.

I slowly pulled away from her and made my way, kissing up her sensual body to her face, her lips.

"I love you," I whispered with arms on either side of her head.

A barely audible "I love you too," squeaked from her lips, eyes closed, arms out to her side, a smile on her face.

Then, in a mere whisper, "I need you inside me," came from her lips.

Without a word, I climbed between her legs and grabbed hold of my incredibly rigid dick. I ran the slick head through her dripping-wet pussy and slid it slowly inside her.

"Oh god."

I groaned with the intense feeling that rippled through my body with the first feeling of her hot, tight pussy wrapped around my cock. My head and fingers were buried in her hair. I kissed her ear.

"God I missed you," I said as I pressed my cock deeper and deeper inside.

She moaned louder.

"You are so fucking hard, so deep."

She grabbed my ass, fingers digging into my skin, pressing me harder into her.

I moved to a kneeling position. I wanted to see her body, her face. I wanted to see my dick moving in and out of her, slick with her juices. Her legs were resting over my thighs. What a gorgeous sight. My wet cock pumping in and out of her, my thumb rubbing her clit, her hands running wildly through her hair. This was too much, bringing me to the point of no return and I could not hold on any longer. The intense feeling took over, and ripples of pleasure ran through me. I grabbed her hips, faster and faster. The sound of our skin slapping together rhythmically is a beautiful new song.

"Baby, oh fuck yeah, mmm, fuck."

I moaned as I came so hard it sent me quivering over the top of her.

Her fingers dragged lightly over my back. She kissed my shoulder. Ran her fingers through my hair.

We walked around New York as much as we could until it became too problematic with the fucking paparazzi. Once they attached themselves to me and her, it was game on. The bubble of Charleston where nobody cared about the Stephen Harlow saga, was wonderful. Since Cassie became a bit more of a celebrity the last couple of days here in the city, and they located me with my big story with the Albanian mess, they put it all together. So, walking turned into Ubers, which turned into private drivers.

I surprised her with dinner reservations, and called and gave them a heads up that we would need a table as private as possible. Fortunately, they accommodated.

"Where are we going?" she asked as our car was pulling up in front of the restaurant.

Our driver came around to open the door, letting us out. She looked up at the sign, looking at me in surprise.

"Ophelia's?"

"Yep." I smiled. "Come on, before we attract unwanted attention out here."

I escorted her inside.

The atmosphere was modern, luxurious, candlelit, cozy and inviting with dark woods and white linens, classic Midtown Manhattan vibes. We were seated at a private table, and the impeccable service started.

"I can't believe you got in here on short notice," Cassie said, looking spectacular across the candlelit table.

She was dressed in a little black sweater dress that she almost didn't make it out of the room wearing.

Damn, she killed me.

"I didn't have too much of a problem. There are two other locations in New York as well," I told her.

Our server came and went over the specials for the night, and we ordered a beautiful bottle of Bordeaux she recommended as we looked over the menu.

"I haven't had French in so long, but having it as a fusion will be different. Going back to my roots," she said, smiling.

"Well, you mentioned this chef before, so I figured I would see if I could make it happen," I said.

"She is a force to be reckoned with, but I don't think I would ever want my career to be this big. It's not in my DNA. She isn't even in the kitchen anymore. It's just her concept now. Her and her husband basically started opening locations as a business venture when her first one became a two Michelin Star." She shook her head. "I still love being involved in my kitchen. I still know my kitchen staff and love being part of the operations. I would love to get back to cooking more, honestly."

She smiled, slightly sad, looking down at her menu.

Our server came back, did our wine presentation, and we placed our order being the four course prix fixe menu.

Cassie had a hard time not watching the inner workings of the restaurant as we sat.

"You can't just enjoy this, can you?" I asked, shaking my head.

"I'm sorry. It's a horrible habit. It's just that I am intrigued by how other establishments work," she said, embarrassed.

I reached for her hand. "It's okay. I love your passion for what you do. It was so awesome to see you on TV doing that cooking segment the other day. You looked like you were having fun."

She laughed. "I was so nervous. I didn't know if I was going to pee my pants or get sick."

"Well, you couldn't tell at all. All that time on camera on your show must be paying off," I said, rubbing my thumb on the palm of her hand.

I was so grateful I was with her, touching her.

Our first course came out, an absolutely divine crevettes a l' Ail. Shrimp, buttery, and the bread was absolutely amazing. I was either hungrier than I thought, or this was that good.

"So, if you didn't have this celebrity gig or Sagi-Shi, what would you do? Would you still be in the culinary world?" I asked, eyes practically rolling in my head with each bite.

Putting her fork down and wiping her lips with her napkin, she said, without hesitation, "I would open an Izakaya."

I took a sip of my wine, then asked, "What is that?"

"It's a Japanese pub. They usually open late night and it's just a little chill spot with cool drinks and beers, Japanese snacks, and where lighter pub food is served. A local's hangout. Small."

"That sounds cool. Why didn't you do that to start with instead of Sagi-shi?" I said, practically scraping my plate before our server took it, saving me the embarrassment of licking it.

"I just couldn't come up with enough of a small concept that made enough money in San Francisco with the real estate prices as high as they are," she said.

"Seriously? That's what it came down to? Not your happiness? It was real estate and making enough money?" I asked in shock.

"Yeah, Stephen," she said, taking her last bite. "I couldn't ask people to invest in my dream if it wasn't going to make money. The restaurant business is exactly that, a business. They fail all the time, and they actually fail more than they succeed."

"I guess I would just want you to pursue your dream. The one you want. That's all," I said.

She reached across the table and caressed my hand. "Well, you are so sweet, but I am, babe. I love my place. I love my life. I'm happy. Now that I have you, It's pretty much perfect."

She smiled.

The rest of our dinner was nothing short of a culinary symphony. Our conversation was harmonious, and we talked about everything, except the subject of Lauren. Either we didn't want to ruin the perfect day, or we didn't feel that it was necessary. I wasn't bringing her up, and neither was Cassie.

Back at the hotel, we slipped in under the radar of cameras. Hopefully, they had grown tired of us. We really weren't that interesting.

Once in the room, Cassie checked her phone.

"Oh shit."

"What?" I asked, nervous.

"Arie. She's questioning a story about us. *Cyber Millionaire Playboy Gets Hot With Celebrity Chef.*" She said, covering her eyes. "There are pictures of us kissing on the sidewalk in front of the hotel."

I wrapped my arms around her shoulders, placing my chin on her head. "Well, it could be worse. It could be pictures of us fucking in the hotel," I said, trying to get her to laugh.

"She thinks this is good for publicity." She sighed. "She's always whoring me out for likes, views, or whatever."

"Well, that's her job as your publicist, babe."

I put my hands out.

"I'm just not used to this at all. I'm a private person," she said. "Oh, wait. She just text me."

She read it in her horrible rendition of Arie's British accent.

"Is he involved in some Albanian drug thing, Cassie? Jesus. You need to call me asap so I can fix this mess if I need to. What the fuck, Cassie? I leave you alone in NY, and you go shag a cyber security drug lord, for fuck's sake." She laughed, doubled-over, asking, "Can I please mess with her?"

"Only if you call her back in your Australian accent."

I laughed.

Chapter 37

CASSIE

Our apartment was perfect. The tree in the corner, with the view of the bay off to the side, the smell of cookies that Cora and I had baked the night before, and now Stephen was flying in. I couldn't believe he agreed to this, coming here for Christmas, sacrificing his family for mine, and sleeping at a hotel for Cora's sake. Even more, Cora agreeing to it, being excited for it. My nerves were all over the place. What if she didn't like him?

"Mom? What time does his flight get in?" she asked, her head buried in the fridge, only flannel pajamas covered legs hanging out.

"One-forty-five. I'm leaving in a minute to go get him. You may want to put actual clothes on before we get back, Cora," I said with sarcasm.

The refrigerator door closed, and I got the look.

"Yes, Mom, I know. That is why I was asking," she answered with a glare and even more sarcasm back.

"Hey. This is going to be fun, right? I'm nervous too," I admitted.

"Yes. I want to meet him. I just need to eat something. I don't know what I'm allowed to eat in here."

She opened and shut the cabinets.

Oh, this was a teen hunger issue.

"Do you want me to make you a quick sandwich before I go?" I asked, sort of kissing ass to make peace.

"Yes, please, Mom," she whined, then disappeared down the hallway, knowing she'd won this little battle.

It obviously went both ways.

I sat in the cell phone lot, patiently waiting until my phone alerted me of his text. My heart leaped.

Stephen: I'm here sexy girl.

Me: Best news all day. I didn't come in. It's a holiday zoo. Sorry.

Stephen: No worries. I shouldn't be long. I didn't check a bag.

Me: Yay.

Even though it had only been three weeks, it had already been too long. His hug, strong and needed. His kiss, pure bliss.

"Hey, you," I said, smiling.

"Hey."

His eyes, gray and green, beautiful.

Another quick kiss before he put his suitcase into the trunk and climbed into my tiny car.

"Ahh, the comforts of the Mini again," he said, making himself uncomfortable in the seat.

"You love it," I said, taking off with extra zip.

"Some day, I am going to buy you a roomier car."

He chuckled.

I laughed.

"It's not about money. I love my car. San Francisco is not made for a big car."

We caught up for the forty-minute drive. He asked me how to act around Cora, what to expect, and about the impending meeting of Jack. This was a very big holiday, and I was asking a lot of him. This was taking things to a whole new level.

"I don't even know what to expect from Cora these days. She is a teen. She's moody as fuck and unpredictable. I threatened her not to act bitchy, and she promised she wouldn't. She asked for this, so there is that." I put my hands in the air. "She has met Beth and is giving her a chance, so she at least owes you that respect."

I took a deep, stressed breath.

He put his hand over mine and looked in my direction. "Hey, do you want to stop at my hotel first and work some of this stress out?"

I looked over at him to see him smiling. "That sounds like a great idea."

I reached over and ran my hand down his thigh, over his crotch.

"Oh god." He moaned. "If you start that, you will have to."

He bit his lip and moved in his seat, reaching over to my thigh.

I pulled into his hotel parking lot. He reached over and took my face, kissing me hard.

The aching between my legs was hard to ignore. I wanted him so much as he slid his hand between them, fingers warm, strong.

"We need to go inside. I am so fucking turned on right now that it hurts."

I moaned into his kiss.

"Okay," he whispered, opening his door, climbing out, and adjusting his dick in his pants, making me smile and shake my head.

He checked in as fast as he could. We took the elevator up silently, hand in hand, with another couple in the lift with us, scrambled down the hallway, and then, with a quick swipe of the room card, and the door closing behind us, he then pressed me up against the wall.

A hand up my sweater, another unbuttoning my jeans. Mine pulling his black pullover up over his head, pulling his t-shirt off, unbuttoning his jeans as I felt him backing out of his shoes. It was as if we were being timed at this. It was a national emergency. We must be naked now, or the world would end. Next thing I knew, my bare breasts were in his hands, pressed together, his teeth, his lips tightly around my nipples. His fingers were in my pussy, fucking me deep, and his thumb on my clit. My hand wrapped around his hard, thick cock, stroking it up and down. We were a frantic mess no more than two feet inside his hotel room. He turned me around, hands and face pressed against the wall, his palm on the small of my back, the swollen head of his cock running up and down the opening of my pussy, teasing me.

"Yes baby, fuck me. Fuck me hard," I begged, looking back at him, hair covering half my face.

This was exactly what I got. His hard cock, deep as fuck.

"Right there, fuck yes. You like that?" he said while fisting the back of my hair.

Then, he held my shoulders, and buried himself to the very root, and let go of every last drop he had. It was so hot to lose control like that. He kissed my back, my shoulders. He backed out slowly, and I tip-toed to the bathroom.

I came out to him leaning casually against the wall.

"This is a nice room."

He laughed, trading places with me and going into the bathroom.

I walked into the bedroom area, laying across the bed, laughing.

"Oh yeah, it is nice."

He came out naked, chiseled, still somewhat hard, sexy as fuck, and laid next to me. He ran his fingers down over my breasts, over my nipples, kissing them, and then ran his hand down my stomach. He kissed my lips, then kissed me harder as he then thumbed my still swollen clit.

He whispered into my mouth. "I know I didn't take care of you."

I moaned with my eyes closed, his fingers running perfectly through my pussy, still so wet. He strummed my clit with rhythm and precision until heat pooled in my belly, and my mind fell away from my body.

"Yes, yes, yes."

I moaned, letting go so easily. He kissed me as I came hard, my pussy becoming so wet under his fingers, and my legs trembled uncontrollably.

"Damn baby, yes, that's so fucking hot," he said, running his fingers through me, kissing me deeply.

I nervously opened the door to the apartment to only be surprised by the smiling, outstretched, hugging arms of a well-dressed Cora.

"Hi, Mom. You must be Stephen," she said.

Who was this child?

I'd take it, watching her shake his hand and the smile on his face. This was going to be great.

The next few days consisted of running all over San Francisco, ducking in and out of stores shopping, which I now knew Stephen loved to do. Him and Cora bonded over burning up a credit card, eating everything in our path, and watching Christmas movies. We did the unthinkable and invited Jack and Beth over for appetizers and cocktails. This was Stephen's idea before he came, and the idea made me personally want to crawl under a blanket and die, but it was for Cora.

Stephen showed up after getting dressed at his hotel, noticing my nervousness. He took me by the shoulders, looked me in the eyes.

"You do harder shit than this every day. You run a Michelin-star restaurant. You have your own show on TV. You have forgiveness in your heart and know how to start over, babe. This is for Cora. I'm here with you, right here." He smiled. "Shit. I should be more nervous."

"That's actually true," I said, laughing. "I love you. You are crazy, the things you will do for me."

Tilting my face up by his index finger, he said, "I only wish I had the years in between back. I'm going to see what Cora is up to while you finish getting ready."

Then he left my room.

How did I become so deserving of this man? I prayed I didn't fuck it up. I always seemed to sabotage this relationship with him and fuck it up.

The doorbell rang. I took a deep breath, and I got a comforting smile and nod from Stephen across the island as we were finishing up preparing tonight's appetizers. I walked to the front door, and there they stood, the new happy couple. The last I saw of them, she was on her knees, and his dick was in her mouth. This was a much better look for them.

A relaxed Jack, hair looking spectacular, black, long in the front, jeans, form-fitting white buttoned-down shirt with the sleeves rolled up. Beth, her blonde hair, shoulder-length with perfect waves, wearing a blue wrap dress, simple, cute.

Jack handed me a bottle of wine as he entered the door, arm outstretched for Beth to enter first.

"Beth, nice to see you again," I said as she walked past me. "Jack," I said to him as he kissed the side of my cheek.

"This is really great, Cass. Thanks," he said, walking down the hallway leading to the kitchen, where Stephen greeted them.

My heart could have melted. Stephen, gorgeous as hell, dressed in jeans, a thin black V-neck sweater, and a kitchen towel draped over his shoulder. My beautiful, perfect sous chef, who was now shaking the hand of my former husband who did look remarkably like him. Fuck. I wondered if they noticed. I laughed internally at how my mind worked.

"Jack, it's nice to meet you," Stephen said, shaking his hand with a nod.

Jack, sizing him up, in his attorney way. "Very nice to meet you as well, Stephen. This is Beth."

He placed a hand on her shoulder.

Stephen shook her hand. "Nice to meet you, Beth. Cora talked a lot about you and how much fun you two had in Vail."

"Oh, she is such a doll. That girl loves to shop," she said.

He laughed. "Yeah, she burned a hole in my credit card for sure the past two days."

"She's playing the two of you," I spoke up, laughing. "Wine everyone?"

I held up a bottle of cabernet.

Cora joined us, and we mingled in the kitchen. I gave Beth a tour of the apartment, and once we were down in the den out of ear's reach, she placed a hand on my shoulder and said, "Cassie, I just want to say I'm sorry for what happened with…"

I interrupted her because I couldn't bear to hear the words spill from her mouth about that day again.

"Beth, I am letting it go. For Cora, and to be able to look Jack in the eye. Also, look what your fuck up led me back to?"

I directed her eyes up to the kitchen where Jack, with a smiling Cora in the crook of his arm, and Stephen stood with wine in hand, talking.

"He is the best thing to step back in my life." I then looked back at her. "So I should be thanking you, actually."

I smiled.

Christmas morning, I was awakened by the smell of coffee and the faint sound of Christmas music playing in the living room. I dragged myself out of bed, brushed my teeth, and there he was, waiting on us, tree lit, presents piled high, and the mood was set.

He handed me my cup, "Merry Christmas, baby."

"I love you, Merry Christmas." I wrapped my arm around his waist, looking out at the view and the living room. "When did you get back here this morning? I feel terrible, you traipsing back and forth, and I miss you in my bed."

He kissed the top of my head. "Only about thirty minutes ago. I wanted to spend some time with you before Cora woke up," he said. "Come down here."

He led me down into the den to the couch.

He sat facing me. My heart started beating faster. This seemed planned, a speech of sorts.

"What, Stephen?" I asked.

"You get so nervous, it's adorable." He chuckled. "I wanted to give you this."

He pulled out a gift shaped like a small box.

I put my hand to my chest and completely froze, "Stephen. I…"

"Just open it, Cass, before you faint, okay?" he said, smiling.

I did. In the black velvet ring box was a beautiful, large pearl set in a simple gold band.

"Stephen, this is beautiful," I said, shocked.

"Cora and I picked it out. She said this was perfect." He ran his thumb over the pearl, then up into my eyes. "I wanted to give you something to let you know that I am serious about how important you are in my life, where you fit in. I never want to lose you, Cass, never again." He laughed, tilting his head as he slid it on my ring finger. "I also wanted to do a test run to see your reaction in case I pop the question one day."

He smiled.

Ugh.

That smile I absolutely adored.

With tears running down my face, I laughed, then kissed him.

"You fit perfectly in my life, our life. I love you, Stephen Harlow.

Chapter 38

CASSIE

The book tour and grueling taping schedule was out. I stared at it, having a meltdown, wondering how I would do it all and still have some resemblance of a life.

My newest target, Johnathan, stood in front of my desk, taking it like a champ.

"What the fuck am I supposed to do with this schedule, Johnathan? I have a goddamn restaurant and a teenage daughter who needs me. Oh, I may need a life of my own at some point, too. I haven't seen Stephen in over a fucking month."

I rambled on with my angry rant.

He blankly responded, arms crossed, "Are you done?"

"Yes." I pouted.

"I can lighten the load. You just have to tell me. They know you have a career outside of this, but you have to communicate, Cassie." He shook his head.

"Okay, I'm calling mercy now then," I said calmly. "Can we spread some of these book signings out, maybe? I just can't leave Sagi high and dry this much."

"Sure. Let's just sit down and come up with a doable plan," he said.

"Thanks, Johnathan. Sorry I exploded. I am so stressed. I am missing so much stuff with Cora. It's spring break coming up for her, and I have nothing planned."

I buried my head in my hands.

I suddenly heard, "Hey, Cassie. It's okay, I got you."

Then he was gone by the time I looked up.

I tapped my phone and looked at the time, realizing that I needed to get to Sagi to help with dinner service for the night.

I sent a quick text message before my exit.

Me: Hey babe. I'm heading to Sagi. I love you

Stephen: Have a good night at work. Love you too.

I seriously missed him. I felt so disconnected from having a life that I felt I had during the holidays, spending time with friends and family.

I grabbed my things and made my way out to Johnathan's desk.

"Hey, I'm heading to Sagi. I'll look over the schedule and see what's doable when I figure out what I'm doing for Cora's spring break. Is that cool?" I asked.

He looked up at me, leaning back in his chair. "Yeah, just let me know soon so I can rearrange these signings, okay? I don't want Arie poured down my back."

I shook my head. "Got it."

I got to my safe place, my sanctuary, Sagi-Shi. I pulled open the heavy back door, and I instantly felt better. I felt at home.

I ran into Kyle immediately in the hallway.

"Good afternoon, Chef," he said.

"Kyle. How are things today?" I replied, happily.

"We have a busy night ahead, so I am really glad you are here. Can you handle finishing this order so I can get this kitchen right, please?" he asked, handing me order sheets.

"Of course," I said, taking them from him and shifting into the office.

The night went so smooth. I was incredibly impressed with how well Kyle ran this kitchen. It had become such a well-oiled machine that I basically just followed his lead. I was his sous, following in his wake.

I eventually made my way into the dining room to mingle with guests after service and then into the bar.

"Hey Marcus, how is your night out here?" I asked, approaching the bar.

"No complaints, Chef," he said, hanging wine glasses.

Then, from the end of the bar, I heard a familiar voice, Adam, our wine purveyor, said, "I came in for a drink on the right night, I guess."

"Oh, hi, Adam. How are you doing?" I said, walking over to shake his hand.

"I'm doing well. You?"

"Busy, overwhelmed, but hanging in there."

I laughed.

He sipped his drink, then asked, "Do you ever get time for yourself? I see you on TV, on the pans I just saw at the home goods store, and here. Do you even sleep?"

"Are you stalking me, Adam?" I joked.

"Hardly, but I don't know how you do it. You have to be exhausted," he said.

Leaning on the bar stool next to him, I said, "I have my moments, but I don't know any better, I guess. What should I be doing?" I asked him.

"Having a drink with me when you get done in there."

He pointed behind me to the kitchen.

I laughed. "Ooh. I should, huh? Well, I will be awhile," I said, tilting my head.

"I'll wait. I have nowhere to be."

He smiled, coy.

"Adam, I am seeing someone, I just want to make that clear," I said.

"I know. I am interested in being your friend, Cassie. That's all. I think you are interesting. Is that okay?" he asked with an arched brow.

I shrugged my shoulders.

"Oh, okay. I just didn't want to give you the wrong impression, that's all," I said.

He emptied the last of his drink, placing the glass of ice on the counter, sliding it to Marcus, turning to look at me.

"So, I'll be right here when you get done."

He nodded and smiled at me.

"Well, okay," I said shyly and made my way back to the kitchen.

It took me about an hour, but I eventually made my way back to the bar, where Marcus was closing up. Adam was there, as he said he would be, looking at his phone, alone at the dimly lit bar, with a full drink in front of him.

"So, you normally stalk restaurant owners until closing?"

I laughed pulling the stool out next to him and climbing up.

He looked up and laughed. "No, I usually stalk them in parking lots, but I like the ambiance here," he said.

"Marcus, I'm not going to keep you, but can I get a glass of cab, please?" I asked.

"Of course, Chef," he said.

Adam and I talked for about thirty minutes about my restaurant and celebrity world, and he answered my questions about the world of wine until Marcus gave me the look that he was ready to head out for the night. I was actually enjoying my conversation and wasn't quite ready to end it.

"One more?" I asked Adam.

"Sure," he said.

"I've got it, Marcus. I'll lock up behind us," I said.

He gave a silent look between me and Adam as if to question, *are you sure that's a good idea?* with raised brows.

"I'm good Marcus."

I laughed and nodded.

"Okay, chef. See you next week."

He proceeded to the front door and locked us in the almost dark restaurant. The kitchen staff all said goodnight and let themselves out the back and locked up as well.

I went behind the bar and poured myself another glass of wine, bringing the bottle out onto the bar, and poured him another bourbon. I made my way back to my stool and kicked off my shoes, getting more comfortable. Our conversation got more personal, talking about family, where we were from, and fun banter. Next thing I knew, my bottle was empty.

"Oh wow. Now I am going to have to call an Uber," I said, realizing my buzz.

"I can give you a ride," he said, shrugging his shoulders.

I laughed. "Really? You should get one too."

He shook his head. "I guess you are right. I've had like, six drinks since I've been here," he said holding up and looking at his empty glass.

I reached for my phone to pull up the app, his hand stopped me. I looked up, his eyes, so blue, looking into mine.

"You are so beautiful, Cassie," he said, leaning forward to kiss me.

I backed away from him. "Adam, I'm sorry. I'm flattered, I am, but like I said, I'm in a relationship with someone."

He winced. "Yeah, you did say that. I'm sorry." He put his hands up. "I'm sorry. You can't blame a guy for trying."

Well, yeah, you can.

I stood with my phone and clicked on my Uber app.

"I'm going to lock up and get that Uber now. It's time I got home."

"Yeah, me too."

He took out his phone and did the same.

We both waited outside and chatted until our rides showed up, then parted ways with a friendly hug. On my way home, I text Stephen goodnight as I usually did after my work nights so he would see it in the morning. I felt good. I had a habit of sabotaging my relationship by now. Me and bad decisions held hands and sometimes shared a bed. I was not doing stupid shit this time, not with Stephen.

I woke up with a lovely wine hangover and a text message from Arie.

Arie: Cassie, call me so you can tell me what to do with this article, and a link with, *Turmoil In the Kitchen?* and side-by-side pictures of me and

Stephen and another picture of me hugging Adam outside the restaurant last night.

"Oh fuck," I yelled, digging my palms into my eyes.

Chapter 31

STEPHEN

Catherine buzzed in over my intercom saying, "Mr. Harlow, just a reminder you have a meeting with the Blanchard Group in fifteen minutes."

Without looking up from my computer, I answered, "Thank you, Catherine," then reached for my phone.

I had two missed texts, one being Allen and the other being Cassie.

Cassie took precedence, of course, and I was always happy to see her morning texts.

Cassie: Good morning, babe. Call me when you can.

Allen's text was just a link to an article. He was always sending me dumb shit.

Whatever.

I found her beautiful face and pressed send.

"Hey baby," she said immediately.

"Hey, honey. How was your night at Sagi?" I asked, turning my chair around to the skyline. Gray Charlotte skies looking like rain.

"Yeah, that's what I was calling about. Sounds like you haven't gotten hold of a certain article yet," she said.

"Oh shit. What is it, Cassie? Allen sent me something, but I didn't open it," I said in a worried tone.

"Stephen, it's nothing. I promise," she said.

I leaned forward in my chair, closing my eyes, elbow on my knee and forehead resting in my hand.

"Can you just tell me what happened, Cass?" I asked.

"So, my wine purveyor, Adam, came in last night, and we were chatting it up past closing." She paused. "When we left to wait on our Uber, someone must have caught a picture of us…baby…"

My heart fell. I sat back in my chair, ran my hand over my mouth, down my jaw.

"Doing what, Cassie? A picture of you two doing what?" I asked in a serious tone.

She said in a low voice. "Just us hugging. I swear, baby. We were just saying goodbye and got in separate Ubers."

"Holy fuck, Cassie," I said, taking a deep breath I must have been holding in.

"They mentioned us. There's a picture of you and I, then compared it to us having trouble in our relationship. I'm so sorry."

She started to sniffle.

"Babe, nothing happened?" I asked.

"Well, to be honest, I don't think I made the best decision to hang out with a guy after hours alone. He kind of made a pass at me…"

"Wait, what?" I interrupted.

"It's okay, I stopped him, and he listened. He's not a dick. I learned my lesson and was obviously punished by my actions with this stupid article," she said.

I sighed. "It's okay. Just ignore it. I'm sure Arie will take care of it anyhow."

"Yeah, she's just going to let it blow over since it's not true. She's going to post some old pictures on Instagram of me and you being all happy," she said.

"See, emergency diverted," I said quickly.

"You are so understanding. Thank you," she said.

"Oh, I'm pulling up the link now so I can see this douche who is hitting on my woman. Then I'm going to send my Albanian Cartel after him to take out his knees."

I laughed.

"I love you," she said softly.

"I love you too. Is there anything else you need to tell me?" I asked.

"No, except I want to ask when am I seeing you next? I also need to plan Cora's Spring break. My schedule just came out, and it's insane," she said, stressed.

I took a deep breath. "Well, let's plan her break and start there. Do you want to come home? Want me to come there? We can take her somewhere tropical. Italy or somewhere kick-ass? Take some of her friends?" I asked.

"I don't want to stay here, and I doubt she does either. Let me talk to her tonight. Italy? No way Stephen," she said.

My phone buzzed. I pulled it from my ear to see the incoming text. It was Lauren's brother Jakob. I hadn't seen his name come across my phone in quite some time. I went back to my conversation.

"I know. I like to go overboard, and you hate it. Well, talk to her, and we will make a plan, all right?"

"Okay, babe. I'll talk to you later."

"Okay. Hey. Manage to stay out of guy's pants for the day, all right?"

I laughed.

She chuckled.

"I'll try."

After hanging up with Cassie, I jumped on a call with Jakob. Instantly nervous that my world was about to change, yet again.

"Hey, my brother," he said. "How are you doing?"

"I'm doing all right, Jakob. What's going on?" I asked, very curious.

He took a beat, then said, "We searched everywhere, man. She was there and I definitely think she is alive. She has escaped, just to where? That is the question. I just don't know where, Stephen, or if someone has her. We haven't gotten anything from her, just silence."

"Someone must have her then. She has to know she is safe because why wouldn't she reach out by now?" I asked him.

"I don't fucking know," he said. "I don't fucking know."

I heard the frustration in his voice.

I let out a small laugh.

"It's kind of like her, you know? She's stubborn as shit. Always has to do things on her terms. Always her way."

"You got that right, my brother. Classic fucking Lauren." He laughed. "Let's just keep the faith this is what it is, okay, my brother?"

"Okay. I will," I said.

"I see you and your Chef lady. Everything good with you two?" he asked me.

"Yeah, we are doing great. I wish we saw more of each other and the cameras weren't shoved in our faces constantly, but we are doing all right," I said, happy he was encouraging me to move on.

"Well, when she visits next time, I want to meet her," he said with excitement.

"You got it, man."

We chatted a bit about his parents before hanging up. He had to come clean to them about him and Lauren's professions since the media pretty much let that cat out of the bag. They haven't lost hope for her safe return either.

I may have pulled that stupid article up a couple of times during the day. Jealousy got the better of me a couple of times seeing her on her tippy toes hugging Mr. Blonde, perfect hair, younger, tall, wine dude. I also looked at the comparison photo they used of us, and it outweighed my jealousy. We looked really fucking happy. We were really fucking happy. I couldn't let this stupid shit sabotage our relationship. We had worked too hard to get there again. Plus, she called me immediately, just like we discussed what we would do going forward, communicating better.

I sat on my dock, the sky an absolute brilliant red and orange. My bourbon, an expensive gift from a client, Whistle Pig, The Samurai Scientist. I guessed they knew I was dating a Chef at a Japanese restaurant. These perks, I'd take them. I swirled the amber liquid in my glass, the ice clinked against the sides. I stared out over my beautiful lake view, feeling fortunate, feeling peace in my heart for once. I took a picture, feet outstretched on the teak table, the bottle of bourbon and glass, the blue water and sunset. Pretty fucking cool. I sent it to her.

My girl's dots danced. My heart did too. Just like every damn time.

She sent me a selfie of her in her dressing room at the studio, alone, brilliantly naked.

Yeah, I was feeling more than peace in my heart.

Chapter 40

CASSIE

Coming off our amazing high from our spring break trip to Maui, I was refreshed and ready to roll into the intense taping and book signing schedule. Cora and her friend Tiffany had an absolute blast. Stephen spoiled us at every turn, from the private jet to the Grand Wailea Waldorf-Astoria hotel stay. Cora and I came back tanner than brown berries, and my photography team wasn't very thrilled when I arrived back at work.

I rounded the corner, looking into the camera display screen with Abby, our photographer, laughing.

"I'm so sorry you have to deal with the most unphotogenic person ever."

"Whatever," she said. "You are so fun to photograph. I just wish we could use some of these fun ones in the cookbook. I think you would come across more real to your readers."

Just then, I practically ran into Johnathan standing, blocking our way.

"Shit. You scared me," I said, holding my chest.

"Hey, Cassie, I need to talk to you," he said in a serious tone.

Abby stopped and put her hand on my shoulder. "I'll edit these and send them to your email. Just let me know what you think when you get a chance."

She then continued down the hall.

I responded slowly to her, but not taking my eyes off Johnathan, "Sounds good, Abby."

"Johnathan, what's wrong? The look on your face is scaring me," I said nervously.

He took a deep breath. "I don't want to be the one to tell you this, but Stephen…"

I interrupted, covering my mouth. "Oh my god. Oh my God. What's wrong with Stephen?"

He placed a hand on my shoulder. "No, Cassie. Stephen is fine."

I let out the breath I had been holding. Fuck. What was happening?

"Stephen called me. It's your friend, Brittany," he said.

My entire body buckled under me. My hands shook covering my mouth, my eyes widened, shock took over my face, waiting for whatever horrific news he was about to tell me.

"Oh shit. Here, Cassie, sit down."

He pulled me over to a group of leather chairs.

"Hey."

He tried to get my attention.

I looked at him, barely visible with the tears filling my eyes. "What happened to Britt? Is she okay? Oh, fuck. Johnathan, tell me she is okay," I muttered.

"It's actually her husband, Cassie." He placed his hand on my knee. "He was stabbed early this morning. I don't have many details. Stephen called me because your friend Britt had left you some messages, and she couldn't get a hold of you. She was frantic, and he didn't want you to find out that way and be alone. When he couldn't get a hold of you either, he called me. He wants you to call him."

My mind was reeling. Someone stabbed Avery? What the actual fuck? I needed to call Britt.

I ran my shaking hands through my hair. "I need my phone. I need a flight. I need to get to Charleston, Johnathan."

I looked at him in a fit of hysterics.

"I know." He calmly handed me my phone he had retrieved from the dressing room. "I already booked it. We just need to go and pack you up, okay? Your flight leaves in two hours," he said, shaking his head. "I'll stay with you, okay?"

I burst into tears and hugged him.

"Thank you."

He then gave me space to make my calls.

I wanted to listen to my messages, but I realized it would be heart wrenching to hear her. I would call Stephen first.

I shakily hovered my finger over his contact, his face. I pressed and closed my eyes. He picked it up immediately. My heart lurched.

"Cass," he said with urgency and sadness.

I began crying instantly at the sound of his voice, knowing I needed him. I needed his comfort right now. I needed him to tell me this wasn't really happening.

I cried, "Oh my god, Stephen, what happened?"

"Some lunatic stabbed him when he was taking the trash out this morning behind the restaurant. It's really bad, Cass. He is in critical condition right now. That is as much as I got from Britt," he said. "She was franticly trying to get a hold of you."

"I didn't have my phone. I was in a photoshoot all morning. Fuck." I whaled, burying my head in my hands. "I wasn't there for her. Where are you?"

"In Charlotte still. I'm heading there now, though," he said. "I know there is a bunch of people with her. You know them. There are probably two hundred people in the waiting room," he joked.

"Yeah, I'm sure. Johnathan booked me on the next flight. You will get there before me, I guess," I said.

"I need to try to call Britt and get going. I guess I'll see you there?" I asked.

"Yeah, I'll see you there. As soon as you know, let me know your information, I'll get you at the airport, babe."

With the sound of desperation in his voice, he said, "It will be okay, Cass."

"It has to be. She can't lose him, Stephen."

Then I burst into a flood of tears.

I hung up, and my heart felt like it is literally shattering in a thousand pieces. I realized I needed to make so many phone calls just to leave San Francisco. I needed to go into business mode and get to the airport.

I dialed Jack.

"Hey. What's up?" he answered, in his friendly, I get laid every day, I'm so fucking happy now, co-parent voice.

"I have an emergency and have to fly to Charleston," I said quickly.

"Fuck Cass. What happened? Mom? Dad?" he asked, worried.

With no time to reprimand him that they aren't his parents anymore, I said, "No, it's Avery. He's had an accident. It's bad. I have a flight in two hours, Jack. I know I am supposed to have Cora starting tomorrow. Can you pitch-hit for me?"

"Of course. Anything you need," he said.

"She may need more things. She has a key to the apartment if she needs to go by. I'll call as soon as I know more, okay?" I said. "But I need to go."

"Yeah, I got it. Just be safe," he said.

"Thanks, Jack," I said before hanging up.

I walked to my dressing room, officially in business mode, wiping tears from my eyes, snot from my nose, and Johnathan walking briskly behind me. I dialed Kyle.

I get his voicemail.

"Hey, Kyle. I've had an emergency come up, and I have to fly to Charleston immediately. I know you weren't expecting me this weekend, but in case you need anything, that's where I will be. Text me when you get this. You can reach me by email or instant messenger once I get on the plane in two hours. Thanks, buddy."

I walked into my dressing room and grabbed my purse and tote, shoving everything in it that I needed. I make a look of, *I'm ready* with my eyebrows and a nod of my head to him.

We made our way out of the studio. He continued to follow as I dialed Britt's number, completely unaware of how emotional this call would be.

"Cassie," she screamed.

"Oh my god, baby," I cried.

I stopped mid track, covering my mouth again, leaning against the wall.

"I'm on the way baby, I'm on the way."

My voice cracked.

"He might not make it Cass. I can't fucking lose him. I just…"

Her voice completely disappeared.

My heart split in half.

"Hey. Britt. He is going to make it. Listen to me," I pleaded into the phone as I pushed forward and walked through the hallway, people walked past us with worried looks.

She recovered enough to come back with anger. "That motherfucker stabbed him. Like…over and over, Cass. Who would do that to Avery? He is the nicest person on the fucking planet."

She sobbed.

We exited the building, and I was now completely disoriented. Johnathan grabbed my arm and guided me in the opposite direction towards the garage. I just followed him now, balancing my heavy tote, wiping tears from my eyes, my hair wildly whipping around my face from the wind, and managing my phone.

"Who the hell stabbed him? This is crazy. Did they catch him?" I asked.

"We have no idea who it was. They are still looking for them. Fuck, Cassie. Are you coming?"

She started bawling again.

"Yeah. I'm heading to the airport right now. Do you have people there?" I asked, knowing that was the stupidest question ever touching my lips.

She almost had a laugh in her response. "There are so many people here, it's a goddamn circus. I just want my family and you. Oh, Cass, I called Stephen. I couldn't get you. I panicked and didn't know what to do."

"I talked to him. He's on the way now," I said.

She muffled the phone, talking to others.

"I need to go. The doctors need to talk to me," she said.

Johnathan unlocked my car, and I climbed in the passenger side, taking off towards my apartment.

"Keep me updated, Britt. Stephen can email me if you can't when I'm on the plane," I said. "I love you."

"I love you too," she whimpered, then hung up.

Just then, I realized, looking next to me, that I had a rockstar of an assistant.

I looked at him saying, "Thank you so much for taking control of all this. I don't know how I even got in this car."

Looking around, realizing that it was my car.

He looked over for a quick second, nodding. "Of course. I got you."

We parked and made our way upstairs where I packed a suitcase so fast, I had no idea what I put in there. I didn't even think or care about what the weather was like in Charleston and the clothes I needed. It wasn't a vacation. Johnathan called two Ubers, one for me for the airport, and one for him to go back to the office, so I would have my car there when I came home. We walked downstairs, and he hugged me goodbye.

I texted Stephen my flight information when I got in the Uber, then, once at the Airport, I raced to my gate. The flight was horribly slow, and my anxiety was through the roof. I messaged him when I hadn't heard anything about Avery's prognosis in hours. He answered, giving me a very in-depth update since he had just gotten to the hospital and spoken to Britt.

His message was terrible.

"According to the doctors, he was stabbed in the back, lacerating his liver. He had turned to fight them off, and then they stabbed him over and over again in the abdomen, hitting his bowel and lung. He's still in surgery. They have a lot to repair at once. Everyone is just waiting. Now and then, they come out to say he's holding his own and vital signs are stable. All I know is that they had to open up his abdomen and repair what they could. The biggest risk is sepsis right now. He's had transfusions for his blood loss as well."

I feel like I was sitting in a flying waiting room with two hundred and fifty strangers. I just wanted someone to hug me and tell me it was okay. Just then, I got another message.

Stephen: I know after reading all that you need a hug.
I wish I was there to wrap my arms around you right
now.

I closed my eyes and held back the remaining tears. This man read my mind.

Me: I will take that hug when I get there.

Stephen: I'll be there when you land, babe.

My flight landed at 10:30, and Stephen picked me up at the curb for the first time, only to save time from the walk to the garage.

He got out, greeting me with his warm, comforting hug, bringing me to tears. I saw him just a week before and was having a great time, and now this.

We parked, and he walked me up to the 5th floor, where it was surprisingly sparse with visitors. Mainly Avery's and Britt's family and a couple of close friends. I located Avery's Uncle Carl.

"Where is Britt?" I asked, hugging him.

"She just went back to talk with one of the surgeons, Dr. Carroll," he said, holding me tight.

I stepped back, looking around. "I thought there would be more people here."

He smiled and silently laughed. "There were. This place was a zoo. Britt came out here and told everyone that she loved them so much, but she needed some breathing room, and it was time to get the fuck out."

"Oh my." I shook my head.

Just then, Britt and Avery's parents walked out, and the room erupted in movement. I made my way to her. When she saw me, she immediately lost her shit, wrapping her arms around me tight. Her body convulsed silently, as if she had run out of tears. I finally pushed her back from me.

"How did the surgery go?" I asked.

She took a deep breath.

"Well, they were able to repair his bowel without putting in one of those bags, you know he would hate that shit, no pun intended," she said with a half-smile.

Only Britt could still make a joke, giving me the dire prognosis of her husband's condition.

She continued. "He also has a chest tube to re-inflate his lung, and they are watching the lab work for the liver function right now. What a fucking mess, Cass. The biggest mess is the sepsis from the bowel laceration."

"Jesus, Britt. So, is he going to be okay?" I asked hesitantly.

She shook her head.

"The next twenty-four to seventy-two hours are critical. They are moving him to ICU right now. They will keep him sedated and on a ventilator, watching his vital signs closely. I feel better that he's out of surgery, but I can't wait to see him," she said.

I brushed my hand through her hair. "Honey, you look so exhausted. When can you see him?"

She side-hugged someone I didn't know, thanking them for coming with an exhausted half smile, going back into her conversation with me.

"Not for a while. It takes them a bit to get him situated in ICU."

"What do you need me to do?" I asked. "Do you need clothes? Food?"

"Maybe some clothes tomorrow. I'm good right now. I'm so glad you are here. Go get some rest. I know that was a tough travel day," she said.

"Seriously? You are worried about me? What is wrong with you?" I shook my head. "Go update your family. I'll be here."

I tucked a strand of hair behind her ear.

She hugged me. "I love you."

"I love you too. He's going to be fine," I said.

As she walked away, she turned and said, "He has to be. He owes me a grand from a bet we made, and he's not getting out of it, not this way." She winked.

I turned, and Stephen was there, with a hug waiting on me, and a cup of horrible coffee. Except for a trip for clothes for Britt, this would be the routine for the next twenty-four hours.

"Hey. Cass," I heard whispered, my shoulder being shaken lightly.

I opened my eyes to see Britt sitting next to me as I lifted my head off Stephen's shoulder.

"Hey, is everything okay?" I whispered.

I could tell she had been crying.

"Yeah, he's more stable, but…" she reached out to hug me and started sobbing.

"Oh honey, what is wrong?" I said.

She sobbed.

"He looks fucking horrible, Cassie. He's so red and swollen, but when I held his hand, he's like fucking, ice cold, like dead cold, Cass." Her voice shook. "There are machines and tubes all over the fucking place. He just doesn't look like him. I just want to hear his voice. I want him to tell me I'm being ridiculous. I just…." she trailed off crying uncontrollably to where I couldn't understand her. She buried her head into my chest as I ran my hand over her hair, and I kissed the top of her head. Then, Stephen wrapped his arms around both of us.

Later that day, we went home to the carriage house. We were greeted by Stephen's mom and my parents with warm hugs and a delicious home-cooked meal. We then went to bed, sleeping for what felt like twelve straight hours.

I panicked when I woke up to missed texts from Britt about a spiked fever of 104, causing Avery's blood pressure to drop dramatically. Stephen and I showered and dressed as fast as possible, racing back to the hospital. We found an emotionally exhausted Britt in the ICU waiting room.

"I brought you a smoothie." I handed it to her. "What is the news now?"

"Thank you, I actually wanted this," she said, smiling and stabbing the straw into the lid. "They have him on infusions to get his blood pressure back to normal. Three different antibiotics to get it back to normal. Fucking hell. I was dead asleep in there last night when alarms started going off like crazy. It was bananas."

"Jesus," Stephen said. "Is the fever coming down?"

"Yeah, they think they can get him stabilized in about twenty-four hours, hopefully," she said, sucking on the straw. "This is good. What is it?"

"Peanut butter banana protein something," I said.

"Mmm, I like it. Thanks," she said, looking over at the two of us. "I honestly don't know what I would do without the two of you. I mean, yeah, family has to be here, but y'all, this…" she waved her hand between us. "This is fucking love."

She smiled.

"We love you. You are our family, Britt. You and Avery," I said, running my hand down her blonde hair. "You need a shower."

"I know, I need to go home. I need to properly hug my kid. I need a proper meal and a fucking drink. I will, just not until Av is stable." She smiled and stood with her shake. "I'm going up to kick someone out of his room now. I'll see y'all in a bit. You don't have to sit here. I'll text you if anything changes. Go back to bed. Go…" she started thrusting her hips and making a fuck face. "Get it on for me," she said and laughed.

We shook our heads and smiled. I mean, she gave us permission.

Chapter 41

STEPHEN

Sitting in Charlotte traffic never seemed to bother me that much. It should, but I just utilized it as if my car were my office. No wasted time. I handled business meetings, caught up with calls I had been needing to make, like my mom or my brother, but today, an unexpected one, a returned call to Merek, Lauren's dad.

"Hi, Merek, I'm returning your call. How are you?" I asked.

"Good morning, Stephen. I'm well," he said.

"Are you sure this is an okay time to talk? Are you driving?"

"Yes, sir, It's fine, I'm heading into the office, but I'm in traffic with plenty of time. Is everything okay?"

I was now worried by his tone.

"Okay, well, Klara, Jakob, and I have made a hard decision to make arrangements." His voice became shaky. "Make arrangements to declare Lauren dead."

He started to cry.

My eyes welled with tears, I took a deep breath and asked, "Oh god, Merek, why?"

He took a big breath, and said, "It's just a financial decision, Stephen. We haven't given up. In the state of New York, you can declare after three years. It's been three years, Stephen. Three years since my Lauren has been missing."

He sniffled.

I wiped the tears that were now streaming down my face.

"Oh, Merek, I don't know what to say. What is the benefit of doing this?"

"Well, we were talking about this and her apartment, her assets. You paid her apartment off. We know this. You took that burden off of us. That was over a million dollars, Stephen. You continue paying the taxes. We would like to sell it and pay you back."

"Marek, no. You don't..."

He interrupted. "Yes, Stephen. You have paid for private investigators. You have done so much, and we are forever grateful. We want you to move on. Jakob told us about your new love. We are very happy for you. Please, let us do this? We aren't giving up. We aren't having a service and burying our daughter without her body. Jakob believes she is alive, and we believe too."

"Well, it sounds like you have made your decision. Is there anything you need me to do?" I asked.

"No. Jakob found us an attorney to handle everything. We just wanted you to know. I wanted to thank you for everything. Klara and I thank you. You are family, Stephen, you are always family," he said, so genuine, so heartfelt.

"Thank you, Merek. I feel the same."

We hung up, and I was left feeling such a mixed bag of fucked up. Declaring Lauren dead. Fuck. We didn't feel that way, but that felt like closing the book before it was over to me.

I walked up to Allen's office and knocked on the open door-frame. He looked up from his computer.

"Hey man. What's up?"

I walked in and sat in front of his desk in one of the plush leather chairs. I told him the news and like the awesome friend he always was, he put all aside and listened to me ramble on.

"Wow. I didn't see that coming," he said, shocked, fingers tented under his chin.

I took a deep, needed breath. "Yeah, me neither."

I covered my mouth with my hand.

"Dude? How are you not a raging alcoholic? Your life makes me want to drink, and it's," he looked at his watch, "Only nine-fifteen."

I laughed. "I don't know? I work out and jerk off to excess." I shrugged my shoulders, then stood to leave. "I have a meeting I need to get ready for. Thanks for the pow-wow, man. Heavy shit for first thing."

"Hey. We will talk more over drinks on the plane tonight to DC, okay? I'm so stoked we got this new government job. This is going to be a good one. Maybe the last?"

He put his hands in the air.

"Like I said, you love this John Wick lifestyle, Allen, you won't retire." I laughed and said, poking my head back in, "And who is going to sit in that stupid air-conditioned fat man's chair?"

Chapter 42

CASSIE

"Cora, I'll be home in two days. It's not that bad," I told her, feeling so guilty.

She whines, "I just feel like you are never home, Mom. Beth is taking me to all my practices now."

Well, that fucking stung, and she knew it.

"Cora, when this contract is up, this will all change, okay? I'm just all behind since I had to take time off with Avery's accident. You can't hold this against me forever," I said, exhausted from fighting with her.

"Whatever."

She stormed off, slamming her bedroom door.

I jumped at the sound. Fucking parental guilt. Fucking teen angst.

Ugh.

My phone buzzed to alert me that my Uber was ten minutes away.

I yelled down the hall, "Cora. I have to go, and I'm not leaving you mad."

She reluctantly came out of her room, walking with the bent over, teen posture of an eighty-year-old, and hugged me with limp arms.

"I love you, Mom," she said, with a monotone voice, patting me on the back.

"I love you too," I said. "I'll see you in two days, baby."

I turned to walk out the door, wheeling my suitcase behind me.

The flight to New York sucked. The airport was crowded, and the flight was delayed. Summer travelers were cranky as fuck. Maybe it was me and my bad attitude, not them.

Here I was, on this book signing tour that got shit reviews. Now, I was basically trying to salvage whatever dignity I had left at this point. It was called everything from boring and basic to the spiceless version of Cassie Buckley. I knew I needed to be more badass. People wanted more complex recipes and stories from me. We knew this from the cooking segments, and we listened. Why wouldn't we do that for the cookbook? So, there I was, wasting my damn time, traipsing all over the fucking country promoting this shit book. I was tired. I just wanted to be me again. I just wanted to cook at Sagi, where I belonged.

At least Johnathan put us up at the Soho Grand Hotel, one of my favorite boutique spots in New York. The garden terrace was to die for, and the cozy candlelit bar was so romantic. I only wished I was sharing it with Stephen, not Johnathan, while I was there. I missed him so much, but he was in DC working tirelessly on a new government project with Allen, and he couldn't get away. Instead, I have to settle for our usual, texts, FaceTime, and calls.

Me: Made it to the hotel. I'm so grumpy

Stephen: Cheer up Buttercup

Me: I'm just over all of this.

Stephen: I know. It's almost over. Just go smile and sell some copies. Enjoy NY at least.

Me: With who?

Stephen: Johnathan

Me: He is grumpy too

Stephen: Well, try. At least we are in the same time zone. I'll call you later tonight, my phone is blowing up and I have a meeting.

Me: ok. Love you

Stephen: I love you too

I decided to change and head down to the bar.

Me: Wanna go grab a drink downstairs in the piano bar?

Johnathan: Ok. Meet you there in 20

While I freshen up, I called Britt on speakerphone.
"Hey. Did you make it to New York?" she asked.
"I did. What are you up to?"
"You know, being the best caregiver ever."
She sighed.
I laughed, looking in the mirror, investigating my skin in the twenty magnifying mirror, horrifying myself.
"Jesus. Why do they put these magnifying mirrors in here? Now I'm seeing things the naked eye doesn't, and I don't want to go out in public. I look like a ninety-year-old gorilla in this fucking thing. I should join the circus, for heaven's sake."
I gasped.
She laughed. "Walk away, man. Walk away."
As I tweezed obsessively, I asked, "How is Avery?"
"Well, currently, bitching that he can't work. It's been two months, and he forgets he almost died a couple times and had a few surgeries. He's pissed he has to be laid up in the bed at home. Poor baby. It's more like poor me. I'm going crazy being trapped here at his beck and call. His mom is coming tomorrow, so I can go to work, thank god."
"He is so lucky Britt," I said.
"No shit. That was so scary," she said.
"Any word on the dude who stabbed him?"
I winced. She got so fired up when anyone mentioned him.
She replied with an angry rant, "Fuckface? Yeah, they had some bond hearing for him yesterday. I didn't go. Fuck him. PCP? Who

the fuck does PCP these days? Hallucinations? I didn't know what I was doing? You stupid motherfucker. Smoke weed, do shrooms. Be chill, you stupid fuck. PCP?"

"So, you are finding forgiveness in your heart? Is what I'm hearing?"

I laughed so hard I was bent over.

She laughed too, to the point she was cackling.

"Thanks. I can't help it. Man, I have anger issues."

"Well, I'm going to meet Johnathan for a drink downstairs before I go to bed. This schedule is going to kill me," I said.

"Well, have some fun while you are there, but not too much, or I'll be jealous," she said.

"I won't have any, I promise. I love you."

"I love you, too," she said and hung up.

I sent her a forgive and forget Gif for an added touch that got me a laughing emoji.

I got to the bar before Johnathan. It was dimly lit. Dark wood, orange and olive velvet fabrics, brass and glass fixtures, swanky, I liked it. The bartender got me a glass of cab, just as my phone rang,

It was Jack.

I always thought something happened to Cora when I was out of town, making my heart drop.

"Hey, everything okay?" I asked, worried.

With a small laugh, he said, "Yeah, everything is fine. I just wanted to talk to you before you got busy with work."

"Okay, shoot."

I took a sip of my wine.

He took a deep breath. "So, I wanted to tell you first. Before we talked to Cora at dinner tonight."

"Tell me what Jack?" I asked.

He took another deep breath. "I proposed. Beth and I are getting married, Cassie."

I froze. My hand still on the stem of my wine glass. I felt like I couldn't swallow. Why was this hard for me to handle? We weren't together. I was in love with Stephen. This is normal progression.

"Cass? Are you there?" he asked.

I took a deep breath, bringing me back.

"Yeah, sorry. That's great Jack. I'm…I'm happy for you two. I am, I'm happy."

Realizing I was trying to convince myself of this.

"Thanks, Cass. That means a lot to me. How do you think Cora is going to take it? Should I be worried? She's been so…"

"Bitchy?" I finished his sentence.

"That is an understatement."

He laughed.

I let out a laugh. "I think it's just a fifteen-year-old thing. Don't take it personally. At least that's what my therapist says." I paused then said, "Well, good luck, and I would feed her first. She does better when fed."

"Okay, I will."

"Congratulations Jack."

"Thank you, Cass."

He hung up.

I motioned to the bartender, pushing my wine to the side. "Can I get a double whiskey on the rocks, please?"

The next day, I had not one but two signings at two different bookstores. I could kill Johnathan. Every time I looked at him, he either gave me his big, white toothy gleaming smile or looked away making zero eye contact. I was impressed with how many people really liked me and stood in line. If you went by the reviews, you would think people hated this cookbook. If you were there, you would think it was a #1 best seller. I just focused on my fans, smiled, and did my Cassie Buckley thing, talking about my passion.

The one thing I loved about New York was the melting pot of people. All the diversity and different cultures meld together in this spectacular city. The food scene was phenomenal, and people lived for it. I signed books for every walk of life.

After my twentieth cup of coffee and fortieth bathroom break, I came to sit back down to a handful of people waiting. I looked at Johnathan and secretly tapped my wrist, questioning how much longer we had. He looked at his phone and mouthed thirty to me. I smiled, looked up, and continued.

I eventually whittled the line down to a beautiful woman, dark hair, almost black, crystal blue eyes, with her child, maybe three. She handed me her book.

"Hi, my fiancé and I are very big fans of you," she said in a beautiful, flowing accent.

Her son, shyly wrapped around her leg, with stunning gray eyes.

"Awe. Thank you. Do you like to cook?" I asked.

"I don't. He does and always wanted a woman who did. I figured this book would help me," she said.

"Do you want me to inscribe it for you or him?" I asked.

"Oh, it's for him, a gift for his upcoming birthday. He will love it," she said.

I wrote a sweet birthday note for him and signed it.

"What is your son's name?" I asked.

"Jonah," she said.

"You are so handsome, Mr. Jonah," I said as he instantly hid behind her leg then peeked out to smile at me again.

Clutching her newly signed book with one hand, she said, "It was nice meeting you, Ms. Buckley."

She reached out and shook my hand with her other.

A few more, and I was done. I was exhausted from smiling and talking to strangers. I wanted to catch up with my own people and call it a night.

I sat at the hotel bar again with my glass of cab this time, scrolling through my phone. I had a text from Cora that she was going out for dinner with Jack and Beth to State Bird Provisions.

Are you fucking serious?

I said feed her, not buy her off with a Michelin star restaurant experience.

Damn.

I guessed they were celebrating. Also, Stephen did just take her on a private jet to Hawaii, so he probably felt like he had higher standards to keep up with these days.

My next text was my man.

Stephen: Hey sexy girl. I hope your day is going well.

You will probably see on the news tonight, they
caught the rest of the Albanian Drug Thugs last night.
Good shit. Call me when you get done.

I smiled and pressed to call him to only hear his sexy voice on
his voicemail. I left a message, ordered some dinner, and carried on.

I went to my room, showered, and crawled into bed. I looked at
my phone. 10:38. I turned the TV on in hopes that he would call.
Sleep took me fast.

I woke up early to a text from 11:35pm.

Stephen: I didn't want to wake you. I had a late dinner
meeting. I love you. See you in the morning.

I put my glasses on, looked at that text, and looked at it some
more. What am I reading? Oh…my…god.

I text him excitedly.

Me: Good morning.

The dots…up and down. He was awake.

Stephen: Good morning. What room are you in?

Me: Ah… 318

I raced to brush my teeth. Oh my god, I loved this man so much.
Who did this? Oh my god, I loved him.

The knock. My heart, my pussy, I squealed. I opened the door.
He was gorgeous…at 8:15am. Who looks this hot at 8:15am? I
wrapped my arms around his neck and kissed him so hard. We were
both smiling underneath.

I unsealed our lips long enough to ask, "What made you do this?"

"I don't know, your text yesterday seemed so deflated and sad.
It was pitiful. You were so close to DC, and Allen had things covered
for the day, so I was like, fuck it."

"I love you so much," I said, taking his face in my hands.

He walked me backwards, pressing his body between my legs,
pressing me back onto the bed. He stood in front of me, peeling off
his clothes, never taking his eyes off me.

"I was thinking about this all night."

"Oh yeah? What were you thinking about?" I asked, biting my lip seductively.

"I was thinking about how hot you are spread out on a big white bed like that. Your hair flowing around you like that," he said, shaking his head, slowly. "Mmm."

I reached down, under my silk pajama shorts, over my pussy, that was now wet. "You like it when I touch myself like this? You like to watch?" I licked my lips.

"Oh, Jesus, baby."

He finished taking his boxer briefs off and was now completely naked, his hand wrapped around his hard cock, stroking it, slowly, watching my hand moving beneath my tiny pink silk shorts. He smiled, then looked at me, climbing over top of me.

"You make me crazy, woman, you know that?" he said, kissing me and his cock pressed into my thigh.

"Yes, I know."

I kissed him back.

He pulled my top off, sucking my nipples one at a time. Then, pinching them as he ran his hot tongue down my stomach as he looked up at me. I gasped and winced at the pain. I liked it. He pulled my silky shorts down and tossed them to the floor, then spread my legs, running a finger lightly through the slit of my eager pussy.

"Oh fuck yes, baby."

I moaned, wanting more, my pussy aching for it. I ran my hands through his thick hair, almost pressing his head into me.

"Baby, fuck."

He slid a finger inside and then licked and sucked my pussy like it is his fucking profession.

"Oh god, yes, yes, yes."

The suction intensified and his tongue was like silk moved about my pussy. The heat rose up my spine. I became lightheaded.

"I'm going to come, baby. Yes."

He slid in another finger and hit my G spot continually until I spasmed and clenched around his fingers uncontrollably. He kissed and made his way up to my face.

"I love you," he whispered.

"I can't feel my face," I said.

He laughed.

"I really like the view you have here," he said, laying half his body over mine.

I ran my hand over his face, chuckling at the odd remark. "Yeah?"

"Yeah, remember how we had sex in front of the window in San Francisco at the Four Seasons?" he asked.

"Uh huh."

"I want to do that again. That was super hot," he said, picking me up and carrying me to the window.

He placed me, knees down, on the small couch.

I giggled. "You get what you want, Mr. Harlow."

"You do too, Ms. Buckley, you do too."

He spread my legs wide, then took my wrists in his hands and placed them wide apart on the window, palms flat against the cool glass. He stood behind me.

"Fuck, you are beautiful," he said in a low growl.

He climbed behind me, running the head of his hard cock up and down my swollen, wet pussy until he found my entrance and pressed it in.

My head went to my chest as his dick slid deep into me. It was thick, hard.

"Oh fuck, baby."

I moaned and went to reach to touch my clit.

"No. Put that back on the window," he ordered.

Oh damn. That was hot as hell being told what to do. I looked back and smiled at him.

He reached around me and massaged it for me, and he knew how hot that was for sure. My head fell, and my back arched. His other hand was on the small of my back. His thick cock slid in and out of me.

I looked at him, whispering, "You can do what you did that day."

I smiled, biting my lip, then dropping my head. The hand that was on my clit was now on the small of my back, his cock, moving slower, deeper, his thumb, wet, now sliding down between my ass cheeks.

"Just relax baby," he said, now massaging my ass. He started pumping his cock harder and harder into me, his other hand reaching up, running through, and pulling my hair.

"Fuck yeah, oh fuck."

He moans, grabbing onto my shoulder, tensing up, and burying himself deep inside me and unleashed streams of hot cum deep inside of me.

He collapsed over top of me, and I could feel him almost laughing.

"What is so funny?" I asked.

"The second you said that, it was over. It's like magic words to my dick."

He chuckled.

"I'll remember that."

I laughed.

Lounging in a five-star bed in Soho and walking around New York City with some paparazzi for a few hours before our flights took off were totally worth the trip. Celebrity status had its benefits after all.

Chapter 43

CASSIE

Sitting on a zoom call with my dad and all our investors, which happened to be some of his friends, wasn't always my idea of a good time. We did it quarterly, I grinned and bore it, and it was how I was able to sit in this very office, at this messy ass-desk, in my very own restaurant.

I hopped off, feeling a bit overwhelmed as I walked out of my office, right into Kyle.

"Oh shit. Sorry, Chef," he said. "How did it go? We still in business?" he joked like he always did after I got out of these meetings.

"Yeah, except two of our investors are pulling out. Fortunately, we have the money to buy them out now, thank god," I said. "I just think it will take away some of my working capital. I don't know. I will talk to our accountant later today. My brain is fried right now. I don't want to talk any more numbers for a while." I breathed out, walking towards the kitchen with him. "I would rather talk back of house."

"I should invest in Sagi. Buy them out and let you go live it up in Charlotte with your man," he said, casually.

I laughed. "Yeah, your knives are currently the most expensive thing you own, Kyle. I think you said they cost more than your furniture? Invest?"

I shook my head and kept walking.

He stopped, and I realized he wasn't next to me anymore. I turned, and he was looking at me.

I laughed. "What?"

"I'm being serious right now, Cassie."

Oh shit.

He was.

I walked back to him.

"Talk to me. What are you talking about, Kyle?"

"I would like to be your partner, Cass. I've earned it. I have the money. Can we at least talk about it?" he asked, totally serious.

I was speechless. I put my hand on my chest.

"Yes. I would love that." I smiled big. "Let's go back to the office," I said, turning him around with my hand on his shoulder.

I sat in the chair, and he leaned on the desk after pushing papers to the side.

He started, arms crossed. "All right, Grace and I have been talking, a lot actually. I think this would be good."

"I am mainly intrigued that you have money." I chuckled.

"I have money, Cass. I live like a poor dude. I have three nasty roommates and pay shit for rent, so I basically just save my ass off." He looked to the side and tried not to make eye contact. "Oh, I also have a bit of a trust fund, and I have been investing the hell out of it."

He then turned to look at me again.

"I just don't need it. I like the way I live," he said, smiling.

"Wait. You are a trust fund kid?" I asked, shocked, sitting up in my chair with my mouth wide open.

He shrugged one shoulder. "Yeah, my grandparents were really wealthy and left me a fuck ton of money."

"Oh, the many sides of Kyle I don't know," I said, shaking my head.

"You second-guessing your decision of dating Mr. I Have A Private Jet now?"

He laughed, tapping my leg with his foot, biting his bottom lip.

I laughed, shaking my head. "Nope." I let out a laugh.

"Anyhow. Me and Grace are moving in together, we are going

to kick shit up a notch, and we think this would be just that. What do you think?" he asked.

I smiled. "I think I wouldn't want to be a partner with anyone else." I stood to hug him. "I want to cry."

He held me out in front of him. "You are always crying, woman."

He laughed, shaking his head.

"I need to talk to my accountant and my dad before I promise you anything. Are you sure you want to do this? You really have the money?" I tilted my head in disbelief.

He rolled his eyes. "Yes, I have the money. Just talk to them and let me know what they say."

"Okay," I said, pulling the black Sagi-Shi hat from his head. "I like your new style, by the way," admiring his freshly trimmed shoulder-length blonde locks, sides now filled in.

He took his hat back, putting it on.

"Yeah, Grace's dad wasn't a fan of the Mohawk, and it was time I grew up anyhow."

He shot me a half smile and a wink.

On the way home in the car, I called my dad and told him about Kyle's grand idea. He thought it was fantastic. He said he would start working on the contract for him. I just needed to tie things up with my accountant and make sure things looked good on our financial end. This was going to be great. This would definitely solidify Kyle never leaving me.

I called Stephen with my excitement.

"Hey, sexy. I wasn't expecting to hear from you this early," he said.

"I know. I'm driving home and I just had some good news and wanted to share it. I had two investors decide to pull out of Sagi today," I said.

"Okay? That's good?" he questioned.

"Well, I came to find out, Kyle is a trust fund baby, and he wants to take their places. He wants to be my partner, Stephen," I said, so excited.

"Kyle? He has money? He eats cold couch pizza and drinks PBR," he said.

I laughed. "I know. I'm just as surprised as you. He would be the best. Maybe this would be the perfect scenario for us. Maybe this would be my ticket to get closer to leaving San Francisco, you know, maybe coming to Charlotte one day?" I said quietly, questioning him.

"Really? You want that, Cass?" he asked.

"I want to be with you, Stephen. This back and forth is killing me, and Cora is going to go to college in a couple of years. It's not that far away. I will have a choice," I said.

"Let's talk about it when you come for my birthday, okay?" he said. "Damn, I can't believe you are even considering this."

"I love you. Of course I am."

For the first time, I was willing to sacrifice my dream for someone else without a second thought. I just dialed his number and blurted this thought out.

"You are a complex, crazy creature, Cassie. I love you."

I sat in my running car at my apartment complex, beaming with joy.

"I'll call you later after I'm done hanging out with Cora. I need to give her some one-on-one tonight. Her and that boy broke up. I have a feeling it's an ice cream, two spoons kind of night."

"Okay, give her a hug for me. Should I text her something sweet or funny?" he asked.

"Send her something funny. She would like that. Thanks."

The night was just like I expected, Cora, full of heartbreak and cherry chocolate chip. I pushed down my happiness and helped her try to understand how this would happen so many more times in her life, but it was okay to feel this hurt right now. Her heart just needed a minute.

Chapter 44

STEPHEN

Today is my forty-ninth birthday, and Cassie was making a huge deal of it. She had family and friends coming to town for the weekend and was on her way to take me to lunch. She was pissed I didn't take the day off, and this is my compromise. Allen and I had so much to do with this new job, I just wasn't thinking ahead when I scheduled back-to-back meetings weeks ago. I definitely wasn't thinking that she would be in my bed, tempting me to stay in it this morning, begging, actually.

I was just finishing up a call with the Blanchard Group when I looked up and saw that she was leaning in my doorway. I could barely finish my last sentence when I saw her standing there in that little green sundress, the one she wore the day I took her to the beach on our first date when we reunited. I remembered sliding my hand up that dress in the car within five seconds of picking her up, making her come so fast, moaning so loud I thought the neighbors all came out to investigate what animal was being tortured.

"Okay, I think…Okay…thank you for your time. We will be in touch."

I hung up. I thought I hung up. I stood and needed to adjust my now hard dick in my pants.

"Baby. You kill me," I said, pulling her into my office and closing the door behind her. Her smile, her kiss, damn.

"So, you remember this dress?" she said, turning from side to side.

"This dress is burned into my memory, obviously."

I looked down and my now hard cock trying to breach my slacks.

"And he remembers too."

I laughed.

She reached for my cock, tracing her long fingers over the outline of it, looking at me, biting her bottom lip.

"You really should have taken the day off and let me play with this. Now I have to torture you in public and here at work, birthday boy," she said, in a low growl.

"Stop Cass. I'm never going to be able to walk out of here like this."

"Ugh, you are no fun in business mode," she whined, still smiling.

"Are we still going to lunch, or am I just locking the door and eating that pussy?" I asked.

"Now we are talking," she said, eyes wide.

"I made reservations, then you can eat my pussy tonight for dessert. Good compromise?" she asked, raising her eyebrows up and down.

"Sounds good." I looked at my watch. "I have a meeting at four, then I will be home early."

I rounded my desk, noticing a FedEx package. "I wonder if this is what Britt sent?" I asked, holding it up.

"Oh my god, open it. She said you are going to die. I thought she sent it to the house, though," she said, leaning on my desk, so cute with her long, tan legs hanging off.

I ripped the envelope open and pulled it out. It was wrapped in basic Happy Birthday wrapping paper. I took care unwrapping it, to only reveal Cassie's latest cookbook. I held it up, and we both looked at each other, laughing in confusion.

"What the fuck? Why would she send me your book?"

I laughed.

"That's weird. Has she lost her marbles? Is that even from her?"

She picked up the envelope and dumped out the contents. A

card fell out, and she handed it to me. I opened the front page of the book and read the inscription, questioning it.

"What? What is it, Stephen?" she asked, worried by the look on my face.

I turned it to her. "You signed this, Cassie. Do you remember signing this?"

It was a book I signed.

To Stephen, Happy cooking and Happy 49th Birthday. Your favorite chef, Cassie Buckley

She said, shaking her head. "Babe, I have signed hundreds and hundreds of books, I don't know. Here, read the card."

She handed it to me.

I slowly took it from her. There was nothing written on the front of the envelope, feeling eerie, I slid my finger under the sealed lip and pulled the card out. My heart fell when I saw the writing... her writing.

"Baby, what?" I heard her say.

My hand went instantly to my mouth, my eyes welled with tears reading her words. Cassie, now by my side with her arm wrapped around me.

"Talk to me, baby," she pleaded.

I just turned and hugged her.

"She's alive. She's okay," I cried. "She's alive."

My phone rang. I looked down and saw that it was Jakob. I knew this was the beginning of a different life than the one I currently had. I kissed Cassie on the forehead and reached for it.

"Hello?" I answered apprehensively.

"Stephen? My brother," he said, so happy.

"I think I was told you got a package?" he said.

"I just got it, yes," I said, still in shock.

"I have someone here who wants to talk to you," he said.

I couldn't swallow. I could barely breathe.

"Stephen?" she said.

My name, coming from her voice, I had not heard in three years. I had to sit down. I put my head in my palm, tears poured from my eyes.

"Oh my god, Lauren. Is that you? Is that really you?" I cried.

"Oh, Stephen, yes, it's me, love. It's me."

She sobbed.

I could feel Cassie's comforting hand rubbing my shoulder, running over my head.

Cassie drove us silently in my car to the police station, where she was located as a base for questioning. I just held her hand and looked out the window.

Her voice broke the silence as we pulled into the parking lot.

"Do you want me to go in with you?" she asked.

I turned to look at her. "Of course, Cassie. I need you."

I gave her hand an extra squeeze.

We were brought back to a conference room, and Jakob quickly came in, hugging me, patting me hard in excitement.

"Best birthday ever, my brother. Best birthday ever. She is finishing up with some questions and will be here in a second." He then turned to look at Cassie. "You must be Cassie." He shook her hand. "I'm Jakob, Lauren's brother."

Cassie smiled. "It's nice to finally meet you, Jakob," she said.

She looked so nervous, so out of place. This had to be awkward. Shit. It was awkward for me. I was there with my girlfriend and about to be reunited with my missing fiancé of three years. There was no handbook for this shit.

Before I could try to even think about how to feel, she opened the door. My mind scrambled because she looked like her but not. The same beautiful, tall stunning Lauren, but dark brown, almost black hair, not the blonde I was used to.

She ran straight to me, straight into my arms and hugged me tight. I reciprocated, and it felt so good to feel her, feel her living body against mine. We cried. I held the back of her head as she buried her face against my shoulder. Her words in my ear between sobs in her beautiful accent I swore I would never hear again.

"I didn't know if I would ever see you again, love."

And

"I'm here Stephen, I'm here, love."

I finally managed to pull her away to get a look at her. I shook my head.

"What happened? I have so many questions."

She nodded. "I know, I know. I will answer them, I will," she said, wiping her tears with her sleeve.

Just then, she took inventory of the room, and that she wasn't alone. She looked at Cassie.

Cassie made a look that she now recognized her. She pointed to Lauren.

"New York. Now I remember. I signed your copy for his birthday." She pointed to me. "You had your little…" She immediately put her hand over her mouth, eyes wide.

I looked at Cassie, then at Lauren.

"What? Little what?" I asked.

Lauren looked at me, then she looked at Jakob, nodding as he left the room.

I put my hands up. "What is happening?" I asked, confused.

Lauren looked at me, then took my hands. "Remember how we were trying to get pregnant, Stephen? Well, I found out I was pregnant after I was kidnapped. I had a little boy."

"What? Oh my god," I said in complete shock.

Then the door opened, and Jakob walked in with a little version of me.

"Mommy."

He ran to Lauren.

She picked him up and turned him towards me, and said with tears streaming down her face, "Stephen, this is your son, Jonah Stephen Harlow."

I looked at her, then him, and then turned to see everyone was bawling, including Cassie.

I reached out and touched his chubby, perfect cheek.

"Hi, Jonah."

That is all I could muster before my hand went over my mouth. I stood in complete disbelief at what my eyes were seeing. I was staring at Lauren and my son. My son who looked exactly like me.

Thick black hair, my gray eyes, and Lauren, alive, healthy, and so beautiful.

I knew I tended to go back and rate my birthdays saying, my 21st was my best, or whatever.

I would definitely say my 49th took the cake

Someone isn't dead, and I got a kid.

Chapter 45

CASSIE

X

The caterers were buzzing in and out of the house, and I looked at the large hanging clock on the wall. Damn, it was an hour before guests got there. I should probably hang up with Britt, but good god, there had been so much to catch her up on.

"So where is he now?" she asked.

"Jakob's visiting with Jonah before there were fifty people here freaking the little dude out. He was obsessed with him, Britt. It's adorable," I said, walking over to hit the control pad to turn the music on for the house and yard.

"I cannot believe everything that has happened and am not there. Holy shit, Cass. Please text me play-by-play. This will be interesting with Lauren there and all Stephen's friends and family. Fuck. What a horrible time for Avery to be stabbed, man. I could kill him."

She laughed.

"You aren't right," I said laughing. "I gotta go, I need to get ready."

We hung up and I looked out to see Stephen's lawn transformed into a backyard birthday masterpiece of tables, chairs, lounges, and umbrellas. A perfect setting for the summer backyard barbecue, complete with boat rides, volleyball, and yard games. Exactly what Stephen envisioned his summer birthday to be at this house. Yay me. I didn't exactly envision his fiancé and two-year-old child being the stars of the show, but I seemed to be good at rolling with the punches these days. The new Cassie, go with the flow. I could do this.

Actually, I was nervous as hell. I was trying not to fall apart inside. I saw how he looked at her. I saw what she brought to the table, Jonah. They would forever have him as a tie to each other. I understood that, having Cora tying me and Jack. The difference was, Lauren didn't cheat on Stephen. She was kidnapped and ripped from his life when they were at their happiest.

I try to push my fears and insecurities aside and head to the bathroom, the one we shared now, our things intermingling now like a couple living together. A toothbrush I kept there, next to his. Clothes in the closet that didn't get packed to go home, lingerie and essentials in a few drawers. I was staking my claim.

I put on a cute one-piece suit since it was a family affair, black with some cute cut-outs, so it was not completely conservative. I chose a cute, flirty floral yellow sundress, a little ruffle for the hem. My hair was down for now. He likes it down, long. Eventually, it would make me crazy, blowing in all directions and would be in a bun or a ponytail, but I'd wait as long as possible. For him.

As I came into the bedroom, I was greeted by his smile, the gorgeous face of my sweet man.

"Hey, babe," I said, walking up and reaching around to hug him. "How did it go?"

He kissed me.

"Great. He actually let me pick him up and carry him around while I talked to Lauren."

He talked fast, with such excitement, that of a new father.

"He high-fived me. Oh my god, Cass, his hands are so small and eerily like mine. I had to inspect them without freaking him out. I have to be so careful not to go too fast with him, he is so shy."

He just kept rambling all over the place, with a smile.

"Oh. I got in a tickle, and he laughed. Oh my gosh, his little laugh."

His head went back like it had melted him.

"I'll see if he will let me do it today. Oh Cassie. Can you believe I am a dad? This is nuts," he said, shaking his head.

I smiled. "I know, it's crazy. You are going to be amazing. Look at you. You are so excited."

I caressed his face with my hand.

He pulled from my embrace. "I guess I should get ready? Everyone is going to be here soon."

He headed into the closet and heard his voice from inside.

"Babe, the yard looks amazing. Everyone is going to have a great time. You did great."

Now he came out with black swim trunks and a light blue shirt.

"Thank you for all you have done and how wonderful you are."

He walked over, taking my face in his hands, and kissed me before heading into the shower.

I walked in and leaned against the counter, watching him continue rambling on as he climbed in the shower, soaping up his incredibly sculpted body while I watched through the glass.

"I know you wanted to drive people around in the boat today, but since things have changed a bit, do we want to maybe ask your brother to do it?" I asked. "You know, so you can spend more time with Jonah and Lauren?"

He dipped his head back, rinsing the shampoo out of his hair. I couldn't help but stare at his glorious cock between his legs that I didn't get to enjoy last night due to his exhaustion.

"Yeah, maybe. We will just play it all by ear, babe. Don't get all stressed. Just let the day happen, okay."

I looked down at my bare feet.

"Okay, I'll try."

I took a deep breath as the water was shut off and the shower door opened. I handed him a towel.

"Thanks."

He leans in for a kiss, wet, warm.

"Look at me," he said, pulling my face up to his with his index finger. "I love you."

I gave him a small smile and said softly, "I love you too."

The yard was filling fast. A lot of familiar faces, some I hadn't seen in years, his brother, some friends, co-workers I was meeting for the first time. Allen and Bianca, Marguerite, and Stephen never leaving my side. It was wonderful. The big news, of course.

"We hear the amazing news of Lauren, and you have a son."

Everyone was anxious with their arrival. Nobody wanted to go for a boat ride or do much of anything because they were worried they would miss their big entrance.

Finally, the big moment happened, forty-five minutes into the party. The place erupted. She had risen. She was stunning in her long, ankle-length, black tank dress that showed curves that holy fuck, how did you have a kid two years ago? Her black hair was straight to her perfect ass. She stood about five foot ten, and what the fuck did she do in captivity? Lift weights like the girl on the Terminator? Her fucking arms.

I mean, this should happen, right? I shouldn't be jealous. I'm being a bitch internally. Unfortunately, this was the moment Stephen left my side...for the remainder of the party.

He didn't even realize it with his excitement.

He stood next to her and Jonah, talking to family members and friends the entire day. I mingled separately.

"Wow. I can't believe she's here. This is absolutely crazy. And Stephen is a dad. My mind is blown girl," Bianca said, shaking her head, sipping on her Prosecco, and holding her plate as we watched them talk to Stephen's brother and kids across the lawn.

They stood next to each other like they were a happy couple with their kid. At one point, he placed his hand on the small of her back for one second.

Bianca noticed and looked at me. I looked at her and made a small smile and a furrowed brow.

"I need another drink, do you need one?"

I looked at her full glass.

"I'm fine. You want me to come with you?" she asked.

"No, thank you."

I turned and marched inside.

I took long breaths as I walked fast, heart beating, heading into the house. I found myself in our…his bathroom. What did I do? I text Britt. Tears filled my eyes, the screen became blurry.

Me: Fuuuuck.

Britt: call??

I did. She picked up immediately, and it made me cry.

"Oh fuck. What is wrong?" she asked.

I told her the shitshow that was happening beyond the bathroom doors. She was appalled, but we came up with somewhat of a plan. I basically needed to stop being a pussy and put myself next to him. I needed to stop being a bystander. He probably didn't realize what he was doing. He was excited, and he was also a dude. Britt claimed they honestly couldn't do more than one thing at a time. If that didn't work, then I could lose my shit. I was to check in if that didn't work.

I got my shit together, and when I walked out into the kitchen. I was greeted by Lauren, who was leaning against the counter, obviously waiting for me to come out.

"Oh, hey."

I was startled.

"Hi, Cassie. I just wanted to talk to you for a moment, alone."

She looked around.

Oh fuck. There was something about her. She was so spy-like. Especially now that I knew what she did for a living. She knew how to handle guns and shit.

Holy fuck.

I couldn't stop looking at her arms that are crossed in front of her. Talk about guns. I glanced down at mine, so puny in comparison. I used to feel so sexy and strong. Now, I just feel so small, so insignificant in her presence.

"What did you want to talk about, Lauren?" I asked.

"Well, I know this is all, well, a lot for you," she said. "I haven't had a chance to talk to you one on one."

I put my glass on the counter and leaned against it, on one hand.

"Okay, I'm all ears." I smiled. "Wait. Can I ask a question first?"

"Sure."

"Why my book signing in New York? Why did you come there first?" I asked, arching a brow.

"I wanted to meet the woman who stole my Stephen's heart while I was gone. I was there, in hiding and well." She shrugged. "I wanted to meet you face to face," she said in such a serious tone.

The accent mixed with the intense look, I instantly changed my mind and didn't want to tangle with her anymore.

"Okay, what else did you want to talk to me about Lauren?" I asked, really wanting to end this conversation now, reaching for my wine and taking a large sip.

"I need Stephen. I need him in mine and Jonah's life. I need you to understand that. I know he loves you. I see the Instagram. I see how happy you two are. He is a wonderful man. I had that from him for two years."

She held up her hand, showing me her ring finger with her engagement ring. "He made a promise to me, but now that seems to be, let's just say...complicated."

She looked at my hand, the one with the pearl ring Stephen gave me. I ran over it with my thumb, protecting what was precious to me.

"Well, we will see what happens, Cassie. It will be nice to get to know each other."

She smiled a devious fucking smile, turned, and headed to the hallway bathroom.

I found Stephen standing on the dock, holding his son on his hip, as if it were completely natural, talking with his mom, his brother Ethan, and Marek.

I made my way across the lawn, my feet melting into the thick, cool grass as I stepped. My nerves grew as I got closer, his back to me, the little leg hanging down his side, a little chubby foot, so freaking cute. I was practically shaking inside from my conversation with Lauren. I just wanted to hug him.

I slid in, running my arm around his waist. He jerked slightly in surprise.

"Oh, hey, babe," he said, leaning over and kissing my head.

"Well, don't you look natural," I said, reaching over to touch Jonah's leg. "Hey, buddy."

Jonah buried his head in Stephen's chest out of shyness.

"Wow. You are his protector now, daddy. Nice."

Stephen smiled and said, "Hey. Jonah, remember, this is Cassie. She is all love and happiness, buddy. She is nobody to be scared of. You can trust her," he said to him and looked at me for reassurance.

Then, I felt her presence from across his shoulder, her stare, her glare, stretching her long arms out for Jonah, saying, "I'll take him now."

Lauren took him from Stephen. Claws were coming out. I interrupted her private family time, so she was punishing him.

A now a deflated Stephen lost his toy, and I felt bad for intruding.

"Are you having a good time? I feel like I've barely seen you. I'm sorry," he said, tucking a stray hair behind my ear.

"Yeah, just catching up with Bianca and Allen," I said with a half-smile.

"Does anyone need anything over here? I was about to go refresh my wine," I said.

I ended up with a full-blown drink order and headed to do my new serving duties. While on the porch, digging through the cooler for random beers and refilling my wine, I was greeted by Allen.

"I'll help you carry all that," he said.

I laughed. "Thanks, my server days have been over for a while."

"So, I wanted to talk to you for a minute," he said, serious.

"Okay. Something wrong?" I asked.

He shrugged and talked low. "Well, it's Lauren. Cass, she's as territorial as they come. I know Stephen loves you." He put his hand out. "There is no doubt about that." He shook his head. "I just don't trust what her intentions are. Bianca told me what she has kind of seen and she is just worried she is going to bully you around. I don't want you to let that happen. Stephen is just..." he ran his hands through his hair, then pointed out to the yard, making me turn to look out.

"Fuck...look at him. He's beside himself. He may not notice what she is doing Cassie, that's all."

"Thanks, Allen. He's a big boy. He can make his own decisions," I said and patted him on the arm. "Plus, she already cornered me and clarified her intentions." I shook my head. "She's scary as fuck."

"Oh no." He put a hand on my shoulder. "Talk to Stephen. Don't let her break you two up, Cass. Please, I know he loves you. I do," he pleaded.

I smiled. "I know, and I will."

He helped me carry all the drinks across, and the circle of conversation continued, but I mingled everywhere Lauren wasn't the rest of the evening.

The party went on until around nine. Lauren, her family, and Jonah left around seven-thirty so they could get him to bed.

Finally, some alone time. We sat on the dock in lounge chairs side by side and just enjoyed the quiet lake night. The clinking of the ice in his glass from one hand, his other hand held mine.

He looked over at me. "I think today was great. Thank you."

I took a deep breath. "You are welcome. Happy birthday."

"I invited Lauren and Jonah over for brunch tomorrow. I hope that's okay?" he said, looking out towards the lake.

I snapped my head around. "Babe, I kind of wish you would at least talk to me before you pass out invites."

"Whoa," he said, taken aback.

"I'm sorry. I just feel uneasy about her. She..."

I stopped myself. I knew I was going to say stupid shit.

"She what, Cass?" he asked.

"She is in love with you, and she wants me out of the picture," I said. "Where was I today? What happened when I came around?" I asked.

"That's bullshit," he barked back.

"The conversation I had with her in the kitchen wasn't bullshit, Stephen." I closed my eyes, putting my head into my hands, pulling my knees up into my chest. "Fuck, I really don't want to fight."

"What conversation in the kitchen, Cass?" he asked.

"She's so intimidating. Do you realize she is still wearing your engagement ring?" I asked.

"I...I didn't notice." He shook his head.

I looked at him. "It's been a long day. I think I'm ready for bed," I said, climbing from the lounge.

He took a hold of my wrist, pulling me into his lap. He made me look at him.

"Cassie, I love you. I am sorry if I have done something wrong. I am sure I have done a multitude of fucked up shit the last twenty-four hours I am completely unaware of. My mind is everywhere." He then pulled me into a tight embrace. "I'm sorry." He kissed the top of my head.

That night he held me tight, wrapped in a cocoon of arms and legs, while I watched the moon move from one side of the room to the other. His breathing against the back of my neck was so rhythmic, peaceful. I never slept, my mind was a tangled mess of memories and thoughts both good and bad. The what- ifs playing reel after reel like a goddamn movie. The ones that had Jonah in it, they made me smile. The ones that had Lauren... I cried silently as his arm was draped across my chest. I periodically kissed his forearm. He slept through it all. Breathing in and out peacefully. My sweet man, dreaming about his new precious life while mine was unraveling just inches away.

Chapter 46

STEPHEN

I woke up to the feel of cool sheets and emptiness next to me in bed. Cassie was gone. I got up and, through my bedroom window, I noticed her in the morning light, curled in a lounger out on the dock. I brushed my teeth, threw on a pair of pajama pants and a t-shirt, and went to head out. I noticed she had started coffee, so I grabbed a cup and another for her, just in case.

The grass, dewy, the air, humid. I reached the dock. She was fast asleep, her legs tucked up into her, and a blanket haphazardly wrapped around her. She was so beautiful with her amber hair flowing down her face, my angel. I placed the mugs on the table next to her now cold, untouched one and sat next to her, and she stirred. Her eyes slowly opened as I tucked her hair behind her ear.

"Good morning, sexy," I said softly.

"Oh, hey," she said in a groggy voice.

"How long have you been out here, baby?" I asked.

"I don't know. I came out to watch the sunrise, but it was in another direction and not that great. I guess I fell asleep," she said, stretching her arms over her head.

She looked exhausted.

"Oh babe, you should have gotten me up. I would have taken you out in the boat for that and put you in the perfect spot," I said.

"I...It's okay." She yawned. "I was just enjoying it out here.

That's all. It's peaceful. I understand why you are always sitting out here and sending me those pictures. It's a good thinking spot." She reached up and cradled my face. "What time is brunch today? I need to go to the store and pick up some things."

"I told Lauren twelve. There's no rush. I put a call into Gloria and she is running to the store. She also wanted to see Lauren and Jonah as well. Gregory is stopping by this morning with a bunch of toys and supplies I'm borrowing from his grandpa's stash. He said he has it all." I told her. "So, you can sit back and relax today, I'll do the cooking. You did so much already, and I feel bad I sprung this on you. It's also not a big deal. It's just us four," I said, running my thumb over her worried face.

She was barely looking at me.

"It's okay," she said softly.

She seemed sad.

"Are we okay?" I asked.

"Yeah. It's just a new phase I'm just trying to adjust to, I guess. I don't know."

She managed a small smile, but she looked down, pulling threads at the blanket.

I handed her the new mug of coffee. "Here. I figured you needed a new one."

"Thank you."

She took it, cradling it in two hands, looking out towards the lake.

"Do you want me to leave you alone or sit with you?" I asked, praying she wasn't going to push me away.

"Stay with me," she said, and a tear slowly ran down her cheek.

"Oh, Jesus, baby. What is it?" I pleaded for her to tell me. "What can I do to fix this?"

She was so sad and it was breaking my heart.

"I just need a minute. I just need you to sit and be with me. I don't want to talk, just hold me," she said.

And that was exactly what I did. I let her crawl between my legs, up into my chest. I covered her in the blanket, and I stroked her hair while she soaked my shirt with her tears. I didn't ask questions, and it killed me. Tears ran down my face as I sat wondering what must be going through her precious mind. My heart was so happy and breaking at the same exact time. It was the most confused I had ever been in my life. I had been on my hands and knees praying for Lauren's safe return, wished and begged for forgiveness of Cassie. I always imagined one of these women to be in my life, and now I had both. I always wanted a child of my own, and I completely gave up on that dream. Here I was, with a son, my little Jonah, my miracle.

I continued kissing the top of her head, stroking her hair, and holding her tight until she had enough. She looked up with her swollen, red eyes and said, "I need to go shower and get ready. I love you, Stephen."

She kissed me and climbed from my embrace and left to go inside.

I sat there for a moment, basically in shock, just breathing in and out, deeply.

No.

This was her walking away.

I grabbed the mugs, dumped the coffee and walked inside, placing them on the counter as I walked past. I made a beeline to the master bedroom, where I heard the shower running in the bathroom. I peeled my tear-soaked shirt off and tossed it to the floor and slowly pushed the door open where steam had already accumulated in the room.

My feet hit the tile, and so did my pajama pants. I slowly pulled the fogged-over glass door open and saw her standing there, back to me, head under the rain head, wet amber hair flowing down her muscular back. Water poured down her strong, tan legs and beautiful ass. She turned her head, water droplets or tears, I couldn't tell.

"Stephen, what are you..."

I turned her, and covered her next words with my mouth.

I kissed her like my fucking life depended on it. I actually felt like it did. This woman was my world, my air.

I ran my hands up to her jaw, I kissed her hard. I could feel her face tense because she was still crying. I let her. I let her let go of whatever it was that was chewing her up. I was not giving up on her.

I was not letting her go.

I kissed down her neck, and her hands came to life. She started to run them over my shoulders. Her head went back as I kissed her shoulders, then down to her breasts. I pressed her back up against the cool shower tile. She gasped. She slid her hand down and grabbed hold of my now hard cock and stroked it up and down.

Holy fuck.

Her touching me and reciprocating.

Yes baby, be here with me, be here with me.

Well, don't come too, because this feels fucking fantastic.

I reached down and slid my fingers into her, felt the wetness pooling between her legs. She moaned, it echoed throughout our tile and glass enclosure. She put her leg onto the ledge, giving me more space to do my job. She was still stroking my cock, now with more vigor.

"Fuck baby, you are going to jerk my dick clean off," I said, laughing into her kiss.

"I'm sorry, I'm so turned on, I'm sorry," she said.

"Is this all I needed to do? You just needed me to fuck you?" I said, smiling.

"I need you to make love to me, Stephen," she said, wrapping her arms around my shoulders.

Fuck, she needed to feel loved, cherished.

Okay.

I turned her around, and I changed all my movements. I washed her body from top to bottom.

I kissed her.

I washed her long hair.

I quickly washed myself before shutting the shower off and grabbing towels. I did this all in silence. I dried her off and carried her to the bedroom, placing her on the bed.

I unwrapped her beautiful body like a present on Christmas morning and kissed and licked her like I never had before. I cherished every inch of her. I found erogenous zones she never knew she had. She had toe-curling orgasm after orgasm. When the sheets were finally a tangled mess between her kicking and her fisting them, I only then dared to climb on top of her now limp body.

"I love you," I said.

"I know baby. I know."

She caressed the side of my face, and one single tear ran from the corner of her eye.

With my forearms on either side of her head, her wet hair surrounding her angel-like face, and her gorgeous body underneath me, I slid my cock inside of her. She closed her eyes, her head bent back slightly, and I kissed her exposed neck.

Fuck, it felt amazing.

Hot, wet, tight.

I pumped my dick in and out of her, and I never took my eyes off of her. I loved this woman. I loved her with all I had.

She wrapped her arms around me, and I could feel her pussy tightening around my cock. I reached under her, taking her ass in my hands, pulling her up into me, deeper into her.

"Fuck, I'm going to come, baby. Are you going to come again?" I breathed into her ear.

"Yes, yes..." she moaned.

Oh damn. Hold off, dude.

How to make French toast. Eggs, milk, fuck, that feels good, dip the bread, fuuuuck don't say dip. Cinnamon, put it in a hot pan, fuck her pussy is so hot. So tight.

I could feel her pussy getting so wet around my cock, getting so tight, her hands in her hair,

"Oh yes," she yelled.

Oh, thank god.

I raised up on my hands and thrust my cock deep inside of her, unleashing a mind-blowing orgasm, leaving me a sweaty, out of breath mess on top of her.

Her hands ran through my still-wet hair, looking up at me.

"I love you too," she said, looking into my eyes. "I love you too."

Tears streamed from the sides of her eyes, her chin quivering.

Chapter 47

STEPHEN

"Good morning, Gloria," I said as I came around the corner of the kitchen to her unloading bags of groceries, the refrigerator doors wide open.

"Good morning, Stephen. How was your birthday party yesterday?" she asked, reaching into bags smiling.

"It was a good time. I'm sorry you couldn't make it," I said.

"I know, I'm sorry about that." She put her hand to her chest. "I still cannot believe the news about Lauren. And you have a son. Stephen, what a gift," she said, mouth wide open.

"I know. I'm in shock myself. Wait until you see him, Gloria. He is adorable," I said.

She looked around. "Where is Cassie?" Then lowered her voice, asking, "How is she handling all this?" arching a brow.

I just shook my head.

"The reporters have the gate absolutely jammed up," she said, shaking her head.

"Are you serious?" I asked, furious.

"They will get bored, just like before."

"Well, not as long as Lauren is back and forth. That's who they are after, not really me. At this point, though, I guess we are a trifecta of popularity though."

I laughed.

She rolled her eyes and continued unpacking the bags in silence as I went back to check on Cassie. She was coming out of the closet, cute as a button with a pair of white shorts and a flowy, navy top.

"Hey, babe, Gloria is here," I said

"Oh, good. I haven't seen her in a while," she said, in a seemingly better mood.

We made our way out, and they went into an instant conversation about family, just as Gregory arrived with a car full of items.

"Man. You didn't have to bring all this," I said.

"We have so much. I am glad to get rid of it. Our grandson doesn't play with it anymore," he said, unloading baskets of big trucks, toys for inside and outside, and essentials like a booster seat and a portable crib.

"This is awesome. I'll get it all back to you as soon as I get all my own," I said, patting him on the shoulder.

"Keep the toys. The gran doesn't come for another couple of months, so we don't need the crib or booster until then. The wife cleaned it all up. You are good to go." He smiled. "Oh, here. These are sheets and blankets, I think go with it."

He handed me a bag.

"Thanks, man," I said, taking it.

"Oh, hey, Cassie," he said as she walked into the room.

"Hey, Gregory, how are you?" she asked. "I haven't seen you since our airport rendezvous."

Laughing, he said, "I'm doing great. Just happily unloading clutter from my house."

He pointed to the pile of things at my feet.

"Yeah, it's been a while, but I remember those times. I can't believe Stephen gets to do this now."

"Better late than never," I said, putting my hands in the air. "I'm going to take this crib into the back bedroom and see if I can figure out how to set it up," I said, lifting it by the handle.

"Can I talk to you, Gregory?" Cassie asked him as I walked away.

"Uh, sure," he said.

Gregory called to me down the hall, "Hey, Stephen, Gloria, or

Cassie can probably show you how to put it up in two seconds flat when you are done with that struggle, man," he said, laughing.

I yelled back, "I'm going to try to keep my man card for at least ten minutes, Gregory. Thanks."

Jakob dropped Lauren and Jonah off, coming in for one quick, "Hi" before heading out.

The tension was thick now that we didn't have the distraction of the party and forty-plus guests. Gloria and Lauren were busy catching up, and Cassie and I got busy showing Jonah some of the new toys that were delivered. Lauren's eyes were never far. I could feel them.

Cassie and I made a beautiful fruit salad and Monte Cristo sandwiches, which was kind of comical since I was just making French toast in my head, trying not to come too fast just earlier. I loved it when Cassie let me be her sous chef in the kitchen, more like her sidekick. She demanded to be in there, trying to stay out of arms reach of Lauren.

"Gloria, please stay and eat with us," I said.

"I wish I could, but I have to get back to the city. I have my other clients this weekend that I'm tending to. Y'all have a lovely time catching up. I'm so glad you are home safe and sound Lauren."

She took her by her hands, squeezing them, smiling.

"Thank you, Gloria," Lauren said.

Gloria bent down to his level as he pushed a car across the floor.

"And I will be seeing you soon, Mr. Jonah, you cutie patootie."

She stood and looked at me. "That boy is your twin, Stephen. Wow." She shook her head. "He is a good-looking boy." She smiled.

"Thanks for everything, Gloria," I said as she left.

We sat and ate with random conversation. Things were going well. Brunch was absolutely delicious, and Jonah was a wonderful distraction between the girls.

"This is delicious. Thank you for having us," Lauren said, cutting up fruit and her sandwich, putting it in front of Jonah as his little hands grabbed it like a hungry hippo, shoving it in his mouth. Lauren reminded him to use his little fork instead.

"Well, I figured it would be nice to have some one-on-one,

unlike yesterday," I said, taking a sip of my mimosa, which I decided was a good idea since I realized my company, and I may need a tad bit of liquid courage.

Cassie looked over and smiled at Jonah. He smiled back. My heart melted. She tickled his little cheek, and he giggled. I looked at Lauren, and she cut her eyes at Cassie.

Oh fuck.

Thank God Cass didn't see that.

"So, how did you manage having him in that situation? His pregnancy and birth must have been so hard. It must have been hell, Lauren?" Cassie asked, never looking up from Jonah, smiling at him, pushing more berries toward his little hand.

I was ready to hear this story and how my son was brought into this world. Lauren put her knife and fork down, wiped her mouth, and sat back in her chair.

"Well, when they took me, they knew I was valuable with my skill set. They were mad, thinking I purposefully messed up the job, which I did, but they honestly didn't know." I shot her a hard look. I was on the other end of that job. I swallowed hard, hearing this news. "I didn't know if they wanted to kill me or use me. Once I realized I was pregnant, and they figured it out, it was a game changer."

She started fiddling with her fingernails, nervous. Lauren was nervous. This was sensitive.

"What happened, Lauren?" I asked gently.

Cassie was now paying more attention. Looking up from Jonah.

She took a deep breath. Jonah started to squirm in his seat, wanting to get out.

"Here, let me clean him up. Let him play while we have this conversation."

She wiped his little face and hands, then let him run around the living room while we sat and talked, sitting on the couches, me on my second mimosa.

She continued apprehensively.

"Once Valton found out I was pregnant, he decided I was his property. I was going to be his."

She was now looking at her feet. This was a vulnerable subject. She looked up.

"Don't get me wrong, he treated me well, like a wife, I guess a captive wife, but he didn't harm me. Meanwhile, I was working for them the entire time. Once I had Jonah, the best doctor, the best care, everything I needed." She took a deep breath. "Valton moved us into his private quarters, his house. He became so delusional. We were now his family. Jonah was his son. We were to never leave his sight. That's when it got hard."

She closed her eyes.

I couldn't help it. I had to comfort her, I knew I was going to pay the price with Cassie, but it was torture to watch her relive this alone across the room. I walked over, sat next to her and placed my arm around her.

"I'm so sorry. You don't have to tell us anymore if you don't want to."

Tears started to fall, and Jonah toddled over to her, curious, placing his hands in her lap, looking at the two of us.

"Mommy?"

"I'm okay, Jonah. Mommy is okay." She caressed his little face.

He just went back to playing, like this was a normal occurrence.

Cassie got up, retrieved a box of tissues, and brought them over, saying with such sincerity, "I'm really sorry, Lauren."

She handed them to her, then made her way to the kitchen.

Jonah fussed, and Lauren decided it was time to get him down for a nap.

"Stephen, would you like to help me? I can show you how I do it," she said to me.

I could almost feel Cassie burning a hole through the drywall between the kitchen and living room, but I did. I wanted to know how to put my kid down for a nap.

"Yeah, I do," I said.

I went into the kitchen, where Cassie was drying dishes and gave her a kiss.

"I'll be right back."

"Okay."

She smiled.

I closed the shades and made it as dark as possible. She told me to sit in the rocking chair and handed him to me.

"He likes to be held like this and just rock. He loves to rock for a while. He likes it when you hum."

She sat on the spare bed and just watched me as I looked down at him. I rocked and hummed, his big gray eyes looking up at me, growing heavier and heavier with the rocking of the chair. Eventually, his little mouth fell open, and he was out. So damn sweet. I did that. I looked up at her like, what now?

She motioned to the crib to place him in there. I covered him with his blanket, and she tucked a stuffed animal in the crook of his arm. We snuck out, taking a monitor with us.

Once the door closed, I said, "That was awesome. Thank you for showing me how to do that." I hugged her just as Cassie walked down the hallway.

Fuck.

She just smiled at us and whispered, "Is he asleep?"

I gave a thumbs up and a smile.

She kept walking by without a care.

Phew.

Maybe this was going to be okay after all.

Lauren and I had a lot to catch up on. I had a lot of questions about the last three years.

"I want to answer all your questions, Stephen. Can we do that in private, maybe outside?" she asked.

I wasn't sure how that would fly, but it was worth a try.

"Let me pass it by Cassie first. Go make yourself comfortable, and I'll meet you out on the patio," I said.

I went to find Cassie, now in the master bedroom, doodling around, busy.

I rambled nervously, "Hey honey, Lauren wants to sit down and have a talk about everything. Is that okay? I have the monitor. I don't want you to feel left out, but I think this is all really personal and…"

She stopped me. "It's okay. I can make myself busy."

She kissed me on the cheek.

I made my way onto the patio, where Lauren was already sitting at the table, waiting on me. Cassie kindly brought us a pitcher of sweet tea and glasses shortly after and slipped back inside. Our conversation started with the horrible events of Valton, pursuing her for two years after Jonah's birth, using her body however he saw fit. Pretending she was his wife in front of staff and around the family. She told me how she continued doing her job, which was using her cyber skills for his trafficking benefit. She did as she was told; she had to keep her and Jonah safe, just constantly praying it would come to an end, that he would get caught, and that they would be freed from this nightmare.

Finally, she had her chance. When my company's efforts with the US government finally paid off, and her skills didn't align, the first ship got through, and Valton lost his mind over it. He became increasingly unstable, and her angel, one of the staff members who had befriended her over the years, had planned to help her escape. Passports were made for them, and a plan was put in place. It was risky, but she had no choice. She already felt her life was in danger at this point. Next thing she knew, she made it safely to Ukraine to a safe house, then to the US to a Ukrainian family in New York. She wouldn't dare let her presence be known. Kastrati's men were knocking on Jakob's door, sitting outside her parents' house, looking for her everywhere. Valton lost it. He made a stupid mistake and came to the US, and she found out.

"I found out where he was, and I made anonymous contact with the Euro DEA. I needed to end it. I was so terrified. If this failed, if he found me, Stephen, he would kill me. He would take Jonah." She cried. I got up and kneeled to hug her in her chair. Comfort her. She had been through so much and trying to protect my child at the same time.

"Shh, it's over now, Lauren. He can't hurt you and Jonah anymore," I told her, running my hands over her head. I backed up to look at her.

"Are you okay?"

She nodded, wiping her tears with a tissue. "Sorry, it's hard to relive it sometimes."

She sniffled.

I stood, and sat back in my seat, pouring her more tea in her glass.

"Here." I slid it to her.

She took a sip, then continued. "So, it worked. Valton, Alban, and Fatmir were arrested with some others, but I knew there were more. I knew I still wasn't safe. They knew I had information that could take the rest of their operation down. When I found out the last of them were finally caught... oh, Stephen, I was so happy. It wasn't until then that I knew it was over and that I was finally safe. I had just gone out a few times. I had known..." she looked down, as if embarrassed, "about you and Cassie, followed her on social media, watched the news and our story come out. I saw that she was going to be at the bookstore, and I was curious. I was jealous."

She looked at me.

I rubbed my hand over my mouth, letting her continue.

"I sent the book. I didn't know what I was coming home to. I just didn't know."

She began to cry again.

I placed my hand over hers.

"It's okay."

"I think I have been rather unfair to her." She looked towards the door. "But I really want you in my life, Stephen."

"Lauren, I need you to understand something." I looked directly into her tear-filled eyes. "I will always love you, but I also grieved for you. That woman in there mended my heart. She has been in my life in so many stages, and this is the final one. I love her, Lauren."

Tears ran continually as she nodded. She understood by squeezing my hand.

"I will always be a part of your life. I will be the most amazing part of that miracle in there, and I promise you that. You know that, right?" I asked.

She nodded, smiling, crying.

"Right now, I think I need to check on Cassie."

I looked at my watch, realizing we had been out there nearly two hours, and I was sure the display of hugging, hand-holding, and crying wasn't going to go over well.

"Are you okay for a minute?"

"Yeah." She whimpered.

I went inside the house. It was so tidy, quiet with music playing so low to not wake Jonah.

"Cassie?" I looked in the kitchen and living room, but she wasn't there. I went into my bedroom, she wasn't there either, but clear as day, there was an envelope on the end of the bed with my name on it.

Holy fuck.

My heart raced clear out of my chest as I ran to it. I tore it open, pulling out a letter. The pearl ring...fell to my feet.

I had to sit on the bed because my feet could not hold me. My hands were shaking.

Dear Stephen,

This may be the hardest thing I have ever done in my life. I want you to know it's not because I don't love you. It's out of love that I am doing it. Lauren and Jonah need you, your love, your guidance, your everything. I don't fit.

This lifetime wasn't meant for us, baby, it just wasn't. Maybe in the next one, you will find me. I sure hope you do.

You are always in my heart, always,

Cassie

Chapter 48

STEPHEN

I raced for my keys, wallet, and the front door.

"Shit, Lauren."

I ran back to the patio and swung the door open, startling her.

"She's gone. I have to go."

And I ran.

As soon as I got to my gate, I saw reporters waiting on me. It started to open, and I yelled inside the darkness of my blacked-out car, "Move out the goddamn way."

I barreled through as they snapped pictures.

I pulled up my apps on my phone as I plowed down my driveway to the one that was currently tracking Cassie, the one she knew nothing about. I stopped my car just as I reached the end of the driveway.

I talked out loud to myself, "Come on baby, where are you going?"

I followed her car icon.

"She's on 77. The airport. Fuck."

I drove and tried to call her through the car. She sent me to her voicemail instantly. I hit the steering wheel.

"Come on, Cassie."

I pressed the phone icon on my steering wheel.

"Call Allen."

"Sup?" he said.

"Hey, can you help me out?" I asked.

"Depends." he said, sarcastically.

"Dude, Cassie hauled ass. I am in trouble here. I'm driving, and I need some information," I said, frantic.

"Oh shit. Okay. What do you need?" he asked.

"Can you look up flights to San Francisco for me out of here? Like, the next ones out. I need to know the times."

I waited.

"Hold up, let me get in front of my computer instead of my phone. What happened?" he asked.

I could hear him walking.

"Fucking Lauren and her, well, me too. It's a fucked up long story. I'm going to try to make it right." Then I yelled, "If this motherfucker would move out of my way." Then, in a calm voice, "Sorry. I'm breaking some traffic laws here."

"Don't kill anyone out there, okay?" he said.

"All right, it looks like the first one is at 3:20, so that can't be one because that's in like... fifteen minutes. She's not there already, is she?" he asked.

I double-checked her icon.

"No."

"Okay, then you have a 5:05, 7:15, and a 9:25," he said.

"It's probably the 5:05. Shit. Okay, she is close, like fifteen minutes to the airport," I noticed, looking at the app. "She is going to get through the gate before me because I have to park. Shit."

I thought for a second, tapping the steering wheel.

"Hey. Can you go into the company account and buy me a ticket, like I don't know, anywhere domestic, cheap? Use my TSA precheck so I can get through faster and send it to me?"

"Yeah," he said. "Give me a few, I'll call you right back. How far out are you?" he asked.

I estimated.

"About thirty minutes, maybe? Thanks, man."

I then hung up.

I pressed the phone icon again, "Call Cassie."

Hearing her voicemail made my heart hurt. This time, I left a message, pleading.

"Cassie, no baby. I am not letting you do this. Answer my call. Where are you going? Please, I beg you. Answer my call, please. I love you."

I hung up.

My phone rang. It was Allen.

"Hey. Okay, you have a one-way flight to Daytona Beach, Florida at 8:20. Enjoy your tan, my friend. I sent it to your email."

"Thank you, Allen," I said, breathing a sigh of relief.

"These chicks you have, they make you work for it." He laughed.

"They have been worth it, but yeah, no shit," I said.

"Anything else?" he asked.

"No, just pray I make it in time and if I do, that she takes me back," I said.

"Go get her. Hey. This is some top-level rom-com shit right here, man."

He laughed.

"Only if I get her Allen." I said.

I hung up and looked at the app. She was only a couple of minutes away from the airport. How the hell did she sneak out without me knowing? Did she get an Uber outside the gate with all the reporters there? Did she have this all planned?

I tried her phone again.

Voicemail.

Dammit.

I parked and ran through the garage like a maniac, pulling up my email at the same time, muttering to myself.

"Where is the damn QR code for the ticket?"

I looked back to the app to see where she was.

This thing was more confusing once I was on the ground and in a crowded place like an airport. I ran straight to the TSA precheck line. Why was everyone so slow?

"Have a nice flight to Florida, Mr. Harlow," the guy said

That was hilarious, nobody ever said anything nice in TSA on a normal day, but today they were.

Yelling in my head to the guy in front.

Dude. Why are you taking your shoes and belt off here? It's precheck. Jesus.

Finally, I was through. I looked at the app. I held my phone, is it right? Left? Wait, right. I ran. My dot was now going in her direction, thank god.

She should be around here somewhere. There was a bunch of people jammed up in front of this place, it said she was there. Then, I saw her, signing some autographs. I slowly pushed my way through, completely winded.

"Excuse me, can I get one too ma'am?"

She looked up from what she was signing and put her hand to her mouth in surprise.

"Stephen, how? What are you doing?" she asked.

"I came to…" I looked around and realized we were now being watched by at least fifteen people around us, and most were holding phones up, whispering, "Is that her boyfriend? Is that him?"

I grabbed her arm, and she grabbed her rolling bag. I looked around and pulled her into the first and only private door I could find. The bathroom.

"Oh my god. What are you doing?" she said, shocked.

"Cassie, I am not letting you leave like this," I said.

"How did you even know where I went, Stephen?" she asked, confused.

I paused a beat, then looked at my phone in my hand. "Um, well, I followed you by the GPS tracker I installed on your phone."

"You installed a what?" she barked, pissed.

"Come on, Cass. My fiancé before you went missing, and I'm in cyber security." I shrugged "I never used it until now, I promise. It was only for emergency, like now."

I waved my phone around and pointed it at her.

She smirked and took a deep breath, which was a good sign for me.

I took her by the face, looking into her eyes.

"Baby, please don't leave."

"Stephen, I am not doing this over and over again, I…" she paused.

I dropped to my knees.

"Eww, that's gross. What are you doing down there? Stephen, this is a bathroom."

She looked around at the conditions, appalled.

I started to trace the bicycle on her ankle with my finger. I looked up at her, "Were you going to go home and put a plane on here too? Maybe next a train? Like, go for a whole anklet of tattoos showing forms of transportation and ways to leave me, Cass." I joked.

She shook her head. "Did you come here to mock me, Stephen? It's not funny."

Her anger built.

"No, Cass, I came here to do this."

I reached up, holding open a black velvet ring box with her engagement ring inside.

She looked back and forth between me and the ring in absolute disbelief at what she was seeing,

"Are you serious?"

She was in total shock.

"Yes, more serious than I have ever been in my life. Cassie Patterson, will you please stop making me chase you and marry me?" I asked, with tears filling my eyes, so much emotion running through me.

I was so scared she was about to say no.

She reached down and pulled me from the bathroom floor, looked me in my eyes, tears welling in hers.

"You are crazy. You just asked me to marry you in a Panda Express bathroom, baby."

Laughing, I said, "Trust me, this wasn't my first choice, I had something really freaking romantic picked out, but you chose this path, crazy woman. Well? You haven't answered me."

With happy tears streaming her cheeks, she said, "Yes. Yes, I would be so honored to be your wife, Stephen Harlow."

She smiled and reached her arms around me and kissed me.

I slid the ring on her finger, and at that moment, I felt like the world became calm again. I could breathe. Everything was in its place once again.

I took her face in my hands and kissed her, my fiancé.

I didn't lose her.

"The people out there are going to have a heyday with this. They think we are having sex in here," she said.

I laughed. "Let's give them something to talk about then. Do you trust me?" I asked.

She let out a small questioning laugh. "Hmm, okay?"

I opened the door abruptly, and there they were with cameras waiting. What they got was me kissing her and holding her hand out with her 2.5 karat diamond ring out for all the tabloids and social media to eat up straight out of the Panda Express bathroom.

Chapter 41

CASSIE

W aking up in his arms and sheets a tangled mess from last night's sexual celebration and feeling my finger, now weighed down by this new heavier ring, had my head spinning.

What happened?

Just yesterday I gave up, sitting in the back of Gregory's car, listening to him try to talk me out of leaving, but I had already made my mind up the night before to set him free before we made love the next morning. I was letting him have this new family he had created. They needed him, and I was the only one standing in the way of their happiness.

He stirred, slowly opening his beautiful gray and green eyes.

"Good morning, baby."

His voice, gravelly, so sexy.

"Hey," I said, smiling, running my hand through his black strands, now, peppered with some extra gray.

He pulled me in closer to his naked chest, warm, so comforting.

"I don't want you to go today...or ever. Just stay, baby," he said, kissing my forehead.

"I wish, but my life continues at home as planned, unfortunately, even though you put this thing on it."

I waved my hand outside the covers above us, laughing.

He chuckled. "Well, as long as you come back, woman."

He flipped me onto my back, pinning me down, arms holding himself up, looking into my eyes.

"You had me so scared, Cass. Please don't ever do that again, okay?"

I shook my head. "I promise. I won't."

He reached down and kissed me. I could feel his dick between my thighs, growing harder.

"Baby. You are something else."

I reached down and felt him, thick, hard in my hand.

He took a deep breath and closed his eyes.

"You make me insane, what can I say?"

He smiled, then kissed me again. He straddled me, then pulled my little tank off over my head, shaking his head.

"I'm the luckiest man. You are a sight."

I looked at him. "Hey. How come you asked me to marry you as Cassie Patterson yesterday?" I asked, running my hands over his muscular chest.

He tilted his head, swirling his fingertips over my breasts and over my nipples.

"Well, that was your name when I originally fell in love with you. Buckley was Jack's name. Was that bad?" he asked.

I shook my head. "No. That was perfect. Absolutely perfect."

I pushed his body over.

"Oh, okay."

He laughed.

I laid over the top of him and kissed him from his jaw down his neck, his shoulder, collarbone, and down his chest.

His breathing deepened.

I licked his sensitive nipples, taking them lightly in my teeth while looking at his facial expressions, wincing and smiling, eyes closed, head tilted back. I continued to kiss over his defined abs, fingers running over his sculpted body, leaving goosebumps in their wake. His pelvis pressed into mine. His cock, harder. I slid my hand down, running my hand down his length.

"Oh yeah," he whispered, as he pressed his hips forward, pushing his dick into my hand.

I wrapped my hand harder around it and begin to stroke it up and down, my mouth making its way down, his hands in my hair.

"Oh, yeah, baby."

He moaned as my mouth wrapped around the head of his cock and slid slowly down. I knew how much he loved this.

I climbed in between his legs to my knees, my hair splayed across his stomach, his hands on the back of my head, guiding me up and down his shaft. Saliva running down his cock, over my hand, down his balls.

"Jesus fuck, that feels so good," he said.

My hand in rapid movements with my mouth, my tongue swirled around his smooth skin as I went.

He pulled at my shoulders.

"Baby, I'm going to come. You need to stop that."

I didn't. I picked up the pace. I could feel him give in. He realized what I was doing. This was for him.

"Oh fuck."

His fingers were in my hair again, grabbing. His body tensed and I buried his cock deep in my throat and ran my hands over his balls, so tight. I swallowed all he had and left him completely drained.

I sat at the kitchen bar in my little pajama bottoms and tank top.

"Here, babe. You look like the cutest Harry Potter ever with those glasses."

He slid my coffee to me as I looked up from my phone.

I smiled.

"Is that a compliment? Oh my god. I have so many messages and voicemails."

I held up my phone, showing him.

"Oh my, Arie."

I hit play, putting it on speaker.

"Cassie, holy fuck. Best publicity stunt ever. You have gone viral, girlfriend. Are you really engaged to your toy boy? The Today Show had your picture up this morning and congratulated you. They want you to do an exclusive on-air phone interview with Hoda and Jenna tomorrow morning. Oh, you may have free Panda Express for life after this too." She laughed. "Ring me as soon as you get this."

I shook my head. "Look what you did."

He pulled an English muffin from the toaster, smearing butter on it and sliding it on a plate in front of me. He leaned on the counter, sipping his coffee. Wearing nothing but his light blue pajama pants, sitting right at his hips, that amazing, chiseled chest, killing me.

He said, smiling, "Look at it this way. We don't have to tell everyone the news one by one."

"Well, I'm glad we told our parents, Cora, Britt, and the important ones last night. They would have never forgiven us finding out on TMZ."

I laughed, taking a bite of my English muffin.

Stephen looked at his phone.

"Hmm."

He groaned, chewing a bite of the muffin.

I look up, asking, "Hmm, what?"

He took a deep breath. "Would you mind if Lauren, Jonah, and Jakob came over for a few minutes before you leave today? They want to congratulate us and say bye to you," he said.

I rolled my eyes. "I'm sure they want to say bye," I said, with a smirk.

"Cass, come on," he said, tilting his head, and an arched brow.

"Fine, I would love to see Jonah."

I smiled.

He leaned across the counter and gave me a buttery kiss.

"That's the spirit."

I was all packed again. I really didn't want to leave, especially now that things were wonderful between us. I just wanted to keep this feeling going. I couldn't stop hugging and kissing him.

The doorbell rang, and I instantly felt nauseous. I swore, I would bitch slap her if she ruined these last moments with me and Stephen. I took a deep breath and enjoyed the moment of seeing Stephen crouch down and Jonah walking into his arms without hesitation. That right there made it all worth it.

"Hey, buddy," he said.

Jonah smiled big. He was genuinely happy to see Stephen. It was so sweet.

Lauren walked up and said, "Jonah, who is that?" pointing to Stephen.

Then it happened, he said, "Daddy," then shyly looked away.

I thought Stephen was going to cry, looking over at me with his mouth wide open. All I could do was cover mine in shock.

"Jonah, that's right, I'm your Daddy," he said, tickling him under his chin, making him laugh.

Lauren then came over to me, leaving the boys to have their fun. "Can I talk to you for a minute?" she asked.

"Okay."

We walked a little further into the kitchen out of ear's reach.

"What's up?" I asked.

"I owe you an apology." She started, looking nervous. "I came back thinking I could have my original life back, Stephen back." She messed with her fingernails out of nervousness like she did before. I also noticed she didn't have her engagement ring on either. She then looked back up at me.

"Before he knew you had left, he made it very clear that it was over between us romantically and that he was in love with you. He will only be in my life as Jonah's father and my friend." She shook her head. "Cassie, he was frantic when he found out you left. I had never seen him like that. When I came into the house, I saw your letter. I'm sorry, but I read it. It was right there on the counter." She winced in shame. "You gave him up for me and Jonah. That was so selfless. Right then, I realized why he loves you so much. I want you to know I won't stand in the way of your happiness." She took both of my hands in hers. "I'm sorry for the way I treated you, Cassie."

I took a deep breath.

"I forgive you, Lauren. It's okay, he's worth fighting for, I get it." I laughed, then I hugged her on my tippy toes. God she was tall. I also saw Stephen behind us, smiling at what he just witnessed.

I walked through the airport feeling very different from the day before, that was for sure. On my way to my gate, I walked up to the Panda Express, where it all went down. I pulled out my phone and took a quick picture of the sign and the bathroom door. We were just standing there yesterday with a crowd of people right there. How surreal. I kept walking to my gate, looking at the picture. I hit send.

Me: This is the place that changed my life forever

Stephen: Did you just confess where you stole all your recipes?

Me: LOL. I can't wait to marry you.

Chapter 50

CASSIE

🍴

Life just sped by like a movie stuck in fast-forward. One month became two, then four became six. All was right in the world; everything was in its place.

Jack and Beth were busy planning their wedding in Vail for this New Year. It was their turn to have Cora, so it wasn't upsetting the apple cart with her school schedule and ours either. A small family ceremony. I was okay...I was genuinely okay. The memory of the horrific night didn't even register when I saw them together now. It was amazing what the mind did when love, happiness, and forgiveness superseded the negative moments.

Cora was doing fantastic. Excelling in high school with great grades, tons of girlfriends, playing volleyball, and with those tiny volleyball shorts, managed to attract a new boyfriend named Owen. Oh, Owen, dumb as a box of rocks but cute as a button and athletic as hell. I could tell he wouldn't last long from the constant arguing from the late-night chats and we would be diving into that cherry chocolate chip before summer again. She was also enjoying her new role as big sister to Jonah. Her toy, her little man as she called him.

I proudly handed Kyle four new chef coats last month. Two crisp pristine ones for the dining room, for mingling with guests. All adorned with sharp black embroidery on his chest saying, "Kyle Berkley Executive Chef-Owner Sagi-Shi".

I cried...of course. Him and Grace plan on getting married in Nappa in the spring, a sweet, intimate wedding on a vineyard.

The vineyard?

Once one of the largest wholesale vineyards in Nappa at over 1,000 acres until sold by no other than, you guessed it, Kyle's grandparents. He was not only a trust fund kid, but a vineyard trust fund kid. He still wore tattered jeans on his days off and was completely unassuming of this wealth. Besides Brittany and Stephen, he was my closest friends and now a proud partner.

Avery was completely on the mend besides some minor PTSD of taking out the trash. Britt said it was just his bullshit way of getting out of it. The m*otherfucker* who stabbed him got three years behind bars and two years' probation. They seemed okay with it. Britt still had anger issues when you talk about it, and I brought it up just for an occasional laugh. I was excited to live closer to my besties in the future. The quick three-hour road trip to visit instead of the grueling plane rides back-and-forth nonsense.

Stephen, oh Stephen.

He decided to sell the glass McMansion. We decided it was time for something in the city, close to schools for Jonah, something closer to Lauren. She sold the New York apartment, paying him back, and bought a cute place in a cool neighborhood. Parks, restaurants, walkable, pretty swanky, and upcoming area. The lake house was his and Lauren's dream house, not ours. I was not going simply to fit into his old life, he said, but rather create one that is ours. Meanwhile, he and Lauren had worked out a pretty good schedule with Jonah, so she could go back to work herself. She was insanely trusting, letting him take Jonah there sometimes. He worked remotely for a week or more and I went there as much as I could. We were making it work the best we could. We had two years before Cora went to college. Then my plan was to go to Charlotte. I'd leave Sagi-Shi behind in Kyle's trusting hands as the main operator, me being a silent partner. Me, silent, that was a running joke.

My taping schedule was ramped up to level ten since I was on the home stretch of my contract. They were squeezing every last second out of me before my eighteen-month sentence was up. It was bittersweet. I had grown close to these people, my friends. Johnathan, his constant organization of my insane life and his secret caring demeanor. Arie, with her tough, sassy, demanding-as-hell attitude. Even though we never went shopping or out for that spot of tea, we have grown a friendship I would always treasure. During this little journey, I had learned so much about myself. I had gotten to do some pretty cool shit, and hell, I'd even gotten to enjoy that celebrity status I wanted for a bit.

I sat here in a daze, feet up, staring out my window at the San Francisco skyline in silence when I heard a knock at my door.

Seriously?

It really never lasted long, this peaceful moment. I turned, and it was Dan Satterfield, Mr. Silky Hands, Mr. Anderson Cooper himself.

"Well. You hired me and ghosted me for eighteen months, showing up my last three weeks?"

I laughed with my hands out.

He shook his head, walking in the door.

"I know. I know. I am terrible, Cassie," he said, coming around the desk.

I stood as he came in for a friendly hug.

"How are you?" he asked, moving back around to sit in one of the chairs in front.

"I'm doing all right. I am wondering what life is going to be like after this."

I looked up, holding my hands in the air.

"I am up for the change of pace, I guess."

"Well, you did an amazing job with us. Out of all of our segments, you had the highest ratings, as you know." He placed his hand out towards me. "And you were quite entertaining to say the least in the social media department, bringing quite the following."

He laughed.

I shook my head. "Yeah, sorry about all that. I didn't ask for most of that nonsense." I smirked. "Actually, any of it, it just seemed to follow me." I shrugged.

He laughed. "It was very entertaining. You are entertaining. We are going to miss you." He looked down between his legs at his hands, then back up at me. "That is why I would like to offer you another contract if you are interested."

Shocked, I said, "Oh Dan...I..."

He interrupted, his hand out. "Before you answer, it's just a year, twelve months. Just taping segments. No cookbooks or cookware lines. Just taping Cassie." He slid a piece of paper towards me. "Also, we are willing to give a nice boost in the money department." He winked.

I took it and flipped it over, looking at the number and taking a deep breath. "Is there the same flexibility in the schedule? Breaks?" I asked.

"Yes, pretty much the same as before," he said.

"I need to talk to Stephen and Cora. I..." I rolled my eyes. "Am I insane to consider doing this again?" I asked.

He laughs. "We are insane to be in this industry, so you are asking the wrong person. Talk to them and get back to me by next week with your answer."

I went in for his hand, which was still creepily too soft like a woman's.

"You seriously are just the closer, aren't you?"

"You now know the secrets of this operation." He laughed and stopped short of leaving. "Oh, congratulations on the engagement, by the way. I hear Panda Express bathroom proposals are the new hot ticket, thanks to you two."

He chuckled.

"Oh, Lord," I said, shaking my head.

I had my nightly FaceTime with Stephen and now Jonah and Cora. Tonight was a dinner date of takeout pizza and salad. This was our new sweet Thursday ritual when we were apart, when we could do it. After Stephen and Cora were done dealing with her pre-calculus issues she was having, and I had my mini-nap, I announced I had something I needed to talk to them about.

"So...I was offered another twelve-month contract today at the studio."

I bit into my mediocre slice that I wished was Ginos.

If there were crickets, they would be chirping…right…now.

"So? What did you say, Mom?" Cora asked, with a less-than-pleasing look on her face.

"I haven't. I wanted to ask you two first. It's only taping. Nothing else. Flexible, and they offered me quite an offer to stay."

I shrugged and ate more pizza just out of nervousness. This shit was terrible, tossing it on my plate.

"Stephen?" I look into the phone that sat in the middle of the table, "Thoughts?"

"Babe, that is the part that you enjoy, right?" he asked.

"Right," I said.

"Well, if it's flexible, it's only a year contract, and if it brings you joy, I think you have your answer already. I just want you to do what makes you happy from here on out," he said. "If it stresses you out, then no."

I took a deep breath and looked at Cora. "I will make sure I'm there for your games and cheer events. Kyle is basically running Sagi. I think it will be okay."

I half smiled, maybe convincing myself.

"Okay, if it makes you happy, Mom."

She hugged me.

"Okay. Cheers to twelve more months." I held up my glass.

"Yaaaaay." Jonah held his cup up with no clue what he's cheering to.

Twelve more months of Ethiopian dark roast with Johnathan, smart-ass conversations with Arie, and taping segments I had grown to love. We figured it would make another year go by faster, even though I was trying to pump the brakes with my daughter slipping away closer to college.

I might have lost my mind but what was new?

Chapter 51

STEPHEN

I open the terrace door, Cassie chatting on the phone. The sun was starting to set, the glow lighting her up like an angel. We scored with this place, which had three stories and a rooftop terrace with the most amazing sunset views of the city in the distance. This rooftop was our sanctuary, and now that it was fall, we found ourselves out there most evenings, soaking up the cool, crisp change of weather, snuggled on a lounge. I missed the lake, but this was pretty sweet. I was getting used to the neighborhood feel, making friends, walking to a café, a bar or restaurant, and a park with Jonah.

I waved at her.

"Babe, we need to go. Your parents and Cora are heading to the restaurant."

I tapped my watch and smiled.

She held up her index finger.

"Hey Britt. I need to go. The birthday girl is being summoned. I'll call you tomorrow. Okay, I love you too."

She hung up.

I held the door open for her.

"I hate that she couldn't come this weekend," I said.

She said in a sad tone, "I know, but we plan on making it up with a New York girls' weekend next month with Bianca too, and that will be awesome," she said, more excited.

"We need to hurry because I wanted to show you that space Allen and I are looking at on the way."

We walked, her arm in the crook of mine, the crunching of newly fallen leaves under our feet.

"I don't understand the logic of having an office on this side of town. You have one in the house," she said, shaking her head.

"Well, I just like to be available for Jonah and you, closer to home. Also, meeting with the occasional client and having him running into my office asking for a peanut butter and jelly lacks the sort of professionalism that Southstar Securities is known for."

I laughed.

Laughing, she said, "Yeah, I suppose."

"Here it is. See? Look how convenient," I said, looking at the front of the building. "What do you think?" I said, holding my hands out.

"It doesn't look very office-like. More like a café or something. What was it before?" she asked.

"A café." I laughed. "But the realtor said with some decent fitting, we can convert it with no problem."

"Cool." She looked down the street. "It is only, what? Three blocks from the house? That's great," she said.

I turned the key and pushed open the door to the dark room, looking for the light switch on the wall as we walked in.

She looked at the floor under her feet. "Oooh, black and white penny tile, I love this already."

I hit the lights, and the room erupted.

"Surprise."

There they stood, all her family and friends from over the years to now.

I thought she was going to stroke out, hand over her mouth, completely freaked out, absolutely caught off guard.

She turned to me, "Oh my god, Stephen."

"Happy fiftieth birthday, baby," I said, smiling hugely at her happiness.

Her hand covered her mouth, still in shock, looking around.

"I can't believe you. Are you really buying this building for an office?" she asked.

"Yes, I already did actually," I said.

"What?" she asked, confused.

"For you." I took her hands and looked at her. "This is your Izakaya, your dream. Do whatever you would like. It's small. You don't need to make tons of money. You don't need to worry about the real estate. It's paid for. It's all yours. Let it bring you joy."

I took her face and kissed her.

She then looked up at me. "Stephen. Are you serious right now? You bought me a restaurant?"

Tears, happy tears in her eyes.

"Yes. Is that okay?" I shook my head. "If you don't want this, hang onto it for about two years, and you can flip it and make bank. This area is poppin'." I laughed. "But it's yours, Cassie, whatever your vision, it's all yours, baby."

She looked around at the people there, in this new space, celebrating her. The love and support of people who have helped make her dreams come true all these years. Her parents, her mentor and friend Mike Tanner, my mom, brother and family, Cora holding Jonah's hand, Avery and Britt, Bianca, Allen, Johnathan, Arie, Kyle and Grace, who was now just starting to show off a small baby bump.

She used to feel like she was alone, in a relationship with her career, making up people like this in her life, but there they were. They travel the distance, they sacrificed for her as much as she did for them. They even broke the law to be with her sometimes.

She looked into my eyes.

"I love you more than you can ever imagine."

"I feel it, baby. I feel it. Happy birthday. Now go be with your people," I said before walking with her into the abyss of hugs and kisses.

Chapter 52

CASSIE

✗

The almost transparent swirl of the hot oil gliding around the silver pan was mesmerizing as my mind wandered to the conversation that Stephen and I had earlier that morning about how happy I was with my new adventure, the one he made possible. His supportive, loving words flowed through my head.

"I feel like you are so content when you are at Yujo; it's your happy place, and I love it."

I smiled as I tossed in the shallots, fragrant fresh ginger, garlic and baby bok choy into the pan.

"What's our special tonight, Chef?" Haruto asked, pulling me from my daze as he moved down the line with a Cambro of fresh chili jam for tonight's service.

"Asian sticky ribs, garlic ginger charred baby bok choy over sticky rice," I said, flipping the bok choy into the air, flames wrapping around my pan as I added soy sauce and sesame oil. "I haven't made this in almost four years," I said. "It's time I brought it back."

I smiled at him.

"Well, we will sell out with your husband tending bar tonight. His whiskey crowd will be here, and they always get whatever is on special," he said passing by me.

I plated the bok choy over the sticky rice, placing three ribs strategically on top, peppering it with diced green onion and toasted sesame seeds.

Gorgeous.

"Hey. Y'all get some of this," I called out to my one server, Vicki, my dishwasher, Alex, and Haruto as I slid it down the counter. They descended like sugar ants to a melting popsicle. Forks digging in, sufficient *fuck yeahs* were said, and nothing but bones were left on the plate in a matter of minutes.

Success.

I leaned against the counter with my tea in hand, looking out at the dining room, soon to be filled with guests, neighbors, and friends. We named it Yujo, meaning friendship. That was our goal in this space, to make new friends there. Stephen even found his place one day a week, tending bar, talking Japanese whiskey, and a lot of fun banter and bullshit.

I looked out at the dining room as Vicki set up the bar that surrounds my entire kitchen. I designed it to be one large Fish Bowl experience. I wanted to mingle with my guests and never miss out on a conversation when included.

Fortunately, I snagged Haruto Seno from Hakucho, a two Michelin-starred restaurant straight out of Tokyo, when it unfortunately closed down after the pandemic. He was not Kyle, but he was fun and talented as hell. He taught me something new every day, and that was what I wanted and needed. I missed Kyle, even though I FaceTime'd him every day and stalked our Sagi-Shi app constantly to see how we were doing.

There I stood, looking out at the white subway tile, stainless steel, clean lines with simple ratan lighting fixtures to add softness, simple. I kept that black and white penny tile at the entrance. I kept the tile that I saw with those first steps into my new life, Stephen, so lovingly bought.

My mind wandered aimlessly as I turned towards the stove, turning the ribs in their sauce. The humming of the kitchen in the background, the back door opening and shutting, dishes being stacked, and the sound of keys being thrown on a counter were the only sounds I could hear.

Then, I could feel the warmth of his body behind me and his voice, so perfect.

"There's my sexy girl."